Heather Peace started her career working in touring theatre, commissioning and directing new plays.

She joined the BBC Drama Script Unit in 1989, later script editing productions in Drama Serials under Michael Wearing, and Comedy under Robin Nash, where she developed Lisselle Kayla's groundbreaking sitcom Us Girls. In 1991 she left the BBC to become Head of Comedy Development at Witzend Productions, returning in 1994 to edit one week in four of EastEnders for a year. From 1994-1996 she was a senior script editor in Drama Serials, leaving to become a freelance editor and writer.

She wrote for the second series of Crossroads and has written a number of short stories; she trained to teach English in 2003. Heather is an Associate Lecturer at the Open University on the Advanced Creative Writing course.

All to Play For

Heather Peace

Legend Press
Independent Book Publisher

Legend Press Ltd, 2 London Wall Buildings, London EC2M 5UU
info@legend-paperbooks.co.uk | www.legendpress.co.uk

British Library Cataloguing in Publication Data available.

ISBN 978-1-9082481-3-8

*All characters, other than those clearly in the public domain, and
place names, other than those well-established such as towns and
cities, are fictitious and any resemblance is purely coincidental.*

Edited by: Lauren Parsons-Wolff

Set in Times
Printed by CPI Books, United Kingdom

Cover designed by Gudrun Jobst | www.yotedesign.com

Legend Press

Independent Book Publisher

Acclaim for All to Play For

'Takes you right back to the intrepid walks round (and round) the baffling corridors of power that were the BBC and offers an insightful, witty glimpse of what really went on behind those doors. And anyone who's ever slipped into the parallel universe that is the Edinburgh Fringe will be instantly plunged back into the heady cocktail of earnestness and debauchery (without the hangover). Endearingly revealing and alarmingly honest.' **Victoria Pile, Writer of *Green Wing***

'*All to Play For* lifts the lid on the inner workings of the BBC Drama department like no other book I have ever read. Written with an insight that can only come from someone who has lived through it. A bitingly honest, funny, poignant, and brilliant debut novel.' **Owen O'Neill, Award Winning Actor, Director and Comedian.**

'The whole book has a wonderfully authentic feel, clearly penned by someone on the inside!' **Tony Grounds, TV Writer.**

'A vivid and passionate evocation of a crucial period in British broadcasting history. The writing is shrewd and funny and fuelled by the writer's obvious commitment and idealism. The characterisation combines unmistakable authenticity with a wicked satirical spin.' **Alison Lumb, Former BBC and ITV Drama Producer**

'Wickedly perceptive, revelatory, funny and at times shocking, this is less a work of fiction than it is an inside job, and all the better for it. This writer certainly knows what she's talking about. A highly credible cast of characters (many of whom you would definitely refuse a Facebook friend request) guide you behind the scenes of the viper world of White City and the TV industry in general. What takes this story up an extra notch is its backdrop, a time of dizzying political, social and institutional upheaval. Landmark pre-millennium changes are rocking the foundations of a boozy, smoke-hazed era of dinosaur practices and unfair privileges. The digital age of television rushes forth with the inevitability of a high-speed train crash, and you read on, not knowing which of your favourite passengers will survive the wreckage, nor how. For those of us who have ever had anything to do with the Beeb, this is an absorbing read; for the remainder, this is just as much a voyeuristic journey of pleasure. The chortle-a-minute ending satisfyingly unites the beginning of the story and leaves only one burning question: when's the in-house screen adaptation?' **Carmen Harris (formerly known as Beeb scriptwriter, Lisselle Kayla)**

'I felt this was more than an honest book, but an absolutely needed breakdown of the industry that we all try to understand. This book is important for men and women both to realize it's actually okay to still believe in what you've always believed in, and although you can't make changes here, you can make changes there.

This should be an industry bible that you read before you enter, just in case you lose hope, this book will help you not to take it too personal.

There are times I felt this book was more of a breakdown of the BBC I had sadly come to understand, a place where a lot of people have lost confidence, and taken their rejection to heart. To know that sometimes there were real people on the inside trying to allow for the creative soul to develop gives us hope.

I love the detail, but felt I wanted more deeper stories from the characters, I felt I was in the lives of the big decision makers, but never understood them enough.

A very thought provoking book, that has left me feeling quite inspired against the odds. I loved *All To Play For*, it allows you to question yourself in all areas of your life, which will make you question, have you ever sold a piece of your soul. This book is excellent and really honest and hopefully for those who sadly put their dreams on hold, after countless rejections will read this book and get back on track, and not let those who don't get it, stop your dreams.' **Angie Le Mar, Comedienne, Actor, Writer, Director and TV Presenter**

'An insider's view of the BBC drama department; Heather Peace could be the Chris Mullin of TV Centre.' **Ian Pattison, Writer of *Rab C Nesbitt***

'A fitting legacy for the Doughnut, brilliantly skewers TV and lays bare the shambles behind it. As honest, shocking and funny as the world of television it satirises; brilliant if you ever lived in the office next to the lift, brilliant if you haven't and want to know what it was like. A gem.' **Geoff Atkinson, Writer, MD of Vera Productions and Producer of *Bremner, Bird and Fortune.***

Acknowledgements

Many thanks to Lauren Parsons-Wolff, Tom Chalmers and Lucy Boguslawski at Legend Press, to Steff Humm for her marketing work, and to Barbara Herbin. Also, for their support in the early stages, Alison Lumb, Andy Croft, Cheryl Moskowitz, Janet Goddard, Dave Fox, Wendy Suffield and Merric Davidson. Not forgetting special thanks to all those who provided my inspiration.

To Robbie

Let's spend less time measuring audiences
and more time enlightening them.

Jeremy Paxman
From The James MacTaggart Memorial Lecture 24/8/2007

Before I Begin

January 2011, Penarth, Wales.

Middle age isn't as bad as you think it'll be. There are compensations. I've reached that stage where life levels out a bit, and the steady tramp uphill finally rewards you with a glorious view back down the mountain. You can pause to rest and congratulate yourself on having made it this far. Retracing the route you discover tiny figures crawling up the path, as if you're looking into the distant centre of the universe, back in time to its first beginnings: there's yourself, an insignificant new creature creeping along with all those other determined little ants, full of hope and enthusiasm and blissfully ignorant of the agony that lies ahead. I'm not at the summit of my Mount Snowdon yet, but I'm well over halfway up. I can afford to sit down for a while and consider my journey, take in the panorama... I'm rambling already. Get back to the point, Rhiannon. Okay.

This is my story, in case that wasn't obvious. The tale of a late baby-boomer from Cardiff, who set off to see the world and arrived in Valhalla, amongst her heroes; who rubbed shoulders with the movers and shakers of her generation before they moved or shook anything. Who found herself caught in the middle of a phenomenal clash of cultures as class war collided with art and commerce in the 1980s and 90s and almost destroyed the BBC – I'm doing it again.

Life's an adventure, that's for sure. You don't really know

where you're going until you get there. Whatever you think is true about yourself turns out to be only the half of it. So, who did I start out as? Rhiannon Jones, second child of two Welsh teachers, (Geography and English) with an older brother and two younger sisters. Dark hair, not skinny. (Not fat though; well maybe a bit since having the children.) Five foot two. I wasn't going to mention that, but it's significant, I have to face the truth. Being short makes you more determined. I wouldn't say I have a chip on my shoulder, mind. Having older and younger siblings makes you stand your ground, and know your place, your rights and your responsibilities. Especially when your parents are teachers, they also give you the confidence to try anything. Encouragement is so important – but I digress again, gentle reader.

By the time I was in the sixth form I realised that good old Cardiff was in fact the dullest, dampest, most tedious old-fashioned city in Britain. Everything colourful and interesting was happening elsewhere, be it Liverpool, London or Leeds, I couldn't wait to get away from my cosy home town that seemed to secrete a relative behind every corner and curtain. Perhaps you felt the same at seventeen? I was torn between acting and teaching. I would have loved a career on the stage, but I had a suspicion that I wasn't the kind of extravert who makes it to the top. I had diabolical stage fright. Plus I was rather short. Okay, it's no big deal. I'm not hung up about that. No, really. Not now, anyway.

So, I went for a compromise, being such a bloody sensible girl. I went to an East London drama school and took a B.Ed. in Drama; that way I got to do lots of acting and professional training, but I would also get a teaching qualification (picture the joy on my parents' faces). I planned to give theatre a try after I graduated, and if it didn't work out I'd go into teaching. I'd be in London – well alright, just outside London – and I would have access to all the exciting stuff going on. I couldn't wait. Life was bursting with opportunity; it was all to play for, and I was up for it.

That spirit was to lead me, against all expectation, into the BBC, the august institution that illuminated my childhood like a second sun. I had never even considered the possibility of working there, it was so remote. When I was young the BBC seemed even more secure than the royal family: it was the veins and arteries of our national culture, even in Wales. Okay, it was rather stolid, overbearingly English of course – but it brought us together, and it was a safe place to come home to. We loved it despite its faults. We could squabble over our places at the table but still feel secure in its patriarchal bosom. When did that disappear? What changed? The BBC still exists, its charter remains the same, but everything about it is different. It's a great loss, to my generation, but of course it had to change. Its anti-quated structure desperately needed reform, but not like that... the baby was halfway down the plughole. It's still stuck there, as a matter of fact.

Looking back I see the two huge powers we call Art and Commerce fighting over the flag of the BBC. As they tear into each other a third sneaks up behind, and snatches the colours: they thought he was their loyal servant, but they weren't paying proper attention and now they've lost control and he's running off with it... I'm getting ahead of myself again, sorry.

I need to go back to the start, to the days when the BBC was stuffed full of talented people rather than overpaid managers and public school interns. Back to the 80s, when art and commerce were the left and right of clashing ideologies, when Britain was still an industrial nation, politics was clear-cut, and we all knew where we stood.

Back then, my new friends and colleagues-to-be were all just as fresh, young and wet behind the ears as I was myself. Our hearts were open and our integrity was still intact. Long before most of us had found our way into the Big Boys Club, some of us unwittingly gathered together in the creative maelstrom that launched a thousand careers: the Edinburgh Festival Fringe...

Chapter One

August 1985, Edinburgh

I remember it was a sweltering hot summer that year. I know it's a literary cliché, but it's true, no use pretending otherwise. I was in my second year as a trainee drama teacher, and was volunteering as assistant director with the Newham Youth Theatre. We'd devised a show with the kids and brought it up to the Fringe Festival with the aim of expanding their horizons, giving them a voice, and having a good time. (You're right, it wasn't just altruism that inspired me to do all that extra work. I was also having a fling with the director, Steve, but I'm not proud of it – he was married. At the time it seemed to me that his commitments were his own responsibility and none of my business; that's another example of how your perspective can change as you get older.) As it turned out, five or six other people whose lives were to become intertwined with my own were there too. One or two would become leaders of the BBC. One or two would win the recognition they craved – and one of these unappealing folk would become the love of my life. So, I'll back off now, and let you get on with the story.

Sitting in the back of the stifling hot police van the two women, the two men, and the boy cursed their luck and their handcuffs, though not aloud, in case they were overheard by the four constables in the front. They shifted uncomfortably, glancing out of the window at the traffic jam they were stuck in on Princes Street, and quickly withdrew for fear of being seen by someone they knew.

They cast embarrassed looks at one another, united by their desperate circumstances. All were strangers from England, visiting Edinburgh for the festival season. None of them had ever been arrested before, and all of them were regretting it like mad.

Jill began to cry quietly. She was furious with herself but couldn't help it. At eight months pregnant, two stone overweight in the hot August weather, and overflowing with hormones, she could just about keep control of her bladder but her tear ducts were incontinent. Hampered by her handcuffs she sought a tissue in her skirt pocket but failed to find one and had to rely on sniffing.

The young woman sitting next to her offered a less-than-fresh hanky, murmuring that she was sorry it wasn't clean, and Jill's tears burst forth again in gratitude.

"Don't worry, it'll be fine. I'm sure they'll let you go straight away. I'm Maggie, by the way." She patted Jill's leg clumsily, her handcuffs jingling. "Are you okay?"

Jill nodded, crimson-faced. "Thanks. I'm Jill. If only it wasn't so hot."

Maggie agreed, and Jill blew her nose as the van began crawling forward again.

"Excuse me!" Maggie called to the policemen, "Can this woman have some water?"

A perspiring neck turned to reveal an impassive Scottish hard man's face, which answered a terse 'no' and turned away again.

"You do realise she's about to have a baby!" Maggie pursued, angrily.

The cop answered calmly, without moving, "We havena got any."

"I'm all right, really" said Jill to Maggie, anxious to avoid any further trouble.

She closed her eyes and practised deep breathing exercises.

Maggie sighed as her anger subsided. This was crazy. She wondered how long they would be detained at the police station, and whether she would be late for the show: she was in Edinburgh with a feminist theatre company, and had directed a play which would be on an hour's time. Fortunately she wasn't in it, so it could go ahead without her if necessary, but she needed to be at the venue for the twenty minute turn-around during which the company preceding theirs removed their set and props whilst her company put up their set and refocused the lights – a mad scramble which took place about twelve times a day in each of the hundreds of theatre spaces on the Edinburgh Fringe. Oh well. If they ran late it wouldn't be the first time. The sun was hot on the back of her neck, her short spiky hair and tatty t-shirt offering no protection. She stretched out her ring-less hands, admiring the look of the light steel handcuffs chaining them together against the faded denim of her mucky jeans. It would make a good image for a poster.

Opposite her the serious-looking bloke in an open-necked shirt and slacks was trying to fix his glasses, which had been twisted in the scuffle. He kept trying to bend the frame so that it would stay on his face, but one arm always stuck out from the side of his head. His concentration was fierce, and finally he forced the frame too far, and one of the lenses shot out and skidded across the floor.

"Shit," he whispered through clenched teeth. He peered around for it, his damp shirt sticking uncomfortably to his sweaty thickset torso.

"Here." The obvious student handed him the lens.

"Thanks," replied Chris, unsmiling. It was scratched. He carried on fiddling.

The student looked particularly depressed, and particularly ridiculous. His face was painted green with purple spots and he wore a chain-mail helmet made of cotton dishcloths sprayed silver, with a crusader-style tabard over his jeans and t-shirt which bore a royal coat of arms and the motto: *Fuck the French*. He still clutched a handful of leaflets for his play, and the kid next to him asked if he could see one. He handed one over willingly.

"Oh, *Henry V*," said the boy. "Where are you from?"

"Cambridge," said Jonathan, biting his lip.

Nicky grimaced. "I'm with Newham Youth Theatre," he said, trying to sound professional, and displayed his t-shirt which was printed, rather ambiguously: *NYT: No Future*. "I've lost my leaflets but we're doing a devised play at Heriot Watt, nine o'clock. It's called *No Future*."

"That's a good slot," said Jonathan, impressed. "We're on at five."

"Actually it's nine in the morning," said Nicky ruefully. "It was the only slot we could afford."

Jonathan nodded, losing interest. He checked his watch: nearly four fifteen. The show would have to go up without him, short by one costume and the director. Of course, today was the day three critics were coming. He was counting on good reviews and hoping desperately to win a Fringe First award to kick off his career as a theatre director. He had been on his way to the theatre to welcome the critics with a glass of wine, only dressing up to try and round up a few more punters in the hope of a full house, and now this had happened. Maybe he could get there before the end of the show and amuse the critics with an entertaining account of his misadventures, enabling them to revise the poor opinion of him, which they would probably have developed in his absence... He just hoped the sound cues would be in the right place this time.

Half an hour later they all sat in a row in a cool waiting room at the Central Police Station. The door was locked, but their handcuffs had been removed and water was provided. They tried to get comfortable on the slatted wooden benches, and waited their turn to be interviewed. First to go was little Nicky, summoned by a huge bull-necked sergeant who strode in, glared dispassionately at them all, and announced: "Right. Let's have the Nit wi' No Future," leaving the others to wait and think back over the incident they had been unlucky enough to get involved in.

*

It had been an ordinary, sunny afternoon in Princes Street Gardens where festival folk and holiday visitors littered the grass eating ice cream, and entertainers wandered around performing or advertising their shows. Edinburgh residents were few and far between.

Jill sat under a tree trying to cool off and rest her swollen legs. She looked up at the castle and tried not to hear the hum of the traffic; she felt her baby kicking and hoped against hope that the play she had written would attract a better audience tomorrow. Today's performance had taken place in front of three people, all of whom were related to a member of the cast. It was enough to make you question whether the public actually cared about new plays. She sucked an ice lolly which dripped onto her cotton skirt, and noticed a young, skinny, punky-looking woman with an orange Mohican stripe in her short blue hair, arrive carrying a soapbox. She put it down on the grass and poked around in a plastic carrier bag, taking out a booklet. She swigged from a can of Coke and climbed on the box, stood facing Jill with her back to the castle, opened the booklet, and began to address anyone who would listen in a strident South London accent:

"Life in this society being, at best, an utter bore and no aspect of society being at all relevant to women, there remains to civic-minded, responsible, thrill-seeking females only to overthrow the government, eliminate the money system, institute complete automation, and destroy the male sex."

It sounded vaguely familiar, and Jill peered at the booklet in the punk's hand. She thought it was Valerie Solanas' *SCUM Manifesto*.

"A woman," declaimed the punk. "Not only takes her identity and individuality for granted, but knows instinctively that the only wrong is to hurt others, and that the meaning of life is love."

A slim woman with spiky hair, feminist symbol earrings and an old Greenham Common t-shirt, who was later to introduce herself as Maggie, paused as she walked past and clapped supportively. She looked round at Jill, who smiled. Sisters recognised one another. Maggie stopped, casually parked her hands on her lean hips, and listened to the punk.

"The male needs scapegoats onto whom he can project his failings and inadequacies and upon whom he can vent his frustrations at not being female."

"What a load of shite!" exclaimed a man sitting on a bench. Jill and Maggie looked at him: he was in his twenties, evidently a local office-worker, wearing a white shirt and grey suit, with his jacket off and his sleeves rolled up. He folded up his *Daily Mail*, spread his knees and leaned his elbows on them, turning a disgusted expression on the punk. His eyes were concealed behind reflective sunglasses, but his mouth curled in pure contempt. Jill and Maggie recoiled from him. The punk continued as if he wasn't there.

"The male is eaten up with tension, with frustration at not being female, at not being capable of ever achieving satisfaction or pleasure of any kind. Eaten up with hate – irrational, indiscriminate hate... hatred, at bottom, of his own worthless self."

Jill saw the man's tension increase. The punk stopped and looked directly at him.

"Don't you agree?" she asked disingenuously.

He laughed, shaking his head. "Here," he called to a teenage boy handing out leaflets, who hurried over thinking he had a potential customer. "Sit down here," he said. "Listen to this bag o' shite." Nicky sat on the other end of the bench wondering what was going on, and the man nodded in the punk's direction.

Jill and Maggie exchanged a glance. This dickhead felt so threatened he was calling on the boy for support. Pathetic.

"The male 'artist' attempts to solve his dilemma of not being able to live, of not being female, by constructing a highly artificial world in which the male is heroised, that is, displays female traits; and the female is reduced to highly limited, insipid, subordinate roles, that is, to being male."

Nicky hadn't the faintest idea what this meant, but he went along with the man and whistled like a builder, laughing at his excellent humour. Jill and Maggie felt uncomfortable. The punk was undeterred.

"Just as humans have a prior right to existence over dogs by virtue of being more highly evolved and having a superior consciousness, so women have a prior right to existence over men. The elimination of any male is, therefore, a righteous and good act, an act highly beneficial to women as well as an act of mercy."

The punk stopped and took a hardboard sign out of her bag, which she held up. It read, *Society for Cutting Up Men*.

"Women, join me!" she shouted. She pointed at Jill and Maggie, challenging them. They hesitated. They didn't want to join.

"A small handful of SCUM can take over the country within a year by systematically fucking up the system, selectively destroying property, and murder!"

It was too much for the man in the suit. He stood up.

"You're out o' your mind, you are," he snarled. Nicky cautiously stood up too. He was shocked by this punk's proposals. Either she was mad or she was very dangerous. He had never heard anything like it before.

"If all men were castrated there would be universal peace," retorted the punk, but Jill's attention was distracted by a tall student dressed as a crusader with a green and purple spotted face, who strolled up to her at that moment and asked her politely if she would like a free ticket to *Henry V*.

"Not today, thanks," she replied, looking round him to see if the man in the suit was advancing on the punk. Things could get nasty.

"How about you?" he asked Maggie, who ignored him. Perhaps it was the silver headgear, but for some reason the student, whose name was Jonathan, failed to pick up on the situation he had wandered into, and he innocently walked up to the man in the suit, put on his best public school smile and offered him and his young friend two tickets for the best show on the fringe.

"Take a hike, pal," sneered the man in the suit. "This kid's nothing to do with me. I'm no poofter."

"I never meant to suggest you were! Not that I'd care anyway!" Jonathan nervously raised his hands and backed away as if at gunpoint.

The punk was vastly amused by this exchange, which was unfortunate because the man in the suit took her laughter as a direct insult.

"You!" he yelled, his face an angry mask, "You had better watch yourself." He began to walk slowly round the punk, who stood firm on her soapbox, glaring at her all the way. Maggie was put in mind of Steven Berkoff. "You are asking to be put in your place." He then pointed at Nicky, who was enjoying the row, "Is that not right, boy?" Nicky's smile faded as he saw the three women and the student stare anxiously at him. Suddenly he wasn't sure what was going on, or whose side he was on.

Maggie wasn't one to stand by and watch a kid being bullied.

"No, mate," she responded. "It's you that needs putting in your place. Who rattled ycur cage, anyway? What's your problem?"

"That woman there's my problem. If you can call her a woman."

The punk remained on her soapbox and held her peace.

"That woman has every right to say what she believes," said

Maggie calmly. "It's a free country."

"Free speech, eh?"

"That's right."

"So I'm free to say, for instance, that all women are second rate creatures and should be kept only as domestic slaves."

Maggie paused. "Yes, you're free to say that."

The man in the suit turned his full attention onto Maggie and targeted her with his venom. "That they're too stupid and emotional to deserve the vote; that they don't even deserve to be educated."

"I've had enough of this conversation," said Maggie. "Entertaining though it's been." She turned to leave, but the man wasn't letting her go so easily.

"That's it, run away darling. I knew you wouldn't be able to maintain a logical debate. You've just proved my point." He cackled gleefully as Maggie turned again and shot him a filthy look.

"Logical debate is fine. Physical aggression is not," she hurled back.

"Who's being aggressive? Have I lifted a finger?"

A stranger suddenly intervened: he was stocky and strong looking, wore a shirt and trousers, and looked like a middle-class professional with his steel-rimmed glasses. He walked into the argument and addressed the man in the suit reasonably and forcefully:

"I think you're overstepping the mark, if I were you I'd leave it there."

"Oh you do, do you?" retorted the man gleefully.

"Yes, I do," insisted Chris. "Otherwise there'll be trouble. There's a policeman up there watching you."

They all looked round and saw that there was indeed a constable standing up on Princes Street, watching the proceedings. This seemed to have the desired calming effect on the man in the suit, who recovered his composure.

"All I'm saying, is *I'm* as entitled to free speech as anyone.

Okay?" he nodded at each one in turn, and they stared back, unable to find the words to contradict him.

Jill stood up. "I have a right to free speech too. And I say you should shut up and let the girl say what she's got to say."

"So let me get this straight," said the man in the suit carefully. "*You* can speak, and *she* can speak, but *I* can't? That's fascism, in my book."

"Maybe we should take a vote on it?" suggested Jonathan with a nervous smile.

Chris snorted. "I have to be somewhere," he muttered, but before he could leave, the punk jumped down from her soapbox and announced: "That's a good idea. Who wants to hear me speak?"

No-one raised a hand.

"Oh, thanks a bunch. There's solidarity for you."

The man in the suit was getting excited.

"No, come on, this is interesting," he said. "Who really believes in free speech? Come on, put your hands up. *Put* your *hands* up!"

Seven hands were reluctantly raised, including the man's own.

"*Thank* you. Democracy in action. Doesn't work unless we all play our part, does it? *Does* it?"

"Nooo," they chorused.

Chris tried to leave again.

"Hang on pal," said the man in the suit. "Just try this. You all believe in free speech, right? So I can say what I like – provided I'm not aggressive," he added for Maggie's benefit.

Chris and the others agreed.

"Okay. Here's a hypothetical situation. You!" He beckoned Nicky closer, and moved so that the two of them were roughly encircled by the rest. Nicky was very confused by now, but interested. He stood facing the man.

"He's a nice boy, isn't he? Pretty." The man invited their agreement, which they conceded. "I should think he's about fifteen. Jail bait, eh? Look at those neat little pecs, that tight little bum."

"What's your point?" asked Jill impatiently, aware of Nicky's discomfort.

"I'm just saying nice things about him! By the way, is anyone here against homosexuals?"

"No, of course not," said Maggie. No-one disagreed.

"That's good, because I'd bet my next pay packet that this kid is as gay as Larry Grayson. Of course I mean that as a compl – " instead of finishing his sentence, the man fell flat on his back, having been neatly head-butted by Nicky, who followed through by throwing himself on the man's chest and grabbing his collar in both hands.

Chris promptly tried to pull the boy off, but his grip was too strong. After a few seconds hesitation Jonathan joined in, and between them they hauled Nicky up, holding an arm each, as he kicked out wildly and yelled abuse.

Jill retreated backwards, mindful of her unborn baby, and tripped over the edge of the grass. She shrieked and sat down suddenly, and Maggie went to pick her up.

The punk unexpectedly went to the assistance of the man in the suit, who brushed her off and rose, his forehead bleeding, to shout at Nicky: "You're oppressing me!"

Nicky surprised his captors with a sudden lunge, which dragged them all into a heap, but the man managed to crawl away on hands and feet. He passed near enough to Jill for her to grab him by the foot, but he wriggled out of his slip-on shoe and escaped.

At that moment, three policemen appeared and swiftly hand-cuffed Chris, Jonathan and Nicky.

"You've got the wrong ones!" shouted Jill, scrambling to her feet. "All the trouble was caused by that man – " she looked round wildly, but the man in the suit had vanished, as had the punk.

"Shit," said Jill. "He's gone!" She shrugged in disbelief, and impulsively threw the shoe backwards over her shoulder, where it struck the fourth policeman in the face. To Jill's astonishment he promptly handcuffed her too, and Maggie for good measure, and before they could say, *Excuse me officer there's been a terrible mistake*, they were being marched up to Princes Street where a police van awaited them.

A middle-aged American couple had watched the whole thing from a bench a little further off. They looked at each other.

"Do you think we should have done something, Fred?" asked the woman.

"I guess. I don't know what, though. Hey, look, honey."

The punk was creeping cautiously out of a clump of rhododendrons. Seeing that the coast was clear, she called, "Come out, Craig. They've gone."

The man in the suit emerged, pressing a handkerchief to his temple and cursing.

"Oh shut up. What's a bit of a scratch in the cause of art?" said the girl. "Serves you right for picking on the wrong one. You were bloody lucky not to get arrested." She took a small hardboard signpost out of her carrier bag, and stuck it into the ground. The man moaned about his lost shoe, and then found it a few yards away. He put it on, and the two of them walked off as if nothing had happened.

The American couple waited a few moments and strolled down to take a look. The sign read:

You have just experienced
ANARKY Street Theatre:
What is Free Speech?

"Oh Fred, it was a happening, just like in the sixties."

"Hell, makes you feel old, don't it?"

"The cops were *so* convincing, I had no idea!"

Fred put his hand in his pocket and pulled out a handful of

change. "They forgot to leave a pail out."

"Maybe it was subsidised," suggested his wife, and Fred kept his money.

*

Whilst the police were interviewing Nicky, Jonathan took off his headdress and tried to remove his face paint with it. He soon looked less like a plague victim and more like ET.

"D'you think we'll be charged?" he asked the others anxiously. They shrugged.

"I can't see why," said Jill. "What have we done wrong? I don't know why we've been arrested at all!"

"Assaulting a police officer?" suggested Chris.

"But I didn't! You saw me, I had no idea he was standing behind me!"

Maggie patted her arm. "Of course. But you can forgive them for the misunderstanding." Jill's eyes brimmed with tears.

"I'm not usually like this at all," she said. "It's being pregnant. I should have stayed at home. I just thought, one more month and I'll be a mother, chained to the cooker till I'm fifty-odd. I've just got to go to Edinburgh with my play."

"You've got a play on too?" said Maggie. "That's amazing. All of us! What about you?" she asked Chris.

"No, actually I'm here for the Television Festival, it starts tonight. I just thought I'd take a walk, soak up the atmosphere. More fool me. I should have stayed in the bar at the George like everyone else."

"Well, to be honest, I'm glad you didn't. Much as I hate to admit it, you were pretty useful."

Maggie threw him a sideways smile that held a shy hint of admiration, allowing her cool blue eyes to linger long enough on his to discover that yes, he was interested in her. He sat a little straighter and put his wounded spectacles in his pocket.

The door opened and Nicky came in. Chris was taken away.

"What happened?" asked Maggie.

"Are you all right?" asked Jill.

"Did they charge you?" asked Jonathan.

"Not yet," said Nicky, swaggering over to the water jug and pouring a cup. He turned and regarded the others, who waited to see what he would say. He evidently enjoyed their attention. "As a matter of fact, they was pretty impressed with the way I floored that geezer. Seems he's been causing a lot of bother round here. I'm the first one to have a go. We was unlucky that he got away."

"So they're recommending you for a bravery award, I suppose," said Maggie drily.

Nicky frowned. "Nah, they never mentioned nothing like that."

"Has anyone got the time?" asked Jonathan.

"Ten to six," said Jill.

"Oh God," said Jonathan. "I'll never get to the theatre before the end of the show."

"Never mind, it's only a student production." Maggie had meant to comfort him, but he looked affronted. "Sorry, didn't mean to sound patronising. I, er, oh fuck it... " She couldn't be bothered with the hurt feelings of a bloody Footlights type.

The door opened again and Chris appeared looking pleased with himself, followed by a sergeant.

"Okay yous lot, you're all free to go. Just mind out what you do, in future. I don't want to see any of you in here again." The sergeant stood at the door and gazed sternly on them as they filed out thankfully, reserving his dirtiest look for Jonathan who sheepishly brought up the rear.

Outside on the pavement they turned to Chris and demanded to know how he had swung it.

"Oh, I just told them who I was and what happened," he said modestly. "That's all. They were perfectly reasonable."

"You were marvellous, then," exclaimed Jill, giving him a little hug and a peck on the cheek. "We're all in your debt." Only Nicky looked sullen. He didn't want to be in Chris' debt.

Maggie noticed and couldn't help commenting, "Come on, Nicky. Don't be a tosser."

"Do what?" he exclaimed.

"Stop pretending you're such a tough guy. Thank Chris for getting you out of there."

Nicky stuck his hands in his pockets and stared at the sky sulkily.

"Never mind," said Maggie, annoyed. "After all, he's only a kid. He'll grow up one day." The others smiled uncomfortably.

"Not at all, don't be silly," said Chris. "Look, there's a cab." He hailed it, and gave the driver a fiver. "Take the lady wherever she wants to go," he said, and held the door open for Jill.

"Thank you, thank you so much," she gushed, overwhelmed by emotion again.

"I say, you're not going towards the Haymarket are you?" said Jonathan, suddenly realising that he had a chance of rescuing his career prospects.

"I haven't a clue, but we will if you like. Hop in."

"How about you, Nicky?" asked Chris. "Presumably you've got somewhere to go?"

"He's just a nit with no future," smirked Jonathan. "Didn't you hear the officer?"

Nicky turned and scowled. "Fuck off you stuck-up twat. I'm just as good as you lot, you know. You ain't heard the last of me." He turned and stalked off up the road. No-one was impressed.

Chris and Maggie shared a feeling that they wanted to remain in each other's company: she loitered behind him and he failed to offer her a ride in the taxi. It pulled away, leaving them on the pavement.

"Well. What's Nicky's problem?" said Maggie.

"He's fifteen. He's working class. And he's a twerp," said Chris succinctly.

"Whereas you turned out to be a knight in shining armour!"

"I don't know about that," he said awkwardly. "I feel in need of a shower. My hotel's down there, d'you want to come back and clean up?" He was fairly sure that there was a promising sexual tension between them, but was uncertain of the correct way to act on it. He didn't usually go in for casual sex, and Maggie was not really his type, but today's events were extraordinary all round, and his triumph over the police force had inspired a sense of omnipotence.

"Actually that would be great," said Maggie, who found Chris something of a curiosity, and engaged in casual sex whenever she felt like it. "I've missed my show anyway."

They walked together into the large modern hotel, and up to Chris' room, where he took a shower while Maggie drank a beer from the mini-bar and watched the local news on television. Then Maggie took a shower while Chris drank a beer. By the time she emerged, wearing the hotel's white towelling dressing gown, a tray of sandwiches had been delivered by room service.

"Wow, this is the life."

Chris smiled, and stopped himself remarking that she was easily impressed. "Feminist theatre has to be low-budget, I suppose?"

"Too right. Lucky to get a mattress on the floor, never mind free crisps with your sandwiches. This is what you get when you're a producer at the BBC, is it?"

"All this and much, much more!" said Chris expansively. He made space for Maggie to sit beside him on the bed, and offered her the plate.

"Well it's very nice," said Maggie, biting the corner off a cheese sandwich. "But I don't know. Do you have, in the words of our new friend, freedom of speech? Artistically, I mean? Or have you sold your soul?"

"Not that I know of, I don't recall that being in the contract."

"I should read it again, if I were you," said Maggie provocatively, "when you've had your specs mended." She poured another beer and wondered whether he was ever going to make a move. They smiled at each other lingeringly, and Chris' nostrils flared a little. Suddenly he put his arm round Maggie, took her in his arms, and kissed her.

Ooh, she thought, he's the strong, silent type. Wants to be in charge.

"Let's lie down," he murmured, and they did.

Forty-five minutes later they said a friendly goodbye outside the hotel, and departed with an equal sense of purpose: Maggie to the Assembly Rooms to further the cause of feminism, and Chris to the opening event of the television festival, to debate with his colleagues on weighty matters of broadcasting.

Chapter Two

Nicky played down the incident when he told the youth theatre about it later; he was worried it might get back to his dad, who was a sergeant at Ilford police station. I could tell he was dying to brag about his street-fighting prowess, but he restrained himself as his mam and dad would disapprove. He asked me and Steve not to mention it to them.

He needn't have worried on my account, because my role in the NYT ended shortly after the Edinburgh trip; I had too much work on in my final year of study and teaching placements. (And yes, if you must know, Steve's wife found out.) I lost touch with them and to be honest I forgot all about Nicky until years later when I read an article on him in a broadcasting paper, which brought back that period of my life in vivid memories. It's funny how certain times become completely closed off to you as you move forward, and then someone opens a door suddenly and it's all there again, laid out in a dusty old room at the back of your mind.

Anyway. Back to the boy.

Nicky had wanted to join the police force ever since he was a toddler. He hoped to become a detective, and planned to join the force as soon as he left school. He worked hard to pass his exams, and his dad, Les, told him there was no reason why he wouldn't be accepted. When the application forms arrived they went through them together.

Nicky's mum, Doreen, watched them through the serving hatch as she cleared up the kitchen after dinner. They sat at the dining table in the living room, heads bent over folded arms. Nicky was built just like his dad, neat and well-formed, and only just tall enough to qualify for the force. He had the same handsome features, dark hair and healthy complexion, but in Nicky flowed all the energy and impatience of youth which had long since evaporated from Les.

Doreen was proud as anything. She and Les had waited ten years to have their baby, suffering three miscarriages before he arrived. Hopes of a large family were put aside as they accepted their fate and celebrated their one great blessing. Nicky was much loved, but never spoiled. They believed in discipline and instilled respect in him. When Nicky was five, they left their council flat in Canning Town and moved to a police house in Ilford. It was a step up for them, they now had two good-sized bedrooms and a garden front and back.

She was delighted for Les that Nicky had stuck to his ambition. They would have been just as happy for him to choose another career – as long as it was a sound one – but Doreen knew that it meant a great deal to Les. While it was nice to be hero-worshipped by a little boy, it was a real compliment to have a young man follow in your footsteps.

They had wondered whether the interest in drama would give him other ideas, but had refrained from warning him against trying to make a career in the theatre. They had the sense not to provoke a reaction, having seen plenty of youths do precisely what their parents warned them against. Nicky had spent four years in the Newham Youth Theatre, and they had attended all his shows, complimenting him without going overboard, and never complaining about the politics, which often struck them as unnecessarily left-wing. Les did, however, allow himself to comment on the director's sexuality.

"Camp as a row of tents, that Steve," he would remark after every opening night.

"So how come he's married with two kids?" was Nicky's usual reply.

"Don't mean a thing, son. Believe me, I've seen it all." Nicky would shrug and accept his father's experienced world-view. He liked Steve and had never seen anything to support Les' theory except larking about, and perhaps touching people more often than most men did – but then again, in the theatre, everyone did. It was a different way of behaving altogether. Nicky understood the rules both inside and outside the theatre, and was equally at ease with either. He was confident and self-possessed; he was liked, and he knew what he wanted. These were enviable qualities in his neighbourhood.

The truth was he had never seriously considered trying to become an actor or anything similar. He knew he had no special talent for it, and feared the prospect of financial insecurity. He had no intention of being gay either. He accepted Les' view that gay men were second-rate, that real men were big, strong and hairy, with rugged faces and stern frowns. No self-respecting man would ever take it like a woman, and women came even lower down the social scale than gay men.

"Look at film stars today," Les liked to point out. "Since they legalised homosexuality they're completely different. They're pretty boys, not proper men." Doreen agreed. She found the likes of Kirk Douglas far more attractive than Tom Cruise. Nicky went along with them, he was content to live and let live, as long as no-one put him on the spot – in which case he would assert himself with his fists. By Ilford standards, he was very easygoing. If ever he felt a twinge of teenage attraction for another man, he dispelled it. A gay boy he would not be.

A couple of weeks before Nicky's interview at the police college in Hendon, he came home one afternoon to find his parents clinging together on the sofa. His father was weeping, but he stopped when Nicky appeared and blew his nose.

"Is it Nan?" asked Nicky, sitting on the edge of the armchair.

"No darling," said his mum. "She's fine. Everyone's fine. Your dad's had a nasty shock, that's all." She patted Les' thigh and sighed.

Nicky leaned back in his chair, and waited for them to tell him what had happened. They seemed reluctant. "Don't tell me if you don't want to," he said, trying to sound mature, but failing to keep a hint of sulkiness from colouring his remark. Les looked at him for a moment and dropped his red-eyed gaze to the floor.

"Shall I tell him?" Doreen asked gently. Les nodded and his face creased up as despair overwhelmed him again, his head dropping into his hands. "Your dad's been suspended from work, along with four other officers. He's being investigated."

"What for?"

"Corruption!" Doreen's anger was apparent. "Can you credit it? Twenty-eight years' impeccable service, and they've got the nerve to accuse him of something like that." Her lips sealed tight and she hugged Les the way she used to hug Nicky when he had been thumped by another boy.

Nicky took a deep breath and blew his cheeks out. He gazed at the pair of them, completely gob-smacked. No-one spoke, and in the silence they heard a distant police siren amid the gentle whoosh of traffic pouring round the North Circular Road.

"Shall I make a cup of tea?"

"Yes please Nicky, that would be just the thing."

Nicky went in the kitchen in a daze. As he waited for the kettle to boil he pondered. There were two absolute constants in his scheme of things: the integrity of his father, and the integrity of the police force. Suddenly, both had been called into question. Either his father or the force was in the wrong. It couldn't be his father. That meant it was the force. It must have made a mistake. But how could it get everything so wrong as to betray one of its own most loyal members?

He took the mugs into the living room and set them on the coffee table, sitting in the armchair again. His father had tried to pull himself together, but looked awful. Nicky had never seen him like this before, and he found it embarrassing.

"Don't worry, Dad, they must have got the wrong man. It'll all come out."

"That's what I told him," responded Doreen. "It must be a mistake. Especially if they've suspended Dick and Terry and Walter as well."

"Have they?" Nicky was amazed to hear Les' old friends named. They were all as familiar and reliable as Les himself. "What are you all supposed to have done, then?"

Les cleared his throat. "Apparently a local villain's been giving us all a bung to turn a blind eye to his rackets." He tried to laugh it off, but the sound he made was more like a sob. He spread his hands and shrugged. "As you can see, we've been living it up for years at his expense. Big cars, fur coats, fancy holidays."

Doreen smiled bitterly. "As if! There you are, you see, there's no evidence. It won't come to anything. I expect they've just suspended you so they can be seen doing the right thing. You'll all be back on the job in no time."

Les nodded miserably. Nicky wondered why he was taking it so badly. Normally his father was totally confident. The shame of the accusation must have hit him very hard indeed.

"No-one's going to think you're guilty, Dad, no-one who knows you could possibly think that."

"Mud sticks, son."

"What about all that *walk tall, walk straight and look the world right in the eye* stuff you used to tell me when I was a kid?" Nicky tried to coax Les back into behaving like the father he wanted him to be. This was weird. Really weird.

Doreen got up. "Nicky's right, Les. Take a bit of your own advice. Show them all you're innocent. The truth always comes out. I'm going to put dinner on." She left the room.

Les glanced up at his son uncomfortably. "I wish it was that simple." Nicky bit his thumbnail. He knew perfectly well that justice wasn't always meted out fairly, and innocent people did sometimes go to jail. But he was amazed to see his father brought so low. Where was his courage, why so much despair?

"Are they framing you?" he asked quietly. Les sighed, chewing his lips. He shrugged. Nicky frowned, then sneered. "Her Majesty's Glorious Police Force. All my life I've been waiting for the moment when I could be part of it. And just when it's about to happen, they turn out to be the bleeding KGB. Well I'm glad I found out in time, Dad."

"What d'you mean?"

"There's no way I'm going to join the organisation that shafts my dad. Not you. How could they?" His grey eyes blazed with anger and disgust, as he sought to reassure his father by affirming his faith in him. Les blinked back at him anxiously, and began to speak, then stopped. He struggled to hold Nicky's honest gaze, then gave up, allowing his head to fall as he covered his eyes with one hand. In that moment Nicky realised the truth: Les was guilty. It swept over him with terrifying clarity and left him breathless. He stared at his dad, unable to marshal his thoughts, then abruptly got up and left the house.

"Was that Nicky going out?" asked Doreen, popping her head through the serving hatch in surprise.

"Yes, he's a bit upset," Les muttered. "Isn't sure he wants to join up, now."

"Well that's understandable. Not to worry, it'll all blow over."

Nicky took the tube into the West End, and sat in a coffee bar off Leicester Square. He stared into his glass of coke and tried to come to terms with the day's revelations, feeling as though his childhood had come to a sudden end in a cataclysmic explosion. He tried to reason it through from his father's point of view: Les had never been a Dixon of Dock Green; he wasn't above pinching a bit of stationery from the office, and frequently parked illegally, he even drove after drinking on occasion. But he had always been very clear on the essential morality which society depended on and the police enforced. He said he knew who the real villains were, he was after them, not the regular citizens who over-stepped the mark by a few inches. It was a game of strategy, he said, you know who they are, and they know you know, but can you find the evidence to convict them? It was this cat-and-mouse game that had always appealed to Nicky. His favourite pastime at home was watching *Columbo* with his dad.

So how come Les was in the villains' pocket? The only explanation was that Les was a hypocrite, a bent cop, worse even than the villain who paid him to keep quiet. He had not only deceived the force and society itself, he had deceived his wife and son. Nicky couldn't forgive him that. Les couldn't even forgive himself. It had been written all over him. Doreen didn't see it, it was easy to pull the wool over her eyes, and her simple-minded blind faith in Les would carry her through, provided he never confessed to her. But Les and Nicky were closer than that, and understood each other better. Father and son, they were almost the same person save for the age difference, or so he had thought up to now.

It took Nicky an hour and a half to break away from his youth. He simply sat and thought, looked at the situation from all the angles he could think of, and came back to the same conclusion. He was finished with his dad, with the police force, with his whole life as he had believed it to be. It was all built on lies. He would start again. He would bury the hurt and the bitterness he felt, he couldn't possibly enter the police force knowing what he now knew. He would find a job, anything, keep looking around until something turned up that interested him. He would keep his own counsel, do as he thought fit, be completely independent. He was his own man now. He wouldn't leave home just yet, he would keep up the charade for his mother's sake, but inside he would be different.

He left the café and bought a copy of the *Evening Standard*, took it to a bench in the middle of Leicester Square and sat down to read the Situations Vacant.

He circled a number of possible jobs, and since one company was based in Soho, he went to look for their office. It was nearly six o'clock when he found it, but all the lights were on in the building – it was in a scruffy, narrow street in which every doorway carried an assortment of bells and nameplates. He pushed the bell marked Magenta Television Productions Ltd and walked in when he heard a buzzer. Magenta was based in two tiny offices on the second floor, up a steep, lino-covered staircase. He found it atmospheric and not at all intimidating.

An Asian man of indeterminate age greeted him and shook Nicky's hand when he said he had come about the advert for a runner, congratulating him on being the first applicant.

"We like people who show initiative. I'm Haris Maqbool, Finance Director. My partner's on the phone in the other office, but if you'd like to wait we could interview you right away."

"Sure," said Nicky, trying to create a good impression. Not wanting to let on that he didn't know what a runner was, he set about asking questions which might elicit the information without betraying his ignorance.

"Can you tell me a bit about the company, and the post?" he asked boldly, sitting himself on an old wooden chair.

"Of course. We're a newish outfit, very small as yet, but we've just won a commission to make a daytime quiz show for a regional ITV station. We're very excited. It's a terrifically good project, and has a wonderful star. Our company is going to do extremely well. As our runner you will be an assistant in all matters, from top to bottom. You will make the tea but you will also learn the business, if you wish. You will earn very little to start with but a very great deal in the long run. This is a truly wonderful opportunity."

Growing up in the East End had not made Nicky naïve, and he knew Haris was embroidering the truth. He also knew that embroidery was a key skill when you had something to sell, and thought Haris was probably rather good at his job.

"Sounds just what I'm looking for," said Nicky.

"Let me fetch my partner," said Haris, and disappeared into the next room. Nicky looked around the walls, seeing little to attract his interest apart from a poster featuring Marilyn Monroe. If Magenta Productions had made any shows so far, they had little in the way of publicity to show for it.

"Alright, me old son?" rasped a cockney smoker's voice, as a wiry man with a boxer's physique and greying wavy hair entered the room, followed by Haris. He wore a creased shirt with purple braces and a loosened tie, blue suit trousers, yellow socks and no shoes. He shook Nick's hand very hard, and scrutinised him.

"Rex Barclay. So you're the new runner, are you?"

Nicky was taken aback. "If you think I'm suitable."

"Haris thinks so. He's a great judge of character. Tell us about yourself, then."

Nicky talked about his experience in school and in the youth theatre, omitting any reference to the police, and said he was interested in a career in television but didn't know much about it so far.

"Of course you don't, how could you at your age?" said Rex. "The point is, are you keen to learn?"

"Yes, definitely," said Nicky, so convincingly that he even believed himself.

"Then the job's yours. On a month's probation. If it don't work out we'll part company. If it does, great."

They shook hands on it, and Rex winked at him. "You seem a likely lad. Handsome too. Matter of fact, you remind me of myself at your age. Now if *I'd* had a Rex Barclay to work for when *I* was seventeen, I'd be running the BBC by now. As it is, it's going to take me a few years yet. There we are, that's life. Alright Nicky, start on Monday, ten o'clock."

"Great. Thanks a lot. I'll see you then."

Nicky felt extremely proud of himself, although he had no idea what he was in for. He liked television as much as anybody, so it might turn out to be interesting. He travelled home feeling at least three inches taller, and entered the house to find his parents eating fish and chips at the kitchen table. His mother jumped up solicitously.

"Oh Nicky, are you alright? I didn't make you dinner in case you was having something out."

"It's okay Mum, I'm fine. Listen, I've got a job. I'm going to be in television."

They stared open-mouthed as he announced coolly that he would be cancelling his interview at Hendon: he had decided on a different career.

"Oh, well done!" said his mother at last, nonplussed. "It's a bit sudden though, ain't it?"

Nicky smiled tightly. "Yeah, well. It's been a funny old day. I think I'll nip out and get myself a burger. See you later."

"Bye dear," said Doreen, and looked anxiously at Les, whose pale face had remained mute. He watched as his son left with only the briefest glance in his direction, and sank even lower into his chair. Doreen, oblivious to their unspoken tension, continued her campaign of jollification.

"Come on Les, eat your chips before they go cold, you know you don't like them soggy." He did as he was told.

Chapter Three

Now I'm going to jump forward a few years to the dawn of the nineties. After I'd been a teacher for a few years I knew that directing the annual school play wasn't going to satisfy my ambitions, and I looked to the wider world. I managed to get a researcher's contract on *Grange Hill*, the BBC1 school drama series, which happened to be set exactly where I'd been working. I was thrilled silly to get this lucky break, which allowed me to work my way up to script editor in the space of two series. I was able to contribute my experience whilst learning everything about television production from the bottom up. I worked at least sixty hours a week and I loved every minute – I was young enough not to suffer physically. I couldn't do it now! *Grange Hill* was a first rate show, and many of the creative staff went on to become famous names, even Oscar winners. I think they'd all agree that we learned our craft there, honing our skills on the strop of the relentless weekly schedule… our young audience demanded that we reflect their lives truthfully, and we spared no effort to achieve that.

Around the same time Maggie, whom I was soon to meet and befriend, was growing weary of touring feminist socialist plays and had begun to see the appeal of a mortgage and a home to call her own.

Maggie didn't see television as a sell-out, as some of her comrades insisted. She saw it as an opportunity to reach a much wider audience. A six-month tour with a successful new play was likely to attract a total audience of six thousand people at the most, whereas a single episode of *EastEnders* could reach up to twenty million.

She approached her career change with typical thoroughness, studying as much television drama as she could whilst working most evenings (few people possessed a video recorder then) and keeping a scrapbook of cuttings from the *Radio Times* in order to learn who were the producers and directors she most admired. She was looking for a guru, someone she could admire unreservedly. She would be happy to take a lowly post at the BBC provided she had access to a brilliant producer who would teach her how to make world-shattering, award-winning contemporary drama. Anything less wasn't worth bothering with. She was confident that she had the talent to succeed, she was willing to give her all in the cause of art, and knew she could climb to the top of the meritocracy.

She had narrowed her list of potential gurus down to two, but had yet to meet either of them. They were Basil Richardson and Stewart Walker, both of whom had been at the BBC for years, and who had between them produced nearly all Maggie's favourite dramas: work which had caught the spirit of the age, given voice to the underdog, and pushed back the boundaries of television. She felt they saw the world from her own point of view, despite being men at least twenty years older than her, because she recognised in their work her own sense of outrage against exploitation and oppression.

She wrote to each man asking if they needed a script editor or reader, but received politely negative responses. Undaunted, she continued to assault the drama department until she was eventually offered a three-month contract as a trainee script editor. She would have to read unsolicited scripts every day, but there was the potential to work her way up to producing. It wasn't exactly the start she had hoped for, but it was a foot in the door, and she intended to make the most of it.

As her letter of employment had given a starting date but not a time, she had thought it wise to arrive at Television Centre at nine o'clock. Finding nothing but locked doors on the fifth floor, she had wandered aimlessly round the circular corridor, reading the names on the doors and the deeply uninteresting health and safety notice boards. At nine thirty she found the Head of Drama's outer office open and a stern but maternal-looking middle-aged woman sitting behind a pile of the day's papers, looking through a huge appointments diary.

"I'm sorry to bother you, but I'm looking for Fenella Proctor-Ball. I'm the new trainee."

"Isn't she in her office? Better come in and sit down then. She's usually here about ten o'clock. I'm Vera, Peter's PA. The tea bar will open soon if you want to get a coffee. I'll keep trying Fenella's office for you."

"Thanks very much."

Maggie sat on a saggy, grubby sofa by a coffee table laden with broadcasting periodicals for most of the morning, listening to the distant battering of pneumatic tools. She tried not to feel annoyed as she sat pretending to read the magazines, but couldn't relax and began to feel a complete idiot as the morning unrolled. Busy people came in and out of the office, glancing in her direction, so she tried to wear a pleasant, unconcerned expression. She had arrived well-prepared and raring to go, imagining that she would be quickly absorbed into the organisation and given a desk piled high with scripts to read and reports to write.

A grammar-school girl from Huddersfield, Maggie had (not unlike myself) grown up regarding the BBC as a magical Olympian paradise which existed somewhere in the ether that was London. It was peopled by urbane, charming men and glamorous women, all of whom spoke like royalty, knew about everything, and conversed articulately with astounding insight and hilarious wit. It never crossed her mind to aspire to work there herself. Instead she worked hard to get into Bristol

University, where she read just enough English literature to scrape an average degree, and fell in love with the theatre, which had satisfied her desire to change the world for ten years.

On hearing that she wanted to go into television a friend of a friend had invited her to spend a day on the set of *Casualty*, a recently-established cutting-edge medical series which had already fallen foul of the government, which was extremely unhappy to see the consequences of their NHS cuts represented to the public in their full glory by the BBC. A day trip to the location in Bristol had turned out to be a fascinating and inspiring experience. The set was a permanent, purpose-built maze in a huge warehouse, teeming with technicians. The actors were friendly, and good-natured banter enlivened the otherwise tedious recording process. Maggie was hugely impressed at their professionalism as scene after scene was taped in a matter of minutes – there was never time for re-takes merely to improve the acting. She observed as the script editor monitored each scene to ensure that no serious errors were made, and checked the running time in case cuts or new material would be required at a moment's notice.

Maggie loved it. She knew she could do the job – including the rest of it, which consisted of working with the writer of each episode to help them achieve the highest possible standard of writing whilst satisfying the technical, medical and serial story needs of the show. She was a good team player and would slot in well here, or on another series perhaps, all her theatre experience was directly relevant. The script team clearly felt a strong sense of achievement and job satisfaction, and had the added reward of VHS tapes of every show they worked on, whereas theatre plays were as ephemeral as conversation: Maggie's only record of her life's work so far lay in a box full of tatty scripts, cheap production photos and programmes.

Perhaps it was the sustained two-year effort she had invested into breaching the walls of the BBC that was responsible for the paralysing wave of boredom and anti-climax which overwhelmed her as she sat waiting for Fenella to turn up. It was nearly half past twelve when Vera finally called over, "Fenella's in her office, if you'd like to pop in."

Fenella's door was open but she was on the phone. Nonetheless she beckoned Maggie in, indicating a chair piled up with scripts and books, which Maggie tried to remove carefully before sitting down. She pretended she couldn't follow Fenella's conversation – evidently an argument with her husband about their nanny – and studied the walls of the little office, which were entirely obscured by enormous shelves labelled at intervals and stacked high with scripts. Novels were heaped around the floor, and Fenella's huge old-fashioned briefcase poured papers onto the carpet. She herself was about forty, Maggie reckoned. She was dressed in a homely but expensive way reminiscent of a senior academic. She wore glasses on a silver chain and a permanent expression of ironic exasperation.

As the minutes passed Maggie felt irritation well up inside her once again, and she forced it back down. She sat in a patient attitude, crossing her chino-covered legs and fiddling with the zip on her ankle boots. She'd bought these GAP casuals thinking they were the kind of smart casual clothes people here would wear, but now she wondered whether she looked dowdy. She was glad she had grown her spiky hair out, and wondered whether she would have to start wearing make-up on a daily basis. She hoped to God that wouldn't be necessary; she felt over-dressed with earrings on.

Eventually Fenella put the phone down and sighed, as if she'd already put in ten hours' work. "Hi. Welcome. How are you settling in?"

Maggie was stumped for an answer. At the very least she had expected an apology for keeping her waiting. Anxious not to get off on the wrong foot, she hedged her bets with a cautious smile and replied, "So far so good."

"Good. Well I'm afraid I'm completely snowed under today,

we've an offers meeting on Thursday, but take that little lot and come and see me when you've read them."

Maggie tried to sound relaxed and enthusiastic as she picked up the pile of scripts she had just put on the floor. "Where shall I do it?"

"Haven't you got an office yet?"

"No."

"Go and see Morag in 5233." Fenella picked up the phone again. "Enjoy!" she said with a gleam in her eye, and turned back to her desk with a frown of concentration.

It was three o'clock by the time Maggie had been found a desk. Well, seven desks, plus three typewriters and a large grey steel cupboard all to herself, because this was an empty production office, and the only available space. Trying to put the frustrating day behind her, she sorted through her scripts and books and made a list of them. Then she organised her desk. She went round all the drawers in the office and acquired a fine selection of BBC pens and pencils, clips and rubbers. Soon her desk was the acme of office furniture, dripping with the tools of her craft, adorned with in-tray, out-tray, anglepoise lamp and phone.

She wandered round the circular corridor and discovered Stewart Walker's and Basil Richardson's offices, but she didn't manage to catch sight of either of them, so she went back to her office and picked up a script. She couldn't concentrate at all. As the window looked onto a roof and a satellite dish she gazed at the walls, enjoying the mystique of the abandoned production charts and schedules which papered them: the last occupants had been making a major costume drama. There was a cast list of thirty names, most of them famous and some of them related. Crates full of box files, drawings and models littered the floor. Wherever she looked she could find no references to 'offers meetings' so she was still in the dark on that front; she would have to wait until she met with Fenella again to find out what she was talking about.

In the last hour, Maggie read a six-page proposal and made copious notes on it. She was interrupted only twice, once by a phone call for someone called Tristram, and once by a hand which knocked gently on the door and opened it displaying a dark sleeve as it extended to put a piece of white paper on a post-tray next to the door. Then it felt blindly round the tray underneath, withdrew and vanished, closing the door quietly. Maggie resigned herself to solitary labour, and went home, taking one of the novels she had to report on.

After two days of reading alone in her office, Maggie was delighted to receive a phone call that was for her.

"Hi! I'm Sally, I'm a script editor here too. Are you free for lunch?"

"Oh, that would be great."

"See you on the bridge at one?"

"Sorry? Where's that?"

"Tell you what, come to my office and we'll go together. It's two doors on from yours on the way to the lift."

"Okay, great, see you then. Thanks for calling, it's really nice of you."

"Don't mensh. Bye."

Maggie felt absurdly pleased, but realised she didn't sound very cool. She must try and act like a professional – so first she must find out how a professional acts in the BBC. Sally would provide clues.

At one o'clock she knocked on the door labelled SALLY FARQUAR-BINNS, SCRIPT EDITOR. She heard Sally on the phone, saying: 'Anyway must go, awfully sorry – got to do some biz over lunch. Call you soon. Kiss kiss.' The phone went down and Sally called, "Hi! Come in Maggie!"

Sally was about Maggie's age, slim and elegant with thick glossy hair and expensive jewellery. "Nice to meet you. How's it going?"

Maggie decided she'd rather be honest than cool. "Actually it's a bit strange. You're the first person I've talked to yet."

"Really? You poor thing. Don't worry, I'll introduce you to a few people."

"You've got a lovely office," said Maggie, admiring the view over the car park. "You can see who's coming and going."

"Not bad is it? Gives me something to do!"

Maggie chuckled. There were scripts and books on every shelf and surface, and videos piled on a trolley bearing a television monitor and VCR. Sally clearly had plenty to do.

The self-service canteen, which Maggie had looked for unsuccessfully up to now, was large and spacious and occupied three floors of a purpose-built extension to the main building. To reach it they walked across a closed-in bridge which was lined with poster-sized photos of a grinning Terry Wogan with many of his famous guests: his live early-evening chat show was the bedrock of the BBC1 schedule. Once in the canteen, there seemed to be an endless range of hot and cold food, and the atmosphere was cheerful and busy. Maggie looked around, hoping to see a familiar newscaster or at least a table of actors amusingly dressed in *Dr Who* costumes, but saw only ordinary people like herself. To a theatre freelance used to having lunch in a greasy spoon café the canteen was rather grand, but those used to eating in restaurants considered it third-rate. Maggie had a large plateful of casserole with chips and peas, pleased to find it was subsidised. It tasted pretty good too, she thought. Sally picked at an avocado salad and seemed more interested in who else was in the room. She asked Maggie about her theatre experience and was intrigued by her Huddersfield grammar school, although she seemed to think Huddersfield was somewhere in the Black Country. When Maggie put her right she shrugged. "Oh well, it's all 't' north, isn't it?" When asked, she said she came from Kingston.

"Cornwall?" inquired Maggie with a grin.

"No, Surrey" corrected Sally, without one.

Maggie learned that Sally also worked for Fenella, and that she had some *very* interesting projects in development. She had joined from a major publishing house and was evidently well connected with their list of writers. Sally thanked God Almighty that she didn't have to slog through the slush pile anymore reading amateur crap. Maggie felt shocked when she realised that she herself had inherited the 'slush pile', as she was giving very sympathetic consideration to each writer and had made detailed notes on every idea, good and bad. Apparently Fenella expected all of them to be rejected.

"The thing is," explained Sally kindly, "there are only so many slots aren't there? And we've already got tons of projects commissioned from writers we know are really good. So the chances of finding anything decent in the slush pile are remote to say the least. Trouble is we have to read everything that's sent in because of the public service remit. Don't worry, when you've served your time some other bugger'll get lumbered with it."

"But how else do new writers break in?"

"They always get through eventually if they're good enough. It's the pyramid system. They all start equal at the base, and the best ones float their way up to the top."

It sounded reasonable but Maggie suspected there was a hidden flaw in the logic. "Like scum, you mean?"

Sally smiled. "Exactly. We skim off the scum."

"From the top."

"No, from the bottom."

Maggie decided not to pursue it. If this pleasant but decidedly snobbish woman had dismissed all those poor writers out of hand, at least Maggie would give them a fair reading. She made a mental resolution to find a brilliant new writer in the slush pile and champion his or her rise from obscurity.

"Hiii Sally," drawled a deep, cultivated voice, as a slim young man with floppy blond hair sat down at their table. "Mind if I barge in?"

"Jonathan my sweet. Meet Maggie. She's the new trainee, started this week. Doesn't know a soul."

"Charmed," said Jonathan with a self-mocking tip of the head and a raised eyebrow. "Well now you know two souls."

"Except that you haven't got one," quipped Sally.

"Ouch! Wicked girl! How dare you?" he replied jovially. He looked quizzically at Maggie. "Haven't we met somewhere before? Were you an actress?"

"No, but I did work in theatre." She didn't recognise Jonathan at all, now that he looked as if he'd just stepped out of Selfridges' window.

He shrugged. "Maybe we crossed paths somewhere or other."

"More than likely," agreed Maggie, uncomfortably – she normally had a good memory for faces.

"How's Basil?" asked Sally. "Still wrestling with the man mountain?"

"God knows why he bothers. The first draft of ep one's in but it's in a terrible state. The guy's spelling is so bad I can hardly tell what he means. I'm thinking of asking him for a glossary."

"Won't it go, then?"

"Probably, Basil wants us to go to as many drafts as necessary before we even show it to Peter. He calls it extraordinary writing. It's extraordinary alright!" He and Sally giggled.

Maggie's attention was riveted by this exchange. How many Basils could there be in the department? This public school twit was apparently privileged to work with her hero, but he obviously didn't appreciate his good fortune.

"Is that Basil Richardson?" she enquired.

"Yep," said Jonathan. "I'm his script editor."

"Lucky you!"

Jonathan's lack of response indicated that luck had nothing to do with it as far as he was concerned.

"Who's the writer you're working with?" Maggie ventured.

"Tony Scott." Maggie hadn't heard of him. "He's the Next Big Thing, according to Basil. Twenty years a miner, two years a writer. Working class hero, all that crap."

"Sounds interesting."

"Yes, *interesting* is about right."

"What's the project?"

Jonathan was beginning to look as if he didn't like having questions fired at him. "It's a four-parter for 2: Love-on-the-dole-type thing. Miners," he said, with a trace of reluctance.

"Sounds great." Maggie felt it would be indiscreet to enquire further. She couldn't help disliking this superior young man. Sally, on the other hand, obviously liked him a lot, and spent the rest of lunch talking knowledgeably to him about people Maggie hadn't heard of: apparently there was to be a new Controller of BBC1, which might have a significant impact on drama requirements for the channel. The best possible appointee would be a man with a drama background, but this was thought extremely unlikely, and there was always a worry that any new controller would favour his particular field at the expense of the others.

The conversation moved on to a discussion of the latest David Hare play at the National, which Maggie hadn't seen, so she made another mental note to go.

"Of course it's absurd that David isn't writing for us," remarked Sally.

"I suppose he just loves the theatre," said Maggie. The others regarded her with amusement.

"Probably got film deals all over the place" said Jonathan, in a tone that settled the discussion.

Back in her office after lunch Maggie felt twice as lonely. Accustomed to the camaraderie of a theatre company, she longed to feel part of a team pulling in the same direction, and the after-effects of her lunch with Sally and Jonathan were a sense of bewilderment and social ineptitude. Although they had both been perfectly pleasant, there was a great gulf between them and Maggie, which she had no idea how to cross. There was no real point of contact. She felt she had nothing in common with them whatsoever. They treated her as a peer, but as a stranger: well, fair enough, she was the new girl.

She wondered how she could get to Basil. Or Stewart. Making friends with Jonathan clearly wasn't a way forward, they were chalk and cheese. Maybe Basil wouldn't like her anyway, if he liked Jonathan.

She looked at her pile of scripts and books, which had hardly been dented so far, and decided to get through them as fast as possible so that she could go back to Fenella soon and talk her through each project with a well-thought-out assessment of their potential for production, thereby earning Fenella's respect and her right to a place on the team.

Two and a half weeks after her first day, Maggie called Fenella to say she'd read everything and could she come and talk about them.

"Goodness, you *are* quick, aren't you?" said Fenella. "Anything good among them?"

"Yes, one or two are very promising."

"Okay. Well I'm really busy this week, can you do me a short report on each one, say a page each, and drop them off? I'll leave your next pile with Anthea."

"I was rather hoping to have a chat. There's a few questions I'd like to ask."

"Really?" Fenella didn't sound keen to squander her precious time on answering silly questions from newcomers.

"Maybe I could ask Anthea instead."

"Yes, do that. She knows the ropes."

Maggie felt disappointed but not downhearted. She spent a day re-writing her reports to shorten them from three pages to one, and double-checked her own notes on each writer so that she could refer back to them if she needed to in the future. Then she called Anthea to announce that she was coming round to see her. Anthea Onojaife was as black as Brucie's twirl-girl Anthea

Redfern was white. She was secretary to Fenella and to another development executive. Tall and straight-backed, her large features seemed even larger in contrast with her very short hair, and her age was hard to guess. She looked bored and pissed off when Maggie entered her tiny office. The connecting door into Fenella's office was open, and Maggie could hear her on the phone, cajoling somebody.

"Hi Anthea. I'm Maggie. These are for Fenella." She plonked the pile down on a chair. "She said she'd leave some more stuff for me to pick up, and that you could answer a few questions for me."

"Did she? Okay, take a seat. She'll be off the phone in a minute."

Yet again, Maggie sat and waited. Evidently Fenella hadn't told Anthea about any of this, and Anthea wasn't going to act on Maggie's word alone. "Shall I get us some coffees?" she offered, but Anthea shook her head. As an afterthought she smiled and added, "Thanks." Maggie picked up a circular advertising the new Drama Discussion Group, which looked like an opportunity to meet other members of the department. Maybe she could join. Maybe Stewart and Basil would be there.

Anthea disappeared into Fenella's office and a muttered conversation took place. She emerged with three large novels.

"Fenella would like you to read these and do synopses. They're all advance copies."

Maggie accepted them happily, "To see if they'd work on television?"

"That's the general idea."

"Great."

Anthea's mouth twitched. "Everything all right?"

"Oh yes."

"Good." Anthea went back to her typing. Maggie felt uncomfortable about pursuing a conversation, but Fenella had told her to ask Anthea, so she did.

"Can you tell me what an 'offers meeting' is?

"That's when the heads of department offer the controllers the new projects they want to make. They happen twice a year."

"Oh, I see. And the controllers say yes or no."

"Sometimes. Mostly they say they'll have a look at it."

"So there's like, two deadlines a year for new shows?"

"Yeah, but they can take projects in any time."

"So – sorry if I sound stupid, but what's the point of having offers meetings?

"There has to be a system." Anthea made it sound crashingly obvious. Maggie decided to quit while she was ahead, and stood up to go, not daring to ask Anthea if she would like to have lunch one day. She was certain Anthea wouldn't want to, and not sure she wanted to herself. She just wanted to have a mate in this forbidding place.

"By the way," she added, "do you know how I might join the Drama Discussion Group?"

"Just turn up. Didn't you get the memo?"

"What memo?"

"That one." Anthea pointed to the circular Maggie had already read.

"No, I haven't had any post yet."

"Aren't you on the rooms list?"

"The what?"

Anthea sighed and produced a thick document stapled at one corner, which listed all the drama employees, their room numbers and so on. She looked at the back page. "I thought as much – you're not on it. Here's a spare one. You need to call Maxine and tell her to put you on it for the internal mail."

"Oh, I get it. Thing. There's this hand that visits my office bringing post for other people. I think of it being the Addams family running the post service." Maggie's nervous attempt at humour had failed.

"You have to look out for yourself here, keep the memo if you like."

Maggie thanked her rather too warmly, felt embarrassed, and

returned to her office wondering what Anthea had meant exactly. It certainly wasn't an offer of friendship. She sat down and devoured the details of the memo. It listed four programmes, all drama department productions due for transmission before the discussion date in a fortnight's time, which everyone was asked to watch. No problem, thought Maggie, noticing with delight that Stewart Walker had produced one of the films. He was sure to be there.

In the next week, Maggie read two of the novels and wrote a six-page synopsis of each. Determined to pin Fenella down to a meeting, she dropped them off with Anthea, with a note to Fenella asking whether she had time to talk about the first pile of scripts yet. Anthea glanced at it. "You're too late, I'm afraid. I've already rejected them."

"Sorry?"

"Fenella told me to send them all back."

Maggie blinked. "*All* of them? Just like that? Even the good ones?"

Anthea smiled. "It's a tough old world, isn't it?" At that moment Fenella's door opened and she came out, chatting to Sally. They walked straight out of the office without acknowledging Maggie or Anthea.

Maggie took a deep breath. She'd been working there nearly a month now, and still hadn't had a proper conversation with her boss. A faint sense of panic began to lurk at the back of her mind.

"I mean, really, it's just that I don't know whether I'm doing what she wants. Do you think she's happy with my reports?"

"I imagine she'd tell you if she wasn't," said Anthea stiffly, and the phone rang. She picked it up, and Maggie decided to leave. She didn't bother saying goodbye; it wasn't expected.

Evidently she hadn't been employed because they valued her opinions; they merely wanted her to stand at the gates of the

BBC with a metaphorical riot shield, turning away the thousands who mistakenly believed that the 'Auntie' affectionately referred to by the likes of Terry Wogan was a kind, friendly organisation with writers' best interests at heart and a sympathetic interest in their work. Nevertheless, she must have courage in her abilities and believe in her own judgement. No doubt Fenella would call her in eventually – she would have to, as Maggie's contract was already a third over, and there would inevitably be some kind of assessment. Or so she assumed. She would be patient. Better not to annoy people when they're busy with important matters. It would be awful if they didn't give her another contract, she'd barely dipped a toe in the water.

After another day or two of reading, during which she found another writer who she thought showed promise, she began to wonder what was the point of her efforts, if everything was to be rejected anyway. Did Sally really mean *everything*? Maybe she should start developing a project on her own, as Sally seemed to be doing. She knew lots of theatre writers, maybe she would call a couple if she didn't hear from Fenella soon. On the other hand, she ought to ask permission first. Damn that bloody woman. She was neglecting her duties. If she was responsible for a trainee, she ought to be training her.

Later that evening, she left her office and walked to the lifts, frowning to herself and jiggling her keys. She pressed all the buttons and waited, gazing automatically at the Ceefax monitor until a lift arrived and the doors pinged open, when she stepped in and turned to face the closing doors. Two men were already inside, discussing the test match. As they travelled down a floor and stopped again to receive more people, Maggie noticed a familiar tone in one of the voices. Unable to turn and look, she swiftly scoured her mental files and remembered a man she'd encountered in Edinburgh several years earlier: a BBC wonk who'd proved unexpectedly capable at the police station, and afterwards, in fact. The unfaltering conversation behind her indicated that he hadn't recognised her, so she dawdled out when they reached the ground floor, pausing in the foyer to pretend to check her bag so she could surreptitiously get a good look at him. Yes, that was Chris. He'd hardly changed at all, but wore a very smart suit – Armani? – and carried an even smarter briefcase. He and his companion walked with total ease and confidence out to a waiting limo, where a chauffeur opened the back door for them.

Maggie shrugged to herself, and headed off to the tube station.

Chapter Four

That's right, I slipped Jonathan in there without warning you. His Cambridge University production of Henry V had led directly to a job at the National Theatre and then the BBC, thanks to a couple of contacts he had – did I mention he was an old Etonian? By the time Maggie and I had squeezed ourselves under the thick glass doors of the BBC, he was comfortably established on a staff contract (that means permanent employment in normal language).

Please don't think I resent the ease with which he strolled through his career. On second thoughts, you can think that if you like. Seeing how it's true.

What about the other bloke, you're probably thinking. What's he up to? Chris was a General Trainee, which is BBC-speak for potential senior manager. (George Orwell worked at the BBC, you know. Do you think that's where he got the idea for Newspeak?) Up to now Chris had neither distinguished himself nor blotted his copybook. He was on the lookout for something that would put him ahead of his peers in the dog-eat-dog race to the top. Appropriately enough, he'd just been given an office in the brand new building on the site of the old White City Greyhound Stadium. Perhaps the frantic rivalry of the dogs lingered on, trapped and circulating round the state-of-the-art air conditioning system.

BBC: the Best of British Culture! Chris wrote on his A4 pad, smiling with satisfaction. He underlined it and made a row of dots below, *bullet points* as they were called. Americans had such a clear, assertive way of doing things, and Chris loved to be on the ball with the latest management methods.

- *Newsnight*.
- David Attenborough.
- Dennis Potter's *Singing Detective*. (Not the other stuff.)
- *Fawlty Towers*.

He paused: these were their best shows, he believed, but bizarrely, he couldn't call any other great shows to mind. He tutted, annoyed with himself. He'd have to do some research. How silly, after working there over ten years – the thing was, he didn't often switch his own telly on.

He tapped his pen on his pad, and stared out of the tinted window as a pigeon flapped down onto a branch of a huge plane tree. He couldn't ask his new secretary for this sort of information, it wouldn't look good. Best to wait for her to collate a list of every series broadcast since the last license renewal, nine years ago, which would refresh his memory. He leaned back in his creaking office chair, wishing he had one of the new leather jobs with upholstered armrests, and castors that rolled. The Orwellian charm of the new White City building did not extend to its interior – which was more Kafkaesque. A massive cube of glass and steel, the new building was a hundred yards up the road from Television Centre. Inside it felt like a cross between an airport shopping centre and the set for Fritz Lang's silent film, *Metropolis*. The building was far from finished, and only one half of one floor was occupied, so it was a bleak and lonely work environment for the moment. He didn't plan to stay there once his current job was finished.

He missed his office in Television Centre where he'd felt part of the department, a cog in the real production machine, developing ideas and features for Current Affairs. Well, *a* feature. As a General Trainee he rarely spent more than a year in any job, since the aim was to pick up as broad a range of experience as he could, on the fast track to senior management. He had joined the BBC straight after achieving a First at Oxford, and intended to rise as high as he could in the corporation. He regretted the speed of his rise, in a way – he'd have liked to become a successful programme maker first – nothing like a couple of BAFTAs to earn you the respect of the staff. But you couldn't get a proper overview from the shop floor, he reminded himself, and overview was what really counted in management.

So he'd accepted a role on the License Renewal Committee without question, it was only for a year or so, and it was a vital task: persuading the government to grant the BBC another ten years of the license fee, at the rate they needed, without too many compromises. He had to review their whole output over the last nine years, and report his conclusions to the committee next week. While his secretary collated the list of programmes he was jotting down some thoughts, and mentally trying them out: you couldn't be too prepared for a boardroom presentation. He wanted to come up with some radical ideas that would make the top brass sit up and notice him – but right now, he hadn't any.

*

That evening Chris and his partner Catherine crunched up the gravel drive of their university friends, and neighbours, Sebastian and Emma. They rang the doorbell and turned to survey the small but beautifully landscaped front garden.

"I think this is the nicest garden in our road," said Catherine. "One of the best in Chiswick. The wisteria's just lovely, isn't it?"

"It is," agreed Chris, sniffing the bulky mauve tresses dangling fragrantly from the wooden porch. The door swung open.

"Aha! The man from Auntie, if I'm not mistaken, and his good lady wife!" exclaimed Sebastian. "Enter, enter!" He kissed Catherine on both cheeks and shook Chris' hand warmly. "Shortest journey, last to arrive!" He joshed, leading them into the drawing room where two other couples were sipping martinis. "You know Cosmo and Bella, of course. "This is my old school chum Toby, and his wife Jessica."

"Glad to meet you," said Chris, shaking their hands.

"Okay chaps, chat amongst yourselves like well-behaved guests, won't you? I've just got to go and tickle the roast, or some such." He wandered out towards the kitchen.

"To *what* the roast?"

"Ignore him, Catherine," said Cosmo. "I always do! Ha!"

Twenty minutes later the six guests had covered all the preparatory ground: property prices, reputable builders, the distribution of babies amongst them, intended schools, and nanny alternatives. They were embarking on a comparison of holiday villas in Provence and Tuscany when Emma appeared in the doorway, wearing a huge blue and white striped apron and a slightly flustered face.

"Do come through, everyone!"

They strolled enthusiastically into the pleasant dining room with French windows opening onto a York stone patio and lawn, and exclaimed at the lovely table setting and flower arrangement. Each guest sat down to a large white dish containing a little pile of pasta balanced on a cushion of leaves.

"It's fresh spinach and goat's cheese ravioli, with wild rocket and pine nuts. Help yourselves to balsamic vinegar and olive oil."

"Absolutely delicious, Emma!" said Catherine. "I don't know how you do it all."

"Sebastian's taken care of the main course, so watch out... Oh he's pretty competent – on a good day! I know he's a rung up on the average pater familias. I cheated with the pasta –

Selfridges food hall, I'm afraid – but I made the dessert with my own fair hands."

"If I had four children I'd be sending Chris out to the chip shop, I expect!" Catherine exclaimed, and the other women added heart-felt murmurs of support as they nibbled daintily.

"Champagne, everyone?" boomed Sebastian. "'Fraid the lamb's going to take a bit longer than expected. The Aga wasn't really hot enough." Emma raised her eyes. "That's enough from you!" Sebastian countered, and she gesticulated her sense of outraged injustice. The guests chuckled happily at this familiar double act.

"Now then Chris, tell us some juicy tales of the BBC," Sebastian commanded. "We city sloggers love a bit of gossip, our lives are so damned dull."

"Traipsing from St James' to St Moritz, and then rushing back in time for Ascot – must be so tiresome for you" replied Chris easily.

"I often wish I'd taken the artistic route, like you. I envy you your little garret at the BBC: having ideas, meeting actors, all that sort of thing."

"Why didn't you, then?" asked Emma. "As if we didn't know."

"Man cannot live by bread alone," Sebastian looked pious for a second. "He needs a good brie and a bottle of plonk to wash it down. Someone's got to make the money that pays the taxes which pay your salary, Chris me old pal. Not that I resent it. Not at all. Delighted to subsidise the old goggle box, what would the kiddies do without the *Magic Roundabout* and all that?"

"Oh do shut up Sebbie, you've no idea what you're talking about. That finished years ago."

"Anything good coming up, Chris?" asked Cosmo.

"Of course, as always!"

"Shame I can't invest, like I do in the West End."

"Cosmo's an Angel. And amazingly, he's made quite a lot of

money. Mainly through Andrew of course," explained his wife Bella.

"You can't beat a good musical," Cosmo nodded. "Cost a fortune to mount, but the returns are phenomenal."

"Sounds like Emma," remarked Sebastian thoughtfully, and they all guffawed as she narrowed her eyes at him. Sebastian picked up her hand and tenderly kissed it.

"Seriously," said Cosmo. "There ought to be room for private investment in the BBC."

Chris grimaced. "It's very difficult. Although the government would love it, they daren't."

"Dear Mrs T, how did we live before she came along?"

"Did you see *Spitting Image*?"

"Yes! Hilarious."

"I detest that show. It's revolting!"

"Thank goodness the BBC doesn't do anything so nasty. At least you can always count on them to maintain standards of decency."

"I've just bought shares in a little Californian outfit called Pixar," announced Toby, "they specialise in CGI."

"What's that when it's at home?"

"Computer-generated imagery – the next big thing." Toby tapped his nose. "You heard it here first."

"Really?" asked Chris. "Are you talking about that little film with the anglepoise lamp?"

"Doesn't sound terribly promising," commented Sebastian, as all eyes turned to Toby, the quietest man at the table and by common consent, the cleverest – he had his own management consultancy firm, and even understood how computers worked.

"The potential is huge, absolutely massive."

"Not just cartoons, then?"

"Not at all. The digital revolution's only just beginning," Toby assured him. Chris nodded, listening intently.

"I'm buggered if I can make our bloody computer do what I want," moaned Sebastian. "Takes me half an hour to switch the damn thing on."

"He's banned," said Emma. "Ever since he spilt coffee over the keyboard. Two hundred pounds to fix it!"

"We're computerising the Beeb, it's a bit of a nightmare," said Chris. "Resistance is terrible in some quarters. Not from the technical bods, of course – but the typing pool's days are numbered, that's for sure. And we shan't need half the number of journalists we've got at the moment."

"The inevitable march of progress."

"Indeed."

They all paused to contemplate the changing times.

"At least you're safe at the BBC, I hear all the ITV companies are having to bid for their new contracts!"

"That's right. Sealed bids. Mrs T's idea; they hate it, and who can blame them?"

"I suppose you still have to make the government love you though, or no license fee."

"Absolutely. She was on our backs about overmanning and wastage from the minute she walked into Number Ten, and we sent a twelve-man crew to film the interview."

"Twelve?"

"Yes, three would have done, she was completely right." Chris smiled ruefully. "She did us a favour, the unions had us over a barrel till then. We've changed a lot since. We're pretty cost-effective now."

"Glad to hear it," said Toby. "But are you leading the field? Seems to me it's all up for grabs. It won't be long till we have hundreds of channels like they do in the US. Where's the BBC going to be then?"

"Packed up in a boat and sent off down the river, I dare say!" declared Cosmo, "And good riddance! People should get out of the house of an evening, and see a bit of proper culture. Not sit about like a sofa-sandwich."

"Couch potato," murmured Bella.

"The future's digital, no doubt about that," Toby confirmed, quietly confident, and Chris took out his Filofax to make a few notes. Now he knew what to say to the License Renewal Committee.

Catherine watched him fondly as he wrote, his brow slightly furrowed, the hint of a smile about his mouth. He was never off-duty, his attention never drifted far from his work. She had always admired that in him, there was something very reassuring about it.

Chapter Five

Reassurance is one of those personal qualities you rarely encounter nowadays, and when you do, you suspect it's false, nothing more than a PR technique. David Cameron is a case in point. In the old days the wealthy middle class, doctors, lawyers and so on, all wore an air of relaxed certainty that totally convinced the rest of us that they had everything under control, and they knew exactly what they were doing. We trusted them blindly. Now we know better. The disastrous invasion of Iraq in 2003, the scandal of MPs expenses, the collapse of the banking system... there seems no end to the ways politicians and elite professionals let us down. Maybe the 21st century, global warming and all, will bring us to a new level of awareness: maybe we'll finally grow up and learn to take responsibility for our actions. Better late than never, eh?

Anyhow. Back to 1991. Little Nicky was still working his nuts off at Magenta, learning the business and doing rather well at it.

"It's a right old game, this television lark, ain't it?" exclaimed Rex as he clinked glasses with Nicky across the restaurant table.

"Here's to *Ten out of Ten*," said Haris, presenting his glass to the show's host Geordie Boy, and inviting Rex and Nicky to join him in a toast.

"We wouldn't be where we are today without it," affirmed Rex, clapping Geordie on the shoulder of his well-tailored sparkly suit.

"Thanks man," nodded Geordie, grinning broadly and tossing his beautiful bleach-blonde hair.

The four men were celebrating in style with a slap-up dinner at the top media-frequented restaurant in the West End, because they had won the jackpot. The ITV regional broadcasting franchises had just been awarded by Mrs Thatcher's government in a revolutionary process which required all applicant companies to submit sealed bids, the highest of which would win. It was a simple blind auction, which had caused no end of fuss in the industry amongst those who felt that broadcasting should not operate purely by market forces. Now it was all over; there were a handful of winners and a lot of losers, including one of Mrs Thatcher's best friends, which was some consolation to many.

Magenta Productions had tied itself in with the Midland Broadcasting bid, promising to supply 200 hours of daytime game shows to the standard of their successful quiz, *Ten out of Ten*. They had rustled up a few smart-sounding ideas, which the newly-promoted Head of Development Nicky Mason had tarted up with celebrity names, whilst Haris costed them as low as possible. That was it. A few days' work followed by some schmoozing by Rex, and they were in the bid: Midland did all the hard graft. If the bid failed, Magenta stood to lose nothing at all. But it had won, Midland were now running one of the largest ITV regions, and Magenta had the daytime schedule sewn up. Their output was about to expand by at least eight hundred per cent. They were all euphoric.

"It's better than winning on the Grand National, ain't it?" Rex chuckled throatily, lighting a huge cigar. "D'you think this makes me look like Lew Grade?"

Haris viewed Rex through half-closed eyes as he struck a powerful attitude, and shook his head pityingly.

"You're right, Haris. I've got too much hair!" Rex laughed uproariously and the others enjoyed his delight, although they also felt he was being just a little too loud for the swanky place they were eating in.

Nicky thought he had never been so happy. He had recently turned twenty-one, and Rex had thrown him a party at a top nightclub. Rex liked to joke about him being the son he never had, especially after Nicky told him how his father died in action during the Falklands war. (He'd almost come to believe this himself, having not spoken to his father in four years.) Rex had treated him well at Magenta, and had been a good boss. Nicky's wages were low, and there was no money to pay overtime, so Rex never required Nicky to work more than forty hours a week. Nicky appreciated this so much that he often did, for no pay, and Rex returned his commitment by sitting and chewing the fat with Nicky over a cigar and a whisky, discussing the business, the people they were negotiating with, ideas for shows and possible directions they could expand in. He believed that work should be fun, and he wanted to unite his life and his work so that the two were inseparable; his colleagues were his family. Nicky was more than happy to trade his old family for this one.

Haris had no problem with Rex's attitude and found it entirely appropriate for a forty-five year-old divorcee with two grown-up daughters. As an equal partner in the business, possessing most of the financial acumen, he himself worked the hours he saw fit, which were basically nine-to-five plus the occasional evening, because he had a wife and three children at home in Neasden. Their household was run on traditional Muslim lines, and Haris stepped nimbly between cultures on a daily basis. There was no conflict in his mind: his duty was to be a good son, husband and father when at home, and a good finance director when at work. He had never let either side down. Rex had failed as a husband and father, (divorce could only be seen as failure) but Haris didn't judge him. Rex was an extraordinary person, as far as Haris was concerned. He admired his energy and optimism, his dynamic determination, his zest for life and shrewd business insight. Haris could see that he and Rex complemented each other extremely well, and by respecting each other's fields of work and domesticity, they had sustained an effective working relationship for eight years.

Nicky's arrival had been valuable, but Haris hadn't seen a great deal of him, since Rex had soon taken the boy under his wing and found more than enough for him to do. The Runner became the Personal Assistant in no time at all, so he appointed his own Finance Assistant, choosing a large, middle-aged Jewish matron, which Rex found perverse, given the availability of nubile young women. Haris was perfectly happy with his choice: the office ran very smoothly, and Essie's calm feminine influence was needed in their all-male team. Essie's outlook on life echoed his own, and they became fond of each other without feeling the slightest mutual attraction.

Essie didn't care for evening engagements, and Geordie Boy had gradually become the fourth most important member of Magenta. Haris saw him as an oddball, another misfit who wished to insinuate himself into the world of entertainment, that generous, all-welcoming, all-punishing arena where everyone ultimately had much the same chance of success: in the end, you either pleased the audience or you didn't.

Rex had discovered Geordie on the comedy circuit. That is to say, after Geordie had spent seven years working up his act and legging it round any club that would book him, Rex turned up in an established venue one night and decide that Geordie's act would work in his daytime television show.

Geordie's real name was Neil Armstrong. While this had afforded him a slight celebrity at school, it was not really useful to a comedian. As the Durham-born son of a vicar he had preferred to adopt a comic persona onstage, and had slipped comfortably into the character of an eager geordie, stubborn but naïve, friendly but ready to react at the first sign of trouble. The accent came easily to him, and he developed standard geordie remarks into swooping musical catchphrases. He was careful not to go too far; he had no wish at all to ever run into a bunch of tanked-up geordie lads who thought he was taking the piss out of them. Offstage his true personality was quieter, his humour ironic, and he spoke with a gentle Durham accent, although Rex liked him to wear Geordie Boy's clothes and regarded him as walking publicity for the show. He would try to provoke him to behave outrageously, to exaggerate his homosexuality and become a full-blown queen, but Geordie resented this and rarely rose to the bait.

Geordie had very mixed feelings about Rex. He quite liked him, basically; he was grateful for the break, and found Rex honest to the extent that what you saw was what you got. Rex was the son of a Hackney market trader, and it showed in every inch of him. He wasn't the most sensitive man in the world, and had often trampled on Geordie's feelings, sometimes deliberately. 'Come on son, toughen up!' he would say, jabbing punches at Geordie's shoulder. 'Spare the rod and spoil the child. You'll never survive in show business unless your skin's as thick as a deep-sea wetsuit. If you've got it, flaunt it! Sell yourself!' Geordie chose not to argue, and tried to comply with his boss' demands, but behind Geordie's mask Neil was storing up resentment, drop by drop. Tonight, however, he would do it all Rex's way.

They had come to The Ivy precisely so that they could be seen celebrating. Rex wanted the entertainment world to know that Magenta was now on the map. Tonight he was playing it cool for a change. Instead of working the restaurant, stopping off to shake hands on his way to the gents, politely introducing himself to people he thought might be useful contacts, he stayed in his chair and graciously received congratulations from people who pretended to incidentally walk past him.

As Rex accepted compliments from the new ITV Network Centre Head of Daytime Broadcasting and promised to have lunch with him soon, he winked at Nicky. As the man walked away, he leaned over and whispered in his protégé's ear, "See that? They're queuing up to give us a blow job, now!"

Nicky grinned broadly. Rex was amazing. He never lost his self-control. He showed the same cheerful bonhomie to everyone he met, looked them squarely in the eye and listened intently to whatever they had to say. As a result he had no enemies so far. Some people thought him a barrow boy, but ITV was built on entertaining the working class, and there was no stigma attached. In the main Rex was well-liked. He was good company, he made a good show, and he was doing well for himself. He was very happy with this state of affairs, but Rex had no real friendship for anyone in the business who was not part of Magenta; he was a self-made man, possessed no old school tie, and hadn't spent long enough in the industry to build enduring friendships. He envied other men these allies, but he didn't grieve over what could never be. Instead, he would privately undercut them, distancing them with a joke.

"I dunno," sighed Rex with satisfaction, "them bastards have made my soup go cold." He slurped a few spoonfuls and abandoned it. "Oh well, I never liked asparagus anyway."

"Why choose it then?" asked Nicky.

"They all taste the same to me, you can't get my favourite here."

"Let me guess, chicken soup with dumplings?"

"I know," cried Geordie. "Pea and ham!"

"No no," Haris shook his head confidently. "It's Heinz Cream of Tomato."

"Absolutely right, that's why we're partners," Rex told the younger men. "Knowing each other well enough to know what he'd say about anything. Worth a fortune, that is. Trust."

As he made his point Rex glanced paternally at Nicky and Geordie, and discovered something he had suspected for some time. He filed the information mentally and continued talking without hesitation. "What's the first rule of business, Nicky?"

"Buy cheap, sell dear."

"Good boy. That's how my old man ran his fruit and veg stall, and it's just as true if you're selling massage or telly programmes."

"Massage?" asked Geordie.

"That's how I got started, mate. Didn't fancy getting up at dawn to juggle fruit and shout me lungs hoarse. So I trained as a masseur."

Geordie smirked. "Bet your old man liked that idea."

"Not much, as it goes," admitted Rex. "He was scared shitless I'd turn out to be a pansy. Eventually I was able to reassure him on all fronts. Within two years of finishing my training I was married with a kid and earning three times as much as him."

"How did you pull that off?"

"Who wants a massage most? People with stressful jobs – people who earn shitloads of money. So first off I change me name. Reggie was too East End. Rex is Mayfair. Then I built meself a celebrity client list. Low overheads – a car, a portable table – and I charged them the earth. They was glad to pay it: a top class massage, wherever and whenever they wanted it. See? – Don't take your jacket off, son."

Geordie was uncomfortably hot in the packed restaurant, but he clenched his teeth and kept it on. "Buy cheap, sell dear makes sense," he frowned, "but surely it's a bit more complicated in a creative industry?"

"You know what?" said Rex, draining his wine glass and banging it dramatically on the table, "It's exactly the same."

He smiled happily and leaned back in his chair as a discreet waiter began clearing their starters away. "We'll have another bottle of that, please mate," he said, waving vaguely at the empty claret bottle. "Whatever it is."

An hour or so later Rex and Nicky stood side by side at the urinals in the lavishly appointed gents.

"You like our Geordie Boy, don't you son?" mumbled Rex in Nicky's ear.

"Eh?" replied Nicky in surprise.

"I can see you like him. And he's been daft about you since he clapped eyes on you, anyone could see that and all."

"I'm not gay, Rex!"

"I never said you was. I said I can see you like him. There's nothing wrong in that, son. I've tried it meself."

Nicky shot him an astonished look and zipped up.

"Didn't expect that, did you?" Rex guffawed, and watched through the mirror as Ted Danson came out of a cubicle and went to wash his hands. Rex finished peeing and went to the adjacent wash basin, nodding pleasantly through the mirror to the star.

"Alright, mate?"

"Sure." Ted looked momentarily troubled, as if he feared a conversation were brewing, but Rex gave him a wink as if to say, don't worry, you're safe, and Ted smiled as he left the room, "Cheers, buddy."

Rex beamed at Nicky. "See that? I got Ted Danson to say *Cheers* to me! Now if I'd noticed he was in the restaurant I would have bet you a pony that I could do that, and I'd have won!"

"You're pissed." Nicky was nervous. "What was you on about just now?"

"Calm down, son," Rex patted him on the shoulder. "Don't worry, no-one's gossiping about you. You're like a son to me, I care about you, and I don't like to see you hung up about this thing. Girls are one thing, boys are another." Rex stretched out his hands and weighed them against each other as if comparing two melons. "Now, I know that back in the wildwoods beyond the Mile End Road one is kosher and the other is definitely not, but here in sophisticated Soho no-one gives a flying fuck. Boys like having fun together. So why not enjoy yourself? That's all I'm saying. It's entirely up to you." He walked to the door and turned, his hand on the knob. "Tell you what, though. If you can get Geordie to sign up for the next two years on the same deal he's had up to now, you can produce the new show."

Nicky gasped. "Really?"

"Yes, really. Come on then, or they'll think we're playing hide the sausage in here."

Nicky was too stunned to speak. Either Rex was a lot cleverer than he had realised, or Nicky's carefully constructed image was not nearly as watertight as he had imagined. Either way, it made him rigid with insecurity. He kept his eyes low, afraid that they revealed his every thought. His feelings swirled. He wasn't gay. He had girlfriends. He'd never fallen in love yet, and he hadn't the least desire to settle down with anyone, ever. He had broken away from his family not long after starting at Magenta. He had no idea what the future held, only that it wouldn't include anything from his past. He had tried to re-invent himself, starting with a blank canvas, and he had thought himself a huge success at this. He had become a bright, hard-working trainee media entrepreneur: reliable, capable, keen. He soaked up all Rex's experience and he wanted, eventually, to exceed Rex's achievements. He didn't know how, or even what kind of programmes he would make, that wasn't important. He didn't have any kind of master plan, although he wondered sometimes whether Rex did. Perhaps one day he would be inducted into that ultimate mystery. For the time being, he was content to serve his time. He was still too young to feel confident about striking out on his own.

He could trust Rex. He knew that for certain. Maybe he should listen to Rex's well-meant advice on his private life too. He did fancy Geordie, it was true. He didn't want to. He wished the feelings he had for Geordie could be re-directed towards Melanie, the pretty girl he had been going out with for nearly six months. It had never developed beyond a casual relationship because he had never got beyond liking her quite a lot.

He was afraid of starting something with Geordie that might get out of control. He didn't know where it would lead. He didn't want to be a queer, to join the gay community, to camp around. He hated all that. He wanted to be masculine, strong. But he would like to screw Geordie. He was there for the taking, and had been ever since Nicky joined the company. Nicky had behaved from the start as if there were no possibility whatever of sexual contact, and Geordie had respected this; he had given up years ago, resigning himself to admiring Nicky from afar, employing the patient self-denial his church upbringing had given him. Nicky was confident Geordie would never turn him down.

And he could be producing the new show in a matter of weeks! That would surely make him one of the youngest producers ever. He thought he could pull it off successfully if Rex was around to help out when he hit problems. He could have it all. Rex was handing it to him on a plate. He felt poised to emerge from his chrysalis, not even sure what his wings would be like, but sensing them folded tight against his back, capable of carrying him up in the sunlight so he could reveal their dazzling colours to the world. It was a heady feeling. He liked it. He would go with it. Carefully.

"Anyone care to join me at the casino?" enquired Rex as he handed the waiter his credit card. Haris excused himself, but Nicky accepted.

"Love to, Rex. You'll come, won't you Geordie? Go on, it's fun. I'll show you what to do." Nicky smiled winsomely into Geordie's eyes, and made him feel wanted – the party wouldn't be complete without him.

"Alright, why not, eh? Don't let me lose me wages though, will you?"

"Don't worry son. We'll take care of you," growled Rex, patting him on the back as they left the restaurant.

Outside, Haris went off to the multi-storey car park to pick up his Volvo, and the rest hailed a taxi. The Soho streets were shiny black and busy with jostling people interested only in their own pursuit of pleasure. As the cab pulled over to them Nicky pondered how he would tackle Geordie. The cabbie leaned over and asked. "Where to, guv?" and Nicky shrank behind Rex. He knew the driver. He climbed into the back seat trying to conceal his face, but couldn't resist a glance forward to see if the man had recognised him too. The cabbie wore a puzzled expression, as if he thought he knew Nicky, but wasn't quite sure.

It was Walter, ex-colleague of Nicky's father Les, one of the four men suspended from the Ilford police force for corruption. Les and the other two were currently on trial at the Old Bailey, but Walter had escaped prosecution by taking early retirement. He had forfeited part of his pension, and become a part-time cabbie. Nicky knew this from his mother, whom he spoke to occasionally on the phone. She longed for him to visit, but he couldn't bring himself to do it, and live the lie. She occupied a fantasy world in which Les was a wrongly accused hero who would eventually be proved innocent, like an old Gregory Peck movie. Nicky intended to go and see her when Les was convicted. She would need support then, once she knew the awful truth. He had decided this four years ago, not realising how long it could take for a case to come to court.

They soon arrived at the casino in Mayfair, but Nicky failed to escape Walter's attention when they got out.

"Nicky Mason! Thought it was you. How's the old man bearing up?" Walter's confident booming voice alerted all three men.

Nicky pretended to see him for the first time. "Walter, is that you? Good heavens. How are you?"

"Mustn't grumble. Is Les doing alright? How's your mum coping?"

Nicky fought a rising panic. "They're fine, fine. You know. It's not easy. Nice to see you, Walter. Got to go." Nicky's ears were burning and he desperately searched for an explanation he could pass off on Rex and Geordie. He hoped that Walter would at least be discreet enough not to mention the trial.

"I hear on the grapevine that the trial's going very well. Very well indeed, if you get my drift. Tell your mum not to worry. Your dad's gonna be alright. Tell her I told you."

Nicky took a deep breath. "Okay Walter. Good night."

"Night, son. Good to see you. It's been a long time. Glad to see you're doing well for yourself."

The taxi pulled away, and Nicky turned, resigned to his fate. Rex and Geordie were staring, intrigued.

"Looks like wor Nicky's a bit of a dark horse, Rex," remarked Geordie, a humorous glint in his eye. Nicky looked coolly at Rex, trying not to betray his anxiety.

Rex studied him through narrowed eyes, then hugged him. "That's right, Geordie. He's just like I was at his age. The spitting image." Then he turned and led them both into the casino. A top-hatted doorman welcomed them, and a receptionist offered them a large leather-bound book to sign themselves in. Nicky was last. After Rex Barclay, Geordie Boy, he wrote: Nik Mason. It looked good. He decided to keep it.

Chapter Six

Having worked on *Grange Hill* for a few years I felt at home in the television industry, and I was ready for a change. I wanted to move into adult drama, and I managed to get offered the job of Series Script Editor on a period drama series about frocks, which was based in Shepherds Bush. It was a big promotion, although the show itself was gentle and undemanding. (It was later parodied mercilessly by French and Saunders, and I've been embarrassed about it ever since. I'm not telling you the title, you'll just have to work that out for yourself. Beware of satirists, that's all I can say.) Being on the spot enabled me to get the feel of how the corporation operated in a way that was impossible when I was continuously in production miles away. The main hive of the BBC contained an army of development producers, script editors and readers, all working on a wide variety of new and potential drama projects; they were assailed on a daily basis by all the agents and writers in the country, or so it seemed. Let's just say it looked rather competitive. I was glad I didn't have to deal with it.

After a few months I received the memo about the new Drama Discussion Group, so I went along to see the action. It was much better supported than I expected. I was too late to get a seat, so I had to stand at the side and lean on a window sill. It was worth the effort though, as it proved very entertaining – mainly because of a new girl with a Yorkshire accent who had some refreshing opinions and no inhibitions in expressing them.

The Bridge Lounge was a large plain room decorated in institution beige with straight-backed chairs arranged in a huge oval. Behind them were a few plastic-covered comfy chairs, so as Maggie was one of the first to arrive, she chose one mainly to avoid being in the front row. Anthea was there, behind a table, pouring wine into dozens of glasses. Maggie didn't like to take one until a few more people had come in. She looked over the notes she had made on the programmes they were to discuss, and watched as people flooded in. She was amazed at the turnout, having expected twenty at the most, and felt a sense of occasion. This seemed to be a major gathering of the whole department. She recognised Sally of course, who was chatting up Jonathan quite successfully by the look of it, as they sat down cosily together in the front row. She prepared to wave if they looked in her direction, but they didn't. There was no sign of Fenella. Morag Fishman, manager of the department and finder of offices for new recruits, rolled in looking harassed and made straight for the wine, complaining to anyone in earshot about the appalling noise caused by workmen on the seventh floor who were re-modelling a suite of offices for the Director General's new cohorts without the slightest consideration for the poor bastards actually trying to make programmes. Distinguished-looking middle-aged men filled up the top end of the oval of chairs, and Maggie guessed they were producers: a few women infiltrated them, but most of the other women were of Maggie's generation and chose the opposite end of the oval. Friendly insults and jokes flew across the room as they all relaxed, and Maggie felt exhilarated. At last she was enjoying herself. She sighed with pleasure, and surreptitiously studied the men, trying to guess which ones might be Stewart Walker and Basil Richardson.

The room quietened as a grey-haired man, tall and craggily handsome, stood up and surveyed the room thoughtfully, apparently unaware that one of his hands was surreptitiously patting his balding patch. Maggie suspected he was also trying to stand up straight so that his stomach didn't hang too far over his belt, and found this endearing.

"Thanks for coming everyone. I must say, it's an excellent turnout. Out of all our producers and script editors, development executives and readers, I think we have virtually half here this evening. Did anyone make it down from *EastEnders*?" Silence fell as everybody looked round. "Evidently not. I'm sure they're all preoccupied with more important matters up at Elstree: I hear the chicken pox has broken out in Albert Square." A murmur of laughter spread round the room. Maggie wasn't sure, but she guessed this bloke must be the Head of Drama, Peter Maxwell. He certainly commanded everyone's respectful attention.

"Okay that's enough from me. I now declare the first Drama Discussion Group open! Over to you, Fenella." He looked round the room. "She is here, isn't she?" A few people giggled and the door opened, so all eyes turned as a well-dressed man entered in a hurry, his schoolboy hair flopping over his lined face. "Well I'm *so sorry* I'm late. I'd just like you to know that I've been in my office since eight o'clock this morning." He took a glass of wine and sat down with a mock flourish as everyone chuckled.

"We believe you, Donald," said Peter. "You didn't have Fenella with you, I suppose?"

"Rumour and calumny!" exclaimed Donald. "I've never touched her." A few people laughed sycophantically.

"Right, well let's start anyway," said Peter, and then Fenella burst in. "I was in a meeting with Salman, I *am* sorry," she said as she bustled past the standing crowd at the back of the room. Maggie was impressed and realised that she had no right to expect Fenella to spare time for an insignificant yob like herself. Fenella sank into a chair near Peter, depositing her briefcase on the floor in front of her so that it spilled open in its usual way, and rummaged in it for a few seconds before producing an agenda. She looked up and addressed the group in her normal tone which suggested that she had seen it all a million times and nothing would shock or surprise her; she would simply carry on flogging herself to death doing a superb job in the face of countless difficulties.

"Now I don't want anyone to feel they're at Programme Review, this is just an idea for bringing the department together to talk about our work in a completely honest way. Hopefully we'll have a stimulating discussion and get to know each other a bit better. Good.

"Now the first drama on the list to talk about is *EastEnders*. Who'd like to start?" Silence. "Well did anyone see it last week?" Everyone looked around, but no-one was prepared to break the ice. "Has anyone *ever* seen it?" Further amusement as no-one raised a hand. "For God's sake, *someone* must have watched the bloody show! From a sense of duty if nothing else!" Peter looked wryly amused and threatened the assembly with detention. Maggie had been watching the twice-weekly soap religiously, of course, but was much too shy to say anything yet; her heart pumped hard at the thought of it.

Eventually someone said they thought the issue of HIV had been introduced very effectively through Mark Fowler, and that public reaction had been favourable, which was an important achievement. Another was enjoying Grant Mitchell's storyline – a real East End thug with a real East End tart on his arm. They hoped Grant and Sharon would marry, making a great replacement for Den and Ange. Someone else said they didn't feel it was their place to criticise, but wasn't the vocabulary somewhat limited – 'Allo Dot, fancy a cuppa? Ave yer seen my little Willy?' being the staple diet of social contact. It looked as though *EastEnders* was held in low esteem here. Maggie was amazed, it was far and away the most successful show the drama department made.

Anthea, standing behind her table of wine, seemed unafraid to contribute to the discussion. She said she thought the Taverniers were sidelined as the black family; a script editor responded that she thought they were too politically correct, and a producer said he found them stereotyped. Anthea said it just wouldn't do to have one token family from each ethnic minority – they would always be peripheral to the central drama between the whites. Most of the assembled group looked a little brow-beaten at this point. Anthea hadn't raised her voice but they behaved as though she had. Maggie was quietly relieved to see that other people found Anthea intimidating too. She would have liked to support her point of view but didn't have anything new to add, so she kept quiet. Anthea, the only non-white person in the room, remained motionless, her face inscrutable.

Fenella tactfully drew the subject to a close, by acknowledging that Anthea had made a very important point, and it was a shame no-one from *EastEnders* had managed to find the time to come this evening.

Next on the list was Stewart Walker's *Death of a Baby*, a hard-hitting portrayal of life on a Bradford council estate in which a young mother's circumstances forced her into prostitution, and then into the hands of a very nasty pimp who ultimately hurled her baby to its death from a fifteenth floor balcony.

Maggie had found it disappointing. It lacked the wicked humour of other films by Stewart which Maggie had admired so much, and she had found it dull and depressing. However, she had some ideas about why it didn't work. She waited for others to begin the criticism, but instead there was praise for its uncompromising truthfulness and a superb performance from the first-time actress playing the teenage mother. Admiration of the photography drew a general murmur of assent, and Donald Mountjoy quipped that the props store must have used up all its stocks of stage blood and vomit.

Jonathan asked whether Billy Trowell, the writer, had drawn on his own experience, and Maggie was at last able to discover Stewart. He was a dark, tousled man who had chosen to sit in the back row. He sat up and drew on his cigarette, ignoring the ash flaking off it. "Of course. I wouldn't like to say which character he might have been closest to, though."

Jonathan nodded and half smiled as if to say he knew exactly what Stewart was saying. "What would you say was the hardest part of working with a writer who is determined to show the underbelly of life in its worst light? Was it fighting to prevent the language being censored?"

Stewart paused for thought. "I'd say the *worst* thing was wondering what he'd do to me if he didn't like the film!"

Everyone laughed. There was a general frisson as the group acknowledged the dangerous forces that had to be negotiated in order to achieve a drama of this calibre. Stewart re-filled his glass from a bottle by his foot. Modesty forbade basking in glory.

Maggie now felt brave enough to join in, so she put her hand up firmly, gaining Fenella's attention as the laughter subsided.

"Yes – ah, Maggie," said Fenella.

"I just wondered why it presented such a negative image of women." Her nerves amplified her voice. There was a shocked silence, which she misinterpreted as interest in what she had to say, so she elaborated, "Every one of the women was a victim. None of them really tried to fight back, apart from the one who got acid thrown in her face."

Maggie's face grew hot as people looked round at her, wondering who the hell she was with her daft opinions. The silence was horrendous. She hadn't meant to launch an attack on Stewart, she merely spoke as she found. She wanted desperately to explain that actually she was a great fan of Stewart's work and that he should receive her criticism in that context... but, fearing it would sound like she was trying to retract her opinion, she said nothing.

Fenella appeared to feel sorry for her: "You found it offensive." Maggie tried to deny it, but Fenella didn't stop. "Well that's a point of view, anyone agree or disagree?"

Sally put up her hand, "*I* didn't think it was offensive at all. The whole purpose of it is to show the endemic violence against women on inner city estates. The women *are* the victims so how else do you want them portrayed?"

Maggie was surprised that Sally seemed so antagonistic towards her, she thought they had established some sort of loose friendship over lunch. She felt the majority mentally gathering behind Sally. She glanced at Stewart and saw him smirking into his wine glass. She knew she was right – maybe she hadn't made herself clear; she decided to try again.

"But it doesn't leave any room for hope. It's all so bleak and nihilistic."

"That's because Bradford *is* bleak!" Sally's tone verged on the superior. "Have you ever been there?" This raised another laugh. Maggie felt furious with this wretched woman who knew nothing at all about Bradford, and didn't realise that it was Maggie's home ground; nevertheless it was Sally who was hitting the right note with the crowd. Maggie wouldn't be walked over.

"I know, but supposing you lived there and you watched the film, how would you feel about it? Wouldn't you want to think that maybe it *wasn't* hopeless and you might be able to over-come the situation somehow?"

Sally had no answer to this so she shrugged as if it were irrelevant, then looked at Jonathan and raised her eyes at him. He politely failed to respond, but his raised eyebrows and down-cast eyes indicated solidarity with Sally. Maggie felt angry. This wasn't going at all the way she had intended. She had hoped to impress Stewart with her insight and her political analysis, but Sally had got to her, and once she was involved in an argument Maggie always felt compelled to see it through.

"I'd be very interested to know how it was received in Bradford," she said. Fenella, wearing an amused expression, looked over her half-moon glasses at Maggie and then turned to Stewart, inviting him to answer. He dropped his cigarette into a half-empty wine glass and glanced shrewdly at Maggie, who held his gaze.

"Unfortunately neither the ratings nor the audience appreciation figures are broken down by regions as small as that. Of course we do know that inner city viewers are inclined to select ITV or BBC1 as a matter of choice, so given that *Death* went out on 2 on a Saturday night, I rather doubt whether we succeeded in diverting very many council estate inhabitants from more urgent affairs down the pub." The audience smiled. "To be perfectly frank, my dear, Screen Two is really for a few million viewers from South East England and the chattering classes in North West London! If we can bring the plight of the inner city working class woman to the attention of those in a position to do something about it, then surely it's our duty! I'm sorry if you found it voyeuristic."

Maggie didn't dare pursue an argument with her redoubtable opponent, often described by the critics as 'the enfant terrible of television drama'. She knew she'd scored a disastrous own goal. Damn. Shit.

From within a red haze she heard a man speaking reasonably in measured tones.

"... traditionally speaking, the working class victim's triumph over adversity is what audiences respond to *most* strongly."

You understood me, thought Maggie, I love you. Who are you? He was a mature, pleasant-looking individual with wavy grey hair. She soon found out when Jonathan put his oar in.

"Basil's right, of course, and we've got *Gas and Boilers* to prove that point." A general nod in Basil's direction credited him with the seminal sixties drama. "But there are some stories which *need* a tragic conclusion – look at the novels of Hardy, or Zola." Basil acknowledged the truth of this by inclining his head in Jonathan's direction.

The theme was picked up and tossed around the room, while Maggie sat back and resolved to keep her trap firmly shut for the rest of the meeting. So this was Basil! She was amazed to find that her two heroes were so different. Basil looked incredibly old-fashioned, not the sort of person she would ever have imagined herself working with. He was wearing a suit and looked almost like a Conservative politician, or at least a Liberal. Jonathan was perfect for him, of course; Basil would never want Maggie in his office, she felt sure. Stewart, on the other hand, was definitely more her kind of person, obviously a bit of a rebel. In fact if he was twenty years younger he would be quite fanciable.

By now she had lost track of the argument as well as her desire to participate, so she looked around the room, thinking there *had* to be at least one woman in the room who had agreed with her but was too bloody pathetic to say so. She caught Anthea looking her way, but she appeared to be wrapped up in her own thoughts. Maggie wondered how long the meeting would go on for. Now that she'd blown it she wanted to go home as soon as possible.

After ten minutes Fenella moved the discussion on to the film adaptation of Max Beerbohm's *Zuleika Dobson*, a novel from 1911 about a young adventuress running amok amongst the eligible bachelors at Oxford University. Maggie hadn't understood it, really, even though she had a degree in English literature. She had found it obscure and unfunny, a parade of men in blazers and boaters who did little but punt girls in long frocks through trailing willow branches in idyllic sunshine – unless they were attending sherry parties at which they embarrassed themselves by hiccuping in front of the Dean's stuffy wife. At the mere sight of the doll-like heroine every man in it was reduced to a quivering wreck, and none of them was apparently capable of having a conversation with her.

However, Maggie now knew better than to say as much, which was just as well because everyone else had loved it to bits. They showered Donald, who had produced it, with praise. It was apparently sweet, enchanting, witty, and compared very favourably with Merchant Ivory films despite the budget being only a fraction of theirs. Maggie tried to damp down her bile by reasoning to herself that the corporation's drama output needed to be broad, and that there was no need to deny audiences who wanted to see this kind of nostalgic escapism now and then, just because *she* thought it a waste of time. But she was puzzled when someone referred to the satire. What satire? It was a satire? What on? Someone was saying that they suspected the satire might have escaped some of the audience if they weren't very familiar with Oxford. Maggie realised that she was one of them. Damn and shit. She felt outraged on behalf of the 95% of viewers who, like her, had never been to Oxford let alone Oxford University, and weren't remotely interested in it.

Sally was defending the film. "Even if the satire *did* go over some peoples' heads, they still enjoyed it on a literal level. My hairdresser *loved* it." People chuckled.

Maggie spoke out without thinking, "On a *literal* level it's totally crass. There isn't a single character you can care about and none of them really communicate with each other. I really don't see what it's got to offer a nineties audience."

Sixty heads seemed to turn as one and glare in disgust at Maggie. She almost gasped, and could hardly believe what she'd done. Her hands and armpits sweated as a drone of disbelief and noisy tutting rippled round the room. She rallied when a sarcastic woman said she presumed Maggie thought the women were misrepresented too. "They were no more stupid than the male characters," she replied. Her heart pounded. She would have to maintain her dignity for now, but this was obviously the end of her career at the BBC. She had managed to impress herself on every member of the department as a whinging, humourless feminist – a stereotype which was evidently about as popular here as maggots in the canteen kedgeree.

After that, she really did keep her trap shut. She couldn't leave early, it would look pitiful, so she sat out the rest of the discussion on *Zuleika Dobson* in humiliated rage, and barely listened to what they all said about the latest classic serial,

Eminent Victorians. No-one else said anything controversial apart from Anthea, who remarked that apart from *EastEnders* none of the shows discussed featured black actors at all; the assembly listened in polite silence and gazed expressionlessly at the stained carpet.

Finally the purgatory came to an end, and Maggie shuffled out keeping her eyes low to avoid Sally and Jonathan whilst telling herself she hadn't liked either of them anyway. A silver-haired man with whisky breath pushed past her and squeezed her arm. She looked up momentarily and he winked at her. What did he mean? Was that some sort of encouragement, or was he just laughing at her? She walked off as briskly as the crowd would allow.

As she neared the lifts she heard her name called, but she pretended not to hear – she just wanted to get out of the hateful place. The caller was not put off, and hurried up behind her.

It was me, chasing after Maggie. I'd watched it all unfold with my heart in my mouth. There was no way I would stick my own oar into that shoal of piranhas. I thought Maggie was right in most of her opinions, and I wanted her to know she wasn't alone. They'd all made her look like an idiot, but she seemed like a good person to me. I caught up with her at the lift doors.

"Hello, I'm Rhiannon. I just wanted to say that I agree with you."

"Thanks for your support!" she snapped sarcastically. I felt terrible. Perhaps I should have spoken up in the meeting – but it wouldn't have helped Maggie, it would just have put me in the same boat.

"Look, I'm sorry. I'm new to this kind of thing too."

"Oh, right. Sorry, I shouldn't have said that. I take it back."

"I don't suppose you fancy a drink?"

"Why not?" Maggie smiled, relaxing a fraction. "Just what I need. Shall we go to the club?"

The BBC Club was a big lounge area concealed on the fourth floor of the Television Centre doughnut (in the middle of the Light Entertainment department, inevitably). You had to join to use it, and there were two bars, tables and chairs, and little else. The atmosphere was relaxed, and it was the place to retreat to after studio recordings (or to spend an hour or two at lunchtime, if you were in the LE Department).

We found a quiet table near the window overlooking the grim redbrick blocks of the White City council estate, and introduced ourselves. We hit it off pretty fast. After half a pint of draught Guinness and three Marlborough Lights, Maggie spilled her despair at the awful impression she'd made in the meeting, and I tried to make out it didn't matter.

"It's not that your opinions were unreasonable, it's just the way you expressed them."

"Too blunt?"

"Just a tad. People here don't say what they think. Not like they do in Wales."

"Nor in Yorkshire. A spade's a fucking spade there."

"Now Maggie, you've got to learn to think of it as a traditional implement for the manual rearrangement of the alluvial crust."

She laughed. "You've got these southerners sussed, haven't you?"

"I've been studying them for several years now. And keeping my ear to the ground."

"Can you hear the cavalry?"

"Oh yes, I know exactly what they're up to."

Maggie looked at me with a sparkle in her eye and went to get the drinks in again. When she returned from the bar she launched into a deconstruction of Fenella's management style. I contributed my own angle on BBC employment practice as I had observed it in operation.

"Did Fenella appoint you?" I asked.

"No, I was interviewed by someone else, who'd already

moved on by the time I started."

"That's it then. Fenella's not interested in you because you've been foisted on her."

Maggie was puzzled. "What's that got to do with it?"

"Just politics. She probably favours the other new girl, her sister's friend from Cambridge, what's her name – Sally."

"Sally Farquar-Binns? I thought she'd been here ages."

"Only a couple of months."

Maggie was gobsmacked. "You mean – she's no more experienced than I am?"

"Rather less, I should imagine."

Maggie looked exasperated, and lit another cigarette. I watched sympathetically as reality emerged for her. Sally had none of Maggie's knowledge of theatre and audiences and the practice of drama, but she had the social expertise to navigate the arcane traditions of the BBC. She knew the ropes, the rules, the manners, the language, and most importantly, the right people. She was a bona fide player while Maggie's arse was glued to the subs' bench. Fenella, whose job surely included responsibility for all the trainees, had no intention of furthering Maggie's career in any way. She was probably hoping that Maggie would stumble off into the sunset after her contract expired. Eventually Maggie sighed and gave me a wry smile.

"What a prat I've been. I actually thought I had some sort of worker's rights. I thought now I was on the payroll I could follow a career path of some kind."

"It is a career path, of sorts. Think of it as a kind of outward-bound challenge. You're on your own, you have to work out the rules of engagement for yourself, hack your way through the jungle with nothing but a knife and fork, and capture a tiny bit of territory by getting your own programme commissioned. Then you're on the map. Unless they shoot you in the back first."

Maggie nodded. "You're right. It's obvious, now you've said it. I've been spoiled, working in theatre. I was daft to imagine that the telly industry would be the same on a larger scale. I've been acting like a bull in a china shop, haven't I?"

"I rather admire that, actually. I'm far too polite. I daren't rock the boat. I'm so chuffed to be working here at all that I tend to keep my head down and get on with the job. It's easy to do that when you're on a show. Being in development's a lot more complicated. I wouldn't wait around for Fenella, if I were you. I'd go and pester all the producers, one of them might take a shine to you and take you on, you never know."

Maggie's face collapsed. "If only I hadn't made such a tit of myself in front of them all this evening."

"Don't assume they all hate you. You've shown the courage of your convictions. That deserves respect. The whole thing was just about arse-licking, wasn't it?"

"You what?" Maggie fixed me with a look of consternation.

"You must have noticed that the only show to get slagged off was the one without a producer in the room. No-one dared criticise anyone's work to their face. Except you, of course! Some people love that. Stewart Walker does, for a start."

"Really?"

"As long as you don't become a bore, like poor Anthea."

"I don't know what to make of her. I don't disagree with anything she says, but I can't seem to get along with her. She's closed off, somehow."

"She's got bitter. She's been trying to get a trainee script editor's contract for years, but they see her as a secretary and that's that."

Maggie's face radiated another shaft of inner sunlight, and a faint smile lifted her expression at the thought of Anthea feeling envious of her own crummy contract. There was really someone in the department who was even more disadvantaged than Maggie – someone who wasn't giving up. Anthea would continue to put her case until the BBC finally caught up with the rest of the arts world, which had treated equal opportunities and integrated casting as standard practice for a decade already.

Maggie was suddenly filled with respect for Anthea.

"I wish I had her tenacity," said Maggie. "I normally walk away from people I don't respect. At speed."

"Anthea's got a bigger battle to fight than either of us."

Maggie nodded. "The only other black faces you see here are serving in the tea bar."

"Or cleaning the toilets." We contemplated this grim fact in embarrassed silence.

"It really makes me angry."

"Imagine how Anthea feels, then!"

"You know who annoys me the most? That Jonathan Proulx."

"Basil Richardson's script editor?"

"What sort of a name is Proulx, anyway? It's ridiculous!" I surprised myself with this outburst; I hardly knew him. Maggie glanced at me quizzically.

"I suppose it must be French. Why don't you like him?"

"He's just so bloody tall and blonde and handsome, he's straight out of *Brideshead Revisited*. Life is so easy for people like him; they glide through it on gold-plated roller skates. It drives me insane. He's always surrounded by posh girls exactly like him. They've all got trust funds and families with three houses, and they've no need to earn a living at all – this is all just a game for them. To the rest of us it's life or death! Well not exactly, but you know what I mean."

Maggie laughed. "I agree. He's a supercilious creep."

"He epitomises everything we're up against. The old boys' network. They just carry on as they always have, they don't really notice the rest of us at all."

"Hmm, I think they've noticed *me* now. There must be something we can do. Let's start a plot!" said Maggie ruefully.

"An old girls' network!"

"That would be great, but there aren't enough of us. What about a grammar school network?"

"Yes, but wouldn't the men try to run it?"

"It's all a distraction from what we're really here for. I shan't care once I've won my BAFTA."

"Imagine beating Jonathan to a BAFTA!" A thrill of anticipated *schadenfreude* swept through me.

"Oh, wouldn't that be satisfying?"

"There's only one way to do it."

"Make better shows."

"Exactly. Beat them at their own game. Prove we're as good
as – we're better than them."

We discussed the kind of programmes we most wanted to
make: Maggie was full of original ideas but they didn't necessarily have mass appeal for a television audience. I'd never
given serious thought to new projects, but I knew all about the
practical needs of a production. We shared a deep admiration for
programmes that mattered, that changed attitudes and became
central to the national culture.

"Wouldn't you like to make the definitive Welsh drama?"
asked Maggie.

I shuddered. "I don't want to be stuck away in a corner. I want
to be part of the mainstream, accepted on the same terms as
everyone else – not be the token Welshwoman."

"You sound like Anthea now."

"Yes, well we've got something in common, haven't we?" I
saw Maggie recoil as if she'd inadvertently stepped on my corn.
I tried to hurry on, ashamed of reacting so chippily. "It's a bit
obvious, that's all – I'm proud of being Welsh but it's a bit
parochial for me, you know what I mean?"

"Yes, of course." Maggie smiled and said nothing more on
the subject. She was beginning to learn the art of tact.

*

The meeting proved to be a turning point for Maggie. Once back
at her desk she felt much clearer. She understood that she would
probably never get a proper meeting with her boss, and she
would have to find herself a new contract some other way. She

had plenty of confidence in herself and her abilities, but very little where the institution of the BBC was concerned, and she wasn't at all sure that she would remain there. Never mind. If they couldn't see her finer qualities, they could get stuffed. The BBC wasn't the only television company in the world, even if it was the best – *that* reputation wouldn't necessarily last for ever, Maggie told herself, although she couldn't really imagine a change momentous enough to shake the BBC from its towering position of superiority.

She rallied herself for an all-out assault. She planned out her remaining six weeks such that she could continue reading scripts and writing reports for Fenella at the same fast rate she had already established – she was determined not to give her boss an excuse for giving her a bad reference – and she also gave a lot of thought to projects she would like to develop, and writers she wanted to work with. She called the writer whose unsolicited script she had thought most promising and invited him in for a chat, and two other writers she had worked with in theatre, asking them if they had ideas they would like to develop with her. They all promised to think about it and meet her within a week.

Then she called various producers' secretaries and succeeded in obtaining appointments to meet five producers for a brief chat, including to her amazement Stewart Walker, who called her back and spoke to her personally. He remembered her and was charming; he obviously bore no grudge, and wasn't the kind of man who took criticism to heart. He raised her hopes by mentioning that he was looking for an editor for his next project, and Maggie resolved that, come what may, she would get that contract.

Finally, just in case, she wrote a letter to the executive producer of *EastEnders*, saying how she loved the show and her main ambition was to work on it, and obtained a huge number of video tapes of old and recent episodes from the film and video library so that she could catch up on the storylines and characters and discuss them intelligently if asked to do so.

The act of phoning a writer from the BBC forced Maggie to behave as if she were a real member of staff, whether or not she felt like one. Paul McEntee, who had received his rejected script from Fenella only four days beforehand, was very surprised when Maggie called, and couldn't reconcile the two events. Maggie wondered if she was doing the right thing. She tried to explain that she had found his writing full of energy and truth, and that she would like to meet him to find out what he was interested in so that she could bear him in mind for future projects. As she talked she felt a fraud: it was quite possible that she would soon be out of a job. He agreed to come and meet her for a chat.

Maggie took Paul to a lively tea-bar she had discovered on the ground floor next to one of the recording studios. The fact that it was frequented by people actually making programmes gave it a much better atmosphere than the one on the fifth floor which was always full of people deep in thought. He was mixed race, still in his twenties, worked in a DHSS office and wrote in his spare time. Becoming a full-time writer was still a dream, but he was serious about it, and listened avidly to Maggie's thoughts on his script. She was encouraging but frank about the odds against his getting an original idea commissioned; he might do better to try and get taken on by one of the soaps. Paul was quiet, and listened to Maggie as if she were a mentor, which made her feel uncomfortable, she was hardly in a position to be that. She decided to come clean.

"To be absolutely honest, Paul, I'm rather new here myself, and I'm not sure they'll keep me on. I can't give you any guarantees at all. I can only offer to put your ideas forward."

"That's okay. At least you're being honest with me. And you're the first person who's ever given me any encouragement apart from my mum." Maggie was charmed. She asked what subjects he would choose to write about given a clean slate, and he began talking about his complex family, which was split between Peckham, St Lucia, and Norfolk. His black mother's family came from St Lucia and his white father had left him and his brother with her in Peckham in order to go off with a Scottish potter and live in the country. His step-mother had another two children, older than him, and now a new baby. His mother had subsequently had two more children herself, with a Rastafarian from Jamaica who had three more children back home. His full brother, Steve, was in prison doing twenty years for armed robbery, which Paul didn't believe he was guilty of, although he had done smaller robberies. Because Steve had refused to take his punishment lying down, he had been in solitary five times in his first two years. He often had bruises when Paul visited him, and lived in fear of villains who thought he might grass them up.

Maggie was fascinated by this colourful story, and convinced there was great material here for a drama of some kind.

"I know they say you should write about what you know," said Paul, "and I know a lot about culture clashes. But it's very hard to use your own family for raw material. It doesn't seem right. That's why I haven't done it before."

"Unless you can use it to right a wrong, or to bring something unfair to the attention of the public," Maggie suggested. "What about your brother?"

Paul smiled and shook his head. "I couldn't risk putting him in an even worse situation."

"It wouldn't have to be his actual story, you could make it a parallel story and change all the details. No-one needs to know it's based on him."

"Maybe. I'll think about it."

Maggie said she would look forward to hearing from him soon, and took him back to Reception. He was genuinely grateful for the meeting, and she felt undeserved satisfaction. Maybe nothing would come of it, or maybe this writer would have the perseverance and talent to make it.

JoJo was completely different. Maggie had directed one of her plays four years previously, and had been vastly amused to discover JoJo's background in street theatre had included a summer of anarchist stunts on the Edinburgh Fringe. She had been the punk girl reading *The SCUM Manifesto* who had caused Maggie and the rest of the audience to get arrested, and JoJo was delighted to meet one of her victims. She swore she had never meant for the police to come along, and was relieved they had come to no harm. The *Manifesto* was only meant to be a way of engaging people in debate; she had never taken it seriously. Regrettably, she said she had given up street theatre and was now trying to develop her creativity in directions which earned money, since it was no longer possible to live on the dole. Maggie and JoJo had become good friends.

As well as writing feminist plays JoJo was now a lesbian stand-up comedian. In her act she claimed that her aim was to make men laugh themselves to death, and if she couldn't do that she would make women laugh themselves to murder. Completely fearless, she was game to try anything. Sitting in the club with her was a tonic in itself as far as Maggie was concerned, and this time her feelings of fraudulence were towards the BBC: fancy their paying her to get pissed with a mate and have a laugh. JoJo had a talent for getting people to like her. A combination of a cheeky grin, diminutive physique, huge brown eyes and bright orange hair helped, but her ready wit was warm, and far less aggressive than she pretended in her act. Maggie felt she would come across well in an interview, if she could get a producer interested in meeting her, they might be in with a chance.

"I suppose there's money for this masterpiece you want me to write?" asked JoJo, sipping a Becks.

"Ah. The money. Umm… "

"I knew it. You don't seriously expect me to do a whole script on spec?"

"Not a whole script, of course not. Just a treatment. A two-page proposal will do, then I can try and get it commissioned."

"Fair enough. Actually I have got a story I want to write, but

I don't know whether they'll like it here. It's about a lesbian."

Maggie smiled. "Good."

Jill Watkins was Maggie's third hope. Ten or more years older than Maggie, Jill was no political firebrand but she had many years' experience of writing plays for a wide variety of theatre companies and audiences, and had recently made her television debut writing for the ill-fated new soap, *Eldorado*. She was divorced and had a little boy aged six; yes, you're right, Jill was the pregnant woman in the Edinburgh fiasco. She and Maggie had run into each other many times after that; it's what happens in theatre.

"Wouldn't it be brilliant to make a community film with the BBC?" Maggie said.

Jill promised to start work on the treatment right away.

With two weeks left on her contract Maggie's cheerful determination started to falter. Two of the five producers' secretaries had called back to say they couldn't meet her after all due to busy schedules, although she was welcome to try again in a few months; however, at least she was going to meet both Stewart and Basil. *EastEnders* had failed to respond to her letter. Fenella still hadn't asked her in, and enquiries through Anthea revealed that there wouldn't automatically be any kind of assessment of Maggie's progress. Maggie tried not to feel disappointed at this crushing lack of interest in her. She ran into Sally in the canteen, and learned that she had a new contract to work on a major Dickens dramatisation. Donald Mountjoy would be producing it. Maggie realised with a shiver that the discussion group had been the arena in which Sally had auditioned. Still, she drew guilty satisfaction from knowing that at least Sally hadn't got any of her own ideas off the ground. Perhaps Maggie would succeed.

Each of her writers had come up trumps, and she had three strong ideas on paper. All were what they called 'left of field' in the drama department. All Maggie needed now was the support of a producer or development executive. She thought it pointless to ask Fenella, and it might be bad politics to go to one of Fenella's peers: producers, however, were not only senior, they were mostly able to commission independently.

The first one she met was Sonia Longbow, a pale woman in her thirties with wispy fair hair and anxious blue eyes. Her office was a mess, and she explained to Maggie that she had just moved into it. She added that she would more than likely be moving out again shortly; it was well known that the last office before the lift was given to people about to get the sack. Maggie was disconcerted by this intimate revelation and clumsily tried to sympathise, at which Sonia suddenly looked embarrassed and brushed it aside as if it was all a bit of a joke, and said she was up for two or three series and might accept a line producer's contract, in which case she wouldn't have much time for development.

Sonia had produced one film. Before that she had been an Associate Producer, which meant looking after the budget. Maggie hadn't seen Sonia's film as it had yet to be broadcast, although it had been completed eight months earlier. She asked when it would go out, but Sonia said the Controller hadn't scheduled it yet. Maggie asked what it was about and who had written it, and Sonia told her in detail; the concept was Sonia's own but it seemed she hadn't been able to get the writer she really wanted. As a result the script, which centred on a Surrey banker's wife, hadn't quite brought out the very real tragedy inherent in the dysfunctional family riddled with communication problems. The Controller feared adverse public reaction to the scene where the banker took his son's pistol and shot seven horses, and the mother and daughter's joint suicide was considered to be in slightly dubious taste, apparently.

Eventually Sonia asked Maggie about her own interests and

whether she had any projects she wanted to develop. Maggie handed her the three documents she had prepared, and Sonia said she'd love to read them and would get back to her as soon as she was able.

Maggie had slightly mixed feelings about Sonia, but had enjoyed her openness and interest in Maggie's own ideas: maybe this was someone she could work with. She felt encouraged.

She didn't hear anything in the next three days. She did, however, receive a letter from a personnel officer brusquely reminding her to hand in her ID card and office key and clear her personal belongings when her contract ended in ten days' time; it also pointed out that she was not entitled to reveal BBC matters to anyone outside the organisation. This struck Maggie as ironic, given that she had discovered next to nothing anyway.

Basil Richardson was charm itself. He welcomed Maggie into his spacious office, gave her a seat on a comfy sofa, and asked his secretary to send for Jonathan and then fetch coffees for them all. Whilst they waited he explained to Maggie that Jonathan Proulx had been his script editor for a year, and that they had a great deal of work on. Maggie thanked him for making time to see her, and he said to think nothing of it, the wheels had to keep turning however busy one was. He asked about her theatre experience and compared it to his own, which began in weekly rep at various provincial theatres in the fifties. He told her that television scripts were essentially no different from theatre scripts, all one had to do was visualise as if seeing through a camera rather than picturing a stage. In his opinion she had had the best possible training by seeing audiences respond, that there was no faster way to learn what works and what doesn't. Maggie agreed with him, and said she was surprised that people inside the BBC very rarely seemed to mention the audience, whereas she was accustomed to thinking of them first – you couldn't have a successful play without an appreciative audience. Basil agreed that too many years in the ivory tower of Television Centre did tend to make drama producers lose touch with their audience. Maggie was just about to say how much Basil's famous dockside trilogy had meant to her when she was a student, when Jonathan and the coffees arrived.

Jonathan was very friendly and interested in Maggie, which was embarrassing given the way she had indulged in bitching about him; she also felt deeply self-conscious about her performance at the discussion group and wanted to make a joke about it, but as she couldn't find a way to introduce the subject she let it go. Jonathan felt once again that he had met Maggie before somewhere, but even when they compared notes on the theatre companies they knew, they failed to find common ground.

Eventually Basil smiled at Maggie over his half-moon glasses and said, "So what is it you'd like to do?"

"All I really want to do is make some shit-hot programmes." Immediately she regretted it. "I suppose that's pretty obvious really."

Basil didn't seem at all put off, although he was amused by her phraseology. "And what would a 'shit-hot' programme be like?"

Again Maggie wanted to mention some of Basil's own work, but she felt it would sound like brown-nosing.

"A drama that's truthful about peoples' lives and means something to them – like certain shows meant a lot to me when I was growing up. I'd really like to do something that changes the world – like *Cathy Come Home*, for instance." Feeling caught between Jonathan's intense scrutiny and Basil's rumina- tive gaze she blushed and picked up copies of her three proposals. "Actually I've brought some ideas along, I don't know whether you'd like to have a look at them… "

"Sure," said Jonathan, and she handed them over. Basil's secretary put her head round the door and made a face at Basil, who excused himself and left the room. Jonathan sat back in his chair and crossed his legs stylishly as he perused the top document, while Maggie looked round at the framed certificates and film posters on the walls. Then he looked at the second one, and the third. "Lesbians in the army aren't really Basil's cup of tea," he said drily. "And I'm afraid your idea of a film starring members of the community is over-ambitious. Equity wouldn't allow it for a start. You might have had a chance with this one," – he held up one of them – "But unfortunately we've already got something on the subject."

"Oh, what a shame," said Maggie, wondering whether he was dismissing her ideas because he despised her. Basil returned at that moment, and looked interestedly at the proposal Jonathan handed him.

"'A film about a young black guy in prison,'" read Basil out loud. "Hmm. Where did you find this?"

"He sent in an unsolicited script I liked. This idea's based on his brother. I think it's very powerful. He's a new writer, so it might be a bit risky, but it's a subject that hasn't really been covered fully. Not on telly, anyway." Basil's bushy eyebrows rose and fell several times as he read swiftly through the proposal. "He'd need quite a lot of help with the writing I expect, the other script of his that I read was a bit rough and ready. But it's full of energy."

Basil handed it back to her. "It looks riveting, although sadly we already have a first draft of a *very* serious prison drama by one of our *leading* authors." He looked meaningfully at Jonathan, who pursed his lips and nodded agreement.

Maggie wasn't sure what all this meant, but the sum total of it all was that they didn't want her projects. She wished Basil had seen the other ideas himself, as she was obliged to accept Jonathan's rejection, but had to assume that he knew what he was talking about. Reluctant to conclude the meeting, she said she was thinking of applying to *EastEnders*. Basil said vaguely that he didn't know much about it, but Jonathan was enthusiastic, "That's a really good idea, Maggie. It can be tough meeting all those deadlines, but you can't match it for production experience. I'd go myself if I weren't embroiled in so many projects down here." She didn't believe him.

Basil wished her the very best and said he would look forward to seeing her again. She suspected he said this to everyone. She shook hands with both of them and glumly returned to her office.

One week left to go and one producer left to see. Maggie could almost hear her time ticking away, and she took to wandering the corridors in case she never had another chance. She noticed that Sonia Longbow's name had been removed from her door and hoped that she had managed to get a line producer contract. Maggie wondered what she'd done with her programme proposals, and decided to forget about it.

She discovered that there were viewing rooms where you could observe what was happening in each of the eight studios. It was fun to watch the progress of sets and technical preparations. *Blue Peter* rehearsals were entertaining: how absurd the presenters looked, squashed together on little boxes in the middle of a vast lino floor, with only a couple of open bookshelf arrangements behind and three huge cameras sliding smoothly in and out at them.

Exploring other parts of the building, she found that the best tea-bar by far was in the News block. She reckoned they needed to keep themselves on the ball, with three shows a day to put out. Or maybe they were just better at getting what they wanted. Once she caught a fleeting glimpse of Kate Adie walking round the corridor, a few sheets of white paper in her hand: she looked exactly the same as she did on television, which was a surprise to Maggie. For no reason at all, she had expected journalists to be like actors and to have a different persona off-camera.

Two days before she was due to leave, Fenella called and asked her over. Maggie's hopes rose again like a hot spring, and she trotted round immediately.

Anthea smiled when she entered the outer office, taking Maggie by surprise, and lifting her spirits further. Fenella was on the phone as usual, but when she finished she asked Anthea to hold any calls, and closed the door behind Maggie; she sat down in her padded office armchair and gave Maggie her full attention.

"I'm sorry we haven't had the chance to get to know each other. I only realised this week that you were due to leave. How have you got on?"

Once again, Maggie was completely disarmed. "Fine, thanks," she replied, and tried to marshal her feelings into a positive shape. "Actually I suppose I was hoping that you'd tell *me* how I've been doing."

Fenella looked surprised. "Oh, very well as far as the script reports go. No problems. Anthea says the slush pile's only half the size it was when you started."

Maggie flushed with pleasure, feeling ridiculous, she was so relieved to find that she hadn't gone completely unnoticed after all.

"Do you have any plans after you leave?"

Maggie's heart sank again. "I, er... I'm seeing a producer on Friday, and I'm still waiting to hear back from *EastEnders*."

"Jolly good, which producer?"

"Stewart Walker."

Fenella's eyes glinted. She paused. Maggie wondered what she was thinking. Did she remember the Discussion Group? In the end Fenella simply nodded, and started talking about *EastEnders*, which she recommended to anyone with a strong constitution, and she knew they were looking for a trainee.

"I'll call the Series Editor and tell her about you, if you like," she suddenly offered. "She was in your job a few years ago."

"Oh, thanks! That's really nice of you." Maggie meant it. "That's bound to help."

"Won't do any harm," said Fenella, almost maternally, and

offered Maggie a Silk Cut, which she refused. "Mind you, you might live to regret it. I worked on *Dr Who* and that was murder – and it didn't have a serial element."

Maggie was amazed and pleased to think that the intellectual Fenella had been on a show as bizarre as *Dr Who*, and the conversation took off.

She came away feeling much better about everything. It lasted until she got back to her office and found a letter from *EastEnders* saying that they had no vacancies at present.

As Stewart Walker was now her last chance, as well as her best hope, she gave the meeting a great deal of thought. She felt sure he would like her prison drama, and wondered what his next project was to be. He clearly loved to court controversy and one or two of his shows had made waves in parliament. He revelled in tackling issues others dared not touch, such as freemasonry and political corruption. There was no question that he was a brilliant producer, and that was enough to make Maggie keen to learn from working with him.

As she approached his office she heard raised voices, so she slowed her pace, she didn't want to arrive at an embarrassing moment. It quietened down so she walked round the door and into the little secretary's office which opened into Stewart's, just in time to see him rip a piece of paper in half and drop it in a waste paper bin. A small, angry-looking young woman yelled, "Do it your bloody self then!" and marched out, ignoring Maggie, who froze on the spot as Stewart glared at her and then stalked into his own office.

Maggie sat down and waited. Stewart's secretary didn't return. Suddenly he shouted for her to come in.

She did, wondering if he was in a temper. Stewart was opening a bottle of wine. He poured two glasses, handed one to Maggie and strode across the room to a sofa with a glass coffee table in front of it. Maggie smiled, then hesitated as there were hardly any chairs and she wasn't sure where it would be appropriate to sit.

Glancing around she was surprised not to see the usual array of scripts and certificates, instead there was a shelf with a couple of plastic and metal awards on it, and one large framed charcoal drawing by a well-known caricaturist hanging above the sofa. Maggie couldn't help looking at it, and realised with a start that it was a nude portrait of Stewart himself, drawn with enormous face, hands and genitals. Her gaze dropped a yard and discovered Stewart regarding her with amusement.

"Come and sit down," he said. "Sorry there isn't much furniture. I find it clutters the place up. Cigarette?"

Maggie sat at the other end of the sofa and reluctantly accepted the Gauloise, wishing she'd brought her Marlboroughs. She managed to inhale without choking. Stewart seemed to be waiting for her to speak. She was afraid of making a fool of herself again, so she waited for him to start. They sat smoking in silence, until finally Stewart said, "So you want to be my script editor?"

"Well, yes, if you think I'd be suitable," she replied cautiously.

"What have you done up to now?"

Maggie recited her cv, wishing it included names or at least theatres that he might have heard of. He nodded without betraying any attitude.

"So you want to change the world."

"Yes, of course."

"Don't we all?" he shrugged, and she grinned, sharing a sense of comradeship. Stewart sighed, stretched and crossed his feet on the coffee table. "I like a woman who knows what she wants," he mused. "It doesn't make you popular, you know."

"I'd have to be daft not to have realised that by now." She began to relax. "To be honest, I was beginning to think I'd never fit in here."

"Who cares about fitting in? Take no notice of all those arse-lickers. They'll never do anything *really* worthwhile. They're only interested in how far they can climb up the corporate ladder: who's got the biggest office, who's got the biggest *cock*." Stewart fixed Maggie with a challenging stare, as if to test her nerve. She wanted him to think she was cool, so she nodded and smiled ruefully.

"What's the female equivalent of that?" asked Stewart. "Who's got the biggest *tits*?"

Maggie laughed. "There's really no substitute for a big cock, is there?"

"I couldn't have put it better myself. We radicals have got to stick together, Maggie," muttered Stewart, as he slid along the sofa, put his arm round Maggie's shoulders and kissed her on the mouth.

Maggie jumped and almost gasped as his wet tongue thrust in and met hers. Astonished, she found herself staring into his eyes at point blank range and wondered what to do as he settled in for a snog. She didn't want to push him off and risk offending him. Neither did she want this situation to progress. Did he think she had been flirting with him? She quickly reviewed their conversation, and couldn't think of any reason why he would. Her breasts were suddenly clasped by a hand so large and exploratory that it could hold both at once, and she knew it was time to act. She gently pushed him back and half-smiled reprovingly. He drew back and looked in her eyes, realised she wasn't overwhelmed, and to Maggie's enormous relief, stood up and walked over to the window where he lit another cigarette and gazed out at the London skyline. She gathered herself and slipped out of the office. Stewart's young secretary was back in her chair, typing sullenly. She looked up at Maggie and said cheerily, "See ya." Maggie left.

By five o'clock she was on the Central Line, watching the stations go by: there were seventeen between White City and Stratford where she lived. Usually she liked to read, but this evening she used it for thinking. Half of her wanted to turn her back on the BBC forever, to go back and work in theatre where creativity was relatively easy, safe, rewarding and enjoyable. And badly paid. With dwindling audiences. The other half wanted to take on the monster and beat it: prove that she was good enough, make some great programme or other which would win a prize and allow her to feel that she had left her mark on the world. She was damned if she would let a git like Stewart Walker put her off. She was a match for him and anyone else whose ego was out of control.

Making television drama was mostly politics, she realised that now. Instead of the 'us and them' game she was used to, this was a much subtler business. It was like trading in your game of snakes and ladders for a chess set. It was all much harder than she had expected. She realised with hindsight that she had been arrogant to think she could walk in off the street and carry on as if this were merely an extension of her theatre career. It was another game altogether; clearly, anyone who really wanted a successful career at the BBC had to be utterly single-minded. You had to take it very seriously indeed if you were going to get anywhere.

Allies, thought Maggie. I need friends I can count on. Rhiannon, maybe. She seems like someone I can trust. I'll call her tomorrow, see if she wants to meet for lunch.

Chapter Seven

At the last minute Maggie's contract was extended by another twelve weeks. She and I lunched a lot over the next few months; we called it our Powder Plot. We always had a laugh and felt better for sharing our frustrations. You need to relieve the pressure now and then when you work in an intense environment. We often bounced ideas off one another, always searching for that great new project that could be our route to the all-conquering BAFTA. One day Maggie arrived with a Welsh idea.

"I saw this news item about Welsh hill farmers. They can't survive, it's terrible."

"I know," I said.

"Did you know the suicide rate's rising faster there than anywhere else in the UK?"

"It doesn't surprise me."

"Someone should make a drama serial about it. Don't you think so?"

I grimaced; it didn't sound much fun to me. "How Grim Was My Valley?"

"Very good. I thought, what if you've got a family farm that goes back generations, and they have a poetic tradition too – bards. Isn't that a big thing? Eisteddfods and all that?" I tried not to look bored as she carried on: "We don't have that in England, I wish we did. It could make very powerful viewing, don't you think?"

"If you say so."

Maggie wasn't going to be put off that easily. "Supposing the eldest son's a poet, and he's really not into the farm, the father's desperate for him to help keep it going but the son knows it's hopeless. They both feel suicidal. So the main storyline's about the farm, and the subplot's all in poetry – it could be a narrative voice-over."

I could see Maggie was really into this idea, and although it wasn't ringing my bell, I thought it had potential. I said she should go ahead, and suggested a Welsh writer I knew of who would be ideal for it.

Whilst we devoted ourselves to the creative rat race, others were similarly occupied at management level, where a volcanic upheaval was imminent. Chris Briggs had made a good fist of his work on the License Renewal Committee, and he was rewarded with a magnificent promotion. It was easily the most challenging post he'd had, and the most public. It was essential to make a success of it, or his career would certainly peak and dive. He prepared himself with great care.

Late one Sunday evening, Chris and his wife Catherine lay cosily in bed after a pleasant session of lovemaking. After twelve years together youthful passion had gradually been replaced by technical expertise and in many ways this was more satisfactory for both of them. It was certainly a good deal less messy and time-consuming, quieter and more efficient. Catherine snuggled into his shoulder, eyes closed, dozing contentedly, her short bobbed hair falling across her face, her mouth pressed against his firm pectorals.

Chris propped his head up with one arm behind it and allowed his gaze to wander round the bedroom. It was a large airy room in a fine Georgian house with all the original fireplaces still in situ. Damask curtains from Heals were swagged casually at the huge sash windows, and lovely Indian carpets covered most of the varnished floorboards. Tomorrow he would begin his new job as Controller of BBC2, and he was looking forward to it. At thirty-eight he was not the youngest man ever to take the job, and he didn't think he was the most brilliant, but he was quietly confident and totally determined to make a great success of it. He had proved to be a notable General Trainee, especially since taking the lead by bravely championing the digital future, and he was now being groomed – along with others – for the top job of Director General. He would occupy that role, and then retire to pursue whatever lucrative interests presented themselves, possibly in the House of Lords. He was well on course and had every reason to feel satisfied.

Downstairs the front door opened and closed heavily. Glancing at the clock on the mantelpiece Chris saw that it was twenty to eleven; that would be the nanny returning from her evening at the cinema. Catherine stirred and roused herself, "Oh God I nearly went to sleep." She sat up, fluffing the pillows, and tried to straighten out the bedclothes on the graceful antique brass bed. Giving up on them she leaned down and picked up her briefcase from the floor, dumping it beside her with a sigh. Her eyes automatically sought out a photo collage on her bedside table featuring happy family shots of their baby Natasha, now four-years-old. She wondered whether this time she would conceive again. She willed it to happen, and began to form a mental picture of a baby boy. Or another girl. Or one of each... then she pulled herself together, opened her briefcase and removed a sheaf of files, and put on the spectacles which were waiting in a professional manner in their place between the photos and the radio alarm.

"Are you in court tomorrow?" Chris asked.

Catherine tutted. "How many times?"

"Sorry."

"It's okay, you've got an important week too. Haven't you any work to do tonight?"

Chris picked up his own spectacles and a heavy book, opened it halfway and began reading. Catherine nosily peered at it and smiled to herself. *Management and the Technological Revolution*. It looked incredibly boring. She gave her full attention to The Crown versus Sanderstead Holdings plc.

*

Selina greeted him with a warm smile and a fresh cup of coffee. The papers were ready on his desk, and a vase of flowers he couldn't identify adorned the coffee table. Chris sighed with pleasure: how marvellous this girl was, she seemed to anticipate his every need before it even crossed his mind.

She had proved to be an effective secretary when they worked together on the Licence Renewal Committee, examining the BBC from every angle and drawing up a strategy which would appease the government's enthusiasm for privatisation, which was well known and widely feared within the industry; it was thought that commercial pressures on the public service broadcaster would reduce it to a carbon copy of ITV. Because of this the Director General had been keen to anticipate the government's every objection and spike their guns. Ruthless efficiency measures and cuts were to be put in place across the board, every department would be instructed to become cost-effective or risk closure, and producers of all programmes were to be told they need no longer use internal resource departments but could go to outside firms for any service they needed, if it saved them money. This was expected to make the BBC such extraordinarily good value to the viewing public that they would consider the license fee a bargain.

The strategy had been spectacularly successful and the government had not put up a fight at all, renewing the BBC's charter for ten years. The Board of Governors were delighted with the DG and the committee. Cynics suggested that the government was equally delighted with them for implementing Tory policy with such dedication – without even having been asked to do so.

Chris had taken a leading role on the committee and had impressed everybody with his clarity of vision and conviction that they must embrace a digital future. He had been given this promotion to see whether he was as good at practical implementation as he was at theorising: the corporation staff were still blissfully ignorant of what was coming, and the changes would not be easy to handle. He, in his turn, had not hesitated to invite Selina Crompton to become his Personal Assistant. She had provided excellent clerical support to the committee and understood the framework within which he would approach the job of Controller. He had learned from the DG that you needed like-minded people around you if you were to succeed in making changes. Selina was totally reliable and showed a level of diplomacy, which promised an exciting future. She was also attractive, slim, blonde and well educated, although Chris, naturally, was not the kind of man to prioritise these factors.

As he had such a thorough knowledge of the organisation Chris lost no time in planning his approach to scheduling Channel Two. He would work closely with the new departments currently being set up alongside him on the seventh floor, devoted to strategy development, policy planning, focus group research and ratings analysis. They would supply hard facts and figures, which would give him a scientific basis for choosing programmes and re-arranging the schedules. Based on American systems which had already proved their worth in the US, they would help to drag the BBC out of its civil service past and transform it, ready to compete in the world marketplace of the 21st century. This approach constituted something of a revolution from the top down, and sooner or later there would be trouble from the staff. However, the DG's stroke of genius was to make every department, whether they supplied resources or made programmes, survive or collapse entirely on its own merit. There would be no announcements of closure or redundancies, which would only precipitate strikes. Targets would be set, and departments would know that they had the same prospects as any business in the outside world: either they would break even or they wouldn't, in which case they would go bust. This meant that market forces would dictate which parts of the corporation were dead wood. Savings made by cutting them away would be put into new technology. It made perfect sense. It also meant that any internal opposition would be hard put to focus on any one aspect; when redundancies came along they would be scattered, and those involved would feel that they were personally at fault rather than the victims of cuts, and would go quietly.

For the moment Chris only had to worry about his own channel, which made a nice change and presented a fascinating challenge: how to improve the results without getting such high viewing figures that he would be criticised for putting on mainstream programmes which ought to be on BBC1. He intended to bring a new approach to a post which was traditionally led by one person's taste and judgement – a system which was naturally flawed. Instead of inviting Heads of Department to propose ideas they wanted to make, choosing a handful, and ultimately arranging them such that an evening's broadcast schedule resembled a kind of variety bill, he would do it the other way around. He would decide what the schedules were to look like, count up the various slots, and tell the Heads precisely what kind of shows he needed: how many, and how much he would pay for them. They would know exactly where they stood. He hated intrigue and this would minimise it.

Chris asked Selina to arrange a series of conferences with each programme department. He would address the producers and staff together in an open meeting so that they could get to know him and ask questions. He was keen to be seen as approachable and hoped to communicate his enthusiasm directly, sowing seeds which would return a nourishing harvest of prize-winning programmes. He had no doubt that every department would survive and prosper under the new system, flourishing like well-pruned trees.

Television Centre lacked a room large enough to comfortably accommodate more than a hundred people and so a new conference room had been designated on the seventh floor: to be more accurate, a boardroom had been extended by knocking two neighbouring offices into it. It was spacious and looked onto the centre of the doughnut, which had a courtyard with a non-functioning fountain in it, where staff would bring their bacon baguettes from the new deli-style tea bar to sit and eat on the little surrounding wall, under the towering statue of Ariel, a dated but inoffensive naked male figure symbolising aspiration of astral proportions.

Inside, the conference room was comfortable without being luxurious; cleaner and with a noticeably deeper pile carpet than was found on lower floors. On the longest wall hung an impressionistic mural depicting a busy television studio with huge lumbering cameras not seen in the studios for thirty years. The mural was unusual in that it had two doors, which met in the middle like a giant cabinet.

The real problem was the seating plan. The room was not only very long and thin, it was curved, constituting about a fifth of the doughnut ring. If Chris spoke from one end he would be unable to see the people sitting at the far end on the courtyard side without a mirror. If he spoke from the middle, with his back to the wall of windows, he would have only a few rows of people directly in front of him and the majority to the side and over his shoulders. If he stood in front of the mural it was marginally better but he would have not only the sun in his eyes, but the glassy golden gaze of Ariel's giant face.

Chris sighed and looked at Selina with exasperation. She agreed.

"There really isn't anywhere better?" he asked without hope.

"Not unless we book a studio, and that would mean paying for it. At least this is free."

Chris walked from one position to another, weighing up the options. How to communicate successfully, maintaining authority whilst inspiring loyalty, in the face of structural disadvantage? He smiled to himself: that was BBC management in a nutshell. He would save that observation for his diary, which he kept so that he could write his memoirs one day.

"What do you think, Selina?"

"Well. If you've got your back to the window no-one will be able to see your face, and if you face the window you won't see anyone else's face, so it might be best to go with the end-on arrangement and try not to use the far corner. If you stand at the mural side of the short end, rather than in the middle of it, that will help."

Chris could see that this was a sensible approach, but he disliked the formality of it. He would feel like a headmaster taking assembly.

"Okay but let's try and break down the barriers a bit, I don't want to sit behind a table, and I don't want straight rows of chairs. They can be curved. I'll just stand at the front." Selina made a few notes on her pad, then checked her watch.

"Time we went back. The DG wants to see you at twelve."

"Yep." Chris smiled and looked into her shrewd eyes appreciatively. "Thanks Selina."

His face was transformed in a way she found very appealing. He was a stocky man of medium height and ordinary regular features, with unremarkable short brown hair and a serious expression, but his smile was soft and shy.

"Can you fix up for me to meet the Drama Department first, and Documentaries last; it doesn't matter how the rest fit in. And not more than three a week. Two would be better."

"Sure. How soon do we start?"

"Next week. We'll hold them in the mornings. Ten o'clock."

Selina nodded, noted, and beamed. He was a really good person to work for: decisive, organised and respectful towards her. He treated her as an intelligent professional which was just what she wanted. She was determined not to be written off as a bimbo, and Chris would never do that. Giving him her full support would benefit both their careers.

At nine forty-five the following Tuesday, Chris sipped a weak cappuccino from a polystyrene cup as he stood at his office window trying to look through the venetian blind into the conference room behind the statue. He couldn't see well enough to know if it was filling up. He wasn't really nervous but he was very concerned that the meeting should go well; he knew the value of first impressions and had prepared his address with great care. He had chosen to start with the Drama Department because he didn't know anyone in it. Over the years he had worked in Arts and Music, Sport, Features and Current Affairs, before being hand-picked for the Licence Renewal Committee. Consequently there were many people who had known him in all kinds of junior roles, who would have mixed feelings about his new seniority over them. Experience had taught him to step with care where they were concerned, as their respect had to be earned. Drama would take him as he was. By the time he had worked his way round to Documentaries he would be better armed to take them on. Certain characters would, he knew, give him a hard time.

At five past ten Selina popped in to say that the Drama Department had assembled and were ready for him. He picked up his notes and walked round briskly, with Selina in attendance. He entered at the farthest door so that he was already in his 'stage' area, noted the water Selina had placed on a small table for him, and smiled to her as she sat down at the side of the room and prepared to take minutes.

He cleared his throat and surveyed the room, which had been filled with rows of chairs on a slight curve towards him, as he had requested. He hadn't anticipated the effect of the contrasting curve of the room on the curve of the chairs, which made him feel slightly sea-sick. Never mind, he would re-consider the layout later on. An expectant hush had fallen as everyone soaked up their first proper look at the new controller, so he smiled tightly at the floating mass of faces and began.

"Good morning everyone. Thank you for sparing your time today, I won't keep you any longer than necessary. I've brought you here to introduce myself and give you the low-down on my plans for BBC2, direct from the horse's mouth; I know what the rumour machine's like here. I think it must have something to do with the circular corridors – never-ending Chinese whispers!" This feeble joke produced a friendly murmur which indicated that the ice had been cracked, if not broken. He glanced at Selina who smiled back softly.

"I'm very keen to establish a good, clear communication between us: I intend to be absolutely straight with you on all matters." He paused, hoping for another ripple of acknowledgement which didn't happen. Once again he found himself looking at Selina: he reprimanded himself for seeking moral support from one so young, and addressed a light fitting half way down the room instead:

"Now, I expect you know a bit about my background. I've been here sixteen years, I've made many programmes in my time and I'm very well aware of the problems you have to deal with. I also believe very strongly that programme-makers are the vital core of the BBC, and while I'm in this job I shall give top priority to getting the best possible quality of programmes for the channel.

"It goes without saying that you, the Drama Department, are one of the great assets of the BBC. I'm afraid I don't yet know any of you personally, although many are of course familiar. I can see some very distinguished faces here this morning. I hope very much that you will throw yourselves behind me and help us to lead BBC2 into a new era." Again he paused, but no response. He realised that the sea of faces was waiting for something more informative than bullshit. Time to offer them something concrete; he departed from his notes, putting them behind his back, and strolled a few paces from side to side.

"One of the *most* frustrating things I've encountered as a documentary producer is waiting for an answer further up the line." He glanced sideways at the assembly and saw a few heads nodding at last. "You've got a fantastic idea no-one else has picked up on yet, you've done the research, worked out a rough budget – and you're stuck in your office waiting for the green light. Every day that goes by endangers your project from rival companies picking up on it, participants getting cold feet, or maybe the issue will lose its topicality if the programme isn't made as soon as possible. What you need is a quick decision. And they tend to be a rare species in the BBC. Well, not in my office! I guarantee you a prompt yes, no or maybe. None of your proposals will sit on a shelf wasting time. And that's a promise."

This went down well, the crowd shifted a little, relaxing. Heads turned toward each other, eyebrows rose and fell, one or two fresh young faces were eager to answer his call. Now he could move on, taking them with him. At that moment a drill started up in the middle distance. He refused to let it put him off his stride.

"BBC2's record in drama is very strong, and I mean to build on that. I shall be extremely clear about what our needs are, and I look forward to working with you to develop the right shows." A look of slight bewilderment flitted across the group. "I also mean to build in new technologies which will radically reduce costs over the next few years, provided we're prepared to work *with* them. We mustn't be afraid to try new ways of doing things." Frowns began to appear, eyes met briefly and looked back to the front.

Chris felt a little nervous now. He was losing the tenuous grip he had barely established, and he wasn't sure why. Why would new technology be considered controversial? He gripped his notes.

"I'm going to give you a broad outline of what I'm looking for next, for the 95/6 season. I think it's very important that you know the way I see the channel working, and I want you to feel that you can discuss it with me. I'll take questions at the end." He paused for people to fidget, and recommenced when pens and notepads were at the ready, speaking as loudly as he could without shouting because there were now two drills competing with him.

"Firstly, a classic serial: I must say I thoroughly enjoyed *The Old Curiosity Shop*. Is Donald Mountjoy here?"

Donald waved cheerily from somewhere in the middle of the room.

"Donald." Chris indicated his respect by fixing eye contact and nodding with conviction. "Of course, I would like another along those lines. Secondly I would like a contemporary serial: a cutting edge, state-of-the-nation piece from a leading writer. Thirdly I would like a long-running series of contemporary adult drama which will make a real impact on the nation – I don't see why the Americans should wield a monopoly on cult hits!" He glanced up and was encouraged to see some of the younger faces near the front looking excited.

"I expect to develop projects at a rate of three to one for the slots, and I shall be able to give you specific slot requirements in a few weeks, along with guideline prices. I look forward *very* much to receiving your ideas. Now, does anyone have any questions?"

Chris slipped his notes into the inside pocket of his dark grey suit and took a drink of water. The atmosphere was not good. In fact, the word to describe it was consternation. The audience looked serious; some frowned, others examined their finger-nails minutely. His armpits prickled and he loosened his tie, which he would have removed except that he knew the DG believed that senior executives should look the part at all times. The builders, wherever they were, abandoned their tools and silence fell suddenly on the crowd. Chris tried to look relaxed but felt like a giant panda newly arrived at London Zoo for mating purposes. There was confusion and tension in the room. What should he do about it? He saw the Head of Drama, Peter Maxwell at the end of the second row and caught his eye: would he like to say a few words? Peter rose to his feet, adjusted his belt and lightly brushed his hand over the top of his head, smiling in a generally inclusive manner.

"Thank you Chris, for a most welcome frankness. I think it's taken us all somewhat by surprise!" The group united in agreement.

"If I may, I… rather think one or two of your remarks may have come across in a slightly ambiguous way. Perhaps we could clarify a few points."

"Of course." Chris was all attention. Peter's reputation was sound: not a difficult man to deal with, and a fine track record.

"I think you may have said you were looking at developing drama for the 95/6 season, when you meant 96/7; of course we have to work a year ahead of other departments because it takes so much longer to make drama."

"Absolutely." Chris nodded sagely, masking his concern. He'd forgotten to take that into account, damn it. But he didn't intend to wait a whole year before making his mark. He would not automatically accept the shows his predecessor had chosen. However, he didn't want to go into this until he'd had time to think about it further.

"Sorry about that, everyone – slip of the tongue! Anything else?" He hoped he hadn't made any other blunders. "I'd be most grateful if you would say your name before putting a question."

A hand waved from the very back, on the window side, and Chris moved sideways to get the best view. A dark-haired man with large features and an open-necked denim shirt lifted his head as high as he could.

"Stewart Walker. I *am* sorry, I don't seem to be able to see you very well. For some reason they've set the room out in this bizarre fashion. It's most frustrating."

Chris steeled himself. He knew immediately that Stewart had sat there deliberately, and that Stewart knew perfectly well that Chris would have approved the seating plan. He would not let Stewart know he knew what he was up to.

"I agree," he replied. "It's a very strange room indeed!"

"My question is whether we can depend on you, as a former maker of *factual* programmes, to *really* support us as makers of *drama*."

Chris knew a baited fish-hook when it hit him on the nose. "Isn't that what I've just been saying?" he asked, disingenuously.

Stewart's face writhed with the effort of expressing himself. "You see I've been making drama here for twenty-seven years, and some of those projects – I like to think the *best* projects – have taken three or four years to develop, and two years to produce. I would like *very* much to feel that you understood how we work."

Chris received Stewart's message loud and clear: no jumped-up kid controller was to stand in the way of Stewart's major works of art.

"I intend, as I said, to work closely with you at every stage. I'm sure we'll soon understand each other very well."

Stewart nodded sagaciously. He had received Chris' message with equal clarity: who's the bloody controller here anyway?

Selina had turned to try and see who was speaking but she couldn't get a good enough view. A handsome young man near the front was also craning his neck: as he turned back to face the front, concealing a distinct smirk, their eyes met full on. They held each other's gaze a moment longer than was necessary.

Chris was glad to see another hand rise nearer the front. "Yes?"

"Penny Cruickshank, producer. Hello. Forgive me for asking this, but I'm just wondering if you intend a radical departure from your predecessor's approach?" This was another loaded question, but coming from this large middle-aged woman with such a sweet face, it wasn't aggressive.

Chris smiled warmly. "It's hard for me to say whether it's a radical departure or not; it's certainly a new approach, and I think, a much clearer, simpler one."

Penny nodded hard, adding: "For instance, you mentioned development at a rate of three projects per slot. That's a great deal less than we currently have on our list."

"Really?" Chris had no idea what their list had on it. "What rate do you normally maintain?" Penny looked at Peter, who looked at Fenella.

"The thing is, Chris, we don't really look at it that way. I'd have to count them up and work it out." Fenella *had* recently counted the number of projects in development as the list was getting out of hand. It came out at about fourteen to one, assuming the same number of hours of broadcast drama as last year. This was obviously not a statistic likely to impress Chris Briggs.

Another hand flapped, and Selina was glad to see that the handsome man was going to speak. He had a poise she admired; confidence in his good looks, articulate cleverness, and impeccable manners.

"Jonathan Proulx, script editor. You didn't mention single drama: am I right in assuming Screen Two will remain unchanged?"

"I'm sorry, I didn't mean to overlook single drama. I'm still considering how best to schedule it. This is something I would like to discuss with you, Peter." Peter looked up in surprise, and consented willingly.

"Sonia Longbow, producer. What about new writing?"

"Again, I shall give that special consideration."

"Morag Fishman, Department Manager. Are you intending to set fixed prices, and how soon will we know?"

"Yes, and soon." Chris pursed his lips inscrutably. "I'm sorry, I don't mean to be mysterious, but it's very early days, I'm sure you appreciate that."

Morag did appreciate that, and a lot more besides. Quietness descended as everyone pondered the implications. Chris was about to close the meeting when another hand shot up.

"Sally Farquar-Binns, script editor on *The Old Curiosity Shop*. Do you mean you want another Dickens, or something different for the classic serial?"

Chris shrugged. "What have you got?" he smiled a happy smile: this was the kind of response he could work with. If only they were all like Sally. This gave him an opportunity to quit while he was ahead, so he drew the meeting to a close, promising they'd hear from him very soon. He caught Peter's eye and mimed that he would call him, then left the room followed by Selina, who was followed by Jonathan's eyes. As the door swung to behind her Chris heard a voice announce as if through a tannoy, "Ladies and Gentlemen: Chris Briggs has left the building". He was annoyed but ignored it, and they returned to his office in silence.

*

That night Chris met Catherine at Covent Garden to see *Cosi Fan Tutte* as guests of her senior partner and his wife. The stalls were hot and stuffy, as usual, but he quite liked the music which was mercifully cheerful – a vast improvement on the Wagner they had seen last time. One great advantage of opera was that you could close your eyes, wear an expression of concentrated pleasure, and think about something entirely different without fear of giving offence or being disturbed. He had been too busy since the Drama Department conference to give it proper thought, and this was a good opportunity.

Clearly it had raised unforeseen problems, which he would have to deal with. The drama crowd as a whole were a race apart from the rest. Any television producer was serious and committed to their work, willing to walk through fire for it if necessary, guarded and sceptical of any proposed change to their work procedures. The drama lot had the reputation of acting like prima donnas but Chris had always thought this a superficial judgement; certainly they would name-drop with the best, but he had known news producers who threw outrageous tantrums, and documentary makers who would lie through their teeth in order to get their idea off the ground. The drama peoples' egos were no bigger than anyone else's, they just expressed themselves more vividly. What made them different?

The music trilled and charmed him as he studied the singers giving their all. They seemed to be discovering the music for the very first time: what a superb skill, he realised, to repeat the same notes, the same expression, the same actions over and over, probably a hundred times before the first night, and then perhaps a hundred more times in performance, and *still* make it fresh. He could never do that. He had a low boredom threshold which required him to find a new challenge every time he mastered a skill. Is that what it means to be an artist? Rejoicing in the music, the thing itself, for its own sake; living in the moment?

Drama producers want to make great art. In fact, they think they do. They see themselves following the same process as the live arts: they pick a script and spend a couple of years making it with the best actors and technicians they can find, refining it and perfecting it in the edit. Factual programme makers had an opposite approach: they would pick a subject and chase off in pursuit with a minimal crew, shooting whatever footage they could. The programme would only develop a structure and a clear message in the editing room, when the material was sorted, most of it being rejected, and the narration would be written last. The drama method was essentially about creating a vision and then realising it as closely as possible. The factual method was about discovering as you created on the hoof. There was very little imagination involved, and that explained why factual producers were easy to work with; they were up-front, pragmatic, sharp and responsive, ready to drop something instantly in favour of something better. Drama producers, in contrast, were tenacious and stubborn, refusing to allow any dilution of the purity of their work, which must flow and surprise and engage as cleverly as any novel, play or film. Most of them had started in theatre, and many no doubt aspired to make feature films. A handful of BBC films had been released to cinemas, but without notable success. There was a very strong lobby to extend into features on a commercial level, but the British film industry was in a terrible state and there was little hope of improvement under the current government, so it really couldn't be justified on any level, as Chris saw it: they were a public broadcasting body, and as such they should make drama for broadcast to the masses, not arty films for trendy little cinemas.

In his view it was absurd to consider television as an art form on the same level as opera, theatre or film. Television was a wonderful medium for bringing all those things into peoples' homes, but even then, the viewing figures for such programmes were always low. High art was not what the masses wanted, as *The Late Show* was currently proving. Set up as a five-nights-a-week arts review it was already reducing its broad canvas and would shortly be on only three or four nights a week. London's finest arts journalists presented the show, and if they couldn't get the public interested, who could?

Chris felt he had found the key to understanding the Drama Department. The hands-off attitude of past controllers had allowed them to believe in themselves as creators of significant art. They had let the viewing figures persuade them that millions of people sat transfixed by their shows, whereas he knew perfectly well that most families kept the telly on the same channel all night and didn't even pay it attention; home-work, ironing, cooking, eating all taking place with the telly providing a pleasant moving wallpaper and a comforting murmur in the background. The drama folk had some hard lessons coming their way. Television in the nineties was no art form: it was a medium of communication, and like the Royal Opera, it was also a business. You couldn't put on obscure new music all the time if you wanted bums on your seats, and the government would be wrong to subsidise that policy. You had to give people what they were prepared to pay to see: a regular diet of Mozart and Bizet, with the occasional experimental piece to satisfy the opera buffs. Culture was all well and good, but the bills had to be paid. The BBC could learn a lot from the Royal Opera House and the way it was run. Maybe there was even a documentary series in it?

After the performance they said goodbye to Sir David and Lady Julia who went straight home to Weybridge. Catherine looked very tired and Chris proposed forgetting their plan to have a Thai meal in Soho, but she insisted that she wanted to go, so they did.

They sat at a first floor window table which gave them privacy and a view of Shaftesbury Avenue, where the theatre-goers were turning into night-clubbers. After ordering and tasting the wine, Chris took Catherine's hand and squeezed it gently.

"Anything wrong?" he asked. She was never one to make a big fuss about anything; one of the most stoical women he had ever met.

She shrugged and sighed. "I've got my period."

"Ah." They looked into each other's eyes sadly and sympathetically. There was nothing more to say.

"It's not the end of the world," he said gently.

"I'm thirty-nine. Natasha's four already. We've blown it."

"Do you want to go for tests? IVF?"

Catherine sighed and shrugged again. "Not really. Yes, I do. No." She cupped her face in both hands, trying to rub her eyes without spoiling her make-up, and shook her head. "I don't know," she whispered.

Chris was concerned. If they weren't in a restaurant he would have given her a hug, but as it was he put his hand on her knee under the table, and rubbed it. Their starters arrived, forcing him to sit up.

"Come on, have something to eat," he encouraged, and she picked at her spicy prawns while he embarked on his chicken and coconut soup. He felt he should be making a kind and supportive speech, but didn't know what to say. Women's hormones had always mystified him. He sipped his soup and watched her.

"If only I'd got pregnant again two or three years ago it would all have worked out perfectly. The family would be complete, Natasha would have a sibling, and I'd be able to concentrate on my career. We should have tried harder when the time was right." Catherine stabbed the last prawn and bit it in two. Her deep brown eyes met his light hazel eyes in unmasked resentment. Chris looked pained.

"Don't try and pin the blame on me, Cathy. You know that's not fair."

"It wasn't my idea to restrict sex to Sunday evenings."

"That's Sarah's night off."

"It might suit you and Sarah, but it doesn't suit my ovaries. Anyway I'm sure most couples find a way to make love when there are other people in the house."

"I can't relax properly. You know that. It just wouldn't work." Chris was tense now; she was walking on thin ice. "It wouldn't matter if her bedroom weren't next to ours."

"Let's move house then."

Chris adored the house, and so did Catherine. They would never find such a place anywhere else unless they had a million pounds to spare. The only other room they could put the nanny in was the little loft conversion currently used as a gym. Even if they did put her up there, which would be a lot less comfortable for her, it would mean that she wouldn't hear Natasha in the night, which would mean that Catherine or Chris would have to get up whenever Natasha wet the bed, which was still about twice a week.

Chris sat back and gazed at his wife gazing out of the window at the lively street. A waiter cleared their plates and refilled their glasses with Sancerre.

"So what you're really saying is that you've *got* to have another baby."

"That's not what I'm saying."

Chris raised his eyes and immediately stopped himself, sensing an angry woman afflicted by hormones about to accuse him of treating her like an angry woman afflicted by hormones.

Catherine spoke slowly and clearly so that even the densest of men could understand, "Even if I got pregnant tonight, I would be forty when I had the baby, which means it would be very hard on my health, not to mention my career and I can't afford to set myself back at this stage if I'm going to make it to QC. And it's hard enough finding time to spend with Natasha. How can I make time for a baby and more time for Tasha and put in all the work I need to do and turn up at all the bloody social events we get invited to?"

"Look. Why don't we quit while we're ahead? We've got a gorgeous little girl and everything else is going really well."

"I don't think it's good for her to be an only child."

"In China they're only *allowed* one child."

"So all the kids have the same experience. British kids have siblings. Natasha needs one. Loneliness is the worst thing that can happen to a child."

"She isn't lonely, she's got lots of friends. Anyway her sibling would be at least five years younger than her, that's not much company for her is it?"

"Exactly!"

Chris was lost. "So what do you want?"

"I don't know!"

The waiter's reappearance was welcome, and the table was soon covered with fragrant dishes.

They ate in silence for five minutes.

Finally Chris tried a new suggestion. "You're under a great deal of pressure at work, aren't you darling?"

"I usually am."

"Have you thought that you could give it up?"

"No. Out of the question. I'd go up the wall stuck at home all day."

"You wouldn't have to be stuck at home, you could work

129

part-time maybe."

Catherine put down her chopsticks. "Have you thought about giving *your* job up? Natasha would love to see her father more than once a week. You needn't get bored, you could find a little job – work for a charity perhaps." Catherine's tone was light but her expression acidic.

"Okay, okay. Point taken. I'm only trying to help."

"Well try harder."

"I'm just looking at the situation objectively, that's all."

"When *don't* you."

"What's that supposed to mean?"

"You never talk about what you *feel*. Sometimes I wonder whether you've got any feelings left."

"Now you're being ridiculous."

"Fine. Tell me what you, Chris, feel about our children, born and unborn."

"Catherine." Chris massaged his forehead with one hand. "What are you trying to do? I love Tasha to bits, you know that. If I had another kid I'd love it too. I'd put up with the noise and the smells and the mess and the expense and the inconvenience for the sake of its little tiny fingernails and its darling gummy smile – " He stopped because Catherine was sobbing silently into her napkin. "I'm sorry." He rubbed her knee under the table. "You did ask." She nodded and hurried off to the Ladies.

Chris finished up a couple of dishes as he contemplated the strange complexity of the female. Catherine used to be one of the most sensible women he had ever met, with a crystal-clear legal mind, and now look at her: there could be no doubt that her hormones were to blame. That would pass eventually, he supposed, but it might take years. What a prospect. He would just have to ride the storm as best he could. He loved her, she was his mate for life. They had met at Oxford, recognised each other as soulmates, and set out together on the path to the top. They had been rock solid together all that time, unless you counted Chris' one minor sexual adventure in Edinburgh, but that was before they married. There were bound to be problems along the way. No matter, he was equal to the challenge.

Catherine returned looking pristine and sat down with care. Chris took her hand. "Look darling. I love you, I need you, I want you to be happy. *I'm* happy, I'm happy if we don't have another kid and I'm happy if we do. But I can't be *really* happy unless you are. I'll go along with anything you want, I promise. Apart from giving up my job."

"I'd never ask you to do that."

"I know."

Catherine squeezed his hand and smiled at him, her eyes watery. Chris noticed that her faint crows' feet were more apparent when she was stressed out. "I love you," he whispered.

She smiled again, wider. "I love you too."

The waiter took this opportunity to move in and clear the table. They ordered coffee and relaxed as they sipped the last of the wine.

"We don't talk enough, you know," Catherine remarked. "Maybe it happens to all couples after a few years, you feel you know the other person so well you don't need to say it. You think they know what you're thinking."

"I'm only a bloke, Cathy. You'd like me to be a new man really. But I'm not cut out for it."

"I know. I don't want a new man, I'd be bored silly. They're not sexy at all as far as I can see. It's to do with power. New men have no power. No power, no sex appeal."

"*I've* got power."

"I *know*". She giggled.

"I know it's not Sunday, but I could probably demonstrate my potency for you if you like."

She smiled affectionately. "That's very sweet of you darling, but I've got my period, remember?"

"Oh yes. Shame." He smiled tenderly, privately relieved.

"I've got an idea," she said brightly. "Why don't *we* move up into the loft room for a while? It might be fun."

Chris was dismayed, but a promise was a promise. "All right. What do we tell Sarah? She'll think we're mad."

"I'll think of a good reason. It'll only be for a few months. I'll start taking my temperature so we know when to do it."

"Great. Just one thing."

"What's that?"

"We can get the bed up there, can't we? I don't want to sleep on the floor."

"Of course we can."

The coffees arrived, and they toasted one another in decaffeinated espresso.

"One other thing," said Catherine.

"What's that?"

"You'll have to start wearing boxer shorts."

Chris groaned. "Anything you say, my sweet."

Chapter Eight

I was able to escape the dreaded frock series when Peter Maxwell asked me to be the BBC's editorial representative on a two-part thriller commissioned from a new independent production company. These little firms were proliferating. Many were set up by former BBC programme-makers who wanted more control over their work. Their existence was very insecure, dependent on the favour of the two BBC Channel Controllers, but they had the freedom to operate as they saw fit provided they adhered to corporation guidelines. Crucially, Mrs Thatcher's government was forcing the BBC to broadcast independently-made programmes – at least a quarter of the total output, in fact.

This was a great experience for me, working with a senior producer and a leading theatre writer. It was a step up to work on a two-hour drama instead of a long-running series, and I learned how a contained structure could carry far more power and impact. The story was about a British couple accidentally caught up in drug running, and the film locations spanned the globe. Sadly the script editor wasn't required on location, so my role only lasted until negotiations on the script were concluded – although this was an unexpectedly drawn-out process as the Australian director didn't seem to speak our language; almost every scene suggested something entirely different in his mind. Layers of subtle meaning went straight over his head, and he seemed to take all the dialogue at face value. It was a valuable lesson. You shouldn't assume that the English languages spoken around the world are the same English that's spoken in the UK. Neither should you take it for granted that anyone can read a script and understand it; it's highly skilled. Scripts aren't like pieces of prose. They're a glorious mixture of dialogue and images, character traits and motivations, themes and stories. The briefest scene can communicate an ocean's depth of significance, sometimes with no dialogue at all. The medium of film is so rich, varied and full of potential that you need to understand all the possibilities inherent in a bare script to appreciate its quality. You have to know about actors and what they need, cameras, lighting, sound – and then there's pace, tone, atmosphere. You have to visualise the effect of cutting from one image to another to recognise the power of juxtaposition. Film can be more truthful than real life, more amazing than dreams, more overwhelming than music, theatre, or any of the arts on their own. It can be pure or it can perpetrate wicked lies. It's the richest, most complete art form we have. Have I persuaded you?

I also realised that you can't make original drama in the same way that you can churn out long-running series, which essentially repeat the same formula episode after episode. New work needs to be made by teams of individuals, each bringing their own personality and a unique combination of skills and experience. That's how creativity blossoms: through the open-minded interaction of imaginative ideas and exploration, not by following rules and procedure – and definitely not by ticking boxes, as politicians believe. Don't get me started...

It was eye-opening to leave the corporation buildings behind for a couple of months and widen my view of the industry, I gained another perspective on the BBC and came to sympathise with the independents' point of view. After all, it belonged to the people as a whole, and yet decades after his death, the pompous patriarchal attitudes of Lord Reith's era still lingered on, as if viewers should be subserviently grateful for whatever they were given. Many people in the industry felt this was absurd, and I agreed with them. There was definitely a need for the BBC to modernise itself and catch up with the rest of us.

The broadcasting press reported on the independent sector and often mentioned Magenta, which by the mid-nineties was in the ascendant with five shows on ITV Midland, three of which were networked across the country. When they ran a photo and profile of the industry's youngest head of production, Nik Mason, I was gobsmacked to recognise little Nicky from the NYT. What a turn-up! I was really pleased to see that he'd done so well for himself.

Magenta had moved to smart new offices in Camden, having a permanent staff of sixty and a large number of shareholders. Since floating the company on the stock exchange, Rex and Haris had become wealthy. Rex had a penthouse suite at Chelsea Harbour and Haris drove his Mercedes in to work from a grand house in Buckinghamshire.

Nik was becoming a bit of a name. He had produced two shows of his own, both quiz formats hosted by Geordie Boy, and their collaboration had proved very successful. Daytime ratings were always low, but they attracted a larger share than BBC1, and the shows were re-commissioned.

Geordie had much preferred working with Nik than with Rex. They were of the same generation, and they understood each other so much better. Nik allowed Geordie to be himself, and helped to draw out his charm and humour so that he became increasingly loved by audiences. As the show's contestants were always members of the public it was essential for the host to have enough personality and charisma to carry the show single-handed. The last couple of years had seen Geordie find his feet as an artist, he was now relaxed on camera and a very dependable performer. He had a new agent, who had great ambitions for him, and a stylist to choose his clothes.

Geordie and Nik had just developed a show format which

moved into a new area: the comedy quiz. Geordie had only been peripherally linked to the new comedy circuit, his material was apolitical and he had never felt fully accepted by the punky, anarchistic comedians who liked to push boundaries over the cliff. At this point in his career he hoped to cross the divide, and align himself with those so-called alternative names who were now starting to become the new comedy establishment.

The show would be called *SOS*, and Rex had needed some convincing that it was right for Magenta. It would still be a quiz, with two celebrity guests who were supposed to help the contenders to win. It required more preparation and scripted material than previous Magenta shows, and more costumes, since all the participants would be seen full length – a radical departure. It also tested the contestants a little more rigorously, for their general knowledge and for their long-suffering. They were required to be good sports. This feature worried Rex: what if they proved *not* to be good sports and spoiled the show, or sued the company? He thought it was dangerous – which was exactly why Geordie liked it.

Rex had told Nik and Geordie that the show would never be commissioned except by Channel Four, and that even there, they only stood a cat in hell's chance. So when Nik received a call from their Commissioning Editor for Entertainment saying that he wanted thirteen episodes he was delighted, and Geordie was ecstatic.

"Yes! Yes! Thank you God! This is the big one!" gloated Geordie, raising his fists triumphantly in front of the tenth floor picture window as Nik replaced the phone.

"Ain't we done well, kid! Our first show that's not for ITV. Growth, expansion. Just what Magenta needs. I must go and tell Haris."

Nik left the office and Geordie swung to and fro in the big executive chair, singing to himself and fiddling with the executive toys on Nik's large steel desk.

A minute or two later, Rex's head appeared round the door.

"Hi Rex. Heard the news?" said Geordie.

"Where's Nik?" answered Rex crossly.

"With Haris. He'll be back soon. Did you hear about *SOS*?"

"What about it?" grunted Rex, stomping in and dumping his briefcase and raincoat on a chair.

"We've been commissioned! Thirteen episodes for Channel Four!"

"How much?"

"Eh? Aren't you going to congratulate your clever boys, Daddy-o?"

"Don't wind me up. I want the figures before I rashly dole out compliments."

Nik reappeared, and clapped Rex on the back as he strode happily up to his desk and sat on it.

"Hi Rex. How was the meet at the Beeb?"

"Fucking terrible."

"Oh. Sorry, mate. Sit down. Have a drink."

Rex allowed himself to be cossetted. He sank into the leather sofa, kicked off his shoes and sipped the large whisky Nik gave him.

"Didn't they like *Give us a Break*?"

"They did not. They think advertising is not a subject for a BBC game show. They live in a world where advertising's like sewage, something other people deal with to keep the world turning, while they keep their dainty hands clean. Stuck-up ponces." He finished off the whisky. "Of course it's really me they don't like. If some Oxbridge type came in with the same idea, they'd love it."

"Aye well, *they'd* be making a clever ironic comment on the modern world, wouldn't they?" commiserated Geordie, parking himself next to Nik on the front of the desk.

"Whereas we actually live in it," finished Nik.

"To them, I'm nothing but a jumped-up masseur. I never go to that place but someone's always got to comment on it, like I'm some kind of funny little native species. I feel like a bloody crested tit marsh warbler. I think they think I'm a character out of one of their bleeding sitcoms."

"Maybe it's the generation gap?"

"No it bloody isn't. I'm not old. I'm experienced. More whisky." He held his glass out at arm's length, and Nik poured him another.

"The actual sticking point," continued Rex with mock earnestness, "is in the subtext, however – as them toffs like to say. The one point they troubled to impress upon me was the issue of rights. Unless we pip-squeak production companies are prepared to give them our copyright – on *our* shows which we have developed at *our own* expense – *they* are not prepared to give serious consideration to any bloody new show at all!"

"How do they expect us to make a profit and keep the company afloat unless we own the rights to our own products?" Nik was disbelieving. It was crazy.

"They couldn't give a ferret's fart about us. It's company policy. They're forced to have independents in by law, but they expect us to act like the hired help! They won't negotiate, they're absolutely rigid about it. They want our profits. But they ain't getting them."

"Second rule of business, eh Rex?" smiled Nik.

"That's right, boy. *Own it!*"

"Looks like the BBC operate by the same rules then, doesn't it?" said Geordie.

"Yeah, well, stuff 'em." Rex concluded.

"A toast, gentlemen," called Geordie, filling their glasses. "Stuff 'em!"

"Stuff 'em!" repeated Nik and Rex. They drank.

"Well. At least there's some good news," said Nik happily.

"Yeah, well done, boys," said Rex, frowning. "Get Haris to bring the sums in, will you?" Nik picked up the phone and called Haris.

"He'll be along in a mo."

Rex couldn't stop worrying over the BBC dilemma. "What

we'll have to do, is make them an offer they can't refuse."

Geordie looked askance. "Surely not, boss. We'd never get away with that at the BBC, would we?"

Rex looked up, bewildered, and then caught on.

"I'm not talking about GBH, you northern moron, I'm saying we need a show that's so completely irresistible they can't turn it down – even without the rights."

The door opened and Haris stepped in quietly. In recent years he had taken more of a back-room role in Magenta, preferring to let the extraverts run the production side of the company while he efficiently ran the business end. He was happy not to take part in public engagements, they seemed to him increasingly tedious. He carried a piece of paper which he gave to Rex, standing by him as he perused it.

"Well this show's a complete waste of time, ain't it?" Rex said finally.

"What d'you mean?" responded Nik sharply.

"The price they're offering's too low."

"It's their standard rate."

"There's no profit margin, you dickhead."

"But we keep the rights!"

"Shows like this aren't going to sell anywhere else, how many times do I have to tell you! The repeat fees'll be sod all! There's only one way it could possibly be worth our while."

"What's that?" asked Nik, now annoyed. He exchanged a glance with Geordie, who had been gobsmacked into silence, but not for much longer.

"Keep Geordie in his old role. He can't be co-producer as well." Rex presented his implacable stare, which they knew signalled the end of any discussion. Geordie slipped down off the desk, livid with rage.

"No way man, no fucking way! That's my show, it's mine. I've worked for you for six years, for peanuts, absolute peanuts! You'd never have got this far without me, I'm the best asset you've got. And I'm not going to be exploited any more. My agent says you walk all over me, and I just go, 'Ooh Rex is my friend, I've got to be loyal to him.' Well not any more. I won't take a penny less on that show. If you're not prepared to pay me what I'm worth, I'm off, me. There's plenty of other companies out there, you know."

"Yeah, yeah," said Rex calmly. Haris looked at the carpet, pursing his lips. Nik remained fixed to the desk, all attention. Geordie strode to the window and stared out of it, steam rising from his head. Rex sighed in a dignified manner.

"Then there's no show," he said simply. "We need to concentrate on mainstream entertainment. This fringey nonsense is a load of crap."

Nik watched his friend struggling to control himself. "It means a great deal to Geordie. He needs to develop. It's a great opportunity to cross into new territory. Expand. Diversify. Surely it's worth doing for that alone?"

"You're not considering the risks, Nik. Do you know what this is really about? Artistic ego. Okay, so artists have egos. They need stroking. But they don't need fawning over to the extent that they make complete bloody fools of themselves! This show ain't funny, is it?"

"We think it will be – and so do Channel Four!"

"Exactly. I've never seen a funny show on Channel Four. They're all mouth and vulgarity, that's all. Turn Geordie Boy into one of them 'alternative' comedians and that'll be the end of him. He'll lose the audience we've been building up all these years. It's crazy to throw that away, unless you're going to make enough money out of it to develop a whole new market. But you ain't going to make a sou. You can only lose. It's a dead end. I knew that when you started with this idea, but I thought, let them find out for themselves. Best way to learn."

Geordie stared, open-mouthed, then left the room in a hurry. Rex looked at Haris, who raised his eyebrows and nodded sympathetically, then returned to his own office.

"I'm sorry, Nik. You liked this one, didn't you? You'll thank me one day. It had disaster written all over it." He looked at his protégé understandingly, waiting for him to look up, smile ruefully, and agree that Rex knew best. It took longer than usual, but eventually Nik did look up.

"It's not that, Rex. I mean, I did like it, but I knew it was tricky. I wanted to do it because Geordie's so keen. He doesn't want to be stuck on ITV his whole career, he wants intellectual credibility."

Rex snorted. "Don't, you'll give me indigestion!"

"He might not get over this, Rex. We might lose him."

"He's contracted. He can't leave."

"He's got a new agent, remember. And this one's good."

Rex stood up and put a heavy hand on Nik's shoulder. "Well then, you'll just have to turn on the charm and talk him round, won't you?"

Nik found Geordie on the roof, in the little landscaped garden area which consisted of a series of potted plants and a couple of trellises. Geordie was leaning on the wrought iron railings, gazing at the sky. Nik walked up and embraced him from behind. He stroked Geordie's hair and cheek, turned him round and kissed his lips. Geordie let go of his tension and hugged Nik tight. Nik patted his back slowly for a few minutes.

"I've got an idea," he said eventually. "Want to hear it?"

Geordie sighed, and continued clinging to Nik. "I'm afraid you'll let me down too," he said, in a small voice, his eyes closed.

"Don't be daft," answered Nik gently. "Have I ever let you down before?"

Geordie shook his head.

"Well then. You know how I feel about you."

"Do I?" Geordie let go of him and stood up straight. His eyes longed for reassurance. "How come this is still a secret then? Why don't you come out?"

"You know why."

"I know your excuses."

"Geordie. Come on." Nik held Geordie's face in his hands. "I'm not gay, I'm bisexual. I don't want to be categorised."

"You mean you want people to think you're straight."

Nik shrugged helplessly. "I can't change the world, can I? I've got to live in it as it is. I'm a businessman. Look darling, you're fabulous, I adore you. I'm going to make you a star. Isn't that enough? What do you want to do, marry me?" He chuckled at this absurdity, and smiled lovingly. Geordie melted.

"Howay then, bonny lad. Tell us this great idea."

"We'll develop a show for the BBC, which they can't resist. I'll sell it to them, and keep the rights. You'll be a star with credibility *and* a mainstream audience, and everyone'll be happy. Simple."

Geordie held out for five whole seconds before he capitulated. "Whatever you say, man. I believe in you." He lacked the resolve to keep pushing his own interests; he would much rather put his faith in Nik, whether he trusted him or not.

"I believe in you too." Nik kissed him again. "Don't try to leave Magenta, will you? I couldn't bear it. I know Rex can be a pain in the arse. And I'm sorry if I've been a bit cold, lately. It's my dad you know." Geordie bowed his head. "The re-trial begins next month. The waiting's doing me in. Half of me wants to be there with him, the other half says no, keep your distance, it'll do untold damage to your career. Anyhow, the last thing *he* needs is the papers latching onto me, and chasing me and you all over London for a picture; it could prejudice his case. I just wish it was all over, decided once and for all, and then we could all get on with our lives."

Nik buried his head against Geordie's shoulder and allowed the hint of a sob to colour his sigh. Geordie cuddled him. "I'm sorry, pet." he murmured, "I've been insensitive."

"It's alright," Nik muffled. "Forget it." He pulled himself together and smiled bravely. "Let's go and work on our new show, shall we? Over a pint?"

"Sure, honeybuns," said Geordie, smiling sadly.

"Just don't call me that in the Bricklayer's Arms, okay?"

Later that day Nik chanced across a panel game format in his in-tray which he hadn't binned, and he thought there might be something in it they could use. It was from a writer called Jill Watkins. Her covering letter was apologetic in tone; it said that she was really a dramatist, but she'd had this idea, and thought it might suit Magenta.

"Look at this," Nik said to Geordie. "It's a panel game for soap stars. You get a team each from two soaps and they have to play acting games and answer questions on the shows. Good idea, ain't it? Viewers would love it."

Geordie nodded as he read it through. "Hard to book the actors, though."

"Only if you contract them individually, not if we do a deal. Suppose we stick to two series, say a BBC soap and an Aussie soap, and get an umbrella deal on both sides?"

"Brilliant. What about me?"

"You're the host, stupid!"

"Is there going to be anything left for me to do? I work best with punters, you know that."

"We'll have punters on the teams too. Two actors, one punter."

Geordie smiled. "Sounds good. But what if this Jill Watkins doesn't want to do it that way?"

"What's she got to do with it?"

"I thought it was her idea?"

"Nah, it'll be completely different. She won't even recognise it." Geordie looked troubled. "Oh god, alright, I'll give her some money for it. I'll buy her out. Watch me."

Nik phoned the agent's number on the top of Jill's treatment, and briskly explained that there was an element in Jill's proposal he liked and that he was willing to offer a hundred pounds to buy her out, as a goodwill gesture. He didn't think the idea had a future otherwise. The agent called back after twenty minutes to say that Jill had agreed.

"Lovely," said Nik. "That means we can't get sued when we've got a runaway hit on our hands. Now for the Aussies."

Nik knew his opposite number in Outback Productions' London office, and met her for lunch a few days later. She was a pleasant, put-upon woman who carried a little too much weight, in Nik's opinion, but there was no side to her and she didn't play power games. Nik found this disarming, and had to hold on tight to his own self-control, or he might not have got the advantageous deal he wanted. Her name was Grace Tullock, which amused him as her staff called her Grice. He had to force himself not to do the same.

"We think this is a great idea," she told him enthusiastically. "It'll be terrific publicity for the show, and the actors – they'll really get on the map here."

"The only problem is shipping them over to Britain. It'll be expensive."

"We might be able to schedule recordings to match up with publicity interviews. And maybe the second series could be recorded in Sydney?"

"Why not!"

"I think the broadcasters will go for it too. There isn't anything else like it. Especially if we can do it with *EastEnders*. Do you think they'll go for it?"

"I can only try. There's one other thing I need to make clear."

"Yeah?"

"It's my copyright. We co-produce, but the rights stay with Magenta. Okay?"

"I guess so." Grace was disappointed, but hers was not the only Australian soap.

Once Nik had sewn up the necessary elements to the show and felt certain the BBC would want it, he gave a great deal of thought to his approach, in view of Rex's bad experience. He decided to avoid everyone Rex had met by going over their heads to the Channel Controller. It was a risk, like putting all your chips on one number, because if he said no, that would be the end of it. That's the difference between Rex and me, Nik thought to himself, Rex always tries to hedge his bets. That's why he'll never get to the top, he'll only get rich. I play for higher stakes.

He talked his way into an appointment with the Controller of BBC2. On the day, he chose his suit with care, selecting a designer label which suggested style, street cred and money, without the least vulgarity. He looked good in it. In fact, he decided, he looked good in practically anything. He had that kind of talent.

Chris Briggs' PA was extremely tasty, but Nik knew better than to try and chat her up. Posh girls like Selina didn't like obvious moves. Anyway, it was too soon. He behaved as if he hadn't really noticed her, whilst being very polite. Chris was exactly what he expected: a boring Oxbridge type in a boring suit in a boring office. Why didn't these BBC mandarins possess any interesting features? How were you supposed to tell them apart? As soon as they shook hands, Nik knew that Chris was in awe of him. Nik had everything Chris lacked. All Chris had going for him was his education.

"Pleased to meet you, Nik, come and sit down," smiled Chris, showing him to a chair in front of his desk, and seating himself in his larger chair behind it. "I understand Magenta is going from strength to strength. You must be very pleased. You've made quite an impression."

"Yeah, well, we ain't complaining, you know," replied Nik chattily. "Can't seem to put a foot wrong lately, everything we touch turns to gold."

"I hope it lasts. So, you've got something for us, have you?"

"I think so, Chris, but only you know what you want for your channel, and I wouldn't dream of telling you your business. To be honest, it's the first time I've been inside the BBC. Never thought it would happen when I was growing up in Canning Town!"

"That's in the East End, isn't it?"

"Yeah that's right. I lived in Ronan Point. You've probably heard of it."

"It certainly rings a bell."

"Half of it collapsed one night, huge gas explosion."

"That's it! My God, how awful. Were you in it at the time?"

"I was, matter of fact. Survived, obviously, but it was very traumatic. Lost my mum and dad."

"That's terrible, I'm so sorry."

"Don't upset yourself, it was years ago. We all just got on with it. That's the East End spirit, ain't it?"

Chris nodded; so he believed. What a remarkable young man, to do so well despite his inauspicious beginnings. He was clearly going to go far.

"Anyhow, as I was saying, I don't know that much about the BBC, but I do know how to put together a show that'll entertain people. That's my speciality. And I have to admit, our shows have done extremely well, given the slot they're in.

"Absolutely," agreed Chris. "So tell me about *The Soap Ashes*."

Nik outlined the show, pretending not to notice Chris's eyes light up as he casually name-dropped the stars and the price. "I've already got the Aussies on board, they're dead keen. They want to put the show out in prime time, and they'll pay half the production costs. All you have to deliver is the cast of *EastEnders*." An anxious look passed briefly across Chris' face. "Naturally Magenta will produce the show, and we'll keep the rights. If you can't live with that, we'll look elsewhere. But no-one else knows about this yet. I wanted to give *you* first refusal."

Chris played it cool. He picked up a pen and scribbled on his blotter. "Sounds very interesting, Nik. I'm not absolutely sure if it's right for BBC2, but I'll think about it."

"Sure. Shall we say, until the 28th?"

"Oh, yes, I suppose so. Just one thing. I'm not sure Geordie

Boy is really a BBC performer, if you know what I mean." He raised his eyebrows at Nik, who smiled and nodded.

"To be absolutely frank, Chris, I wondered if you would say that. I like the guy, of course I do, and I think he's very good. I think he could do a fine job, in fact. But I know what you mean. This show could use – well – a bit more class."

"That's exactly it," said Chris, feeling they were working together now. "Let's consider some of our own presenters."

"Of course. Geordie's been good for Magenta, but he's not tied into this show. I mean to say, much as I like the guy, we're not joined at the hip."

Chapter Nine

While Nik was betraying his friend for thirty pieces of silver, and I was swanning around the West End with my new mates in the independent sector, Maggie was busy working on her new project with a distinguished Welsh writer on board. It was developing well and she had high hopes. If the Controller of BBC2 commissioned it she would very likely be allowed to produce, and if it was a success her career would take off. Success bred power, in the sense that you would be in demand to some extent. Everything depended on the Controller's opinion, whether you were a first-timer or a producer of thirty years' standing.

Chris had spent months holding conferences with the various departments. Each went a good deal more smoothly than Drama, since the changes Chris was introducing would have far less impact on the quantity of work they produced. Fears about redundancies were rife, but staff were generally positive about the prospect of staving them off through their own efforts. The departments had characteristic qualities. News and Current Affairs were astute and serious, whilst Entertainment were chirpy and laughed a lot, cheering him when he assured them of a swift decision on every idea. By the end of it all he had a useful overview of the programme departments as a whole, and he was confident they would help, not hinder, his ambitions for BBC2.

He was very pleased with the new Magenta show, *The Soap*

Ashes, which was about to begin production, and felt he had made a shrewd move in picking it up promptly. He had also received a superb proposal for a new late-night drama series from another independent, (composed of some talented young BBC producers who had recently quit to set up their own production company) which put the in-house offerings in the shade. The Drama Department remained something of a problem. Chris had fixed up to do lunch with Peter but it had been delayed twice. Finally they were to meet at a smart restaurant a short cab-ride away in Notting Hill. Chris decided to take Selina with him, it wasn't entirely necessary but she deserved a bit of a treat for all the thankless work she did for him. And he might need to talk it over afterwards; she was intelligent and discreet, and very clever at picking up subtext.

It was much easier to be friendly and relaxed on neutral territory, and the continental atmosphere of the restaurant was just what they needed. Chris found Peter to be a very decent chap and quite good company. Selina contributed amusing remarks now and then, and a pleasantly convivial air had been established by the time they had finished the main course and Chris judged it time to get down to business.

"Now then. The Drama Department." He grinned at Peter as one pal to another. "How would *you* like to work more closely?"

Peter nodded and looked thoughtful. In truth he didn't want to work more closely at all, he wanted to see as little of Chris as humanly possible. His staff wanted it even more, he had been pestered by every one of them since the dreadful conference, demanding to know what was going to happen to: a) their projects, b) their contracts, and c) the department as a whole.

"I think you're absolutely right, of course," he said, "we need a lot more communication."

"You and I should meet regularly, every three weeks perhaps, to start with."

"By all means."

"Can you come up tomorrow with your development list? I'd like to pick out the projects I can use, give you the prices, and talk more fully about what I want."

"Absolutely. I'll bring my Development Executive, Fenella Proctor-Ball. Forgive me if I seem to have misgivings, it's not that – I'm just thinking of the list. I'm afraid a lot of shows are going to bite the dust. It always happens when controllers change."

"The new broom doesn't want the old dust. I know, I've been there myself."

Peter didn't believe him, but pretended he did, and that he recognised Chris' empathy with gratitude.

"What I'd like most of all, Peter, is for your people to come up with some really terrific ideas that I can commission straight away. We all know that 25% of broadcast material must come from independent production companies by law now. *My* aim is to put out the best programmes I can get, *wherever* they come from. I certainly wouldn't discriminate *against* the Drama Department, if that's what your staff are concerned about."

"It has been mentioned," muttered Peter.

"I thought as much. The 25% is across the board, not specific to each part of the BBC. I can fight for your programmes if they're the ones I want."

"That's good to hear."

"I really don't want to see anyone get laid off, Peter. But it could happen. It's up to us all to make sure it doesn't."

"Absolutely."

"I'd like to tell you something which, strictly speaking, I probably shouldn't. I've actually got a project on the table from a leading independent which is perfect for my new adult slot."

"A cult hit?" enquired Peter, no trace of irony perceptible.

"That's right. It's great. It's contemporary, cutting edge, young, sexy, dynamic. It could run indefinitely and it only costs £150,000 per hour."

Peter looked alarmed. "We couldn't match that. Our overheads are massive. Everything has to be charged now, there's no way we can compete with small companies."

"Don't give up before you've tried. That's not an attitude I can work with. That slot belongs to you, Peter; I want you to win it. I want you to bring me a better, cheaper idea."

"I'm not sure we have anything in development which would lend itself."

"Get the team working on new ideas."

"But I *do* have some really excellent projects which are all the things you want. I just can't say offhand whether they could be returning series, or could be low-budget. We'll look into it."

"I like *new* ideas, Peter. We're only five years off the millenium. Ideas you've had floating about for a few years already are hardly likely to be up-to-the-minute."

Peter's heart was heavy. Chris expected them to start from scratch and come up with a fully developed 'cult hit' in a couple of weeks. If he could do that he would be running his own drama empire by now.

"What about something to do with clubbing?" Chris continued. "Selina here's a bit of an expert. She could probably kick you off in the right direction."

Selina froze; she could see that Peter felt patronised. "I'm sure there are plenty of people in Drama who go clubbing as much or more than I do," she put in.

"Of course," said Chris. "I mustn't try to teach my grandmother to suck eggs!"

"Actually we have a couple of terrific films about clubbing in development," said Peter brightly. "I think you'll like them. I wanted to ask what your plans are for single drama, you mentioned a scheduling query?"

"Mmm. Single drama. I've been looking at the ratings, Peter. They really are very poor. It costs me up to 900K for a film which may well attract less than a million viewers. I can buy in an American film for a fraction of the price and get five times the viewers – and I know what I'm getting. Looking at it objectively it's very hard to justify to the licence-payer. What do you think?"

Peter took a deep breath before replying. "I think for us to stop making films would be a tragic loss to British culture. BBC plays and films have always been a training ground for our best film directors and writers, not to mention countless actors and technicians... "

"Yes of course, and where would Alan Parker be if it weren't for the advertising industry? Ha! That could be an argument for introducing adverts on the BBC! Don't worry, I don't subscribe to that view. But I've got to think of the licence-payers' interests. Is the BBC here to train film-makers or to broadcast the best programmes we can get?"

"There's a big difference between licence-payers and share-holders, Chris. I sometimes think the DG sees them as one and the same. What our films need is *more* investment. How else can we compete with America?"

"Sure. We need to look into private investment. I'm sure we can find a way round this, Peter, but it will take time. I'm going to put single drama on hold."

Peter was horrified. "No films at all?"

"Just for the time being. I want to concentrate on returning drama. That's where television comes into its own, people love a really good series that they can get totally involved with over a period of months. It gets talked about at home, at work, in the media: films are here and gone in a moment, Peter. They don't have the impact." Chris felt almost sorry for Peter, whose drooping shoulders betrayed his despair. "You can't make *Cathy Come Home* in the nineties. It's a different world."

Much as he would have liked to argue the point, Peter saw discretion as the better part of valour. "I suppose new writing comes under single drama?"

"Yes, but I would like to set up some sort of competition: a national event open to anyone, linked with the millennium. Call it *New Writing for the 21st Century* or something a bit catchier. I know it's still some way off, but I think we might capture the public's imagination this way, don't you? Get people thinking about new beginnings, even science fiction."

"That's a terrific idea Chris. How do we fund it?"

"Your department can look after the whole project." Chris evidently regarded this as an honour.

"We'll need half a dozen readers and editors and support staff dedicated to it for a year if it's to be a national competition. You have no idea how many entries are generated by things like this."

"Details we can sort out later on. Or I can put it out to an independent… " Chris was beginning to feel irritated by Peter's defensive attitude. "The bottom line, Peter, is that I have to make a success of BBC2. I have to pick the right programmes for the schedule. It's not *my* job to keep the Drama Department going, it's *yours*."

Peter smiled wistfully and sighed. How times were a-changing. When he was singing along to Bob Dylan, Chris was a schoolboy in shorts, and this girl he seemed to think so highly of was unborn. He had better make the best of it.

"I'll do everything I can, Chris. You can count on it."

"Great."

"If we've covered everything, I really need to get back to the office. I don't mean to rush you… "

"Not at all, Peter. Go ahead. We'll follow on when we've had coffee."

"Okay. Thanks for a splendid lunch."

"I'll call Vera about that development meeting tomorrow," said Selina.

"Thanks very much," said Peter, and left, trying hard to walk with an air of relaxed confidence – not that his companions were paying him any attention.

Chris smiled at Selina. "That went rather well, I think. How about you?"

Selina agreed. "He's a pushover."

"I wouldn't go that far. But he knows when he's beaten. He's got to dance to my tune now." He chuckled happily and stood up to go to the gents, adjusting his underwear. He noticed Selina look away tactfully. "Sorry – new boxers."

"Oh," she replied, nonplussed.

The development meeting with Peter and Fenella also went smoothly. The classic serial was easy; there were two major dramatists working on novels by Mrs Gaskell and Charlotte Bronte, but Chris asked for some proposals on Dickens follow-ups to give him a wider choice – he was concerned that it shouldn't be too depressing. The contemporary serial had several strong contenders, with leading writers already at work including the controversial Billy Trowell.

There was unfortunately nothing Chris felt would supply him with 'a cult hit in a post-watershed slot of 45 minutes to be supplied in series of ten episodes with returning potential at a cost of £150k per show'. Peter was very stubborn about the costs, which irritated Chris. He advised Peter to give 'blue sky thinking' a whirl by bringing all the editorial staff together to brainstorm ideas, but Peter resisted. He said his people were used to working in small teams, not sharing ideas with all and sundry. He also commented that the phrase 'cult hit' could only be applied in retrospect, but Chris told him not to be pedantic. In the end Chris told Peter it was up to him, but however he did it he had better get a move on, because there was a leading inde-pendent with a terrific show all ready to go. "Be creative," he encouraged. "Find new ways of doing things. Hand-held cameras, digital editing – there are all sorts of new products out which I'm certain can be used to shortcut." Peter and Fenella promised to investigate.

Chris hoped he wouldn't have to deal with the Drama Department for a while, as life at home was rather demanding.

Catherine had found that their brass bed was too big to go up the stairs to the second floor after all, so she had bought a sofa bed and a thick Chinese carpet. The gym equipment was put away and with a couple of lamps the room was really quite cosy. Their move upstairs was accepted without question because their bedroom was being decorated. Chris knew better than to grumble that he liked it as it was; Catherine was determined that the work would take at least two months, maybe three or more, and had decided on original built-in wardrobes and a mosaic floor.

Her next ovulation fell on a Saturday, and they gave Sarah an extra night off by giving her their tickets to a play at the RSC, which they said they didn't want to see after all. They had sex three times that weekend, which they hadn't achieved since their first months together. Unfortunately it didn't result in pregnancy, so Catherine's enthusiasm remained unabated. However, she was confident that effort would be rewarded in the course of time.

Not having access to their bedroom and clothes from 8.30 to 5.30 was rather inconvenient, and Natasha had become fascinated by the mosaic tiles and kept laying little trails of them all over the house, to everyone's annoyance. They got everywhere and splintered if stepped on.

They also acquired a guinea pig which lived in a hutch in the back kitchen. Catherine felt Natasha needed a pet, although it seemed to Chris that Catherine spent far more time with it. He was content for her to be a mother hen if it made her happy. There were times when he envied colleagues with old-fashioned wives who wanted only to keep a lovely house, bring up a family and look after their husbands. Life would be a lot easier.

It was very pleasant to quit the chaos of home every morning and arrive at his well-ordered office. To be greeted with a smile and a cappuccino, and sit down to work in peace. He had only to give Selina the word and he would be undisturbed for as long as he wished, although even Selina had no power to stem the construction noise which continued to resound through the building in fits and starts. They were adding a massive extension to the side of Television Centre which would accommodate a large foyer, a state-of-the-art music studio, and extensive news-rooms which were part of the DG's plan to combine all the news services into one massive centralised system.

Chris was now able to concentrate on his favourite occupation, collating all the information provided for him by the focus groups and ratings analysts and studying similar data from the US, along with their schedules. He pored over them looking for ways to advance his own channel, and was becoming enamoured of the aggressive scheduling techniques the Americans used to fight off intense competition. Granted, he was only competing against Channel Four at the moment, since satellite and cable television had made precious little impact on the public so far. Some channels were watched by no-one at all, and the top figures rarely reached a million. They were bound to get going eventually though – especially since the BBC was setting up cable channels of its own. He had to make BBC2 as strong as possible for its future security.

He wanted to pick up on new trends and build on them, and he saw that lifestyle shows were starting to do very well. They were cost-effective so he commissioned more. Daytime chat shows and quizzes were also very popular: he commissioned more. He encouraged producers of travel shows to get comedians to present them, thus attracting two sections of the viewing public to the same show, gambling that the higher fees would be worth paying. He bought in top American sitcoms, which were streets ahead of British comedy shows. They were slick, upbeat, wise-cracking and altogether superior, as he told the Head of Light Entertainment in no uncertain terms. The wretched man had whinged on about the Americans' massive development budgets, and the importance of letting new shows develop through two or three series before writing them off as failures, but Chris told him the modern world of television didn't have time for that.

He liked discussing programmes with Selina, who always had

an intelligent opinion, and he unconsciously began to rely on her in much the same way as he relied on Catherine at home. She kept the office machine running smoothly and mopped up tedious bits of business so that he could concentrate on the important, over-arching task of executive achievement. She was so loyal and devoted that it came as a shock to him one day to see her flirting with a handsome young man who had the temerity to sit on her desk while she was working at her computer. He was so taken aback that he retreated into his office and closed the door before they saw him.

He told himself not to be ridiculous. Selina was gorgeous, she was bound to have men all over her – but she had never mentioned a boyfriend and he had never asked. He had enjoyed the cosy illusion of her constant devotion. Now it was shattered. Why was he upset? He was jealous. He could hardly believe it. His first reaction was to get rid of the boy immediately, but he didn't want to make a fool of himself in front of Selina. He decided to be casual, and opened the door again. He strolled out asking, "Any chance of another coffee, Selina?" and was surprised again because she was on her own.

"Of course. Cappuccino?"

"If it's not too much trouble." It *was* quite a lot of trouble, because she had to go down to the ground floor to get one, whereas filter coffee was available from their own percolator. While she was gone he glanced around her desk for clues to the identity of the boyfriend, but found nothing. He felt annoyed with himself and went back to work.

At lunchtime he decided to eat in the canteen, although he didn't like it much. It would make him seem a man of the people, one of the workers. He still wanted people to feel he was accessible, although he'd prefer they didn't access him often. He went down ten minutes after Selina, piled a tray up with food and sat down by the window with *The Independent* open in front of him. He could see Selina a few yards away, chatting with the same boy beauty, as he named him privately, and soon remembered that he was in the Drama Department. The two of them made a perfect couple, both slim, elegant and blonde. Chris had always envied people like that. His solid, celtic physique and lack of style had always left him out of the running whenever sexual competition was the game. Maybe he should have tried harder? It wasn't in him. Catherine had been only his third girlfriend, and the only one he had fallen in love with. He concentrated on his paper until someone sat down opposite and he had to move it.

"Oh I'm sorry, I didn't mean to disturb you," said a cultured voice unconvincingly. "Oh, it's Chris Briggs, isn't it! Sally Farquar-Binns. Script Editor in Drama – we met at the conference."

"Oh yes." Chris resigned himself to conversation. She fiddled about with her plates and cutlery until she was comfortable, and leaned towards him. "It was a super meeting, and Peter's told us all about your exciting new plans. We're all going berserk in development!" Her chirpy enthusiasm took the sting out of what he might otherwise have perceived as sarcasm, and he suddenly recalled who she was.

"You worked on *The Old Curiosity Shop* didn't you?"

"How sweet of you to remember."

"You did an excellent job on it, Sally."

She shivered with pleasure. "Thank you so much. You'll be glad to know I'm working my way through the whole Dickens canon. Whew! There's an awful lot of it. But they're *marvellous* aren't they? I can hardly believe I'm getting paid for doing it! Tell me, which ones are *your* favourites?"

"Oh, I don't know. *A Tale of Two Cities*, *Nicholas Nickleby* perhaps." He could barely remember them. "*David Copperfield*, of course."

"Yes that's *my* favourite, too. But it's been done so well so many times, hasn't it?"

"I suppose so." He was beginning to feel out of his depth and made a mental note to ask Selina for a set of Dickens synopses.

A new arrival saved him from embarrassment.

"Hi Sally, mind if I join you? – Oh sorry Chris, I didn't see you there!" A thin pale woman with large anxious eyes sat next to Sally and unloaded her tray.

"I'm *so* pleased about the new writing initiative!" she enthused. "I've been banging on about it for years, but you're the first person who's ever recognised its true importance. A nationwide trawl for new talent, what a marvellous idea."

"I'm glad you think so."

"I don't mean to sound presumptuous but have you decided who's going to run it?" Chris looked surprised. "No no, of course not. How would it be if I drew up a few plans, designed a proposal?"

"That would be very helpful," said Chris, trying to sound at once gracious and noncommittal. "You are… ?"

"Sonia Longbow, producer." She went to shake his hand but changed her mind – it wasn't necessary in a canteen. "I've been at *EastEnders* for a year. It's a bit like going abroad, going off to Elstree; you don't see anyone until you get back. But new writing is my real love."

"Splendid," said Chris. He looked up to see Stewart Walker approaching and quaked inwardly, to his relief Stewart sat down with a few men at a nearby table. They were sniggering about something.

Penny Cruickshank was the next person to steam over, and as her bulky figure squeezed into the space next to him he stood up. "I'm just about to leave, why don't you sit here?"

"Oh, thank you," said Penny, disappointed. He left them to complain about leaving his dirty plates for them to clear away, and tried not to hurry back upstairs.

Later on that afternoon Selina came in with his tea, and mentioned that she'd been reading some Tony Scott scripts sent by Basil Richardson's office and that they had completely knocked her out. "It's such *real* writing," she said. "So warm and tragic and funny. It's about these miners who lost everything when their pit closed, and how they try and make new lives for themselves. You *must* read it."

"Sounds intriguing," said Chris. "But it doesn't sound like a cult hit."

"No. But it could be your cutting edge contemporary serial."

"Let me have a look. By the way, did I see you having lunch in the canteen?"

"Yes," said Selina. "That was Jonathan. We've been seeing each other for a few weeks."

Chris tried to be avuncular. "Great!" That sounded ridiculous, he was certain. She smiled, amused and flattered by his obvious liking for her. He smiled tightly and nodded repeatedly, unable to think of a single remark.

"Actually, he says you once did him a big favour, but you probably don't remember."

"Really?"

"About ten years ago, when he was a student at the Edinburgh Festival. He says you both got arrested when some nutter started a fight in the street. You can't have forgotten a thing like that!" Chris looked bewildered, and then it began to come back to him. He remembered the green-and-purple-faced student, and could see that he might have turned into Jonathan. "Apparently you sweet-talked the police into letting you go, and then paid for a taxi so he could get to his theatre in time to meet some important people. You probably saved his career."

"Good heavens. I had no idea." Chris tried to recall what had happened after they all left the police station, but could only bring to mind that he had shagged a feminist, which was a first for him, and that it was his only act of infidelity to Catherine. How ironic, he reflected, that his boost to Jonathan's career should be repaid by having his secretary stolen from under his nose. Such were the rewards of philanthropy.

"Can I get you anything else?" asked Selina, to fill the silence.

Chris pulled himself together. He was being melodramatic. Selina was her own person. Anyway, he was happily married. "No, thanks very much Selina, I have to go and see the DG in fifteen minutes, don't I?"

"That's right," she turned and walked to her desk.

He found that the Drama Department was suddenly ubiquitous. He met producers in the restaurant, development executives in the foyer and script editors in the lift. Every one of them had a fabulous idea they were sure he would like. None of them actually made an appointment to see him as that would be going over Peter's head, but they lobbied him assiduously until he was sick of the sight of them. The last straw came when he took a phone call from an apologetic Selina: she had put this woman off so many times, would he mind having a word? It was an agent called Muriel Barnet, calling about her client Billy Trowell.

"You *have* to *do* something Chris," she began, before he had a chance to say hello. "It's *absolutely disgraceful* what's going on. I've *never* had a client treated like this in thirty-five years in the business, and I can tell you, *none* of my clients will want to work for the BBC when this gets out."

Chris sighed. "Would you like to tell me what the problem is?"

"Billy's written the most *wonderful* four-parter for you. It's *exactly* what you want for your contemporary serial slot. *Very* on the edge. It's dark, hi*lariously* funny and *so* moving. *I* think it's his best work yet, and I'm *sure* you'll agree."

"I look forward to reading it."

"I *can't wait* for you to read it, Chris."

"So what's the problem?"

"I'm sure you know that Billy's always worked with Stewart Walker, they go back a long way." Chris didn't know, but somehow he wasn't surprised. Muriel rattled on, "Stewart has behaved *abominably* to Billy. He's refusing to accept the final episode, won't even authorise payment on it."

"Doesn't he like it?"

"So he says. He wants a complete rewrite. Billy and I think he's *totally* wrong."

"It really isn't for me to interfere in this kind of matter," said Chris, allowing a little irritation to show in his voice.

"The point is Chris, Billy *won't* change the ending, he feels *very* strongly about it. *Very* strongly. More strongly than he feels about *Stewart*."

"You want to change the producer."

"I *knew* you'd understand! I know it's not normal procedure, but it *really* would be in your best interests, Chris. It's a fan*tas*tic project."

"You'll have to talk to Peter about this, er, Muriel. It's not my area."

"Well I know Chris, but Peter can't seem to make up his mind whose side he's on. If you would just have a word, I'm sure it can be sorted out."

Chris took this to mean that Peter had taken Stewart's side.

"Okay Muriel. Leave it with me," he said, and hung up without the least intention of doing anything at all.

"Selina!" he called, and she hurried in apologetically.

"I'm awfully sorry, was she a real pain?"

"That's all right, it's not your fault. How am I going to keep them away? Why are they pestering *me*?"

Selina pursed her lips. "I'm sure it'll stop when you've chosen your drama projects. Perhaps you could turn some down soon, put them out of their misery?"

"Hmm."

"What about another meeting? Maybe they could pitch their ideas and you could make a shortlist or something?"

Chris thought she had something there. Kill all the birds with one stone. "Good idea. Get Peter on the phone, would you?"

She did.

"Peter, how are you?" began Chris.

"Never better. You?"

"Fine, fine, although I have to say your lot aren't backward at coming forward when they want you to know about their bright ideas."

Peter smiled broadly and winked at his PA Vera, who was with him. He switched his phone to conference mode so that she could hear the conversation.

"I do hope no-one's made a nuisance of themselves," said Peter mildly. "Funnily enough *my* office has been a good deal quieter lately."

"Yes, well, I do draw the line at masonic handshakes."

"No, really?" said Peter, glaring at Vera who was rocking with repressed laughter.

"I want to have a meeting with the whole lot of them. They can pitch their ideas and I'll respond on the spot, yes, no or maybe. We've got to put an end to it."

"Whatever you say, Chris. Will your office organise it or shall we?"

"Selina will take care of it. Okay Peter. Bye."

Peter put his phone down and raised his eyebrows at Vera, who pulled a face.

"He knows what he wants, doesn't he?" she said.

Peter nodded sadly. "Is he going to get it?"

Vera shrugged. "It wouldn't surprise me."

*

Catherine still wasn't pregnant and their bedroom was almost ready to move back into.

They had been to a private clinic for check-ups, where the consultant had assured them that there was no physical reason why they shouldn't conceive. He suggested that they were too tense and should try to forget about it for a few months. Very often, he said, the Through-the-Looking-Glass approach was the one that worked.

Unfortunately for Catherine, the effort of trying not to think about it increased her tension markedly. One day she arrived at work, opened her briefcase and found a little note from Natasha: *I love yoo mumy from Tasha*. It was too much for her and the tears streamed down her face. Terrified that her colleagues and clients might interpret her emotional incontinence as a sign that she was no longer fully reliable, she feigned a migraine and went home again. It was her ovulation day. She knew her cycle so well now that she couldn't help recognising the signs even though she wasn't supposed to be looking out for them. She lay on the sofa bed and wondered whether to call Chris and ask him to come home, but reluctantly decided against it. He would be annoyed and probably think she had a screw loose, it was very uncharacteristic behaviour for her. In any case, he was bound to be busy. Instead she went to her health club for a sauna and massage; then she bought oysters for dinner, and a new dress.

When Chris arrived home at eight o'clock he thought she looked radiant, and felt a great relief. At last she was getting over it. Oysters for dinner made a nice change, and he appreciated the effort she had made. She said she wanted to put it all behind them, and he agreed heartily.

They were watching *Newsnight* together when Sarah the nanny dropped her bombshell: she was giving in her notice because she wanted to move north to be with her boyfriend. There was little they could do to keep her; they were truly sorry as she had been with them since Natasha's birth. She was sorry too, especially to part with Tasha, but she wanted to start her own family and who could blame her? They all feared the impact on Tasha, who was very attached to Sarah. It was a severe blow, not only to their tremulous domestic tranquillity, but to the pleasant evening which Catherine had so subtly constructed in order to seduce her husband without him noticing.

When they were in bed she snuggled up to him sexily but he kissed her once and said he wasn't in the mood tonight. She tried to conceal her disappointment but he knew her too well.

"Okay let's give it a go."

She turned to him and smiled. "Only if you really want to."

"I do," he lied, and began foreplay. Beneath his exploring hands she felt like a velvet cushion full of bedsprings, but he persevered manfully. She did all she could to help him, but ten minutes later he rolled over to his own side of the bed and gave up.

"Sorry Cathy." He stared at the wall.

"Never mind." She stared at the ceiling.

In the silence they heard Natasha downstairs, coughing in her sleep. Chris struggled with his feelings. He was angry, humiliated, inadequate. He realised now what Cathy had been up to, and hated her for putting him through it. How dare she treat him like a performing seal? He steamed in silence. Catherine merely felt despair, coupled with the humiliation of having been rejected when at her most vulnerable: naked and aroused. She tried to forget her own feelings and figure out what he was going through, he must feel a terrible failure.

"It's all right darling," she whispered, stroking his shoulder. "There's always another time."

"Don't fucking patronise me!" his outburst amazed them both.

"What do you mean?"

"Sex isn't something you do on demand," he replied tersely. "It's supposed to be a spontaneous act of love." He sat up. "I can't remember the last time I made love to you just because it felt right and I wanted to. It must be months ago. There's no *joy* left in it."

Catherine's body turned to stone. Oh God, she thought, it's all fallen apart. Maybe this is the beginning of the end. He had never spoken to her like this before. She had nothing to say.

"I'm sorry," she whispered.

"I'm fucking sorry too. I'm really, really fucking sorry that our happy, relaxed, satisfying love life is out the fucking window. You've turned it into *sex by numbers*. The only thing I want, the only thing in the whole fucking world, is for you to get fucking pregnant so we can get back to normal."

Catherine was too stunned to cry, but she was no doormat. "We both want the same thing then. What do you suggest?"

He glared at her.

"I know," she continued. "Why don't you wank into a bottle, stick it in the freezer, and I'll inseminate myself with the turkey baster once a month. Then you won't have to touch me at all." She held eye contact defiantly until he had to leave the room, unable to think of an appropriate response.

Downstairs he poured himself a large whisky and put the telly on. His mind was blank with fury. He carried the bottle with him and slumped on one of the huge sofas, wishing he had some cigarettes, although he hadn't smoked for years. He switched the telly over to the satellite dish and began surfing through the channels, looking for anything that would occupy his mind. All crap. He settled for a Dutch entertainment show that was so bad it comforted his bruised ego. BBC2 was the Shakespeare of channels, and it was *his* channel. He poured another whisky and relaxed a little.

The programme finished and was followed by an erotic performance of extraordinary explicitness by British standards. He watched, fascinated and embarrassed to start with, and then realised that he actually found it quite titillating. In fact he was becoming aroused. He gazed objectively at this very attractive woman as she undulated for the camera as if she was enjoying herself, and had an idea.

Twenty minutes later he climbed back up to the loft room and put a turkey baster and a cup of semen down next to Catherine. She was lying awake, re-playing the row in her head and trying to make sense of it all.

"There you are," he said irritably. "It's all yours. I'm sleeping in the living room," and stalked off again. Catherine's jaw fell open and he had gone before she thought to reply.

At breakfast the following morning the atmosphere was dire. Sarah tried to keep a low profile, assuming that it was because she was leaving. Chris felt bad for her and tried to lighten up by asking her whether she would look for a new post in Edinburgh right away, unfortunately Natasha was listening and wanted to know what was going on. On realising that her beloved Sarah was leaving her she wept inconsolably and Chris set off for work feeling a total bastard for not waiting so they could break the news to her gently. Catherine said nothing about it but he knew exactly what she would be thinking.

Even Selina's pleasant smile failed to crack his misery, and the prospect of a morning with the Drama Department was enough to make him seriously consider calling it off. He wasn't *required* to go through this process, he could deal entirely through Peter if he wished. However it would look a lot better if he saw it through. This time the conference room had a huge table down the middle, equipped with water jugs and stacked plastic beakers. The woody smell of French tobacco hit him as he crossed the threshold. "Let's have a vote on smoking. All those in favour?" A few hands began to rise as people caught on. He continued quickly. "All those against?" Twenty hands went up. "That's clear enough. Cigarettes out please gentlemen." Chris briskly opened the meeting, reminding them that he was looking forward to hearing their pitches for all the slots he had available. "Okay," he concluded. "Let's start with the contemporary serial. Who's first? Or shall we just go round the table?"

There was a brief pause, then Peter asked Fenella to summarise the situation.

"We have a number of projects under option, with two leading contenders ready to go, more or less. One by Tony Scott, one by Billy Trowell." Chris nodded, remembering his recent conversation with Billy's agent with distaste.

"Yes, I'm aware of both projects," he said confidently. I have the Scott scripts in my office I'll be reading them shortly. What about the Trowell scripts?"

"Ah… how are they coming on, Stewart?" Fenella innocently passed the buck to Stewart Walker, who always produced Billy's shows, although she knew perfectly well that they had fallen out badly and were not currently on speaking terms. Stewart adopted a thoughtful expression.

"It will be compelling. Original. Dark, perhaps very dark. Challenging, certainly. Controversial. Powerful."

"When can I see the scripts?"

"When they're ready. I never circulate scripts before they're at final draft. You can take my word, Chris. I always deliver what I promise." Chris absorbed Stewart's words sagely, and saw an opportunity to rid himself of the whole problem by simply doing nothing.

"That's fine, I understand. You must work in the way you choose. Who am I to interfere with the artistic process?" He smiled pleasantly and Stewart inclined his head in acknowledgement, his vanity allowing him to believe that Chris had come round to Stewart's point of view. Chris was relieved that the Trowell problem could be shunted out of sight into the future. He already expected to go with the Scott project. Selina's enthusiasm meant more to him than the egotistic hyperbole of those he considered drama queens. He was about to ask for cult series proposals when another voice piped up.

"Actually I have another project for this slot, may I show you?" A young woman half-hidden down the side of the table waved a proposal and slid it up the polished mahogany surface, he caught it neatly and read the front page aloud: "*Poetic Justice*, by Geraint Vaughan. A story of Wales: of farmers, poets, national identity and struggle." He turned the page and read swiftly. Nothing grabbed his interest. It looked dull, as far as he could see. He sighed. "Is Wales interesting right now?" No-one replied, taking his question as rhetorical. "I'm not sure this really hits the contemporary cutting edge nerve," he offered, deciding that it was time to show how decisive he could be: he would turn this one down. "Poetry, sheep... it's a bit *Under Milk Wood*, isn't it?"

"Not at all!" Maggie leapt in. "It's completely original, it's absolutely on the nail in terms of rural life. Why does contemporary drama always have to be about urban deprivation?"

It was a good point. It deserved an answer.

"I want something more... how can I put it... sexy?" Maggie leaned back in her chair and blew out her cheeks. She and Geraint had worked really hard on this proposal. She knew it was good, and different. And now unwanted. "I'm sure you know what I mean," said Chris, sliding the proposal back down the table a little too hard so that it sent a stack of beakers rattling onto the floor. It had to be passed back to Maggie, who was frowning furiously at it. She kept her own counsel, tight-lipped.

Peter chose this moment to suggest, in the mildest possible tone, that it was regrettable there were to be fewer opportunities for authorial contemporary drama. "These projects are so often the cherries in our fruit cake. We've never allowed them to compete against each other like this. Do we really need to rule any out at this stage?"

Chris felt irritation rise from his stomach, he wasn't going to keep going over these arguments. "I promised you all a clear yes, no or maybe. If I give everyone a maybe, nothing's changed, has it? I think it's quite wrong to have masses of expensive projects sloshing around which are never going to reach the screen. This is the nineties, not the seventies. We need new ways of managing development. Let's move on to the cult slot." He looked to his right and saw Penny Cruickshank looking calm and collected. She was a cheerful, matronly woman who would have made the ideal Brown Owl. "Penny?" he said expectantly.

She hesitated, prefacing herself with a thoughtful look. "I don't quite know how you plan a cult hit, I always thought a cult following came afterwards – but I *do* have something which might fit the bill, Chris. It's a series based in a recording studio, somewhere like Abbey Road, right now. *Music* you see. It will feature in every episode, not just as a soundtrack, but actually part and parcel of the action. We'll appeal to a *lot* of people that way – after all, *everyone* likes music don't they?"

Chris frowned. "Music is divisive, not inclusive."

Penny stopped short in surprise. Around the table people considered this aphorism: there was some truth in it, music had become so diverse these days that the audience was fragmented. Penny was lost for words. "Oh," she said.

"Do you have anything else?"

"Not right now, I'm afraid," said Penny, who had so loved this idea she had put all her eggs in the one basket. She stared at it on the table in front of her. It was dead in the water already. This had never happened to her before.

The next person was a smartly dressed young man, who had what he described as a tongue-in-cheek pot-boiler about the sex lives of footballers. Chris cut in with, "Too mainstream," and moved on. Fenella was next.

"I've been working on a sci-fi idea," she said, covering up the treatment in front of her with her forearms. "But it needs more work. Do you think sci-fi would fit the bill?"

"If you can do it on the budget, why not?"

"I'll let you have it by the end of the week," said Fenella.

"Donald?" invited Chris, trying to sound as if he cared.

"Sally and I are also developing a kind of sci-fi idea," he said in his normal untroubled tone. "But I'm not able to give you concrete details yet. However, it would be an advantage to know, as we put the budget together, roughly how many episodes you would want: the more we make the cheaper it becomes."

"Good point, Donald. The answer is that it depends. I know that's rather awkward for you, but I suggest you cost several alternatives, say ten episodes, twenty or thirty."

Two dozen pens scribbled this down. The meeting progressed in the same vein until everyone had spoken, although a number of people were rather vague, preferring not to see their precious projects shot down at such a tender age. Chris rejected the vast majority and accepted none. He had four 'maybes' piled in front of him. The group was bitterly disappointed and a number of cynics were exchanging dangerous looks across the table. Chris had fulfilled their worst fears. They had no faith that any of them would win this slot. Neither did Peter, although he had maintained absolute discretion, standing aside to let Chris run the proceedings in the way he wanted. With luck he would shoot himself in the foot sooner or later, and things would get back to normal. Peter's quiet assent was mistaken for insouciance by some of the producers, and there was a faint rumble of revolt in the air. It was too much for one young woman.

"I'm sorry Chris," she said. "But may I say something?"

"Go ahead." It was the girl whose Welsh project he had rejected earlier.

"I have to say, I'm amazed that you're dismissing all these projects without even reading them. I'm sorry, I know it's not my place to say so, but it means hundreds of hours of work are going straight down the pan. It seems such a waste." The group was silent in her support.

Chris found himself floundering with a bad case of déjà-vu. He knew this young woman. He felt it strongly, although she was looking at him as though he were – well, the Controller of BBC2, that's all. He frowned slightly, completely forgetting what she had just said, and then it dawned on him: she was the feminist he had slept with in Edinburgh that time, after they all got arrested... so she had gone into television. She didn't seem to recognise him. Was she just pretending? Was she putting the knife in on purpose? Hadn't he been any good in bed? Had she told everyone in the department about it? What a great piece of gossip it must have been. His mind raced, while his face remained still, mouth open.

"I agree with Maggie," said Stewart unexpectedly, bringing Chris back to the present. Maggie, that was her name. "It seems the department has spent the last ten weeks frantically chasing its own tail. Was that what you had in mind, Chris?"

"I hope very much that's *not* the case," rallied Chris. "I can assure you that I have *always* wanted the Drama Department to win these slots, as I've said on several occasions. I still hope you do. How you go about it is your own affair."

"I must say," said Penny, who had not yet come to terms with his perspective on music. "It's quite difficult developing shows your way. To be quite frank," she became a little emotional in spite of herself. "It feels back to front. Great ideas don't fit into rigid slots. It's like trying to make *drama by numbers*. Somehow it takes all the joy out of it."

Many people nodded gently. Chris closed his eyes, clasped his hands under the table and tightened them until they ached, grinding his teeth to control his temper. Penny's words echoed his own mean accusations at the height of last night's trauma. He felt his brain dislocate: how come his sex life was suddenly so intimately wrapped up with the bloody Drama Department? He felt as though he were sitting there in front of them in the nude. These people really knew how to get to you.

The room waited, agog to see what he would say. Fifty people followed the sequence of Chris' tortured expressions and drew their own conclusions. Penny wished to God she'd kept quiet. Was he going to explode?

Finally he looked round. "Thank you all for your hard work. I'll let Peter know what I've decided by the end of the month." He stood up and left, with Selina close behind, carefully appearing not to have noticed anything amiss.

In the normal run of things, Chris could cope with criticism. He believed that constructive debate was essential to progress of any kind, and a few months earlier he would have engaged the drama producers in discussion and won them over – or at least explained himself in the attempt. This time, he didn't feel up to it. He thought he could hear skeletons rattling in his closet, although he had nothing to be ashamed of. He felt he was losing control, as if there were people out there who might have it in for him. He felt raw-nerved and insecure to the point of paranoia.

Sod the lot of them, he had enough on his plate without nannying the bloody Drama Department. They could damn well look after themselves from now on. Sink or swim with the rest. Why did everything have to go wrong at once?

Selina brought in a coffee and left him alone in his office, where he swivelled his chair round to look out over the court-yard and the golden statue, which had been resprayed so that it glinted too brightly in strong sunlight. He lowered the venetian blind.

His thoughts turned back to Catherine. Last night's disaster wasn't entirely her fault. And after all, she might even have impregnated herself, in which case they could be back on course. Perhaps the only problems they would have to deal with from now on were the usual ones associated with a geriatric mother, as the doctors attractively described pregnant women over thirty-five.

He resolved to be magnanimous. He would buy her a bouquet and propose that they take a month's holiday abroad in September. It was always a quiet time for him, as most television executives took their summer holidays after the Edinburgh TV Festival at the end of August. It would also be their last chance to go out of season as Natasha would start school the following January. The new nanny could come with them so that they would have plenty of time to themselves. They could go to the Bahamas or somewhere truly relaxing, wherever she wanted. The tension would evaporate, and she would probably come home pregnant.

Chris buzzed Selina and asked if she would be kind enough to nip downstairs and collect some travel brochures from the in-house travel agent, and also order a large bouquet. Then he picked up the new ratings lists and began to study them.

*

The following week was as good as the previous one had been bad. Catherine was back to her usual self, having been thoroughly mollified by Chris' sudden conversion to her cause. Her chambers had granted her leave without any trouble, and they had a glorious month at a luxury resort in the Maldives to look forward to.

Chris' new schedules were standing up well in the ratings. He had begun pitting like against like, such that audiences for a particular kind of show had to choose between BBC2 and Channel Four. In most cases he won the war and beat Channel Four into second place. There were a few complaints from viewers who wanted to watch both, but after all, they could always get a VHS recorder and tape the other side. A few of his American purchases proved hugely successful, and he also began putting out archive material such as top sitcoms from the sixties which appealed enormously to older audiences and cost him next to nothing.

The DG was very pleased and invited him to lead top-level strategy discussions on the future of programming. He developed his ideas into a complete theoretical system which he planned to publish once he had been in the job a full year and had indisputable statistics.

He had no personal contact with the Drama Department for a month, thanks to Selina's superb sentry skills. The last meeting was never mentioned, he merely told her he wanted to concentrate on other matters, and it was all taken care of.

Their relationship had become a shade more formal. Life was far too complicated when sentiment got in the way. He was no longer inclined to discuss much with her, and preferred the objective approach. The weight of responsibility on him was enormous, and he wanted more than anything to justify the DG's faith in him and exceed his expectations. He knew he was seen as the brightest rising star by some of the governors. His future was very promising indeed.

Eventually he had to communicate his drama choices for the next season. Peter and Fenella were summoned to his office, where he remained behind his desk while they sat on upright chairs in front of him. They listened politely while he repeated his intentions, which they already knew, and tried to look impressed. Then he got down to the nitty gritty: commissions.

"Firstly, I want to green-light Basil Richardson's four-parter about the ex-miners for production. Er, Tony Scott – *Down and Up*."

"Oh that *is* good news," Fenella said, genuinely, and Peter smiled too.

"I think it will be a fine authorial piece for the contemporary slot, and I want to put it out in the New Year."

"In the New Year?" said Peter. "That's cutting it very fine. We'd normally take at least nine months, preferably twelve."

"I have an independent project lined up for the autumn. I need it in January. In any case, it's not going to need star actors is it? Do it like Ken Loach. Keeps the costs down."

"Very well, Chris. I'll speak to Basil about it. He's an old trouper, I'm sure we can find a way round it."

"Good. For the next classic slot I want *A Tale of Two Cities*. That's Donald Mountjoy again."

Fenella's face fell. "Does that mean it's no to Charlotte Bronte and Mrs Gaskell? Two Dickens serials in a row?"

"I believe in building on our successes," answered Chris. "Audiences adored the first one, so give them another!"

"Don't you think they'd adore a bit of a change? Jane Eyre's *hugely* popular." Fenella had been counting on getting this one through, it was going to be her own show, her debut as a producer.

"It's a bit soppy for the nineties. Single drama, as I said, I'm still considering, but I *do* want to move forward on the new writing initiative. This proposal from Sonia Longbow seems very sensible, so I propose to go ahead with it. I shall earmark a regular five-minute slot before *Newsnight* for a month in 1999."

"Splendid," said Peter faintly. That was four years away, and Chris was bound to have moved on by then. There was no guarantee his successor would honour the commitment.

"Finally, I'm afraid it's bad news on the cult slot. None of your proposals matched up to the one I have from the independent company I mentioned before. I'm sorry. Some of them were good ideas but too expensive. Those that were cheap enough just didn't excite me." He handed back the little pile of documents to the despondent pair. "If I were you I'd cut your development list down radically. I can't commit to increasing the amount of drama, we're already fulfilling our charter requirements, and the money just isn't there. Concentrate on the big names. Audiences love them."

Peter and Fenella took their leave with faces like thunder.

*

The new bedroom looked magnificent. The mirrored wardrobes were a dream, and the mosaic floor was unique as far as they knew. The patterns were inspired by period Georgian ceiling murals, with ribbons and swathes round the skirting boards, and clusters of flying birds and posies in the middle. It was too pretty to cover with rugs, so they had to wear slippers all the time as the surface was so cold to their feet.

One Friday evening Chris arrived home at ten thirty, after dinner with the DG at his club. He was a little drunk and quite elated. As the house was silent he climbed the stairs quietly and looked round the bedroom door to see if Catherine was awake. She was working in bed as usual, she looked up and smiled. "Hello darling. Good day at the office?"

"Certainly was." He beamed and wobbled slightly. "How are you, darling?"

"Fine. Have you something to tell me?"

"Fancy a cup of tea?"

"Alright. Camomile."

"Coming up." Chris disappeared. Catherine wondered what it could be. The last time he had looked that cheerful he had been promoted to controller, but he'd only been in the job for six months so surely they wouldn't be promoting him again yet. She put her work away and removed her spectacles, intrigued.

He re-appeared with a tray bearing a teapot, two cups and saucers and a plate of biscuits, and even a single rose in a tumbler.

"I say, it *must* be good news!"

"I couldn't find a vase," he said. "Where do we keep them?"

She smiled. "Did you cut that rose off the bunch on the hall table?"

He smiled back mysteriously. "Might have. Might not."

She giggled. He was sweet when he was tipsy. He sat next to her on top of the bed and removed his shoes, dropping them heavily on the floor, and stretched out, sighing with satisfaction.

"Who's a clever bastard, then?" he asked.

She pretended to have no idea. "Einstein?" He shook his head. "Stephen Hawking?" He shook it again, beaming like an idiot. "Not you, surely?" He nodded like a toddler. "You can't have been promoted again already?"

"Not promoted exactly. Not yet."

"*What* then? Tell me!"

"I'm going… to Harvard."

"*Harvard*? Whatever for?"

"To study business management at the highest level in the world. Alongside the top – the toppest people in the world!"

"Really? How wonderful! The DG wants you to do this course, does he?"

"He is *desperate* for me to do it. He's already done it himself."

Catherine hugged him. She understood that this was the highest accolade imaginable. It would cost the BBC a small fortune to send him, and they would only invest that money in a person they were certain of.

"Is anyone else going on the course?"

He beamed at her again. "No!" and laughed. She hugged him again.

"Well done. Well done, *DG-in-waiting!*" They kissed, and then settled back. Chris poured the tea.

"I shall be away for ten weeks, I'm afraid. Will that be alright?"

"Of course, don't be silly. We'll miss you lots but we'll be fine. When do you think you'll go?"

Chris grimaced. "That's the bad news. It starts on September 2nd."

"We're going on holiday that day."

"I know."

"Surely you don't have to do it immediately?"

"I can't leave it till next year. I'll be too busy to go. They might send someone else. It's too big an opportunity to turn down." Chris stared at his tea.

Catherine's face fell and she went limp as the full implications gradually sank in. No holiday. No relaxation. No conception. No husband, in fact, for ten weeks, and no doubt his work commitments would keep increasing if he was being fast-tracked to the top. The moment had passed for them to consolidate the family. They had missed that boat whilst running to catch another. She pondered in silence, dry-eyed, and realised the war was lost.

"Don't worry darling," Chris took her hand and squeezed it. "We'll have a holiday. We can go for a fortnight in August, and another fortnight at Christmas. I told the DG – I told him straight – I can't deny my family their holiday, and he agreed. 'You've got to take care of the staff!' he said." Catherine smiled but didn't care for this summary of her role. He raised her hand to his lips and kissed it. "We'll get pregnant, Cathy, just don't worry about it. Please?" She smiled wanly and nodded. She snuggled down into his shoulder feeling suddenly exhausted, closing her eyes so he wouldn't see her sadness.

"Tired darling? I'll let you go to sleep. I'll just go downstairs for a little while, look at some papers." He kissed her head, extricated himself, and left her alone.

Chapter Ten

I managed to spin out my time at the independent production company for the best part of a year; it was entertaining to hear Maggie's account of Drama Department politics from a comfortable distance, but eventually I had to return and engage with it all myself. I was recalled to Shepherd's Bush with nothing definite to work on. With my thirtieth birthday behind me I was conscious of the need to move my career up a gear, and my ambitions were growing. Maggie's brand of energy found the frustrations of development hell intolerable, so she got herself a job on *Casualty* and went off to Bristol to gain production experience.

At the time I was living in Archway, near the bottom of Highgate Hill, where Dick Whittington had his 'turn again' moment. I felt a certain empathy with him. I'd managed to get a mortgage on a tiny flat in a Georgian house, nothing very special but it was homely and in walking distance of Waterlow Park, Highgate Cemetery and Hampstead Heath. Three places I'd come to love dearly as a substitute for wild and woolly Wales. I might not have much time off, but being able to walk from my own front door and enjoy so much natural beauty in the middle of London was a great substitute. I don't how people manage without it, I really don't. You must go and see for yourself, if you don't already know the area.

I lived alone as none of my boyfriends had been long-term enough to contemplate moving in with. You could say that was down to my bad experience with Steve, the director of the Newham Youth Theatre. I'd really fallen for him, and I was naïve enough to believe that he'd leave his wife for me. That's what he'd told me, of course. Maybe he even believed it himself, until the crunch came. (Did he hell, I can hear you thinking. Okay, you're probably right. He was just another fantasising narcissist. Or was he a narcissistic fantasist? I suppose he was like Bill Clinton: he did it 'because he could'.) I learned my lesson, I was determined not to let another man make an idiot of me and I grew more and more independent. I earned my own living, paid my own way, owned my own flat, made my own fun. Sorted.

Turning thirty was a bit of a surprise, I have to admit. It crept up on me. The whole cliché of being left behind because I was still single, plus the next milestone along the road being the appallingly old *forty* – it was too much. I worried myself sick for a day, and then realised that the only way to avoid turning into my unfortunate namesake Bridget Jones was not to care about it, so I set it aside. If the right man ever came along I would reconsider, but for the time being I was very happy with my career.

It was terribly important to me that I prove myself as good as anyone else. The BBC seemed dominated by posh people from the Home Counties, who would be terribly polite and interested in you for as long as they maintained eye contact, and then leave you feeling like a llama chewing on an apple they've unexpectedly shoved in your mouth. They acted as though you were fascinating, and then briskly moved on to the next exotic creature, however charming the encounter there was no doubt who was in charge. They were on their home ground. You weren't. It didn't matter which part of the UK you came from. The prevailing culture was that of the English ruling class. (It still is, but they disguise their accents.)

That's why I didn't want to work on stories about Wales. I didn't want to be pigeonholed, I wanted to be a purveyor of fine drama, universal drama, not the obvious stuff. I didn't want to be told I could have that little corner to myself whilst they – the men, the white men, the posh white men and women – got on with the important programmes. Do I sound chippy? Well, I'm sure you don't expect me to apologise.

The BBC is always saying its role is to reflect the diversity of voices we have in Britain. Whether or not it fulfils that role is another matter. To me, it's not just about voices, it's too easy to interpret that as a range of regional accents. Now that posh people have stopped telling us accents are a sign of inferiority, they like to collect them; you hear that on Radio 4 all the time. How quaint, how historical, how amusing these old folk sound! Quick, tape them before they fall off the perch. Presenters always assume that the listener shares their point of view, that of observer/consumer. They never imagine listeners might share the subject's point of view. The only people presenters really address are those just like themselves.

Point of view is a central issue in all things televisual, we even abbreviate it (POV). In theatre there's only one, and that's the audience's, whether they're arranged neatly in rows or wrapped around the stage. As soon as you start using cameras you have a complex situation. There are many different ways you can look at – and represent – your subject. It's as big as moving from two dimensions to three. Perspective changes everything. Add in time (the fourth dimension) and you're on the verge of losing any concrete sense of truth. Don't quote me, but I believe they've identified as many as eleven dimensions now. Just trying to get my head around that leaves me reeling. It's bad enough trying to write a novel with five main characters and lots of minor ones – trying to see life through all their eyes in order to build a rounded picture of a huge institution at a time of national change, trying to tell a story with depth and complexity, and make it a good read – to be perfectly frank it's doing my head in. So many risks... confusion, obscurity, tedium, lack of point... what *is* the point of a story? What's the

point of this one, for a start? Well I'm not going to tell you half
way through, am I? Obviously. Skip to the end if you're bored.

Where was I? POV. I've changed mine as I've got older, like
we all do. Getting older is a bit like climbing a mountain (stop
me if I'm repeating myself). Your point of view keeps changing
the higher up you go. At the start you can't see a lot, but you're
focussed on the journey and you have a clear mental image of
the summit, which you don't doubt you'll reach in due course.
By the time you're half way up you've accumulated experience
and distance, and you can look back as well as up. You can also
remember your initial POV and place it in the context of your
present situation. I find that so interesting, don't you? Did you
know that scientists have made carbon fibre so strong that
they're now working on a cosmic elevator, an actual lift that will
carry people miles up in space to an orbiting satellite, and it
should be working by the middle of the twenty-first century?
Imagine what our point of view will be like from there! Perhaps
it will even lead to a new level of consciousness? Anyway, back
to me and my brilliant career at the BBC.

Better Be Cheap seemed to be the driving force in 90s broadcasting. As the free market dogma ran riot across the planet, all
British public services – from schools to railways to hospitals –
were made to function as businesses, proving their cost-effec-
tiveness and creaming off profits for their new shareholders. The
BBC's fixed income forced it to fund its new digital services
through internal cuts and extra sales. Staff, resource departments,
development budgets – everything possible was pruned back
hard, to two shoots above the root. Every department had to pay
every other department for the services it used, in an endless
round of internal market accounting in which only managers
were allowed to proliferate. The need to attract additional
funding and world-wide sales meant that no show would get
commissioned without star names attached.

The Drama Department received a clear message regarding
its new status within the corporation when it was given notice to

leave Television Centre. The fifth floor of the doughnut was at the hub of the BBC; to work there was to be next to the beating heart of the organisation. Suddenly the management decided on a transplant. Drama was to make way for Sport, which was considered the new key to balancing the schedules and the corporation budget. There was a massive shift in attitude at the top of the BBC. The seventh floor no longer housed the finest specialists in culture and entertainment, promoted to guide others further along their own path; men like David Attenborough and Michael Grade. The new leaders knew little about making programmes, but a lot about politics and business management. A tabloid ethos began to creep in as the target audience grew larger and larger, and 'dumbing down' was a term heard increasingly from those who could see standards beginning to fall. The managers denied it, accusing critics of elitism and justifying their decisions with statistics. The irony was that the poor old Beeb desperately needed reform and modernisation in its working practices, no-one could deny that – but what we got was closer to napalm.

It seemed to me that the managers on the seventh floor were like a double-thick layer of icing on top of the doughnut, dripping down stickily over the entire building until everything wholesome in it was overwhelmed.

The Drama Department's move was presented as a positive event, as there was much more office space available across the road. Half-concealed behind the tube station stood a four-block office complex which pre-dated double-glazing, air-conditioning, and even window blinds, although it did have its own canteen. The unexpected benefit was a drawing-together of the staff. With only each other to talk to, and a sense of rejection from the main hive, morale took a sharp dip and personal survival instincts kicked in. Some felt they had been exiled to St Helena, shamed for some unknown misdemeanour. Others relished the view from the sidelines, and redoubled their cynicism. Most just felt terribly sad, knowing that the quality of programmes would inevitably slip and slide until their distinctive values fell away, and BBC drama would end up no better than any other. It would be years before the viewing public would notice, since programmes take years to make. By the time they started asking what had happened to the quantity – and possibly the quality – of BBC programming it would be too late. The stable door would be safely bolted but the horse would have legged it over the horizon.

All that's by-the-by. Now that I was no longer the up-and-coming youngster, I was determined to put myself on the map by producing a drama of my own. I had a great idea based on my experience of being a teacher – nothing to do with Wales at all. If I could squeeze it onto the development list and keep it alive I'd stand an excellent chance of being allowed to produce it. (First-time producers were more popular with the management than you might think, yes, you've got it – they're a lot cheaper than experienced producers. In fact you don't even have to give them a pay rise, there's a jargon phrase for it: *acting up*. No doubt it goes back to Reith and the civil service set-up that launched the BBC in the first place, if not further back to the navy and the cat-o-nine-tails… we should be grateful they don't use that, I suppose. I bet they'd like to.) So I was throwing my hat into the ring, risking my reputation and all that, a bad first film or serial could mean the end of your career. A prize-winning first film gave you at least three years of professional celebrity before you had to prove yourself again. (And then again, and again.) Everyone wants to win a BAFTA. You pretend you're not bothered so that you won't be crushed by disappointment, but we're all human.

I nursed my great idea in secret until I'd picked my writer. I didn't have the confidence to write it myself, not even the proposal. I needed it to look really good, to do the idea justice. I decided I wanted Jill Watkins to do it, so I met her in Crouch End where she lived, just a mile or two from my own place. We talked the concept through and she liked it. She was more than ten years older than me and had lots of experience of writing for mainstream audiences; with a son of her own she understood teenage boys, which was crucial to making the script convincing. She agreed to develop it for me on spec, I would be credited with the idea, and would then try to get it commissioned. She needed no persuasion, we shared much the same attitude to the story and felt it would be a very productive partnership. She promised to send it to me in a few days.

Back in my office I already knew who I would take it to: Basil Richardson. He was everyone's favourite, the producers' producer. He was so well-respected that he existed on a level above the politics of ego which many of us were mired in. His judgement was universally admired, his good taste undisputed. That's why I wanted him to oversee my project: for his wisdom and sound advice. His endorsement would also be the quickest way to getting the scripts commissioned. If he liked it, it must be good. It would also boost my own self-confidence no end. I waited anxiously for Jill's treatment to arrive, and was relieved when it came, as promised.

Lover Boy
Proposal for a three-part drama serial for television
by Jill Watkins
From an idea by Rhiannon Jones
3 x 60 minutes

SHARON is an English teacher in a comprehensive. She's in her mid thirties, married to JOHN who is in charge of advertising on the local paper, and they have a two-year-old baby, CHLOE. They are contented rather than happy. They live in Epping. Nothing extraordinary has ever happened to them, their problems are everyday ones.

LUKE is just sixteen, about to sit his GCSEs. He loves art and making things, he wants to study ceramics. His parents are in their early forties. His father is a manager at Ford and his mother works in a chemist's shop. He has a sister RACHEL two years younger. His school record is good and his future seems bright.

Sharon teaches Luke. She notices that he is maturing more rapidly than the other boys; he is big-boned, smooth-skinned, tall and attractive without being conventionally handsome. His long hair is always tied in a ponytail, his brown eyes have grown decidedly sexy, and his gentle manner and slow smile are enchanting. He has a poise and inner confidence which is rare in sixteen-year-olds. She finds she is developing a crush on him, and is horrified.

Luke has always counted Sharon (Mrs Morrison) his favourite teacher, because of her sparkling eyes and sense of humour. He is now much taller than her, which he finds slightly embarrassing, but enjoyable. He loves her long curly brown hair, and the way she dresses. She's very special, he feels he knows her, and he knows he wants her. Girls his own age don't interest him, they're immature and superficial. He'd rather go out with Mrs Morrison. In fact he wants to spend the rest of his life with her.

Lover Boy is the story of their relationship; how they start seeing each other, how they declare their love, how they cope with universal dismay, how they break up and break down, how they finally commit to each other and start a new life together.

Above all it is the story of a great love.

I was delighted with it. And before you ask, no – I never had feelings for any of my pupils (apart from wanting to strangle a couple of them). It's fiction, right? I made it up. And back then it was original, no-one had broken these taboos on telly before. Now there are none left to break. The biggest problem storyliners have is finding new versions of the same old tales, they've all been done so many times. The viewing public is practically unshockable now. The most horrific news items are casually reported in the middle of the day, and dramatists can't compete with that. It's difficult to believe that back then, only fifteen years ago this idea about a teacher and pupil falling in love was quite radical. Hopefully it would ruffle a few feathers.

I made an appointment to see Basil about the proposal, and managed to meet him without the Proulx boy getting in the way. His new office was in the furthest of the four office blocks, which now housed the Drama Department. It had previously contained the Youth Department, under which regime it had been refurbished in grey steel and tinted glass – no doubt a very costly process, which hadn't improved the building in the slightest, but the Youth people evidently couldn't make fashionable television unless they were in fashionable accommodation. The renovations were barely complete when the entire department was relocated to Manchester for political reasons, and the block had been empty ever since. Now it was home to Basil and the drama folk, who took an instant dislike to it on finding that nothing could be stuck on the walls. (It's impossible to make drama without sticking notes, lists, charts and pictures on walls.)

Basil was his usual charming self, despite his office being strewn with boxes. A brand new computer sat in the corner, unconnected. I wondered whether Basil knew how to use it. There was a rumour that he was once found with a video tape, trying to turn it over and play the other side. We younger ones found our elders' technical incompetence hilarious. I suppose it'll happen to us one day, and it'll serve us all right. He could afford to be casual about such details; his latest BAFTA stared blankly down from a filing cabinet, a Best Drama award for his serial about unemployed miners by Tony Scott, *Down and Up*. I knew Tony had been a first-time writer, after being a miner for a decade or more. It was Basil's quiet influence that had brought his writing to such a high standard, and Basil who had realised such an honest and cathartic production.

I waited expectantly for his pronouncements on Jill's proposal, while he skim-read it again and collected his thoughts. Then he looked at me over his specs.

"An intriguing choice of subject," he said. "Do you think the world's ready for it?"

"I think so, yes," I replied without drawing breath. "Why not?"

He smiled. "I think so too. Depending on how we handle it." My heart beat fast at this hint. "I want to know more. I do have some reservations." I nodded furiously and waited for pearls to fall from his lips, ready to catch and save them on strings. "I like the simplicity of it," he continued. "But I wonder what the tone will be, given it's about a controversial relationship. I wonder whether it might be very romantic, or have an edge to it. I'm not sure there's enough going on to sustain three hours of drama. Tell me how you see it."

He'd put his finger on the missing element, I saw that immediately. "What I want to do is make it utterly truthful and involving. It should be romantic but not sentimental – it should tear Sharon apart. It would be really awful breaking up her family, but she has to do it – and the audience must be with her every step of the way, regardless of their moral opinions. She breaks three taboos, but I want the audience to feel that in spite of everything, this relationship is so strong that the tragedy would be to deny it."

"Like *Doctor Zhivago*."

"In a way, yes!" I was thrilled by the analogy. "I want it to be funny here and there, and happy as well as sad. There should be a sense of triumph at the end, rather than escape – there are no baddies and goodies, it's about fully rounded people. The point is that you have to engage with life and live it, not settle for half a life because convention dictates. That's a message she wants to pass on to her little girl, even though she has to leave her behind."

"Not easy," commented Basil. "Not many people would agree with that."

"Fine," I said. "I'm not sure I agree with her myself, but I respect her decision. It has to be challenging, otherwise it's just another soppy love story. It's a fine balance, we'll have to get it right."

"What about Sharon's husband?"

"He's pretty appalled of course, and cut to the quick, but their love isn't that strong otherwise she wouldn't have found her true partner elsewhere. He comes round, up to a point – he'll find a better partner too, in time. But he does feel very betrayed because he's a decent bloke and he's never let Sharon down. He's a good father too, and he's damned if he's going to let her take Chloe away from him."

"Hmm, it's very linear, isn't it?"

I sighed, realising how right he was. "We could use flash-backs? Or make things more complex – what if Luke's connected to Sharon and John in another way – maybe Chloe's actually fifteen, and he's going out with her – then he falls in love with her mother?"

"*Romeo and Juliet's Mother*!"

"Yes, well, maybe not. Shall I take it back to Jill and see what she can come up with?"

"Yes, do that. The other issue is the shape of it: it seems that three-parters are going out of style with the controllers, especially if we want to get this on BBC1. It'll have to be twice ninety minutes instead."

"No problem," I assured him. "We just structure it with one cliff-hanger instead of two. Can we commission Jill at this stage?" I mentioned this with false nonchalance.

"Yes, as soon as possible," was the unexpected reply. "I can still commission treatments without running it past this new

190

editorial board they've set up, but who knows how long that'll last. We must smuggle as many good projects through as possible while we can."

"Wonderful, thanks so much!" I could have hugged him. Whilst it was going so well I risked another step, "I was wondering whether I might possibly be able to produce this one, if it gets that far?"

"I think that would be a very good plan," said Basil, astonishingly.

"Would you be Executive Producer?"

"Certainly."

"Wow. Thanks so much!" I couldn't think of any other response. I was bowled over. You could have knocked me down with a flicked paper clip. I really hadn't expected it to be this easy... it wasn't.

"There's another project I'd like you to have a look at," he said. "If you wouldn't mind."

"Of course."

"It's something of Jonathan's," he said, and I held my breath. Oh no. "It's going to be his first role as producer, and he needs a good experienced script editor. Preferably a Welsh one. I thought of you right away."

What could I say? It had to be yes.

I tried to forget about Jonathan's project whilst I got on with my own. Ordinarily I would have gone straight to his office to introduce myself properly and offer my services, but I decided to let him find me instead. I resented the idea of his being above me in seniority, given that my own experience was much greater. He might have worked with Basil for five or six years, but I had many more broadcast hours on my cv. To put it bluntly I considered myself better qualified than he was to produce his show, but I was expected to assist, hold his hand in case he made a bad decision, and tactfully save him from disaster. Add that to my Welsh chip and my dislike of posh

Englishmen, and it made an explosive brew. Poor Jonathan!

It was a couple of weeks before he knocked at my door. By that time the editorial board had commissioned both of our projects to first draft. I had made up my mind that my show would go ahead, and his would be dropped. Mine would be a howling success, win BAFTAs galore, and his would be quietly forgotten. Does this sound a tad arrogant to you? Me too. Embarrassingly so. But that's what happens when people are set against one another to compete for living space: they fight to the kill. Clever people are just as bad as anyone else. They knife one another metaphorically, which can be a fate worse than death.

He stuck his head round my door and said, "*Jones the Script*, I presume?" with a half-hearted twinkle and jolly eyebrows. I detached my eyes from what I was reading and stared at him, open-mouthed. How long had he spent working on that line? It was worse than I'd expected. He looked embarrassed and asked if he could come in. I recovered myself, gave him a seat and offered coffee, which he refused. He began making small talk in a polite effort to find common ground.

"Nice office you've got here."

"Yes, not bad. Not much of a view, but at least it's not too small."

"Is that Snowdonia? Looks beautiful."

He was looking at a little print my dad gave me that I like to keep on my office wall. "Cader Idris, actually. Have you been there?"

"No, but I know the tune, I think – it rings a bell from my schooldays."

I was beginning to feel guilty for having made him do all the running. There was a status imbalance in making him come to my office, as if I were the senior officer. I rather enjoyed playing the cactus, if I'm honest. The truth is that the irritating aspects of Jonathan's poshness had by this time evaporated, but I hadn't noticed and didn't want to know. I was happy to leave him in the box marked *rejects*. However, part of the script editor's role is to act as the producer's assistant, it's understood that you're on that career trajectory and you learn an enormous amount that way. It's up to the producer to decide exactly what tasks you carry out, the more willing and versatile your response, the better. I had no right to give Jonathan a hard time, however prejudiced I was. I decided to start afresh.

"I'm really sorry I haven't been to see you before. I've been so wrapped up in my own project – "

"Don't worry, I wasn't expecting to see you before it was commissioned," he assured me. It was gracious of him, there was no edge of sarcasm at all. "I don't want to interrupt you, I'm just dropping off the proposal for you to look at. Maybe we can have lunch soon and talk about it?"

"Yes of course," I said, surprised. "We can talk now if – "

"No no, that's fine. When you're ready." He smiled again and got up to go.

"Thanks, I'll look forward to reading it."

He left, and I thought with relief, that wasn't so bad, he's not going to power-trip me. Maybe he's alright. I glanced at the proposal and decided to read it, I was expecting Jill to come in for lunch, and I had time to spare. I leaned back and propped my feet on the desk.

It was called *The Medical Miracle* and was by Jim Johnson, a writer I knew only by reputation. His story began with a Welsh hill farmer attempting suicide because of mounting debts. His son found him just in time and his GP managed to save him. The farmer then explained it was impossible to make a living from farming any more, and how he felt a failure since the land had nurtured many generations of his family. It was much bigger than a simple business collapse; it was a matter of identity, of national history…

I threw it down, stood up and walked to the window. I could hardly believe what I'd read. It was practically a carbon copy of Maggie's Welsh project, which she'd put so much effort into, and which had been cruelly rejected by Chris at the big meeting. That was why she'd given up on development and gone off to *Casualty*. Jonathan was at the same meeting, wasn't he? He must have heard it all. He'd pinched the idea, changed it a bit and flogged it under another title to BBC1. Outrageous! Did he think I wouldn't notice? Perhaps he didn't care. Maybe he thought it was acceptable to steal ideas. I picked up the slim proposal to finish reading it, but the phone rang, it was reception to say that Jill had arrived. I stuck the thing in a drawer and stomped off.

The canteen occupied the ground floor of one of the office blocks, and offered part of the menu available over the road in Television Centre. As we waited in the queue Jill pointed to a tiny newspaper cutting that someone had stuck on one of the pillars. It was the logo for the new national lottery, a hand with the first two fingers crossed. Someone had written underneath it: *The New BBC Logo*.

"Who said satire was dead?" I said. A few people around us laughed, and then Morag the sour-faced administrator stepped up and tore it down without a word. I looked at Jill and pulled my mouth down.

"Watch your step," she whispered. "Don't rock the boat."

"You're right," I answered, shrugging pleasantly towards Morag. "Never attract the attention of Medusa. Not until you absolutely have to." We moved forward and put our trays down by the till operator who checked off our dinners, and then headed into the seating area. A hand waved from the far corner.

"Oh look, there's my friend Carmen Phillips. Do you know her?" Jill said. She was writing for *Eldorado* when I was there. She's with Anthea Onojaife from *EastEnders*. Shall we join them?

"By all means."

"Hi! Sure we're not interrupting?" Jill greeted her friend with a peck on the cheek, and nodded to Anthea, whom she had once met at Carmen's house. "This is Rhiannon Jones."

I knew Anthea by sight from her time as a secretary, so it was nice to meet her properly now that she was a script editor too. We unloaded our trays as they made room for us.

"This is the only thing I really like about Centre House," I remarked. "It's as if the department has its own canteen. Great for running into people."

"Yes, good for gossip," said Anthea, her eyes slipping above and beyond me. "But it does have its downside, if you know what I mean."

"Who's just come in?" I had my back to the door.

"Donald Mountjoy and a bilge tank."

Jill and Carmen giggled and stole glances at the two men, one lean and elegant, the other soft and saggy.

"Who's the bilge tank?" ventured Carmen.

"How dare you call him such a thing!" said Anthea. "I'm sure he's a perfectly nice tank."

"He's a management consultant," I explained. "He's been brought in to assess the department and find 'efficiency measures'. I'm surprised Donald's even giving him the time of day."

"Maybe he knows something you don't?" suggested Carmen, and I feared she could be right.

"So how come you've got time to sit around in Shepherd's Bush when you've got three shows a week to turn out?" I asked Anthea.

"My contract's up in a couple of weeks, and it's just been confirmed I'm coming down here to do development for six months."

"Brilliant! Who are you working with – not Fenella?"

Anthea's eyes widened at the thought of working for her old boss again. She shook her head firmly. "Just on my own, working directly to Peter. He wants me to find black and asian writers and develop projects with them." She glanced toward Carmen who took a mock bow, and I allowed my jaw to drop open – this was new. "They've just realised that they're way behind the times and have to make up a lot of ground. The Commission for Racial Equality embarrassed the hell out of the governors recently, and the buck's been whizzing from office to office ever since. Then I turned up at the right time, I suppose, Peter practically kissed my feet. He had to have a black script editor on the job or he would have looked ridiculous."

"Surely you're not the first black editor?" asked Jill.

"No, there have been a couple, but they didn't stick around long. For one reason or another."

"Now's your chance!" Carmen raised her eyebrows and looked mysterious. "You're up to something, aren't you?" said Jill.

"We have had rather a fine idea," admitted Carmen, looking at Anthea. "But is it safe to speak?" She looked under the table. "Can't see any bugs. It's about racism in the Metropolitan Police."

I remembered Jonathan's project and sat up suddenly. "Shhh! Don't tell us here."

"Why not?"

"People might be listening. It's not safe."

"Come on, it's hardly an issue of national security," said Anthea.

"I don't mean that – people here have no compunction about nicking ideas and passing them off as their own. Really. I was given a proposal this morning that's just like Maggie's project. Hers got turned down, but this one comes from the golden boy so it's been commissioned."

"No!"

"Who's the golden boy?" asked Jill. I shuddered dramatically.

"Don't make me say his name... d'you know how he greeted me? Jones the Script!"

They all laughed, as much at my indignation as at Jonathan's feeble joke.

"So who is he?" Carmen also wanted to know. Anthea's eyes drifted beyond me again.

"*Proulx the Prick*, of course!"

Amid their laughter Anthea murmured, "He's behind you... "
I froze.

"You're joking," I whispered.

"Sorry, I'm not. He just sat down."

"Did he hear?" She shrugged. I dared to turn round briefly, and found that Jonathan was alone at his table, his back to mine. He must have heard me, but he was tucking into his dinner, pretending he hadn't. I beat my head with my fists. What a stupid cow! Jill and Carmen thought it was very funny.

"Don't worry, he'll cope."

"Doesn't matter, does it?"

"I'm supposed to be his script editor on it." They gazed at me, commiserating. I wondered what to do. Should I turn and apologise? Yes, I should really. But I would look such a complete and utter fool.

Anthea patted my hand. "He might not have heard. It's noisy in here."

I smiled weakly, and decided to take that chance, avoiding certain humiliation. "Let's change the subject."

"You know my office is next to Stewart Walker's?" Anthea said. "He's not in today. Guess where he is."

"Bangkok?" suggested Carmen.

"No."

"Having a nose job?" I asked.

"No. That's funny, though."

"Where, then?"

"He's defending himself at a tribunal. The last temp but one reported him for sexual harassment."

"No! What'll happen to him?"

"God knows. I just hope he gets over his filthy temper before he gets back. I can hear him shouting through the wall." We grimaced at the thought of what his secretaries had to endure. There was a pause.

"Shall I get some coffees in?" I offered, getting up. I carefully avoided looking in Jonathan's direction, collected my crocks and took my tray away. I returned with another loaded with four coffees, by which time I was relieved to find him gone. He had more sense and sensitivity than to stick around. I felt I'd let myself down, despite his despicable crime. I like to feel I'm on the moral high ground so I resolved to be more discreet – and to avoid him as much as possible.

Chapter Eleven

Jill felt truly happy knowing that she'd been commissioned to write the first draft of *Lover Boy*. Sharon and Luke had got under her skin, and the commission was somehow equivalent to giving them permission to live. She couldn't wait to get started. Writing the treatment had been relatively easy. It had all flowed out of her in a satisfying stream, rather like reaching a toilet when you're bursting for a pee, she observed to herself with a smile, as she took a little watering can out onto the balcony to water her pots of marigolds and tomatoes. The project marked a step up in her career, being her first BBC1 drama serial, and it was great to be working on something she felt a hundred per cent enthusiastic about. However she couldn't start right away as she had to attend a parents' meeting at Sam's school that evening.

She'd lived alone with her son in her pleasant Crouch End flat since a relatively amicable divorce around five years previously. Her ex lived locally and saw their son every week. Sam was near the end of his first year at secondary school, and there were signs of adolescence beginning. Jill was conscious that she needed to give him space, but it was difficult.

The doorbell rang while Jill was washing up and Sam was on his PlayStation. He went and opened it, "Hullo Dad. Hullo Gran."

"Hello son. Is your mother ready?"

"Dunno."

Jill dried her hands as they entered the living room. "Hi. How are you?" She kissed her ex-mother-in-law. "Thanks Ivy. It's really good of you to come. We shouldn't be more than a couple of hours."

"Don't even mention it," replied Ivy, settling herself on the sofa. "I'm always glad to spend time with my favourite grandson."

"I'm your *only* grandson."

"So?"

Sam snorted in exasperation.

"Female logic, eh son?" said Neil. "What can you do?"

Ivy tutted at him. "Go on then if you're going. Do you mind if we watch *Coronation Street* Sam?"

"Course not, Gran." Sam looked furtive. "Long as I can *you know what*."

She pursed her lips conspiratorially and glanced at Jill and Neil. "Shh. Not in front of the parents."

Sam laughed and waved them off. "Bye Mum and Dad. Have a lovely time."

"What was all that about?" Neil asked Jill as they walked downstairs to his car.

"God knows. I'm just glad he's friends with his Gran. He's entitled to have a few secrets from me. Us, I mean."

Neil agreed. They got into his comfortable car and set off down the road towards Sam's comprehensive school.

"How's Sandra?" asked Jill.

"Fine thanks. She sends her love. Actually we're, er, we've decided to get married." Neil glanced sideways at his ex-wife but he needn't have been concerned as to her reaction.

"About time." She hesitated. "Congratulations, I suppose!"

"Thanks," he grinned sheepishly.

"I suppose you'll be starting a new family," observed Jill, looking out of the window. Neil didn't answer as he negotiated a clogged junction where several drivers were exchanging insurance details. Jill watched him: his face was lined now, but attractively, his hair was pepper-and-salt, and his neck flopped a little on top of his shirt collar. He was a good deal less handsome than when she had met him, and she allowed herself a small sense of satisfaction. Much as she liked Sandra, she preferred to feel that she herself had had the better part of Neil.

"Actually that's not part of the plan at the moment. I've decided I want to be an MP." He held a determined, responsible expression, but it didn't fool Jill, who laughed.

"An MP? Surely they have to be the organised type, selflessly devoting themselves to other people, giving up weekends to sort out visa problems and get council flats repaired."

"I can do that."

Jill looked at Neil again. "You're serious, aren't you? Which party?"

He frowned. "Labour of course. I wouldn't leave Labour, would I?"

She shrugged. "I wondered why you'd started wearing suits. I thought perhaps your allegiance had shifted."

"Don't insult me. I'm New Labour. I really believe we can win the next election, provided the party gets its act together. I'm an economist. There's a lot I can contribute." He drew up in the school car park, and put the handbrake on, turning to face Jill as if she were a voter he had to convince. "I've grown up, Jill. A lot of us radicals from the seventies have realised that persuasion is more effective than confrontation. Look at Clinton. Who'd have thought someone like him would beat Bush? He used to smoke dope, for God's sake! He's a groovy guy! Tony Blair's our Bill Clinton. We're determined to pull the country round again."

Jill nodded and smiled, almost impressed. "I hope you do," she said, and meant it. "Which constituency are you standing in?"

"I haven't been selected yet."

A light went on in Jill's head. "So *that's* why you're getting married! Oh Neil, how could you?"

"It's not just that," he muttered. "It's what we both want. Come on, we'll be late." He climbed out of the car and locked it after Jill, ushering her towards the main entrance.

In the school hall dozens of parents were milling about.

Jill and Neil joined a short queue for Sam's form teacher, a very thin, bespectacled man in his thirties.

"Mr Speed? We're Sam Watkins' parents."

"Glad to meet you, sit down – I'll get another chair," he said, fetching one. "It's not often the kids have two parents nowadays! Lucky old Sam."

Jill and Neil sat down feeling slightly fraudulent, but didn't feel it was the time or place to discuss their domestic arrangements.

"He made a good start in the first term, but his work's tailed off considerably since. Seems to have lost interest rather. Do you have any idea why that is?"

Jill was taken aback. Sam had always been a model pupil. She had no idea that anything had changed.

"He hasn't said a word about it. He does his homework, doesn't he?"

"Ye-es. More or less. How about you, Mr Watkins? Have you noticed anything?"

Neil shook his head, feeling guilty. He'd been concentrating on his own life lately, and had taken it for granted that Sam was getting along well. Sam spent every other weekend with him and Sandra, but they had got into the habit of having fun together and treating it as holiday time. He left the main tasks of parenting to Jill. He looked at Jill questioningly, hoping she would come up with something. She didn't.

Mr Speed carried on. "He doesn't appear to have made friends within his form, hangs out with a group of Year Eights. Did you know that?"

"No!" said Jill in surprise. "I thought his best friend was Tom, they came through primary school together."

"These kids like to think they're stylish, you know the kind of thing. Into hip-hop."

"And what else?" asked Neil. "Not drugs, I hope?"

"Not that I'm aware of. If they are then at least they've got the sense not to bring any to school." Jill started to feel cold. She swallowed. "If I were you, Mr and Mrs Watkins, I'd have a talk with him. I'm not saying these kids are a bad influence on him, but it may not be ideal. Sam has a lot of potential. He could do very well if he applies himself."

Other parents behind them shifted their feet, and Jill and Neil took their leave in a state of mild shock. They drifted round meeting a few other teachers who had little to say and left the school feeling depressed.

"You'd hardly believe he was the same child," mused Jill, remembering the glowing reports Sam used to receive.

"I suppose we got complacent. It's my fault. I haven't been giving him a strong enough role model."

Jill's silence endorsed this view. They drove home lost in their own thoughts.

*

SCENE 1 / 2 INT. CLASSROOM

ABOUT THIRTY FIFTEEN AND SIXTEEN-YEAR-OLDS LAZE AROUND IN THEIR PLACES, GOSSIPING. LUKE AND RICKY SIT TOGETHER BY THE WINDOW. THE DOOR OPENS AND SHARON ENTERS CAREFULLY, BALANCING A LARGE PILE OF BOOKS AND HER BAG, WHICH SHE MANAGES TO PLONK ON HER DESK JUST BEFORE SHE DROPS THEM.

SHARON: It's alright, thanks, I can manage.

THEY ALL IGNORE HER. SHE LOOKS UP, EXASPERATED, AND ADDRESSES THE GIRL NEAREST THE DOOR.

SHARON: Shut the door for me, would you Eleanor?

ELEANOR LEANS FORWARD AND SHOVES THE DOOR SHUT. THE BOYS SITTING BEHIND HER TAKE THE CHANCE TO LOOK UP HER SKIRT: SHE GIVES THEM A FILTHY LOOK.

SHARON: Right. Good morning everyone.

ABOUT HALF OF THEM RELUCTANTLY MURMUR SOMETHING IN RESPONSE.

SHARON: (AS IF THEY HAD POLITELY ASKED AFTER HER HEALTH) I'm very well, thank you for asking. Right. King Lear. I've marked your essays. Not bad, most of you, pretty good, some of you, completely useless, one of you. (SHE HOLDS UP AN A4 PAGE HALF FILLED) What's this supposed to be, Jack?

JACK SMIRKS IN THE BACK ROW

JACK: It's my character study, Miss.

SHARON: (WALKING DOWN THE ROW TO JACK) You mean it's the first two paragraphs of your character study. Do it again please. I want two full pages by Friday.

JACK ACCEPTS THE PAGE WITH A GRIMACE. SHARON HEADS FOR THE FRONT OF THE CLASS.

SHARON: Next is… Luke Woodward. Nice work, Luke.
            Carry on like that and you could get a top grade.

SHARON HANDS LUKE HIS WORK AS A FEW BOYS SAY
"OOOHH!" IN FRIENDLY MOCKERY. LUKE SMILES AND
GAZES INTO SHARON'S EYES. SHE HESITATES FOR A
MOMENT, THINKING HE'S GOING TO SPEAK, BUT HE
DOESN'T. HE JUST LOOKS AT HER AS IF HE KNOWS
SOMETHING. SHE'S PUZZLED.

LUKE: Thanks Miss.

RICKY: It's your superb teaching skills Miss. He's hope-
            less at everything else.

HE MAKES A FACE AT LUKE, WHO LOOKS PAINED.

SHARON: Shame they don't work on you, then Ricky. Yours
            was uninspired. You weren't watching the foot-
            ball while you wrote it, were you?

RICKY: Dunno Miss. Might've been.

SHARON: Because Lear's youngest daughter's name is
            Cordelia, not Chelsea.

THE CLASS LAUGHS AT RICKY. LUKE'S EYES FOLLOW
SHARON PROUDLY AS SHE CONTINUES WITH THE
LESSON.

The phone rang, interrupting Jill's flow. She scribbled a note to
herself, clicked on *save*, and picked up the receiver.
    "Hello?"
    "Jill? It's Paul at YTS. Good news!"
    It was her agent, she forced herself to focus on him.

"Hello Paul, how are you?"

"Fine thanks, you? – The BBC want to commission a script!"

Jill smiled. Bless him, she thought. "I know, Maggie called me three days ago. I've already started."

"Oh." He sounded disappointed, as if he had wanted some of the credit for getting her the work. "Great. It's a pity they won't commission both episodes at once. Apparently that's the policy now, take everything one step at a time."

"I know. Tight bastards, aren't they?"

"Did the *Casualty* office call you as well?"

"No. What do they want?"

"Availability check for next month. What do you think?"

Jill sighed. If she said yes, she would have too much on. If she said no, she might find herself without anything at all in three months' time. She wanted to say no, she was sick of it, but continuous financial insecurity was hard to live with.

Paul tried to help, "After this there won't be any more *Casualties* until next season, you know."

"But I won't be able to give *Lover Boy* enough attention, and it's my big break. I'd better say no, Paul."

"Sure?"

"Yes. Thanks."

He rang off, disappointed again. Jill felt a sense of power mixed with anxiety. She had never turned work down before, it was a new experience. I could get used to this, she thought. Then she got back to work.

The script flowed easily until she reached the parents' evening where Luke's mum and dad discussed his future career with Sharon. This presented difficulties as last night's experience was fresh in her mind, and she had not yet talked to Sam about it. She found herself identifying more closely with Luke's mother than she wanted to. She had intended Linda Woodward to be an annoying, old-fashioned woman with narrow-minded views. Instead she had a hard time giving Sharon a convincing argument.

SCENE 1 / 4 INT. SHARON'S SCHOOL HALL
MANY PARENTS MILL AROUND AND QUEUE TO SEE
STAFF. IAN AND LINDA WOODWARD SIT TOGETHER IN
FRONT OF SHARON'S DESK. THEY LOOK CONCERNED.

LINDA: Luke's always been good at English, hasn't he?
            It's a valuable subject. If he took a degree in
            English there are all kinds of jobs he could go in
            for, aren't there?

SHARON: Yes there are. But I thought he didn't want to
            carry on with it?

IAN: He likes his handicrafts, but he's very bright.
            A-level Art's fair enough, but we want him to go
            as far as he can with proper studies.
            Qualifications are the most important thing these
            days, aren't they?

SHARON: (SMILING) Absolutely, Mr Woodward.
            Especially if you're not sure what you want to do
            in life, university gives you more time to make up
            your mind. But I thought Luke had made up his
            mind – Ceramics and Woodwork?

IAN: He thinks he has, but he's only sixteen. What does
            he know? He doesn't want to wind up in some
            dead-end carpentry job, or making pots. Pots, I
            ask you!

SHARON: How times have changed. Ten years ago parents
            were telling me they wanted their sons to learn an
            honest trade, not stay on at school. You're saying
            the opposite.

LINDA: There you are you see. There aren't the jobs for skilled craftsmen any more. Ian knows, look at Ford: there's nowhere near the need for skilled labour there used to be, is there Ian?

IAN: That's right. Will you talk to him, Mrs Morrison? He'll listen to you. Tell him an English degree's the thing.

SHARON: I'll try, but I can't promise he'll change his mind. It's his life, in the end, isn't it?

LINDA: Tell him it's about keeping his options open. He's too young to leave school.

Jill heard the front door slam. Sam was home.

"Hi Sam," she called, receiving an inarticulate response. She followed the sound into Sam's bedroom and sat on his bed; Sam was switching on his computer.

"How was school?" she asked.

"Okay".

"I thought we might go to the Music Café for tea."

"I'd rather get fish and chips."

Jill paused. She much preferred the Music Café. "Okay darling. Fish and chips." Sam said nothing as he logged on to the internet, so Jill answered herself: "Great. Thank you mother dear."

Sam grunted, concentrating on his search.

"How's Tom? You haven't brought him home for ages."

"Alright."

"You haven't fallen out with him, have you?"

"No."

"Have you got some new friends?" No reply. Jill persevered, cautiously. "If you have, why don't you ask them back for tea?"

Sam sighed an *it's hopeless expecting you to understand* sigh. "I don't think so, Mum." He ran his hand through his gelled hair. "Mum?"

"Yes?"

"Is it okay if I get my ear pierced?"

"Don't be silly, you're much too young."

"Loads of kids my age have pierced ears. And that's not all – "

"I don't want to know."

Jill didn't see why Sam should get his own way with everything, the least he could do was open up a bit and talk to her. Sam turned and looked at her, wearing the incredulous expression of a boy who has just been told he will have to marry a rich but ghastly old lady.

"I'm not a kid anymore, you know," he said.

"I know, darling. But you're not grown up either."

"You don't *want* me to grow up!"

"Of course I do."

"Not really. Not deep down." Sam stood up, still wearing his jacket. "Give us a tenner, then."

"No, Sam."

"Don't you want fish and chips?"

The phone started ringing again, disconcerting Jill who felt suddenly wrong-footed. She pulled some money out of her pocket and gave it to Sam.

"Skate and chips and mushy peas, please."

"Okay." Hands in pockets, he walked out of the flat whistling.

Jill shook her head quickly to clear her confusion while she answered the phone. "Hello?"

"Hi Jill, is this a bad moment?"

"Oh Carmen, hi. No, it's fine. I was just having a slight altercation with Sam."

"Oh dear."

"He wants to have his ear pierced, for God's sake."

"Is that a problem?"

"He's twelve!"

"Twelve already. Amazing, isn't it?"

Carmen was missing the point, so Jill changed the subject. "How are you, anyway?"

"Fine, great. I got an invite to the BBC writers' party today – did you?"

"Oh yes, I did actually. Are you going?"

"Course I am, I wouldn't miss a chance like that. It's the first time they've asked me. I've arrived!"

"It's only standing about with a glass of cheap wine, you know."

"Sure, but standing about *with whom*?"

Jill smiled out loud. Carmen would have a whale of a time, she was a party animal, able to approach anyone and chat comfortably.

"I wish I wasn't such a wallflower," said Jill.

"Stick with me girl, I'll show you a good time! I better let you sort out the family stuff. Call me sometime."

"I will," promised Jill. "Take care."

When Sam came back with the fish and chips they sat down to watch the news. Jill noticed Sam's new shoes.

"Nice trainers. Did Dad buy them for you?"

"Uh huh."

"They look very expensive."

Sam shrugged.

"Are you happy at school, Sam?"

He shrugged again.

"You don't seem as happy as you were at Shepherd's. And, er, Mr Speed seems to think you're not doing as well as you could."

Sam ate with intense concentration.

"I wish you'd talk about it, Sam. You used to tell me everything."

"That was then. This is now," said Sam enigmatically.

"So what's changed?"

He shrugged. Jill decided to quit before the conversation became a confrontation. She told herself not to get uptight about it, it was probably just his hormones, and made a mental resolution not to talk to him as if he were a child. "Fruit salad or cinnamon cheesecake for pudding?"

"Yuk. Got any Fab lollies?"

Jill gave up.

Chapter Twelve

The BBC Writers' Party is an annual tradition, intended as a thank-you to acknowledge the vital contribution they make. Generally very badly paid and frequently messed around, writers work alone with no security of any kind; they have agents to look after their interests but they pay them a high price. You won't find many writers enjoying the same standard of living as the average agent. Apart from the few who hit the big time writers tend to be nervous and introverted – and who could blame them – they're powerless until the public cries out for them, and how often does that happen? So they like to be noticed by their employers once a year, and to come and enjoy some free plonk and a good gossip with the outside chance of making new contacts and picking up more work.

I was there, along with a few senior script editors and most of the drama producers, to be nice to them. That year it took place in a large art gallery in The Mall which was deeply trendy but not especially smart, so there was little to fear from clumsy revellers in the way of damage. On the walls hung a series of large unattractive canvases which no-one paid any attention to. I was looking out for writers I knew, and hoping to avoid Jonathan, as I'd succeeded in doing for a couple of weeks since my faux pas in the canteen. The room was filling up quickly as people entered through a security cordon at the top of a short flight of stairs. I saw Jonathan arrive with his girlfriend Selina, Chris Briggs' assistant. They looked like a pair of film stars on holiday, casually elegant and entirely relaxed, in contrast to the neurotically tense demeanour of the guests. I found them horribly fascinating. It's not that I wanted to be tall and slim and blonde and socially adept – I've always been happy with who I am, honest – I just resented the pecking order, that's all. Looking back it seems pathetically small-minded. I pretended to look at the art until they had been safely absorbed by the crowd. My avoidance strategy didn't work; two minutes later Jonathan approached me and I had to say hello.

"I just wanted a quick word, Rhiannon," he said, and I braced myself. "I've been thinking, it's really not fair to expect you to work on my project when you're so busy. I'm happy to find another editor if you prefer."

I was speechless for a moment, and then delighted. His expression showed concern for me and gave no sign of ill-feeling, so I took his words at face value and accepted gratefully. I knew he was letting me get away with bunking off – but what producer wants an uncooperative script editor? He was doing the sensible thing in the circumstances.

He smiled regretfully. "Maybe another time?"

"Maybe, yes," I replied, not sounding too keen. I watched him ease himself politely through the crowd to Selina, and breathed a big sigh of relief. Now I could enjoy myself. I watched the staircase for new arrivals; they were coming down thick and fast now.

Jill came with Carmen, who looked beautiful with her hair up and gorgeously coloured African jewellery set off by a tiny blue dress. Jill wore a silk outfit, a black dress with a light grey jacket, and pearls. She'd had her hair cut short and styled round her face, which suited her and made her look quite youthful. At least, she had thought so until Sam said she looked like her mother. They paused at the top of the stairs before descending into the now heaving mass of people conversing in a patchy haze of cigarette smoke.

"Can you see anyone you know?" Jill asked Carmen.

"Anthea's at the far end. Rhiannon's over there. Oh – there's Tony Scott!"

"Really? Do you know him?"

"No, I saw his picture in the paper. Let's go and say hello."

"Hang on – he's talking to Billy Trowell. Can we wait until he's gone?" but Carmen was already beetling down the stairs. Jill followed.

Jill was introduced to Tony, the miner-turned-writer, who was built like a small rugby player, handsome yet diffident. She thought he was gorgeous despite his broken nose, and was keen to talk to him. She was denied this pleasure by long-haired, overweight Billy, who put his huge arm round her and gave her a sloppy kiss which spoiled her make-up.

"Thanks, Billy," she said sarcastically, wiping her face with a tissue.

"Sorry darling. May I say how incredibly attractive you look tonight?"

"Thanks." Jill swiftly assessed how much Billy had had to drink; she reckoned four or five. How was she going to keep him at arm's length? Carmen was already in animated conversation with Tony about his award-winning debut, but Jill couldn't quite hear it because Billy was whispering loudly in her ear, inviting her to sneak off with him for a quick shag in St James' Park.

"Billy, darling, I've just got here. I need a drink."

"Let me get you one," said Billy promptly, swinging round towards the makeshift bar at the back of the room, and spilling the drink of a stout woman who was berating Peter Maxwell.

"Billy, for Christ's sake!" said his agent, wiping her suit down.

"Sorry Muriel, I'll get you another."

"I don't *want* another. Get me some water. *That* doesn't stain."

"Fizzy?"

"Of course fizzy." Muriel turned back crossly to Peter only to find he had vanished.

Jill shuffled up to Carmen and Tony but was pursued by Muriel, who read her name tag. "Jill Watkins. I'm sure I know that name. What have you written?"

Jill took a deep breath. "*Eldorado* and *Casualty*. At the moment I'm writing a two-parter for Basil Richardson and Rhiannon Jones."

"Very good, very good," said Muriel, impressed. "May I ask what it's about?"

"It's a romance, really; star-crossed lovers." She didn't want the idea spread around after what had happened to Maggie's project. Until now she'd thought it was silly to be precious about ideas, but now she felt it was wiser to play safe.

"Ah yes," said Muriel wistfully. "You can't beat a good weepie."

Jill was stuck for an answer to this, but it didn't matter.

"Who represents you?" asked Muriel, never one to beat about the bush.

"Paul Grant, YTS," replied Jill reluctantly. Muriel raised her eyebrows briefly in a superior manner.

"Any time you're thinking of moving up, give me a ring dear." She winked at Jill, who smiled embarrassedly, both flattered and appalled.

"I'll get you three times what they get you. They're far too polite. Far too polite." She nodded and widened her eyes, which were additionally magnified by her large spectacles. It was alarming.

"Here we are," shouted Billy, lurching towards them with three glasses in his hands. Muriel and Jill took their drinks with alacrity before the liquid and containers parted company.

"Come along Billy, I want you to meet Chris Briggs," announced Muriel, leading him off to Jill's great relief. She turned to Carmen and Tony again, and managed to join in this time. "I loved your serial Tony. Really loved it."

"Thanks very much," he said, smiling at her softly. His

Nottinghamshire accent was straight out of DH Lawrence and sent her weak at the knees. "I couldn't have done it wi'out Basil and Jonathan. They taught me everything." His lack of affectation charmed her.

"I'm sure that's not true," said Jill, "But I hope it is – I'm working with Basil at the moment, I'd love some of his genius to rub off on me!"

"Tha couldn't do better," said Tony. "What's it about?"

Jill launched into a description which was more detailed than it needed to be, to keep Tony's attention. She glanced at his left hand to see if he wore a wedding ring; he didn't. His hands were thick and gnarled.

"You have amazing hands," she remarked. "Not like most writers – soft and sappy!"

"Awful aren't they? Miner's hands. Covered in scars."

"Oh no, they're beautiful," said Jill too warmly. "They're real, working hands. You should be proud of them. I think you are really, aren't you?"

Tony smiled sheepishly. "Tha's too bloody sharp by half. Can I get thee another glass of wine?" Jill accepted happily and turned to Carmen as he left. She was talking to a smart young woman Jill didn't know.

"Hallo, I'm Sally Farquar-Binns," she said. "Lovely to meet you," and shook Jill's hand.

"Aren't you a script editor?" asked Jill.

"I used to be," explained Sally. "Now I'm a development producer, on the lookout for new projects."

"Oh," said Jill. "Anything in particular?"

Sally pursed her lips and shrugged. "Series, serials, films. There are a few actors we're very keen to find vehicles for."

Jill nodded. It sounded terribly vague, but she seemed a nice woman.

"You're working with Basil and Rhiannon at the moment aren't you?"

"Yes. It's going well so far – but it's early days."

"Sounds super. From what I've read about it in the lists, you know."

It was news to Jill that the department circulated details of all its projects, but perhaps that wasn't surprising. They smiled at each other. Jill felt obliged to elaborate. "Thanks. I'm in the middle of the first draft at the moment, and I'm sort of falling in love with the main character. He's kind of my dream lover."

"Oh wow!" said Sally. "Amazing!"

Jill wished she hadn't said anything. It sounded ridiculous. She was glad when Tony arrived with a drink for her, and took a gulp. Sally was in there like a shot, shaking Tony's hand and giving him the best angle of her most intelligent expression. In a matter of seconds she had commandeered him so successfully that his back was turned completely to Jill. She sighed and looked at Carmen, who commiserated with a grimace.

The crowd's attention was called for the host's speech, which Jill had been looking forward to ever since Maggie told her who he was. She was keen to see the young producer who had been so nice to her when she was pregnant and under arrest in Edinburgh all those years ago. Apparently he had now become a BBC mandarin. The party took a minute or two to quieten down, as many of the writers were well-oiled and enjoying their rare opportunity to sound off in person instead of in print. Finally a non-descript man in a grey suit, standing at a microphone at the top of the stairs, coughed and lifted his hand.

"Hello everyone, and welcome. This is my first writers' party as Controller of BBC1, and I hope you like the decor – a bit of a change from the usual!"

Jill was surprised, she would never have recognised him. Then again, she hadn't paid him much attention at the time. She wondered whether he would recognise her, and decided it was very unlikely. They had both changed in their transition to respectable middle-aged media types. Jill frowned at this reali-sation; her younger self would have been very critical of her older self. She would have seen her television work as drearily mainstream, and even now she saw Chris as a faceless manager, a bean-counter with power. It dawned on her that she had a genuine connection with Chris which she could use, if she wished. Granted, it wasn't a strong one, but it would be enough to start up a conversation. What could she gain from it?

She realised she had missed the beginning of Chris' speech, and castigated herself for fantasising about self-interest instead of paying attention.

"As you know, the BBC values its talent very highly indeed, and we're delighted to see so many fabulously gifted people here tonight. After all, we wouldn't win any prizes without you lot writing the scripts!" He paused for a reaction, and the crowd obliged half-heartedly. "I know we don't always pay the highest fees – " this brought a much louder, spontaneous response – "But rest assured, we care the most. We believe in writer-led drama, and always will."

As he blathered on Jill's hopes rose. Chris was evidently one of the good guys. Perhaps he *would* be interested in her and speed her project along.

Carmen nudged her. "Look, it's Salman Rushdie!"

"Where?"

"Over there. He's with Basil."

Jill scanned the crowd and was excited to see a short, balding Asian man in a group of distinguished older writers and producers; she was amazed that he was attending despite the fatwa against him.

"You're right! God, I hope no-one takes a pot at him here."

"I expect he's got bodyguards."

"Can you see them?"

"Must be those tall serious guys who look incredibly sober."

"I thought they were from the Nation of Islam."

They turned and listened to Chris again. He was telling the writers that they were the life-blood of the BBC and he was looking forward to all the fabulous top-rating shows in the pipeline. He also hoped they would have a great evening, but to please refrain from molesting the ducks across the road, as they were the property of the Queen. The assembly chuckled gamely at his awful joke, seeing no point in upsetting Chris. It was always best to humour the top brass.

A blonde woman with wispy hair excused herself as she eased past Jill to get near the bottom of the stairs, down which Chris was walking to accompanying applause. Descending into the light fog of tobacco smoke he pretended not to see her until she grabbed his arm. Jill eavesdropped, admiring her doorstepping technique.

"Chris, hello, I did enjoy your speech."

"Thank you, er... "

"Sonia. Longbow."

"Ah yes, of course."

"The art gallery makes a lovely change. Far more interesting."

"I'm pleased you think so."

"You remember the new writing initiative? I wonder if I might have a quick word about it."

"Actually I'm in a bit of a – "

"It won't take a moment, and I know it's very close to your heart, as you said at the time."

"Indeed."

"You see, I have a terrific list of really talented new writers, drawn from all over the UK; twelve are shortlisted and they all have projects they're ready and waiting to write for us. The trouble is the development funds have stalled. The new controller hasn't released them."

"That's really a matter for him, not for me Sonia."

"Yes I know, but I thought since you'd kicked it off you might have a word."

"It really wouldn't be appropriate, I'm afraid."

Sonia's voice became a fraction more vehement. "The thing is we're breaking a promise. When the initiative began we told all the applicants there would be twelve commissions offered to the winners."

"I don't recall it being a competition."

"No, not as such, but we did promise commissions to twelve successful applicants under the scheme. It's all the same."

"We haven't announced any winners, though. That's the main thing."

"No, I haven't told any of them yet. That's why I want the assurance of funds, so that I can get them started."

"I'm sorry Sonia, it's out of my hands now. Excuse me."

Chris politely left Sonia and tried to walk purposefully into the middle of the crowd. She glared at his back, mouthing an unmistakable swearword.

Jill took a deep breath and spurred herself into action. Now or never, do a bit of schmoozing, that's what parties are about, she thought, tapping Chris on the shoulder. "Hi!" she said shyly. "Remember me?"

Chris frowned. "Sorry," he said, shaking his head.

Jill patted her belly and grinned. "I was eight months pregnant last time we met," she chuckled, not really knowing what she was going to say next. "It was in Edinburgh. We got arrested."

Chris looked pained, then half-smiled. "That's right. How are you?"

"Oh, fine, thanks."

"Your baby'll be big now."

"Yes, he's twelve. I must say, you've done awfully well for yourself!" She wanted to kick herself for sounding such an idiot.

"Thanks!" said Chris, "Lovely to see you again!" and he was gone.

Jill sighed. Effing useless. She'd never get anywhere, she might as well stay at home.

In the corner near the toilets there was a slight disturbance, and a couple of bouncers were heading for it. It was Billy, waving his fist at a disdainful, louche man. Jill could just about hear Billy drunkenly upbraiding him.

"Don't patronise me, you smarmy intellectual git. I know when I've been royally shafted. Channel Four won't fuck me about, you know!"

The quietly controlled response appeared to indicate that Channel Four was more than welcome to Billy's talents.

"Peter! Tell this bastard he's a bastard."

Peter Maxwell, looking a little tired and emotional himself, resignedly joined the pair and putting a hand on his shoulder, attempted to calm Billy down. Jill was fascinated. The other man must be Stewart Walker, who she knew had produced most of Billy's work. Billy was no longer a rising star – in fact he was a falling star. Jill sympathised to that extent. Whatever Peter was saying had the required effect, and the bouncers withdrew. Billy looked up morosely and nodded. Then he kissed Peter, Russian style, tweaked Stewart's cheek in a manner bound to irritate him, and strode towards Jill, who hastily hid behind Sally Farquar-Binns and pretended to be busy.

Sally didn't disappoint her.

"Hello, it's Billy Trowell, isn't it? May I say how much I admire your work!" she began. *Death of a Baby* was *so* moving."

"Thank you my dear," growled Billy, cracking a world-weary smile. "It's good to know there are still people in the BBC who can recognise talent. Sally." He acknowledged her name tag and twinkled his eyes at her, swaying ever so slightly.

"I'm in development," said Sally. "But I expect you're terribly busy."

Billy summoned up his most charming smile for her. "Not as busy as you might think."

"Really!" Sally returned it. "Perhaps we should meet for lunch."

"Nothing would please me more," said Billy, rashly picking up her hand and kissing it, which she allowed but didn't enjoy.

"I'll call your agent tomorrow," she said, hoping to disentangle herself. Billy hung on to her hand. Sally felt obliged to make small talk.

"So – what made you decide to start writing?"

Billy thought for a second. "It all began with masturbation fantasies. I thought, these are so good I should write them down for other people to enjoy."

For once Sally was lost for words.

Jill decided to rescue her. "And you've never looked back, have you Billy?" she said, putting her hand on his shoulder and laughing. Sally looked relieved and laughed too. "I think I saw Muriel looking for you," Jill continued, attempting to steer him away.

"She's an old cow, Muriel," muttered Billy.

"Don't be like that. She's a very good agent."

"She hates me."

"Of course she doesn't."

"Everybody hates me."

"They don't, Billy, stop it."

"Apart from you. You're lovely, Jill. Marry me, Jill. Please marry me."

"No, Billy. Definitely not."

"What's wrong with me?"

"Nothing. You're pissed. Shut up." Jill finally caught Muriel's eye and delivered her client up. Muriel looked annoyed.

"Alright Billy, let's find you a cab."

Jill thankfully left Billy protesting that he wasn't ready to go home yet, and found me seeking her out.

"Bloody hell fire," she exclaimed, "I hope we've seen the back of Billy for the time being."

"It's hard not to feel sorry for him," I said.

"Yeah. One minute you're the big cheese everyone wants a taste of, and the next you're stinking and riddled with maggots."

"Yuk."

Jill sighed and shrugged. "It's a daft way to make a living, it really is. Why do we put ourselves through it?"

"Why *do* you?"

"Because we can. Because we have to, because it's all we can do... stop me before I say something really stupid!"

"Because it's a sight more fun than doing a proper job, let's face it." We looked to where the husky cockney voice had come from, and found a short man in his thirties, wearing a sharp charcoal grey suit with no tie and several earrings. Jill smiled at him.

"You're right, why don't I stop whinging?"

"It's a lark ain't it?"

"Yes, sometimes."

"I suppose life's what you make it, in the end," I contributed, hoping I didn't sound like a Sunday School teacher.

"Too right," he said. "I'm on my fourth career already." He had an energy and warmth about him that was irresistible, and we both wanted to hear more. "I've been a floor trader in the city for the last five years, shouting futures. What a game that is. Made a packet though."

"I couldn't do that in a million years," murmured Jill.

"Nah, it's no place for a nice girl like you," he said. "They'd trample you underfoot like a bit of bog paper." His honesty was kindly meant, and we had to laugh.

"Thanks!"

"I started out as a street trader; a valuable apprenticeship that was."

"Really? Selling what?"

"Anything you like. Some of it was even legal." He grinned and winked, we didn't know whether he was joking or not. His eyes sparkled with native intelligence and the confidence that comes from knowing you can hold your own in the roughest pub. The kind of man who could bounce back from any situation and turn it to his advantage. "Now I sell words. I make stuff up, and they pay me. I get up when I like, I fart around all day, spend a month in the pub and then knock off a script the night before the deadline. Nobody gives a shit as long as it arrives on time. What could be better than that?"

"Shush," said Jill, laughing, "don't give your secrets away!"

He wasn't put off. An innocent frankness, no doubt reinforced by wine, drove him to confess. "I'm still getting used to it, I was brought up believing work was work, you know? Physical labour. If my old man could see me now!"

"What would he say?" I really liked this bloke, he was a breath of fresh air.

"He'd say, 'you lucky little bleeder.' Or words to that effect."

Just then Tony Scott put his hand on our new friend's shoulder. "Ready, Jim?"

"Yep, whenever. Fancy coming to Groucho's?" he asked. We didn't need to discuss it. Carmen was behind him, beaming.

"Sounds great," I said. "Okay Jill?" Jill nodded, checking her watch; her mother-in-law Ivy was babysitting, but she wouldn't mind. We headed for the door, and found ourselves in a small crowd on the pavement waiting for taxis.

After five minutes standing around we decided to walk there. We set off towards Admiralty Arch and Trafalgar Square, the men walking behind the women. It was a fine summer night and the air was fresh after the smoky gallery. The square was busy as usual, with tourists sitting on the lions drinking from cans and generally hanging out as if it were a happening place rather than a monumental roundabout. We headed briskly up Charing Cross Road, sharing gossip about people we'd encountered at the party. By the time we reached Shaftesbury Avenue, the Groucho Club no longer seemed such an appealing destination; the mood was changing and we'd had our fill of crowds. I could sense Jill's interest in Tony, and I wanted to help.

"Is anyone else hungry?" I asked.

"I am," said Tony. So was Jill.

"Let's go for a Chinese, shall we?" said Carmen. "I don't mind."

We settled into a corner of a Gerrard St restaurant and selected a dozen dishes between us, then tucked into a bottle of wine. Jill sat opposite Tony and smiled shyly. He responded, but I couldn't be certain whether he was really interested in her or if he was just being friendly.

"I wasn't sure," he began. "Whether you were with that bloke Billy."

"Oh no," said Jill. "Definitely not. He's sort of a friend. Well actually, I once spent the night with him after a do at the Writers' Guild. I've been regretting it ever since." We all laughed.

"We've all been there," said Carmen.

"Speak for thaself," said Tony.

"Go on," said Carmen. "You must have slept with someone and wished you hadn't?"

"No. I've never regretted any of them. I've always been grateful!"

"Last of the great romantics, are you?" said Jim.

"You are, aren't you!" exclaimed Jill. "How marvellous. We're all so callous aren't we, thinking we're sophisticated and cosmopolitan."

"Cherish thy love," said Tony wisely. "One day it might be all tha's got left."

We all paused to take this in, and Jim laughed it off.

"Yeah, well," he said. "More wine, please waiter!"

After we had eaten most of the food and dropped the rest on the table, Jim began to press Carmen on the subject of the screenplay she was writing for Anthea.

"I don't talk about it," she said. "I'm superstitious."

"Come on," wheedled Jim. "I'll show you mine if you show me yours. I swear by my last gram I won't tell a soul."

"Okay. It's about racism in the police force, and it's based on the Stephen Lawrence murder. You know about that, presumably?" Everyone nodded. "I'm showing it as accurately as possible, without using any of the real people or events."

Tony and Jim looked puzzled.

Jill laughed. "It's brilliant," she said. "It's so simple. Tell them, Carmen."

"To get round the legal problems and everything else," continued Carmen. "I've swapped the races round. The victim is a white boy, and the police force is virtually all black. So are the accused murderers, and most of the population."

A slow smile lit up the men's faces as they shared a look and nodded their approval.

"That sounds very powerful," said Tony.

"And funny," said Jim.

"I hope it's both," said Carmen. "It's not really a new idea, role reversal's been done before, but not on telly. We think it'll work."

"The main worry is whether the BBC will get cold feet about it," said Jill. "Because the government's going to hate it. Just imagine!"

"Maybe there'll be a new government by the time it's broadcast? If there isn't, there's no hope for any of us, is there?"

No-one wanted to argue with Tony's analysis.

"Okay, your turn," said Carmen to Jim. "Spill the beans."

"Mine's not in your league, but it'll be neat if it comes off. It's a bit naughty." We all gazed at him expectantly. "It's about a doctor who takes cannabis as treatment for his multiple sclerosis. It's very good for that, you know. He wants to prescribe it for his patients, but of course he can't. He feels a total hypocrite. So then he gets this farmer who's going bust to grow it and make herbal tea-bags, and he sends his patients round to buy them: job done! Until the plods catch up with him, that is. But then at the end, when it goes to court, the film stops when the jury are sent out to discuss their verdict. Then it's up to the audience to decide what they think about the situation – we're hoping *Newsnight* will run a debate straight after the broadcast."

We all agreed it was a wonderful idea. I loved it. "What's it called?"

"*The Medical Miracle*," said Jim.

I stared, horrified.

"What?" he said.

"Nothing! I, er, just remembered something." What could I say? I'd spent the last five hours congratulating myself on being removed from this show, which now turned out to be the best idea I'd heard in my whole career. I realised to my eternal shame that I hadn't even read the proposal right through. It wasn't at all like Maggie's project, and I could have been working with this delightful, funny, original writer; it wouldn't have clashed with my own project at all, and Jonathan knew that as well as I did. It was set in Wales and Jim was a cockney: that's why they wanted me on it. I'd assumed Jim Johnson would be Welsh, or at least middle-aged and worthy. It hadn't entered my head to connect this Jim with it. What a complete and utter idiot I'd been! I broke out in a cold sweat.

Jill noticed it was ten to twelve and guiltily got up to go, explaining about her babysitter; Carmen said she'd share a cab, and I stood up to go too. Jill's eyes lingered hopefully in Tony's direction.

"I'll stop for a last one with Jim, and get the last train." Tony said. "It'll get me home just before Tracy goes to work."

Jill caught her breath, "What does she do?"

"She's a staff nurse. Bless her. She's been supporting me since the pit closed in '85. I'm hoping to earn enough for her to retire soon. She deserves it."

Jill took her leave, disappointed. Carmen kissed the boys goodbye, and I just tried not to cry before I got home.

Chapter Thirteen

While I was busy swanking round west London destroying my best opportunities, young Nik Mason was making a far better job of his career. Chris Briggs had picked up *The Soap Ashes* as his first new commission on being appointed Controller of BBC1, scheduling it before *EastEnders* with a Radio One disc jockey as host. It had proved a great success, and since Nik had managed to keep the rights, Rex and Haris were overjoyed and gave him a seat on the board of directors. Geordie had been devastated at being dropped, but Nik explained how he had tried and tried, but the BBC were adamant that they must use one of their own top presenters, and in the end he couldn't lose the project over that. Geordie reluctantly accepted this and Nik took him for a weekend in New York to console him.

Proud as Rex was of his protégé, he found himself outshone at his own game, and it gradually sapped his confidence. He couldn't throw his weight around the office with quite the same conviction; he wasn't always the last resort for consultation by production staff, and he saw a lot less of Nik, who was always tied up in one meeting or another. Rex began to arrive at the casino earlier and earlier.

Nik had become ambitious. For the first few years he had allowed Rex to guide him, never really thinking about his career beyond achieving the next goal. After all, he had entered the industry by accident. Now he felt he was swimming with the current, it was easy, and he felt very aware of his own strength and power. He was a top professional and had earned his fortune already. He had a superb loft apartment in Wapping with a river view and a Porsche in the subterranean car park. He liked night-clubbing and dabbled in designer drugs, although he was very disciplined and never took too much or indulged too often. He had seen enough to know that he must never let the drugs take control.

He lived alone. He preferred the bachelor life. He brought men or women home when it suited him and Geordie was still a regular visitor, but he had never yet fallen in love. He wasn't looking for love. He didn't need it in his life – in fact he knew it would only get in the way. He was perfectly content to live alone indefinitely. He enjoyed his own company and liked to relax in his apartment, playing loud rock music and sipping a cocktail while he enjoyed the river view. He would look up the Thames towards the City and Westminster, thinking of the famous people who also watched this river flow past their luxury homes – people like Michael Caine (his favourite actor) and Jeffrey Archer (his favourite novelist) – and wondering what the future held in store. Where might he be at the age of 40? Working for Rupert Murdoch? Dining with Rupert Murdoch? Buying out Rupert Murdoch?

Nik lacked a good enough sense of overview to put his daydreams onto a substantial footing. He was good at dealing with people he could see, at working on his feet, but not so good with paperwork and long-term planning. Politics bored him, as did fine art, opera, and anything else that required a dinner jacket but wasn't a casino. On the whole, he felt that whatever his approach to life had been so far it must have been the right one, because it had proved phenomenally successful, so he carried on in the same way without attempting to analyse anything. 'Don't look a gift horse in the mouth' was another valuable maxim he'd picked up from Rex.

When Nik's father Les was finally acquitted of corruption by the appeal court, no-one was more surprised than Nik. He even felt a twinge of guilt. Maybe he should have stood by the old man like his mother did? It made his nine-year absence from the family home all the harder to explain, and he reluctantly went to Ilford to visit Les and Doreen for Sunday lunch, taking a magnum of champagne and an exotic bouquet for his mother.

"How wonderful!" she blushed. "Oh Nicky, you shouldn't have. You really didn't ought to spend your money on us, did he Les?"

"He can afford it woman, look at him!" Les admonished, thoroughly uncomfortable in the company of this young man of the world who looked like a male model and carried himself like a senior businessman. He had never imagined that Nicky would turn out like this. Thankfully, he still sounded more or less the same.

"Actually I'm known as Nik, now. Without a 'c'."

"Ooh!" squealed his flustered mum, as if he'd been renamed by royal command. "However will we remember to call you that?"

"Don't worry about it."

"Oh, thank you," said Doreen, embarrassing him still further.

By the time lunch was over, the atmosphere had relaxed, and the three were beginning to get used to each other. For Doreen it was as if they had lost their son as a teenager and had been sent an angel in compensation. For Les it was an excruciating ordeal of suppressed emotion. For Nik it was painful and tedious. He still had feelings for his parents but he didn't know how to express them. He wanted them to be proud of him, but he didn't want to commit to visiting Ilford on a regular basis. He didn't know how to sit and chat with them. He felt terribly restless.

Later he was glad to escape with Les, even if it was only down the road for a pint in the Dog and Duck. He had to submit to being greeted and admired by various old codgers before they could go and sit in a corner by themselves, but soon the beer began to work its magic.

"Listen Nicky – Nik," began Les, "I want you to know that I'm terribly, terribly sorry for letting you down all those years ago. I've never forgiven myself, and I don't expect you to forgive me neither. I know I can't make it up to you, but if I could, I would. There. Nine years I've been rehearsing that speech!" He tried to laugh.

Nik shook his head. "No dad, really, no. It was me that let you down. I'm sorry. You see, to be absolutely honest, I thought you was guilty. What sort of son does that make me?" He smiled ruefully. Les understood that he was forgiven, that Nik was proud of his dad again. Nik respected the triumph in the appeal court and was now complicit in the pretence that Les was innocent. He gripped Nik's wrist tightly for a full ten seconds, as they both stared into their beers.

"New beginnings?" Nik raised his beer mug, and Les chinked his against it. They caught each other's relieved gaze as they drained their glasses.

Nik came home with a new point of view. In the end, it didn't really matter whether his father had been guilty or innocent. The only vital thing was the result. The final verdict decided your character in the eyes of the world, and that was far more important than something that might or might not have taken place years before. It seemed to Nik that you could be one person at home, and another in public, but the public persona was the only one that counted. It dictated everything about your life. It was the real you, because it was the one other people related to. The inner you could be safely ignored, kept private; trouble only came from journalists prying into peoples' lives, pointing out the anomalies.

Whatever his dad had done and been through, and it must have been pretty damn tough, he had survived and conquered. He was still the same nice geezer, still had his health, his reputation, his house, and his wife. He couldn't have his job back as he was now too old for it, but he'd been awarded a five figure sum in compensation and a full pension. He was well set up for a top quality retirement. He was a winner. Nik realised that he was, after all, his father's son.

The Soap Ashes had gone like a dream, as far as Nik was concerned. It had catapulted him into the top band of up-and-coming producers; he laughed when he compared himself to the 'old school' staff in the BBC's own Light Entertainment Department, whose power decreased in proportion to the rise of 'Johnny come lately' independents like himself. Young BBC producers were even denied royalties on their own work nowadays. They developed shows for a pittance and argued for them until they were hoarse, whilst a guy like him strolled in behind their backs, secured the gig, and strolled out again dripping gold. He loved it. All those public school accents silenced, those receding chins hanging open. He never showed it of course – that would be vulgar – but alone in his loft apartment he smirked into the mirror.

At this point in his life he had more or less forgotten the Edinburgh incident, and he certainly had no idea at all how close those individuals were to him whenever he visited the BBC. The humiliation had been swiftly overshadowed by events immediately after it. All that remained was a vague memory of having got into a fight for reasons he never quite understood, and being arrested with a group of strangers who then patronised him outrageously. One was an Oxbridge student of the worst kind, and another a boffin from the BBC, and there were some women too. He'd been a child of fifteen, they had no right to put him down so cruelly. This thought spiked his mind one evening as he relaxed on his leather sofa and zapped through the television channels, catching a report from the current Edinburgh Festival. A flicker of anger hurt his chest, and he realised that an ember still glowed deep inside him. He poured another Jack Daniels and pondered this discovery, wryly observing to himself that he must be getting old, if he'd started reliving the past. Dynamic young men only looked forward. It was irrelevant now, and he decided to put it behind him.

As the television presenter rattled briskly through a round-up of new comedians Nik's thoughts turned once more to his own career, and what his next step would be. How could he improve on *The Soap Ashes*? How could he make bigger profits, and put Magenta at the top of the ratings chart? Could he keep on making hit shows, or was he a one-hit wonder? He wanted very much to become a notable figure, but on his own terms. He would not bow to the powers that be, nor change himself to suit them. He'd happened on exactly the right way to handle Chris Briggs by sheer intuition, so he would stick to that strategy, and trust his own talent.

The Soap Ashes would take care of itself now. It was a fixture in the schedules of BBC1, gaining up to ten million viewers per week, and it no longer challenged him. Time for a new departure. Not from Magenta. He was happy there and was making a small fortune so there was no reason to move, but he needed a new project, something big. Preferably at the BBC. Despite his feeling towards it, he'd always believed the BBC was the best broadcaster. He had to admit it represented the Best of British Culture, despite the arseholes who ran it. Now if he were in charge... a smile began inside him. What a shake-up he'd give it. All those frightfully charming toffs out of the seventh floor window, one by one. Not literally, but nice idea. He liked a good horror film.

He picked up an A4 pad and began making notes: *New hit drama/entertainment show: GIVE EM WHAT THEY WANT.* (Another of Rex's handy hints for budding businessmen.) What do they want? What do they like? What they already have, apparently. So give them more of it. He wrote a list of his own favourite shows, wondering whether he could somehow copy them: *STAR TREK, COLUMBO, THE PRISONER,* and – he hesitated, but wrote *SUMMER HOLIDAY*, feeling slightly foolish for admitting how much he'd loved the film since he'd first seen it on telly, aged ten. Cliff, his mates, and a bunch of girls having a whale of a time together, driving a bus across Europe: his fantasy throughout adolescence, never realised. He stared at the four iconic titles and was instantly overwhelmed. Better try another approach. What would make this series a commercial winner? The current buzzwords were: *LOW COST, HIGH VOLUME, DIGITAL, INTERACTIVE*. He drew circles round the eight words and phrases, and a big question mark. How to fuse them all together into a show? He needed a writer, but he also wanted to own this project entirely (Rule Two). If he were the sole creator of the show he could claim copyright in perpetuity, and if it ran for years he'd become as rich as Croesus, whoever he was. He needed to bash something out before he let a writer near it. *SERIES PROPOSAL BY NIK MASON* looked good. He only needed a couple of paragraphs.

Next day Nik arrived late at the office, having stayed up till two a.m drafting and re-drafting his proposal, screwing up discarded pages and hurling them, Hollywood-style, at the waste paper bin. Finally he'd had a brilliant idea: that woman who'd written *The Soap Ashes* concept which he'd bought for peanuts. He'd forgotten her name, but she would be the ideal writer to knock this proposal into shape, and she wouldn't expect much money. His secretary was soon able to find her contact details and put in a call.

Jill was very surprised to hear from Magenta. She'd seen the success of *The Soap Ashes* with a sinking heart, kicking herself mercilessly. The one decent commercial idea she'd ever had, sold for a mess of pottage. She was so depressed about it that she'd never even mentioned to anyone else that it was her idea. She'd toyed with asking Magenta for more money occasionally – mostly when bills arrived – but knew she'd be wasting her breath, so she was intrigued when Nik Mason wanted to meet her urgently, and went straight out into the summer heat and caught a bus to Camden Town. The High Street was thronged with catatonic young tourists, and it took a while to weave her way up to the sixties office block where Magenta occupied the top two floors.

Nik was pleasant enough: a smart, attractive young man with the face of a twenty year-old and the confidence of a forty year-old, he was polite, professional and disarmingly modest.

"Ain't it funny how we've never met before?" he exclaimed, as if he'd been longing for it. She shrugged and sipped the coffee she'd been given, which was very nice.

"I normally work in drama."

"That's right, I remember. Well. I have a very small job I need doing – a day's work, no more – and I thought of you right away. I just need a new series proposal tarting up a bit."

"Okay... " Jill frowned, wondering whether to say something about how much money he'd already made out of her.

"I'll pay generously," he continued swiftly, "I'm not looking to exploit you. How does five hundred sound?"

She nodded, relieved. It sounded a lot for a day's work.

"Good!" Nik gave her his most appreciative smile. "Here it is." He pushed a sheet of writing towards her, and she studied it carefully. "Any questions?"

"'A London bus, full of sexy kids, travels through time'" she read thoughtfully.

"It needs to be unique. And very cheap. It needs enough legs to run for decades, and it'll lead the field in interactive digital technology."

"Oh!" Jill had no idea what he was talking about.

"You needn't worry about that. Just write me a page about the basic storyline, make it sound irresistible. And make sure there's a slot for a different guest star every week, like *Columbo*. But we won't do murder – just now and then, maybe – keep it wide open. Just fill this piece of crap out a bit, can you? Keep the bus central – a big red one. It's important for overseas sales."

Jill said she'd do her best.

"Can you do it today?"

"Today?!"

"I'm in a bit of a rush." The rush was to prevent Jill from

discussing the deal with her agent, who was liable to query it this time. Best to get it all sewn up as fast as possible. "You can work here."

Jill agreed, surprised by Nik's brisk enthusiasm, but she was keen to impress him. It was a new way of working, and rather refreshing. What a contrast to the tortoise-like BBC. Nik showed her to a well-furnished but baking hot office, and she sat down at the desk.

Nik returned to his own office to find an unexpected visitor had arrived. Since Nik had appointed line producers to look after Geordie Boy's show their relationship had cooled off to some extent. He hadn't seen Geordie for a few weeks, and wasn't entirely pleased to discover him helping himself to the silver box of cocaine he kept in his filing cabinet. He stopped in the doorway to watch Geordie surreptitiously, noting that his hair was limper than it used to be, his face more lined, and his tan less natural. Instead of looking slim and lively, he was thin and agitated.

"You ain't hooked on that stuff, are you?" he asked.

Geordie smiled humourlessly without turning round. "No man. Don't you worry. I'm not on it every day, just when I'm tired. Have you seen the schedule I'm on? I haven't had a holiday in two years." He sighed with satisfaction as the drug uplifted him. "That's better. I've brought you a new series idea. What d'you think?" He passed a folded bunch of pages to Nik, who sat behind his desk to read them. After a couple of minutes he looked up, waggled his head from side to side, and grimaced.

"I like it Geordie… "

"But. There's always a but." He couldn't resist adding a murmured: "But never the one you want."

"It's a bit bloody camp, ain't it?"

"So?"

"It's not really Magenta." He checked his watch. "I've got a meeting soon." Geordie stuck out his lower lip and pondered.

Then he got up and walked out.

"Geordie, come back mate. Let's talk about it. I wasn't giving you the brush-off, I just wanted to know the time!"

Nik followed Geordie out of the office but found he'd vanished. He checked with reception and then took the lift up to the roof garden, where he saw Geordie standing at the railings in what Nik thought of as his sulking spot. He didn't notice that Jill Watkins was sitting on the fire escape below with her notes, seeking relief from the hot office. He walked up to the railing and stood next to Geordie, watching the canal traffic creep through Camden Lock.

"You needn't have anything to do with it," said Geordie emotionally. "Can't it be *my* project? Haven't I earned that, after all these years?"

"It's a question of company profile."

"No it's not, it's a question of *your* profile, you bastard!"

"Geordie, Geordie, come on love." Nik put his arm round him.

"Get off me! Don't pretend you love me! I'm sick of it!"

Sitting beneath them on the black metal steps, Jill kept very still.

"You know how I feel about you," Nik tried to soothe him.

Geordie turned to face him. "Yes, I do. I've been kidding myself for a long time. But deep down, I know I've never been anything but a shag to you. It could have been so much better Nik, but you wouldn't let it. You think you're twice the man because you screw men as well as women. But you're just another pathetic closet case." Nik's face was tight with anger. "This is it, Nik. This is breaking point. If you don't back this show, I'm getting out of Magenta, and I'm taking it to a company that respects me." Geordie's hurt face struggled to maintain determination. Nik's was icy calm.

"Fine. If that's what you want, I can't stop you."

Geordie stared, tried to speak, then gave up and walked back to the lift, pulling a tissue from his pocket. Nik called, "Good luck," and turned back to the view.

Jill's eyes resembled golf balls as she sat without moving a muscle, wishing Nik would leave. Eventually she heard him turn and walk back indoors, so she scurried back inside her office and quickly spread her work out on the desk. Seconds later his head appeared round the door.

"How's it going?"

"Oh, fine, thanks!"

Nick gave her a thumbs-up and withdrew, to her relief.

A meeting of the board of directors had been called for that afternoon, and Nik needed to prepare himself. He went for a wash and brush-up in the company bathroom, put on his dark suit and re-gelled his hair. A light squirt of good aftershave, a check in the mirror, and he was ready to greet the board members as they arrived.

The boardroom wasn't grand, but it boasted the most beautiful polished rosewood table they could find, with a dozen matching chairs. As Rex said, the essential feature needed to be classy, the background didn't matter so much. That proved you had your priorities right, and you wouldn't waste shareholders' money. In this day and age a lovely table and views across London were worth more than wood-panelled walls and oil paintings.

The distinguished board members were largely drawn from the fields of banking, business, and the media. Rex, red in the face, was the last to arrive, bustling in whilst they were all perusing the papers assembled by Haris and the company secretary. He sat down and removed his jacket, muttering, "I hope nobody minds," revealing huge sweat marks on his shirt.

The main topic for the day was acquisition. It was understood that Magenta needed to keep growing continually, and they had been looking for other production companies to take over. Rex had used the subject to pass on his third rule of business to Nik: Apply Pressure. "That's how diamonds are made," he intoned, leaving Nik to work out the connection for himself.

Haris was proposing that they invest in a new production company called *Sisters in Synch*. They were small but had a number of commissions, and the word on the grapevine was that they had the most exciting talent and ideas around.

"Who are they?" frowned Rex, reading the notes Haris gave him. "Anthea who?"

"Onojaife. I don't know how it's pronounced."

"Are they all women?"

"I don't think so. Anyhow, it doesn't matter," sighed Haris. "Call it a niche market."

"Sisters in the sink! Best place for 'em!" Rex cackled.

Nik exchanged a look with Haris. This was not the first time Rex had attended a board meeting with half a bottle of whisky inside him. Haris tolerated him with a resignation that was beginning to wear thin.

"Do you oppose, Rex?" he asked tersely.

"Suppose I oppose," said Rex, chuckling at the rhyme. "Suppose I propose to oppose!" he beamed at the small assembly, especially at the distinguished representatives of legal and financial concerns whom they had gone to a great deal of trouble to recruit, when first assembling the board. They regarded Rex without amusement. He smiled pleasantly at them and continued firmly.

"Suppose my toes, tiddley pom,

Which nobody knows, tiddley pom,

Have lost their clothes, tiddley pom... how does that song go? Anyone remember it?"

"No mate, no-one's got the foggiest what you're on about," retorted Nik.

"It has a familiar ring," mused the chairman, Sir Geoffrey Spence. "I think you'll find it's from *Winnie the Pooh*."

"I do believe you're right, squire!" exclaimed Rex. "There!" he turned to Haris. "I told you this twat would be useful sooner or later." He burst into gales of laughter as a dozen mouths fell open, staring at him. Haris put his head in his hands and apologised profusely to the chairman, who brushed it off with polite irritation.

Nik took Rex by the elbow and said loudly, "I don't think that new medication the doctor prescribed agrees with you, Rex, why don't I take you home?" Rex was hauled to his feet protesting, until Nik hissed into his ear: "Shut up you stupid git before you halve our share value. Say sorry. Now."

"Actually I do feel a bit funny. I think perhaps I will go home. Please excuse me, gentlemen."

"Not at all. Go home and rest, Rex. Get a good night's sleep." Sir Geoffrey was nothing if not gracious.

Nik drove Rex to his home in Chelsea, which was a mess.

"Why don't you get someone to clean up?" he asked.

"I had a cleaner but she left. I dunno why. I don't care. No-one comes here but me."

Nik parked Rex on a big sofa and stuck the television remote in his hand, then made a cup of tea and put it down next to him.

"Look here, Rex," he said sternly, standing above him with folded arms. "You're losing your grip, mate. You need to pull yourself together. What was it you used to say about dead wood?"

Rex tried to focus his befuddled eyes on Nik, who seemed to sway like a genie. "What?"

"Cut it out. That's what you said. To keep a company healthy you got to prune out the dead wood. Make room for new shoots. Think about it." He leaned down to make sure his point went home. "You, Rex, are becoming a real liability." He patted Rex's cheek gently, then turned and let himself out.

The next day Rex stayed off sick, and the next day, and the one after. Nik called Sir Geoffrey to warn him that it might be necessary to re-structure the company and give Rex time off, or even offer him a retirement package. He hinted that he personally would be happy to take on a more substantial role in the company, but he wouldn't dream of acting against the interests of the man who had given him a start and had taught him all he knew. Sir Geoffrey said to leave it with him.

*

"'Eight young people, including a four-piece rock band and some close friends, decide to spend the summer driving round Europe in a London bus, performing on beaches and in town squares. Four boys, four girls, all attractive but mixed in personality, talents, and racial background. In the course of the series they will fall in and out of love, write songs, have adventures, and grow in life experience and maturity.

"The summer looks bright, but it takes an unexpected turn when the bus drives through a worm-hole in the space/time continuum whilst travelling through a rocky pass in northern Spain. They emerge to find themselves in a small but beautiful fertile valley, with a river running through it.

"At first they don't realise they've left Spain, and they're delighted with the place; however, they need an audience. They explore the area and find to their amazement that they're in a gigantic biome, from which there's no escape.'" Chris looked up, "A biome – that's one of these self-contained eco-systems, is it?"

"That's it exactly," replied Nik. Chris continued reading.

"'They are able to survive quite easily as everything they need is available, but they need to find out where they are, and how to get home. This mystery and motivation underlies the entire series. Once they discover they're in a biome they realise it could be anywhere in the universe, and it must have been created by someone – or something – for a purpose.

"It's not long until others find themselves in the biome via the same route. Later, other worm-holes link the biome to other parts of the universe and the possibilities are endless. Romance, humour, warmth, music, fun, fear and conflict: all human life is here, and quite a lot of alien life, too.'"

Chris paused and nodded, then flicked through the following pages which included costings.

"Very impressive price, Nik. A drama series for the twenty-first century, for sure." Nik thought so too. "But I couldn't possibly commit this far ahead."

"If we start by making thirteen eps, the price triples."

"I realise that, but still… "

"This show has everything, Chris. You can see that, I can tell. It'll knock the soaps into oblivion. It's sci-fi, drama, *and* entertainment – all wrapped up in one fabulous show, with great music. It'll have a big name guest star every week – we can put anyone in, sports stars, celebrities – not just actors. And we'll find eight new young faces and turn them into big stars."

"Like *Friends*."

"*Friends* in space! But much better stories, Chris. This ain't a little sitcom, it's a major drama series. Ambitious, I grant you, the story potential's infinite. I'm going to be completely honest with you. I know I can sell this show, and it's going to be massive. But I'd like you to have it. I've enjoyed making *The Soap Ashes* for you, I really have, and I want you to have this one. BBC1's the place it should be. But I do mean to keep the rights, you know that's non-negotiable where Magenta's concerned. I'm giving you first refusal. You've been very happy with *The Soap Ashes*, and I'll guarantee you'll be even more pleased with *Bus Stops Here*. That's the working title, by the way – we'll find something more charismatic."

Chris nodded. There was no denying that *The Soap Ashes* had been very good for BBC1, and he was very tempted to snap this project up. It smelled of success. Never a man to throw caution to the wind, however, he reminded himself that Nik had no experience of drama whatsoever, and the show could only be made if he committed to a staggering 26 hours from the outset, which was unheard of outside the USA. It would soak up a large proportion of his drama slots, and other shows would have to make way for it. On the other hand, if he let this go, he might lose the precious ratings lead that BBC1 was fighting to maintain against its old rivals ITV, and he was all too conscious of ever-increasing competition building up from Channels 4, 5, and the proliferating cable channels. Supposing he declined this show, and one of them picked it up and scheduled it against *EastEnders*? It could ruin him.

The price for this series was cheaper per hour of drama than any other, if he accepted the volume. Magenta really knew how to cut corners. Their entertainment shows were good quality for popular, accessible entertainment, but could they deliver drama which would match BBC standards?

"Who produces, Nik?"

Nik picked up this signal that Chris had identified a significant weakness, and leapt to strengthen it. "Not me, that's for sure – I'll be an exec producer but this needs a drama pro."

"An in-house team. A co-production."

Nik wasn't giving half his show away that easily. "Very happy for you to name the producer, Chris, you have the best in the world here, and I'm happy to give you the last word on the most vital member of the team." Chris' eyes brightened, surprised to hear Nik backing off. He was the toughest negotiator Chris dealt with. "But I need them on *my* team, they'll have to resign from the BBC and become a freelance employee of Magenta. Anything else just gets too complicated, you know what I mean."

Chris was disconcerted by this proviso, but it sounded logical. It would give him the best of both worlds, in a way. He nodded thoughtfully. Nik saw that he was going to capitulate, and he chose to show respect for Chris' higher status.

"Would you like me to commission some scripts? I realise it's a big ask, expecting you to make a decision on the strength of an idea and a successful working relationship – "

"No no, I can see the potential. And I know how fast you work at Magenta. Enviably fast!" He shared a wry smile, took a deep breath, and put both hands flat on his desk as he looked Nik in the eye.

"I'm in," he said, simply.

Nik restrained his smile and offered his hand: "You've made the right decision, Chris. This show will be the making of us both. It's going to be the biggest ratings winner since *Morecambe and Wise*."

They shook hands warmly, if a little nervously, and Nik took his leave. Chris wandered to his window overlooking the car park and Wood Lane. His heart was beating rather fast and he questioned his decision. Should he have consulted his staff? That would have entailed weeks of meetings and arguments, ultimately a waste of time. Chris' intuition was clear, the future of television lay with Nik, and those like him. The industry was changing radically, with de-regulation, globalisation, and the new digital media. Sink or swim. Ride the waves or drown beneath them. It was up to Chris to ensure the BBC stayed in the lead, and he sensed that Nik was not just swimming with the current but out in front. 'Keep your friends close, and your enemies closer' he reminded himself, as he watched a tiny, ant-like Nik emerge into the car park and get into a cab. He decided to trust Nik's judgement where drama was concerned: he reckoned it was a risk worth taking.

Chapter Fourteen

Looking back from the twenty-first century I'm reminded of *Chariots of Fire*. We were like those muscular young men in their prime pounding along the beach in slow motion, full of innocent youthful ambition, forging through the wind and spray. It didn't feel like a rat race at the time; rather a heroic pitting ourselves against one another to achieve our utmost. We had energy and resolve to spare, and we weren't distracted by children and financial pressures like we are today. Now that young graduates have to start their working lives up to their eyes in debt they miss out on that glorious decade or so of working for love, not money. We've robbed them. As a parent, the one thing you want above all is to give your children a better life than you had yourself – or at least a life that isn't any worse.

Jonathan and I were both struggling to make the pace as we developed our scripts, desperate to win our heat and move up to the next stage. I had successfully avoided him since the writers' party, burying my embarrassment and regret at having effectively removed myself from his project. I was completely focussed on *Lover Boy* and determined to make my mark with it. I had total faith that it was going to be brilliant, as if letting doubt creep in would undermine it. I'd stayed in close contact with Jill, and we'd become good friends, I admired her life as a single parent and a writer. She had a successful career and Sam seemed a nice boy, if rather reserved – he didn't chat when I was around, at any rate. From where I was standing Jill seemed to have the work-life balance sorted pretty well. In retrospect I realise that she must have been fairly reliant on her ex-husband financially, which must have been more of a strain than she let on.

At this point it was Nik Mason who was pulling ahead of the bunch, he was almost level with Chris in the metaphorical mile. *Bus Stops Here* promised a sea-change in the early evening schedules and this affected the Drama Department radically as we were pushed aside. With a plummeting demand for in-house drama it became impossible to keep all the staff, and a quiet purge began to take place. Offices were suddenly empty, as if thieves had broken in during the night and stripped out their inhabitants as well as their contents.

Jill was blissfully unaware of this as she finished the first draft of *Lover Boy*. Whenever she was in the flow of writing she lost all sense of herself as an individual and became caught up in a kind of bliss, as if dreaming but aware and in control, detached from daily life, but fully alive. She found it immensely fulfilling.

Finishing the last page, she leaned back and sighed with satisfaction. She clicked save and print, and went in the kitchen for her reward: a piece of chocolate cake and a cup of coffee. It was a great feeling, finishing a script, although it usually only lasted a few hours before the doubts and anxieties set in. Enjoy it while you can, she thought.

A key turned in the front door, and Sam slouched in with his father, who was carrying Sam's overnight bag.

"Hello darling," welcomed Jill. "What great timing. I've just finished. Had a good time?"

"Yeah," said Sam.

"Give us a kiss, then."

Sam gave her a peck on the cheek with poor grace. Jill tutted. "Coffee, Neil?"

"Yes, why not."

Jill poured another cup and they sat down at the kitchen table, while Sam went and put the television on. Jill cut two slices out of the cake.

"How's the selection procedure going?" she asked.

"The first lot turned me down. The second – well they did too, but it was a close contest. I'm up for another one next week though, which is a much better bet."

"Where is it?"

"Birmingham."

"Not too far away."

"No. I really want to get this one. It has a Conservative majority of two thousand at the moment. I really think I could win it."

"Good luck, then."

"Thanks."

"I suppose it'll mean a pay rise?"

"Yep. I suppose you'll be putting in for increased child expenses."

"You suppose right."

"Mind you, you can't be short if you can afford to buy Sam Nike Airs."

"You what? I thought you bought them."

"He told me it was you! So where did he get them?"

"Don't ask me." Jill's appetite for chocolate cake receded. She sighed heavily. "Has he talked to you about these new friends at all?"

Neil shook his head guiltily. "I didn't want to push it, Jill. Sorry."

"Let's ask him now, then."

"Do we have to?"

Jill shouted for Sam to come in, and he shouted back inaudibly.

"Leave it for now, Jill, it's late. I'll definitely talk to him next time."

"Alright then. I'm pretty knackered myself."

*

When I read Jill's first draft of *Lover Boy* I was very pleased with it. It needed some work, but essentially the characters and dialogue sprang off the page and were immensely likeable and believable. I called her to say so, and arranged for her to come in and discuss it with me and Basil. I then settled down to work through it carefully, identifying where there was room for improvement and possible solutions. I had a suspicion that she might be too closely involved, there was a lack of suspense because Sharon and Luke were so nice.

Two days later I went to Basil's office for our pre-meeting, to go over our notes before Jill arrived. I went along the corridor humming, feeling bright and cheerful, looking forward to hearing Basil's thoughts which were bound to be valuable, and hoping he'd think my own points were astute. All being well, we were on course to get Episode Two commissioned.

Basil's PA was on the phone arguing with someone about the mail. Since the service had recently been privatised, nearly all the long-standing posties who worked out of the post room in the bowels of Television Centre had been replaced. Those discreet men and women knew everybody in the building, and would re-direct mail promptly to anyone who moved office. As this happened to most of us several times a year, according to the demands of production, they were invaluable. The management flatly refused to recognise this and sold off the franchise to a private company which brought in new, uncommitted workers on much-reduced wages. Now the mail was slow and unreliable, and something important of Basil's had disappeared completely. His PA didn't seem to be getting anywhere with her enquiries. I went through to Basil's office and found him looking unusually despondent.

"Sit down Rhiannon," he said, like a doctor with serious news to impart. I wondered what had been lost.

"I'm afraid it's bad news," he said simply. "*Lover Boy* is no more. It's been dropped."

For a moment I couldn't take it in. I hadn't realised its existence was under threat at that particular time. "But they haven't seen the script yet!"

"No, they don't intend to. Chris told the editorial board yesterday that he's chosen his serials for next year and he sees no point in continuing development on anything else. He sees that as a waste of money."

"So that's it? Just like that?" I couldn't believe it.

"I'm sorry, there's nothing I can do."

I just gawped at him like an idiot. He looked sympathetic and strained. I realised he probably had much bigger problems on his plate and I ought to get out of his hair, so I got a grip on myself.

"Okay, I understand. That's life. What about Jill? She'll be here in half an hour. Do you still want to meet?"

"There's no need. You may as well break the news yourself."

"No problem. Thanks Basil, for everything." I smiled ruefully and left in what I hoped was a professional manner. In the corridor I passed Jonathan on his way in. We muttered hello to each other, then I slunk off to my office and closed the door behind me, grateful I didn't have to share it as I sank to the carpet and had a little weep. Then I kicked myself for having put all my eggs into this one basket, which had just been flattened by a tank.

I went to Centre House Reception to meet Jill and take her to the canteen for coffee. Sitting on the foam-upholstered bench wondering how to break it to her I was struck by her pink-faced glow of happiness as she pushed open the glass door. I put on a neutral smile and greeted her with our customary double kiss, then we went out through the car park which was clogged with people standing around.

"Is there a fire drill?" asked Jill.

"No, they've banned smoking indoors."

She chuckled and noticed that each person nursed a fag end,

sucking on it with furtiveness, embarrassment or defensive boldness.

In the canteen I parked Jill at a corner table and went to fetch some coffees, then sat down and went through the usual pleasantries before breaking the real subject as gently as I could.

"The fact is," I explained. "There's no room for it now. The controller's decided he doesn't want it after all. The slot's been filled."

Jill looked horrified and bewildered. "But I've got a contract! Don't they like the script? Can't I rewrite it?"

"No-one else has read it, Jill. It's really good, so don't imagine it's got anything to do with the quality of your work, it hasn't. Basil will sign the acceptance so you'll get all your money on Episode One, but there's no point doing any further work on it. I'm so sorry."

Jill stared at her coffee and shook her head. "I can't believe it. Just like that!"

"Yeah."

"Did you put up a fight?"

I wasn't expecting that, and was taken aback. "I didn't get the opportunity." She didn't look convinced. "They made the decision and passed it down the line. That's how it works these days."

Jill frowned, trying to make sense of it. "But what about these big meetings, and lobbying, and development for new slots? Didn't you say that's the new way? I thought we were on track..."

"I know. So did I. Believe me, I'm more upset than you are." Jill's eyebrows flickered up and down again as she failed to meet my eyes, and I knew she thought I was pretending. It was horrible. I was just being professional, after all, I was a BBC employee, not a freelance, and as such I couldn't slag off the management, especially to an outsider on the premises. She sighed heavily and leaned back.

"The worst of it is I turned down a *Casualty* a few weeks ago, so now I'm out of work altogether."

"Maybe you can take *Lover Boy* to ITV? Talk to your agent about it." I said this altruistically, it would be a big wrench to give it up, but Jill took my words differently and her guard went up again.

"Is that why it was rejected? Too downmarket? Too sensational?" She looked at me sharply.

"No I told you, no-one read it."

"Perhaps they didn't need to."

I began to feel Jill was suggesting that I'd scuppered the project myself, and I resented it. I considered reminding her that it was my idea in the first place, and me that got her the commission, but I couldn't, so I said nothing. Jill probably took this the wrong way too, since she stood up to leave. She shook my hand – a bad sign – and said, "Oh well, thanks anyway. See you around." She left briskly, while I sat there like a lemon.

I soon began to feel more annoyed than sad. She hadn't given a moment's thought to my side of it, or my feelings. Writers! They take people like me for granted. They think we're part of the establishment, with big salaries, pensions, psychic stability. They're egotists. Not all, obviously, but nearly all. Self-oriented. Perhaps they have to be, or they couldn't do what they do. They're deeply insecure and often neurotic, longing to be adored, and terrified of the limelight. They look for conspiracy and read between the lines, even when the truth is plain and simple. There wasn't much I could do, I wasn't responsible for Jill's feelings, and I needed to think about my own employment prospects. It was a real shame, but I had a feeling I would never be close to Jill again – and as of today, I didn't really mind.

Sam was already in by the time Jill returned, doing homework in his room. She put her head round his door.

"Hi Sam. You okay?"

"Yeah." He didn't turn around. Feeling the need for human contact she approached him at his desk and put her hands on his shoulders, reading his book.

"Is that maths?"

"Yeah."

"Doesn't look anything like the maths I used to do. It's lucky you don't need me to help you."

Sam sighed. He seemed tense. Suddenly she realised why. She gasped.

"You've had your ear pierced!" A tiny gold stud sat in his right ear lobe.

"How could you do it Luke?"

Sam spun round. "Luke?! Who's *Luke?*" he glowered at her accusingly. She hesitated, caught between anger and disappointment in Sam, and remorse for her mistake. She felt weak. She wasn't up to a confrontation right now. She sat down on the bed.

"Sorry – he's a boy I've been writing about."

"Is he me?"

"No. He's a bit like you in some ways – but he's older, wears a ponytail. He wants to be a potter." She smiled faintly.

"You love him more than you love me."

"Don't be silly, how could I? He isn't even real!"

"You do, because you think he's perfect. I can see you do. And I'm not."

Sam got up and left the room. Jill remained on his bed, stunned. She heard him open the front door.

"I'm going out. I'll be back later."

The door slammed.

Jill made herself a cup of tea and took a chair out onto the balcony. She sat watching the traffic and the kids hanging out on street corners, wondering if Sam was one of them. She mentally listed her failures: marriage, work, motherhood – a disaster in every camp. Where had it all gone wrong? Maybe Sam had a point. Did she prefer Luke to him, in her heart of hearts? Had she used him as a substitute for her imperfect son? She went back in, lay down on the sofa and cried herself to sleep.

"Here you are, mum."

Jill roused herself painfully. "What?"

"I made you a sandwich."

She rubbed her eyes and saw a tray bearing a cheese sandwich garnished with a tomato cut in half, a glass of orange juice, and a cup of tea. Sam put it down on the coffee table.

"Sorry mum, I knew you'd be cross. I was waiting for it. That's why I flew off the handle."

Jill looked up at her son and saw he had grown up behind her back. She felt a wave of love rush through her and hugged him.

"Alright, alright," he said, pulling back.

"I'm sorry darling," she said, trying not to cry. "I love you so much. But you're right. I've been too wrapped up in work lately."

"It's alright."

"Not any more, though. The show's cancelled, I'm out of work!"

Sam looked sympathetic. "I'm really sorry."

"Never mind. Something'll turn up, I expect."

"So what do you think?" Sam modelled his earring for her.

"I suppose it looks quite nice, in a way," she said reluctantly.

"I thought I'd get it done for Dad's wedding."

The wedding was taking place on the following Saturday. Sam would be in the photos wearing an earring. Her mother would never get over it.

"Does he know?"

"Not yet."

Jill decided to leave Neil to sort that one out.

Carmen was very sympathetic when Jill called to tell her the news about *Lover Boy*. She was feeling good, since her own project was still very much in development. Anthea had suddenly left the BBC, taking Carmen's project with her, and was now heading a new independent production company called Sisters in Synch. They had funds to see the script right through, and the slot was still open at the BBC provided the controller didn't change his mind, which was always a possibility, but they were fast-tracking it since it was a topical subject. If they turned it down after all there was an excellent chance that Channel Four would pick it up; there was even a possibility of turning it into a feature film. Jill was miserably delighted for her.

"You need to get pissed." Carmen proposed. "JoJo's on at the King's Head tonight. Why don't we go?"

Jill quite liked that idea. She had grown to appreciate JoJo in the years since their first bizarre encounter in Edinburgh, even though she sometimes found her humour a little hard to take. Stand-up comedy would take her out of herself a bit without requiring her to talk a lot. She agreed to meet Carmen there and rang Ivy, who promised to come by after bingo and keep Sam company, then she spent an hour or so playing a Jurassic Park computer game with Sam, wishing she was better at it and could give him decent opposition. She strongly suspected he was being kind to her and not playing his best. Who's the kid in this relationship now? she thought to herself.

The King's Head was busy and full of smoke. Jill didn't often go as the comedy was mainly for twenty and thirty-somethings without children and she felt superannuated when the stand-ups' material consisted entirely of jokes about school, drug-taking, and sexual insecurities. She rather wished there were comedy clubs for the over forties, with comfy seats, nice food, and jokes about bringing up kids and mid-life crises.

JoJo was always entertaining. She was petite and pretty, and had a slightly different angle in that she was a lesbian. She had managed to develop a persona which appealed to everyone. Her catchphrase was 'Oh, my aching fanny!' which made some of the audience uncomfortable at first, but by the end of her set they would be joining in.

She sat down with Carmen and Jill afterwards, lining up a

couple of pints and drinking them faster than Jill would have thought possible.

"Thirsty work," she explained. "Anyhow, a comedian who wants to get ahead has to have an alcohol problem or no-one takes them seriously."

Jill related her bad news again, and JoJo commiserated.

"They're all bastards," she declared. "Sonia Longbow called me the other day. You remember I applied for that new writing initiative the BBC were setting up last year? I met her and did loads of work on a treatment, which I never got a penny for. Then there was silence for months – I'd almost given up on it. Well Twinkletits casually rings up and says I was on the short-list and would have won a commission, but they've pulled the plug on the scheme and it's all off."

"No!" exclaimed Carmen and Jill. "Just like that?"

"Just like that. All that effort. I felt like suing them for wasting my valuable time. Then I thought, get your revenge by telling jokes against them which are so funny they'll just curl up and die of humiliation!"

Jill liked that idea. "I wish you'd done some tonight."

"So do I. Only problem is, I can't think of any."

"Actually I heard Sonia having a go at Chris Briggs about it at the writers' party. At least she tried her best. I'm not sure Rhiannon did."

"Who cares? What's so special about Chris Briggs anyway?" She grinned. "If I never achieve anything else in my life, at least I'll always have the satisfaction of knowing that I once got him arrested! He's hardly likely to put work my way after that, is he? I don't need the BBC, they can take a running jump. In any case, Channel Four's my natural habitat. I'll just have to stay in the ghetto."

By eleven thirty Jill felt lot happier. It made all the difference to know she was part of a fellowship. She hugged her friends goodbye, and staggered up the hill to her flat. Ivy had dropped off with the television on but Jill pretended not to notice and closed the front door a second time, more loudly, allowing her to wake with dignity intact.

"Got your outfit for Saturday, Ivy?"

"Thought I'd wear the same dress I wore when he married you."

"He wouldn't even notice."

"He will when he sees the photos!" They both laughed.

"There's only a little do, you know. Very informal."

"You know why, don't you?" asked Ivy rhetorically. "'Cos it's only for the bleeding Labour party. And he can't invite all of that lot because he wants to give the impression he's been married for years."

"Well he has lived with Sandra for seven years."

"I've a good mind not to go."

"That would be a real shame."

"I know," Ivy sighed. "'Course I'll go. I just can't stand this New Labour type he's turning into. New Labour, New Tory if you ask me. Mark my words, see what he serves up at the reception. It won't be beer and pickled eggs down the pub this time, you know – it'll be champagne and sushi whatsits in some poncy wine bar."

Jill laughed, and as it turned out, Ivy was absolutely right.

*

A fortnight later, Jill was sitting at her computer thinking up possible storylines for *The Bill*, which her agent was trying to get her an interview for, when the phone rang. It was Sally Farquar-Binns.

"Jill! Do you remember me? We met at the writers' party, and you rescued me from that ghastly man."

"Billy Trowell?" Jill smiled at Sally's heartfelt description.

"Who else!"

"He's alright when he's sober."

"I'll take your word for it. Listen, I'm frightfully sorry to hear your project was put in turnaround."

"Thanks. So was I."

"I was wondering – are you doing anything else with it?"

"No, no I'm not." Jill had been trying not to think about it, it was too painful.

"Only I've got an idea. Would you like to have lunch one day and I'll tell you about it?"

Jill thought she had nothing to lose. They arranged to meet the next day.

Sally took her to Albertine's, a wine bar in Shepherd's Bush whose clientele was almost entirely BBC drama people, and apologised for not being able to pay for Jill's meal.

"We can't lunch writers unless they're commissioned," she explained, "and even then we have to get permission from Morag beforehand. *So* embarrassing."

Jill felt slightly annoyed as she was broke, and chose the fixed menu, hoping Sally wouldn't pick something pricey and then suggest splitting the bill equally. Fortunately Sally followed her example.

They tried to relax at the tiny cast iron table. Jill was agog to hear what Sally had in mind for her script, but Sally made small talk until they had eaten their starters.

"Now then, this is all very nice but we're here to talk business!"

"Absolutely," agreed Jill.

"You'll probably think this is a terrible idea and run screaming into the street," she hesitated while Jill murmured vaguely. "But there are a couple of possibilities."

"I thought the slot had gone?"

"Yes, *that* slot has," said Sally. "But I thought it just might work in a different slot. It would mean a few changes. "There's a really big push to establish a new precinct drama, for a start."

"Does that mean set in a shopping centre?"

"No, it's like *Casualty*, basically. The precinct is where it all happens."

Jill was at a loss to see how *Lover Boy* could become a returning series.

"Well the precinct would be the school, obviously, and the central story would have to be different – the love story could be a long-runner through the whole thing."

Jill thought about it. "I'm not sure Epping's interesting enough," she said at last. Sally agreed instantly.

"Oh no, it couldn't be set in Epping. It would have to be an inner city school, lots of problems. Gangs, immigrants, that kind of thing."

Jill wrestled with the concept. "To be honest Sally, it's taking me a long way away from what I originally wanted to do with it. If I were writing a new series I'd want to start from scratch."

"Fair enough. I thought you might say that. Okay." Sally tossed her blonde hair and tucked it behind her ear. "I think you'll like this idea better. They want ninety minute films, especially thrillers. That's rather exciting, isn't it?"

Jill was stumped. "Is it?"

"I'm sure you could get it down to ninety minutes."

"Maybe, but it's not a thriller by any stretch of the imagination."

"I bet it *could* be though, couldn't it? All it needs is a hook and an anti-hero, you know, a bit of a chase and a cliff-hanger ending."

Jill's shell-shocked mind pictured Luke being chased over a cliff by Captain Hook, and hanging by his fingernails. "I'm not sure."

"You could really push it dramatically, you could have, say, steamy sex in the staff room!" Sally giggled. Jill stared.

"It's a lot to take on board, I know," said Sally as their main courses arrived. "Why don't you think about it?"

"Okay," said Jill cautiously.

"If you have any brainwaves you could fax me."

"Yes," said Jill faintly, and turned her attention to her pissal-adiere.

They munched in silence for a minute, gazing vacantly at the mirrored partitions.

"The other angle," continued Sally. "Is that it would be absolutely perfect if you could write a role for one of the stars we'd like to find vehicles for. That would *really* make it attractive to the controller."

Jill braced herself. "Anyone in particular?"

"David Jason, of course, for one."

Jill scanned her cast and arrived at Ian Woodward. "He could play Luke's father," she suggested.

"Oh no, he'd have to have a bigger part than that."

"He's a bit old for Sharon's husband," said Jill doubtfully.

"What about the Headmistress? She could be a man. You could develop the part, maybe, make it more central."

Jill tried to make the idea work for her. "Any other actors?"

"Apparently Julie Goodyear's leaving *Coronation St* soon. It would be a bit of a coup to get her."

Jill pictured Bet Lynch and shook her head. "Nothing against her, she's a great actress, but I really couldn't see her – not even as Luke's mum."

"Well I think you'll love this idea. One of Take That to play Luke!"

"Mmm. Do they act?"

"Oh one or two of them are bound to."

As Jill didn't know much about Take That she felt obliged to accept the proposal.

"Great," said Sally, scraping her plate clean. "I knew we'd come up with something! I have to get back to the office now, got a two o'clock. Can you send me something by next Wednesday?"

Taken aback, Jill said, "I'll try," and Sally put a ten pound note on the table.

"Do you mind awfully taking care of the bill? I'm *terribly* sorry to rush off like this, I just noticed the time. It was *really* nice meeting you." She shook Jill's hand enthusiastically, and hurried out.

Jill ordered a coffee and contemplated the meeting. Her immediate reaction was to forget it as soon as possible, but as it began to sink in ideas occurred to her, and she thought it might be possible to come up with something she could get interested in which would also suit Sally.

The bill arrived with her coffee. With service it came to thirty seven pounds. Jill asked the waiter for a cork so she could take the remaining half bottle of wine home.

Chapter Fifteen

Losing *Lover Boy* was a low point for me. I crashed emotionally, and realised I needed to re-think my attitude. It's not enough to be tenacious and try try try again: you could scrape away at a rock face with a pick axe until you dropped dead, but if you stood back and thought about it you might find a way round the mountain that takes a fraction of the time and effort. There's nothing immoral about abandoning the hard route for an easier one and sometimes it's just common sense. I'd been fixed on working my way up the ladder on a strictly democratic, meritocratic basis. Perhaps it was the moral influence of my chapel-going ancestors in my DNA. I don't know why else I made life so hard for myself.

I was feeling very lonely. I'd thought I was close to Jill, and it turned out I wasn't. It was naïve of me. After all she was at least ten years older, with a different background and life circumstances. From her point of view I was just another BBC insider with the power to give her work. Supposedly. I longed for the team fellowship I'd known at *Grange Hill*. Being stuck in development really was a kind of hell; you were in a constant state of waiting, compounded by being in competition with all your colleagues, like a flock of pigeons ready to descend on the same soggy biscuit. I really missed Maggie, who was still in Bristol. She was a colleague I felt no rivalry with. She was too straight to bother dissembling. Her Yorkshire bluntness, which got her into trouble in the mannered society of the south east, was refreshingly easy to deal with if you knew where she was coming from, and I did: Cardiff and Huddersfield were far more like each other than London. I called her one evening for a chat, and she sympathised with my situation and pointed out that I needed to ally myself differently.

"Why don't you make it up with Jonathan?" she asked. "He's on your level."

"Hardly!"

"I think you've got a lot in common."

"You're joking! He's the enemy!" I retorted.

"You have similar tastes in drama. Both close to Basil. He wouldn't have put you with Jonathan if he thought you'd hate each other."

I hadn't seen it like that. Maggie's words stayed with me, though I resisted taking them on board for a while yet. My armour had cracked, though. I considered going to see Jonathan to apologise. Would that be too humiliating? Under the circumstances I didn't know how to offer my services without looking ridiculous. I played out a variety of conversations in my head, none of which felt comfortable, so in the absence of a plan I did nothing about it and occupied myself with routine department tasks.

A few weeks later there was a drama producers' meeting to discuss the all-important matter of contracts. The little conference room at the top of Centre House was packed to its polystyrene ceiling tiles.

Peter Maxwell was outlining the new employment policy: "Less is more. That's the idea." Staff contracts were to be discontinued in future. Instead, they would be offered fixed-term freelance contracts for specific productions as and when their shows went into production, or fixed fees for developing approved projects. For the first time ever, the producers were unanimous in their response. They were utterly appalled. Peter scratched his bald patch and sipped a glass of water as the news sank in. Departmental manager Morag, sitting beside him, beadily eyed the gathering with pursed lips, waiting for the complaints to rain upon them.

"What happens to those of us who are currently on staff contracts?" enquired veteran producer Donald Mountjoy politely. Peter looked to Morag to take over.

"As a matter of fact there aren't all that many, and you will be spoken to individually by Personnel. There will be retirement and redundancy packages available." A dozen or more older producers stiffened. No-one had ever been asked to retire before. They had always been able to carry on until over-whelmed by ill health or the lure of their rose gardens. "Actually," continued Morag, "that process has been underway for some time."

Donald nodded slowly. He had of course noticed that quite a few producers had moved on lately, but he had put it down to their dislike of the new regime at the BBC. Stalwart producers of the old school, whom he would never have expected to quit, had jumped ship to ITV and various inde-pendent production companies. Evidently they had decided to leap before they were pushed. Perhaps he would have to think about doing the same.

Stewart Walker lit a cigarette. No-one felt inclined to remind him of the no smoking rule, but a woman by the window opened it ostentatiously. He inhaled, exhaled, and frowned.

"Are we to know what this fee for developing 'approved proj-ects' is?"

Morag sighed. "It will be in the region of three thousand pounds."

"In total?"

"Yes."

"Regardless of how many months – or years – it takes?"

"Yes."

"Regardless of how long the controller cares to sit on the project, failing to make a decision? Regardless of how many times he changes his mind about the format, the script, and the writer?"

"Yes."

"Well that's marvellous," said Stewart cheerfully. "Isn't that good news, everyone?" He looked around the room. "Thanks, Peter and Morag, for negotiating us such a terrifically good deal." He scowled at them in disgust.

Peter had feared this. "Come on Stewart, don't blame us. You know perfectly well there's absolutely nothing we can do about it."

Stewart's lip curled, but he said nothing. He got up and stalked out of the room.

Peter blinked hopelessly. "It goes without saying that I'm terribly, terribly sorry to see this happening. *Of course* I argued against it."

"We realise that, Peter," said Gillian Makin, a middle aged woman from Pebble Mill. "We know you've done your best to stop the department falling apart."

"It isn't falling apart," replied Peter. "It's being streamlined. We're simply too expensive, and the number of slots is being reduced. We have to be more efficient, more competitive."

"Is there anything else we should know?" asked Basil shrewdly. "Will we be supplying our own stationery, I wonder?"

Peter flinched and exchanged a worried look with Morag. "I doubt if it will come to that, Basil, but there will be further economies in the office. I can't say more than that at the moment. It's under discussion."

A ripple of disbelief spread through the room.

"More staff cutbacks?" suggested Sonia Longbow.

"It's a possibility, we hope not."

Sally Farquar-Binns decided to look on the bright side. "Well I think we should be positive. We learned to live with Producer Choice and it turned out to be quite useful in many ways – "

"Extremely useful," cut in Jeremy Simon, a senior producer. "So useful we no longer have a design department, a props department, a costume department – need I go on?"

"But we can still use most of the people who used to work there, and at a much cheaper rate!" exclaimed Sally. Jeremy shook his head. There were tuts and sighs, but no-one could be bothered to argue with Sally over the value of forty years' accumulated skill and experience, which the in-house resource departments represented. Most of them ignored her. She was something of an interloper in any case, since she was a 'development producer' and had no project commissioned yet.

A despondent silence fell on the room, and Peter drew the meeting to a close. "I'm afraid we must knuckle down and make the best of it," he said, trying to inject a tone of encouragement into his voice. "Market forces have to be reckoned with nowadays. We're too big, too unwieldy. To be absolutely honest I could fill the schedule requirements on my own with just a handful of producers. We have to think about making less drama but making it count more. We no longer have the right to fail, so we can't take so many risks. We don't have a monopoly, we have a lot of lean, hungry competitors, and the controllers aren't interested in favouring us. But we *do* have a huge amount of talent, experience, and guts, between us. Let's pull together and show them we can still make the best programmes! Thank you very much, everybody."

Peter left briskly, followed by Morag, glad to escape this roomful of angry, depressed talent.

It was Jonathan's first producers' meeting, and ironically enough he'd looked forward to it, like a sixth-former allowed the privilege of entering the staff room. Now he felt as if he'd won his pilot's wings on the day the RAF was disbanded. Something akin to war survivor's guilt hung over him: his serial *The Medical Miracle* had been accepted for BBC2, and was about to go into pre-production. Thrilled as he was by this, it was dreadful to see his elders and betters brought low around him, particularly Basil of course. He had been Basil's script editor for four years, and had come to regard him as a father-substitute.

Jon's early career hadn't been *entirely* easy. After leaving Cambridge University he had put on a few plays and then become an assistant literary manager at the National Theatre, developing the work of the most talented new writers he could find. Some of them he had recommended to producers at the BBC, making contacts on his own behalf at the same time, and in this way he had got to know Basil, who invited him to come and be his script editor. Working with him had sanded off the veneer of superiority which he had grown up with and rein- forced during his tenure of a post which was relatively powerful in the small world of intellectual theatre. Basil never behaved as if he was better than anyone else. He had proved to Jonathan that great writers didn't necessarily have O-levels, never mind first class degrees from Cambridge.

Getting Jim Johnson's scripts green-lit meant that Jonathan's first show would receive a lot of attention. It was a controversial issue and he hoped it hit the zeitgeist. It was a great way to start his producing career, even though he had been told he must do it on his current salary. That had been a blow, but Morag had made it clear that he was fortunate to get the opportunity to produce at all. He had agreed without putting up much of a fight, and Selina hadn't been at all impressed.

They'd been going out for three years now, and were getting engaged soon. Her family was wealthy and well-connected and they liked him so he didn't mind going along with whatever Selina said was necessary. There was to be a grand engagement party at their country mansion in the new year. He would need to buy a proper diamond ring. He'd tried to drop hints that he wouldn't be able to afford a big one, and Selina always laughed. He wasn't sure whether she minded or not – or whether she thought he was joking. His own parents had a lovely house but they weren't as well-off as they appeared. He didn't think Selina had any idea about money really, for all her educated social skills. He sometimes wondered whether she was as intelligent as she looked, but she was very beautiful, elegant and charming, and he loved her.

The privilege of attending the producers' meetings now seemed like a ticket for the Titanic. In the aftermath he looked round gloomily at those who were furiously discussing the issue in twos and threes, and slipped out of the room; he had a great deal of work to get on with, and wasn't in the mood for the producers' favourite activity of debating the hidden agenda.

Jonathan's small grey third-floor office overlooked the new foyer which had been built onto Television Centre. This was a grand glass structure accommodating a lot of marble and an area for studio audiences to assemble in – an improvement which was long overdue. Jonathan had often wondered at the submissive obedience of the general public who for decades had queued up outside, whatever the weather, in order to spend four unbroken hours on a hard chair watching the recordings of countless light entertainment shows. Above the foyer were the new bi-media newsrooms, which were empty as the radio journalists were still fighting tooth and nail against their removal from Broadcasting House. Jonathan didn't blame them – for a start, they would be on view through the huge windows to anyone exiting from White City tube station. He wouldn't like that at all.

He settled at his computer to write a blurb for the Drama Brochure, a glossy catalogue of the forthcoming year's productions. As none of the cast or crew had yet been appointed it was tricky; he was supposed to supply a photo as well, but would have to make do with a library shot.

THE MEDICAL MIRACLE is Jim Johnson's first drama serial for the BBC. He is best known for his critically acclaimed novel THE END OF THE ROAD, winner of the Horlicks book prize.

Dewi Griffiths is a 38-year-old GP in mid-Wales: he saves the life of a local farmer who attempts suicide because of mounting debt. Dewi wishes he could help the plight of the farmers, whose centuries-old lifestyle is now unsustainable in the modern world of supermarkets and worldwide agri-business. Dewi suffers from multiple sclerosis, and takes cannabis to relieve his symptoms despite the fact that it's illegal. He would like to prescribe it for his patients but of course he can't. It occurs to him that he could solve two problems at once, and he decides it's worth risking prosecution. He proposes to the farmer that he grows cannabis and makes it into tea bags, and then he sends his patients to buy the medicinal herbal tea. It works a treat, and word spreads. The 'miracle tea-bags' as they're known become very popular. Eventually however, some kids work out what they are and begin smoking them; the secret is out, and the farmer is arrested. Dewi turns himself in and they are both charged without bail. Their customers unexpectedly rally in their support, and crowds gather outside the Old Bailey when the case comes to trial. The story ends when the jury returns to deliver its verdict to the court.

THE MEDICAL MIRACLE is a funny and powerful drama which challenges society to address its attitude towards drugs, and to reconsider the relationship we have with farming and the environment. The open ending provides the opportunity for audience participation in a phone-in vote or a television debate following transmission.

Jonathan fiddled with his synopsis until he was satisfied with it and then took it to Sonia Longbow, whose office was a few doors away. He found her on her knees gazing distractedly at several piles of paper arranged on the floor, with a box of bulldog clips in her hand. She looked up as he knocked and entered.

"Oh God, not another one."

"Hi Sonia. How's it going?"

"Don't ask. Can you hang on a minute? I've *got* to get these in the right order or I'll lose track of it all again."

Jonathan loitered by the door, casually reading Sonia's pinboard which was filled with a complicated chart listing over a hundred productions which were all to appear in the brochure. At least seventy had been crossed out and replaced with something else. He found his own, and felt a tingle of satisfaction.

Sonia clipped her piles of paper together and numbered them with a red pen, then stood up. "Sorry, Jonathan. Is that your entry?"

"Yes." He handed it over and she glanced through it.

"That's fine. I might have to cut it down a bit. You've got a week to find a photo."

"Okay," said Jonathan, turning to leave.

"Since you ask, it's *not* going very well. It's the worst job I've ever taken on, and I wish to God I hadn't."

Jonathan sympathised. Editing the brochure was a rotten job but someone had to do it. It traditionally fell to a script editor, but Sonia had taken it on rather than lose her post altogether.

"Not long to go," he said. "Doesn't it come out soon?"

"Yes but they're threatening to delay the launch. Which means it'll probably all change yet again, and everyone will have finished casting and got production photos and the whole bloody thing'll have to be updated. As it is half the sodding producers won't get on with writing their blurb, and those that do, make mistakes – they can't even be bothered to check the spellings of their own casts! I have to double check *everything*. And look at this rubbish." She picked up a sheet of paper. "This show is 'set on a site skirting the sea in Suffolk.' Don't they realise how crap that sounds? What do I do – rewrite it for them? Or ask them to do it again?" Jonathan smiled, it was certainly clumsy. "On top of that Peter keeps changing his mind about which shows are going in – there are at least twenty projects in here that haven't had the green light, you know. They'll probably never happen, especially given the way slots are disappearing. No-one knows what'll vanish overnight. It's complete bollocks, most of it, or else it's departmental politics. I don't know why we bother with it. And then there's the co-productions. Which producer do you ask, and do you check it with the other lot? Naturally, Stewart bloody Walker's the worst. Would you believe he and Jeremy Simon are bickering over whose name comes first in the credits? They're both Executive Producers, for Christ's sake! *I* can't decide for them, can I?"

"Maybe you should ask Peter to arbitrate?"

"Actually that's a really good idea. Thanks, Jonathan. Sorry to rant at you."

"My pleasure," he smiled, and made his getaway.

At three o'clock Jonathan sauntered into Peter's outer office, where his reassuringly mature PA Vera was on the phone as usual. She looked up at him over her half-moon specs and seemed too weary to smile, although her voice was kind as ever.

"Hello Jonathan. He's got Basil in there at the moment. Might be a few minutes yet."

"I'll wait, no problem. How are you, Vera?"

"Mustn't grumble." The phone rang again, so Jonathan moved away from her desk towards the newspaper rack. He couldn't help overhearing Basil expressing delight at something and strained to listen in.

"Best Drama, of course!" Peter was saying.

"I didn't know it had been entered. You must have forgotten to tell me," Basil replied. Peter's voice continued at a lower, apologetic level, and Jonathan picked up *Broadcast* and sat down to read it. Ten minutes later Basil emerged and closed Peter's door behind him.

"Jonathan!" he hailed. "Congratulations. Our last production just won another gong."

"*Down and Up?*"

"Tony will be so pleased."

"What's the prize?"

"Best Drama at the Banff festival."

"Fantastic! Congratulations, Basil." Jonathan beamed as he

gathered his documents and prepared to enter Peter's inner sanctum. He paused as Basil held his eye mysteriously, strolling behind Vera and leaning over to speak quietly into her ear.

"Tell me the truth, Vera. Who *really* put *Down and Up* in for Banff?"

Vera leaned back and pursed her lips. She patted Basil's hand, which was resting on her shoulder.

"The American co-producers, Basil."

Basil continued to look at Jonathan, letting him understand that the BBC had taken so little pride in the show that they hadn't even bothered to enter it for an international festival. It was the Americans, who had put up half the money and interfered hardly at all, who believed in it. But it was not Basil's way to make a song and dance about such things. He squeezed Vera's shoulder.

"It's good to know *someone* appreciates us."

"Take it where it's offered, Basil."

"Oh I do, Vera, I do," said Basil walking out with his usual dignity, winking at Jonathan as he passed.

Jonathan raised his eyebrows at Vera, who shrugged: none of it was her doing.

"Bit of a back-handed compliment, really – something like that anyway," said Jonathan. "Bit depressing, really."

"You think *that's* depressing," said Vera quietly. Glancing at Peter's door, she whispered loudly, "Basil's been asked to give up his office and take a small one. And he can't have a PA any more."

Jonathan was shocked. He shook his head. "Why?"

"Cut-backs, what else? He's not in production."

Jonathan was disgusted. It was a terrible affront to Basil's dignity; the rest of the entertainment industry would wonder at his apparent demotion as soon as they realised he was answering his own phone and writing his own letters.

"He can't even type, Vera!"

"Lucky *I* can, isn't it?"

"You're far too busy."

"True," said Vera, as the intercom buzzed. "You can go in now."

There was a hint of whisky in the air when Jonathan approached Peter's desk, but no sign of a bottle or a glass.

"Jonathan! Come in. Make yourself comfortable," welcomed Peter, who seemed droopier than usual. He looked at his watch. "Three twenty. Not too early, is it – fancy a drink?"

Jonathan was embarrassed. "Not really, thanks awfully – but don't let me stop you."

"No no. I'll get Vera to fetch us some teas. *Vera!*" he yelled. She opened the door. "Two teas please my sweet. And get one for yourself, you deserve it."

Vera acknowledged his humour with a sarcastic smile and disappeared.

"Now then," said Peter, throwing himself into an armchair as Jonathan leaned back on the corduroy sofa. "*The Medical Miracle.*" He paused and rubbed his temples; Jonathan wasn't sure whether he was going to continue. Uncomfortable at the silence, he opened his mouth to speak just as Peter asked, "Directors. Who have you got?"

Jonathan wasn't prepared, they were supposed to be discussing the budget, but Peter had evidently forgotten. Never mind, he would go with it.

"Well, it's basically a choice of young, trendy and cheap, or experienced and expensive."

"What about your brother?"

Jonathan was taken by surprise. His younger brother Roger was just beginning to establish himself as a director, but he hadn't put him on the list of possibles.

"Well I do think he's very good," he began. "But I wouldn't want to be accused of nepotism."

Peter laughed sourly. "Who cares about *that* these days? Look after your own, that's what I say, because no-one else is going to. I thought he did a very good job on that thing of Gillian's."

Peter was referring to a series of short single dramas produced at Pebble Mill, which Roger had directed.

"So did I," said Jonathan. He liked the idea of working with Roger, who at 28 was three years his junior and would be easier to work with than most directors available to him. "He's certainly young and cheap, and he *thinks* he's trendy! I'd definitely like to consider him, if you think that's a good idea."

Peter nodded assent. "Who knows, you might become the British Coen brothers."

Jonathan liked that idea even more. Vera came in with the teas at that moment, and he took the opportunity to get the meeting back on course. "I need to talk to you about the budget, I've been working on this draft." He put it on the table but Peter didn't look at it.

"Where's your script editor? Why isn't she here?"

"Oh." Jonathan's face reddened. "I don't think I mentioned… Rhiannon's been very busy, so I said not to worry, I could manage."

"Don't be ridiculous," snapped Peter. "D'you think you can do everything on your own? First time out?"

"Well, I thought I could save a bit of money if I edited the scripts myself."

"The point of having an editor is so that you can discuss everything with someone who knows what you're talking about and can work with the writer while you solve other problems. You need her. Go away, and come back when you've got her on board."

Jonathan was somewhat shocked by Peter's tone, which was a good deal sharper than he was used to. He realised he must have made quite a big error; he'd thought his handling of Rhiannon had been diplomatic, but now he saw that it was weak. He was only a learner producer in Peter's eyes. He excused himself and walked straight back to his office without speaking to anyone, not even Vera who had just made him a cup of tea.

I was on my computer, trying to get the hang of the new script software that was supposed to make our lives so much easier, when Jonathan knocked on my door. I called, "Come in," hit *save*, and spun my chair round to see who it was.

"Hello," he said, and walked in rather diffidently. Surprised to see him, I took the opportunity to be nice: not only did I regret not being on his show, I still hadn't found anything else to attach myself to.

"Hiya, have a seat! Would you like a drink?" I caught myself – was I gushing? He perched on a sofa I'd filched from a departing producer's office.

"What's this?" he asked, looking at an embroidered blue plaque I'd sewn onto the back like an antimacassar. "'Alan Bennett, Jack Rosenthal, Andrew Davies... '"

"It's a list of the famous bums that sat on it. It's supposed to be like the ones they put up on houses where famous people lived." I felt a bit daft, but he seemed to get the point.

"Brilliant!" he laughed. "What a list. Is it true?"

"I reckon – I can't be sure, but they all worked with Geoffrey over the years, so it's more than likely they sat on his sofa."

"Makes you think, doesn't it? Imagine if every office door listed all the productions that were made in it down the years."

"Yeah. Sometimes I don't know whether to laugh or cry." We smiled sadly at each other, and all the awkwardness that had existed between us seemed to have evaporated. He cleared his throat.

"I was wondering – I haven't got a script editor for *Medical Miracle*, I've been doing it myself, but I could really use one now. I just thought I'd check whether you were available before I asked anyone else."

"Oh, yes, actually, I'm pretty free now. My show got dumped."

"I heard. I'm really sorry. I didn't want to rub salt – "

"No problem! Don't worry about it. That's life, I've already forgotten about it!"

He smiled his handsome smile, and I smiled back. "Shall I come and pick up a copy of the script?"

"Great!"

I was grateful to Jonathan for making it so easy for me. Of course, at that stage I didn't know what Peter had said, and I thought he was generously overlooking my rudeness and giving me a second chance. Whatever the reason, we seemed to have made a fresh start, and by unspoken agreement we never mentioned what had gone before. Each of us breathed a private sigh of relief and got on with the job in hand. We had no idea what we were in for.

Chapter Sixteen

The Harder They Come
Proposal for a ninety minute thriller by Jill Watkins

SHARON (35) teaches English in a tough East London comprehensive. She has been married to JOHN (58) (*David Jason*) for ten years and they have two little girls (5 and 2). They are more or less content. John runs a local advertising paper. He is the kind of man who seems to have everything under control, who never raises his voice; the sort whom people are afraid to cross.

LUKE (16) (Take That) is about to sit his GCSEs. He loves anything to do with art and making things. His parents both work at Ford Dagenham. He has a sister RACHEL (14).

A murder has recently taken place locally: a woman was raped and left for dead in the local woods. The murderer's identity is a mystery.

Sharon teaches Luke. She has always liked him, and can't help noticing that he is growing up into a very sexy man. He's tall, good-looking, wears a long blonde ponytail and has an inner confidence unusual in a boy of his age that Sharon finds very attractive.

Luke has had a crush on Sharon for months and believes he's the right person for her. He wants to start a relationship.

Sharon and Luke begin an affair. She's riddled with guilt, but can't help herself, realising her marriage is hollow. Luke wants to run away with her, but she won't leave John, it wouldn't be fair to him.

One day they take a walk in the local woods, and are overcome by passion. They don't realise John is in the woods too, we don't know why, he sees them but doesn't let on.

John starts stalking them. The suspense builds. Sharon is on the horns of a dilemma. She wants to run away with Luke, but can't make the decision. John knows what's going on and he's as nice to her as he knows how, hoping it will blow over. Another body is found in the woods.

Whilst the police conduct investigations, Sharon and Luke meet in the woods, followed by John. Sharon promises to leave John, hears a noise, tells Luke to go. She waits a few minutes before she leaves.

John has a knife. He creeps up and attacks her for betraying him. Luke's dog hears something and wants to go back. They do, and catch John struggling with Sharon. It's a tense fight, but the dog's barking attracts some police searching the woods, and they come to the rescue.

It turns out that John is the psychopathic murderer. Sharon and Luke settle down together with the girls. John goes to prison.

Jill was quite pleased with her effort, although she felt it would take a little time to grow on her before she really liked it. What would Basil and Maggie's comments have been? A fleeting regret passed through her, was she betraying them? Hardly, she reasoned. How could you betray people who had dropped your project? All the same, she had changed the title so that they would think it was a new idea, if they ever heard about it.

Sally called back the day after she got the fax and declared it super. However, she wanted Jill to make one or two tiny changes before she took it further.

"Firstly, the boys in Take That have short hair, so can Luke? He'll only look silly with a wig on."

That was tough. Jill had always seen Luke's ponytail as an integral part of his personality, a low-key statement of individuality. She made a Herculean effort and mentally chopped it off.

"Great," said Sally. "Now I've got this idea, it's really very exciting. I think it's a bit dodgy to make David Jason the baddy. I'm really not sure audiences will wear it, so I thought, wouldn't it be a terrific twist at the end, if it turned out that *Luke* was the murderer! Then *John*'s the one who saves Sharon's life, and she realises it was all a sort of mid-life crush on *her* part and goes back home with John, who's really mature and kind and forgives her?"

Jill couldn't speak.

Sally interpreted her silence to suit herself and rattled on, "If you could possibly write that up by the end of tomorrow I can give it directly to David's agent, I'll be seeing him at a dinner party. If David's on board we can get the controller behind it and then we'll be able to sort out your contract."

The magic word *contract* lodged in Jill's mind, and she muttered that she'd try.

"You're a brick, Jill."

"By the way," Jill said before Sally's phone went down. "I'd really like to have a go at developing a precinct drama set in a school. What do you think?"

"I'm afraid that's out of the window now," said Sally airily. "They've already got two: one's set in a police station and one's about a hospital. Speak to you later. Bye."

Jill paced up and down the kitchen while she made coffee. Sally's 'tiny' changes ripped out the heart of the original story. They turned her ideal youth into a neurotic obsessive, and Sharon into a weak-minded fool. She didn't want to write it.

Then she thought of her ever-increasing overdraft, and her ambition to move into a house with a garden, if she could ever make enough money. She thought of Sam and the Nike Air trainers which she suspected were stolen.

Jill gritted her teeth and decided to give it a try, for purely commercial reasons. She would write exactly what Sally wanted. If Sally could get it going then it would be worth it. She wasn't compromising her artistic integrity, she was writing for the market.

She returned purposefully to her computer, and re-wrote the proposal again, incorporating all Sally's suggestions. She worked and honed it over the next day to the most economical, appealing pitch she could.

The Harder They Fall
A Thriller by Jill Watkins

Hainault Country Park, East London: a killer stalks an anonymous woman on her way home in the dark. She is assaulted, raped and left for dead.

JOHN MORRISSON (David Jason) reads the report in the local paper, which he runs. His wife SHARON (Anita Dobson?) shivers as she hears about it on her way to the local comprehensive, where she teaches. LUKE WOODWARD (Gary Barlow?) thinks only of his favourite teacher, Sharon.

Sharon and Luke fall in love. He is sixteen, she thirty-five, but this doesn't seem to matter. She stands to lose her job as well as her family, but in spite of this she can't help embarking on the affair. They meet secretly in the wooded areas of the park.

Luke wants Sharon to leave John and their two daughters. She adores Luke but can't bring herself to abandon them.

John realises something is wrong. One day he is in the woods (we don't know why) and he sees her with Luke. After that he stalks them secretly. He's nice as pie to Sharon at home. Too nice. Our sympathies tend to make us wish Sharon would leave him for Luke.

Another body is found in the woods. The police hunt intensifies. The audience's suspicions fall on John.

John follows Sharon into the woods for an assignation with Luke. He watches them make love and then argue. Luke wants her to run away with him, but she's torn apart by loyalty to John and the kids. We see John peering at her from a bush, he steps on a twig and the sound scares them. Sharon sends Luke away, says she'll follow when the coast's clear. She sits alone, worrying. Suddenly someone jumps her from behind, there's a struggle and a knife flashes. Then someone else joins the fray, we see that it's John, wrestling with Luke to make him drop the knife. Finally he succeeds and punches Luke. He lies on the ground unconscious.

John speaks into a mobile phone, and hugs the weeping Sharon as police with dogs arrive and take Luke away. They thank John for his assistance. John takes Sharon home, and we know they'll be happy together after all.

Sally was pleased with Jill's work and sounded very confident about it. Jill tried to put it out of her mind over the weekend, although she was haunted by the fear of actually being commissioned to write it.

*

Neil arrived to pick Sam up on Saturday morning in ebullient mood. He informed them that they were looking at the new Labour candidate for Birmingham South East, and offered to take them both out for a slap-up breakfast. They went to Banner's, a favourite haunt of Jill's and Neil's: a relaxed café-bar which served great food accompanied by world music. Sam was sniffy about it, dismissing it as seriously uncool and full of old hippies, but he was outnumbered and silenced with a plate of pancakes.

Halfway through the meal Neil said casually, "Sam. You know I'll have to spend a lot of time in Birmingham in the run-up to the election, whenever it happens."

"Yeah?" answered Sam suspiciously.

"There'll be an awful lot of campaigning work."

"Don't tell me. You'll be too busy to see me every fortnight." Sam looked sullen.

"I wanted to ask you a huge favour."

"What?"

"I wondered if you'd be my youth advisor. Join the committee. Come to Birmingham with me every weekend."

Sam's eyes popped. Jill was just as surprised but bit her tongue. Eventually Sam said casually, "Yeah, okay."

Neil grinned. "That's brilliant. Thanks. It'll help me no end."

"S'alright" said Sam, finishing his pancakes. He sat up, suddenly interested in the conversation. "That's the trouble with politicians today," he announced. "They don't know what's going down on the street. They don't know shit about real life."

Jill and Neil exchanged a wordless glance which confirmed a depth of shared understanding.

Sam turned to his mother. "Will you be alright on your own, mum?"

"I'll cope," she smiled.

"You can always get Gran to come and keep you company."

"Thanks, Sam!"

*

Sally's call came a week later. Jill picked up and greeted Sally in trepidation.

"Jill, darling," Sally began. "I'm terribly sorry, but David Jason passed on it after all." Jill collapsed in relief. "He liked it ever so much, but he's booked solid for the next three years."

"What a shame," Jill murmured. "Never mind."

"I've got another idea, though," said Sally, to Jill's alarm. "There's a rumour going round that Ross Kemp's leaving *EastEnders*. It would be a super role for him, don't you think?"

Jill didn't see why not. She felt a little faint, and let Sally rabbit on while she wondered how to get out of it.

"... I can't decide whether it would be better for Ross to be a goody or a baddy. What do you think? He'd be jolly good as either. I suppose if he's the murderer it's a bit close to Grant Mitchell. Maybe we should keep it as it is for now. What about Anita Dobson, though? *Two* actors off *EastEnders* would look a bit odd, don't you think?"

"Yes, it might," agreed Jill, wondering if there was a limit to Sally's obsession with famous faces. A sudden light-headedness made her reckless, "What about Dawn French?"

"Hmm," replied Sally, seriously. "I'll have to think about that one, Jill."

Jill felt it was time she took control.

"Actually, Sally," she said firmly. "I'm not sure about the whole project. I'm afraid I've rather lost my enthusiasm for it." To her surprise, Sally didn't seem to mind too much.

"Really? Oh. Well that's understandable. Without David it's sort of lost its heart, hasn't it?"

"Yes," said Jill, grinding her teeth.

"Okay darling. To be honest I was sort of losing faith myself, but I didn't want to let you down."

"That's very sweet of you."

"Well, look. *Do* stay in touch, and bring me *any* ideas at all. I'm *sure* we can get something off the ground if we keep trying!"

Jill said she would, although she knew perfectly well that she wouldn't, even if Sally was the last producer left in London. She hung up, and went into the kitchen for a cathartic Lion Bar.

She doubted whether she would ever approach the BBC directly again. She had found the whole experience traumatic, and was left with the feeling that getting a show on there was harder than pulling out your own teeth with a pair of nail clippers, and less entertaining. Instead, she would focus her efforts elsewhere.

She returned to her computer and continued with an idea she was writing up for *The Bill*; her agent had set her up with a meeting and it seemed positive so far. She also had some thoughts on a returning series set in a secondary school, which she planned to develop and take along to Anthea Onojaife, Carmen's producer, at Sisters in Synch.

An hour later Sam came home, and offered to make her a cup of tea. Delighted by this novelty, she rewarded him with her company while he watched television. Leafing through the *Radio Times* she noticed *The Soap Ashes*, and a wave of self-reproach washed through her yet again for her loss of royalties. She contemplated her nice but inexperienced young agent Paul and compared him to Billy Trowell's guardian dragon. Muriel would never have let her sell all her rights for a hundred pounds. Her thoughts drifted to the *Bus Stops Here* proposal she'd reworked for him recently, at least he had paid her well for that. Or... had he? Was he up to something? An intangible sense of dread began to develop in her belly. Could she have been finessed a second time? She racked her memory to find out just how significant her contribution to the show had been, and remembered Nik's conversation with Geordie Boy on the roof garden. Poor lad, she sighed. At least I didn't get shafted as comprehensively as you did.

Chapter Seventeen

I liked Jim's scripts for *The Medical Miracle* very much. I'd never seen anything quite like them before. They had an immediacy and relevance to life as people really live it, with all its inconsistencies and absurdities. They were a bit messy, the spelling was idiosyncratic (to put it kindly), and the structure of the story was rather irregular, but the characters and scenes had real verve, and his dialogue had tremendous energy. The scripts had an improvised flavour to them that told me that Jim was one of those writers who don't plan beforehand. This is a hit-and-miss approach which can produce top quality writing, but on other days it produces nothing worthwhile. Writers like him are usually unsuitable for a returning series, unless they happen to know it inside out – for instance you'll find a few great cockney writers on *EastEnders* who won't be much use on *Monarch of the Glen*. People like Jill Watkins can turn their hand to a range of shows, but Jim Johnson was definitely a one-off.

There was certainly a role for me, he'd re-invented Wales to save himself the trouble of research, as far as I could see. I could put that right easily enough. He'd used a lot of names that needed negative checks to make sure they were fictitious, and the plot needed attention. The characters and dialogue were terrific, I didn't want to interfere with those in any way except to tweak a few lines to give them an authentic Welsh feel. I timed the scripts as running ten and twelve minutes short, so we needed some new scenes.

I talked through my thoughts with Jonathan and he was very happy as we saw eye to eye on all the important points. I was relieved to find that he was quite easy to work with, after all; he didn't stand on ceremony, he was simply professional and pleasant. I did my best to be the same. His office was just like him, somehow: extremely tidy, with matching furniture, which was fully functioning, even the blind. I wondered how he'd achieved this and put it down to administrative talent – until I realised that the girls in the admin block would be a lot more susceptible to Jonathan's charms than they were to mine.

Jonathan called Jim in for a script meeting, and we met in his office one Friday morning. Jim knew me already from the writers' party so the formalities were brief, and Jonathan even went out to fetch the coffees himself instead of asking me to get them. I appreciated the gesture. While we waited Jim pottered nosily round the office, and lit upon a framed photo of Selina.

"Who's the tart?" he asked cheerfully, picking it up. I responded with a reproving smile which I hoped would warn him to be more careful in front of Jonathan, and told him she was his fiancée. Jim responded with an expression of appalled disgust which made me laugh out loud.

"She's very beautiful," I said, loyally. I'd never spoken to Selina and knew little about her.

Jim waggled his head as if to say he disagreed. "Debutante. They're all over the city like cockroaches." I was on tenterhooks in case Jon came back and heard him, but Jim didn't seem to care. Seconds later Jon did appear, so the cheeky sod smirked admiringly as he replaced the photo. "What a lovely girl!"

Jonathan smiled modestly, "Thanks, that's my fiancée Selina."

"She's PA to Chris Briggs," I added.

"Actually she's just been promoted. She's going to be part of the new Department for Policy and Planning."

"Not just Miss Kensington and Chelsea, then," said Jim. He grimaced at me while Jon's back was turned, and it was all I could do to keep a straight face. He was so outrageous, he didn't seem to have any sense of decorum. I kept chatting to cover for him.

"I don't know much about Policy and Planning, do you Jonathan?"

"Not a lot. They're going to have an overview of all programme making, make sure it's in line with policy, keep the staff informed with new directions, that sort of thing."

"Sounds a bit of a yawn," I said, and Jon shrugged.

"That's a bit cheeky," said Jim.

"Why?" I asked, starting to blush.

"Fancy describing the future Mrs Proulx's work as a *yawn*, how rude!"

I fixed Jim with a warning look of exasperation: he was clearly trying to wind me up like a clockwork toy.

"Take no notice, Rhiannon," advised Jonathan. "He's incorrigible." I realised that he already had the measure of Jim, and I needn't worry.

We settled down to go through the scripts, giving Jim notes to take away and work into the second draft. It was very enjoyable, as Jim observed afterwards naming us the toff, the chav and the sheep-shagger. I told him he'd regret saying that.

Jonathan then announced that he'd booked a table for lunch in a Notting Hill restaurant, which he'd cover the cost of somehow, so we were duly appreciative. We set off with a sense of excitement and pleasure, feeling we were going to make a great team, and the show would be something very special.

One One Three was busy as usual, and hummed with media folk networking. We sat in a panelled booth which allowed a measure of privacy, and ordered spritzers. The restaurant had a good balance of comfy relaxation and delicious-but-not-too-fancy food and service. It was both friendly and discreet, and at the same time it was a fashionable place to see and be seen. I was easily impressed, places like this made me feel very provincial.

Over lunch we got know each other better, and our working

relationship really began to gel. You might think it extravagant to spend even a fraction of a production budget on restaurant bills, but that underestimates the significance of the creative spark and how it travels round a team. The difference between a standard drama and an exceptional one can be down to these small but vital events, where interaction goes deeper than it does in normal working patterns. Creative leadership is about nurturing the right assemblage of people in the right atmosphere, so that they feed one another and enter a new place together; in this way the individuals act like ingredients in a cake, and combine to produce a magnificent confection. I saw that Jonathan already understood this and knew how to achieve it. I was impressed. I asked Jim if he'd always wanted to write.

"Not till I had kids," he said. "Never crossed my mind till then. It makes you think about the future, and how much time you spend in the office. I thought, these scribblers have got it made. I fancied writing a bestseller and living off the royalties."

"So you did."

"Yeah, well it wasn't as easy as all that, but yeah, basically. I'm a lucky bleeder, gift of the gab like my dad."

"Does he write too?"

"No! He can hardly write at all, only in capital letters, bless him. He'll talk the hind leg off a donkey though. He can tell a story, he can. Generations of market traders in my family. Blag anything you like."

"Proper cockneys."

"You could say that. I've had to clean up me act since I met my missus though, married into the Old Bill, ain't I!" Jim didn't seem to have got over this fact yet.

"You have to mind your P's and Q's now?"

He sucked in his breath with a comically serious expression. "It's murder. *Both* in-laws are coppers. You can't get away with nothing. I bought a new kitchen table. They come round, eye it up: 'So where d'you get this, then?' –'Heals, actually' – 'Oh yes? How much d'you pay for it then?'" Jim reproduced the suspicious gaze of a 1950s police constable. "I'm constantly expecting to get my collar felt and a quick march down the nick!" It was a lovely image; we laughed.

"What about you, Rhiannon?" asked Jonathan. "Do you write?"

"No, too busy," I said, "but I'd like to write a novel one day. Everyone says that though, don't they? How about you?"

"It's not for me. I can't imagine it anyway. Maybe I'm too reserved. I like telling other peoples' stories."

"You don't want to expose yourself," suggested Jim.

"Maybe that's it," agreed Jon shyly. I wondered what he wanted to hide, but didn't like to ask. Jim, quick as a kestrel, read my face.

"She thinks you've got a skeleton in the closet," he put in.

Luckily Jon wasn't offended. He smiled charmingly at me, "In my family nothing's ever revealed publicly. It just isn't done. Not that there's anything dreadful to conceal, as far as I know! It's about showing a public face of respectable happiness."

"Good manners."

"Exactly. You pretend everything's absolutely perfect, regardless of whether it is or not. You sail through life confidently. You're very successful, that goes without saying. And you don't reveal your feelings, that would be a kind of betrayal."

"Wow," I said, incautiously. "I don't think I could live like that. So – if you *wanted* to be a writer, you couldn't?"

Jon pursed his lips. "Risky. It would depend on what you wrote. Biography, academic work would be perfectly fine. Spilling the emotions: all rather embarrassing."

"Makes me realise how lucky I am," I said. "My parents always encouraged me to do whatever I want. Both my grandfathers were miners, and my dad managed to become a school teacher. Our family's really keen on education and bettering yourself, and they don't worry about anything I do impacting on them. They're really proud of me. They never care about gossip."

Jon looked kind of wistful, and I felt sorry for him, for the first time.

Jim, of course, couldn't resist a comment, "Poor little rich boy. It's no wonder he's got a lobster up his arse."

"Nobody else could get away with the things you say." He just grinned, and Jonathan looked tolerant and signalled for the bill. I realised he quite enjoyed being treated like this, perhaps it made him feel one of us. I supposed teasing wasn't done in his family either, and he enjoyed the warmth and acceptance that it implies. I'd learned a lot about him over lunch. I'd had a glimpse of his vulnerable side, and had seen him in another context – it had taken Jim's scathing wit to show me what I could have found out on my own, if I hadn't had a crab up my own arse since I'd been at Television Centre.

The bill arrived, Jonathan paid, and as we got up to go I noticed a familiar figure at the door. "There's no escaping the Drama Department," I remarked. "Here's Penny Cruickshank – ooh – who's that?" Jon glanced over and saw our generously proportioned senior colleague with two fashionably-gelled young men half her age, being shown to a table.

"She's on a date," offered Jim.

I ignored him and surreptitiously watched the waiter seat them in an alcove and give the wine list to one of the men. "I know that bloke's face from somewhere."

Jonathan sneaked a peek, "I think he runs Magenta."

"D'you think she's leaving? I can't believe it. She's been at the Beeb forever." We left, discreetly ignoring Penny, though normally we'd have had a chat. There was evidently something afoot and we didn't want to put a spoke in her wheel, Penny was one of the few people everyone liked.

Penny had noticed us immediately, and was now taking care not to look around, being keen to avoid catching anyone's eye on this occasion. She preferred to keep negotiations private until the deal was signed and sealed. Her companions' eyes, in contrast, swept the room periodically like lighthouse beams.

Nik watched as the champagne was poured by the sommelier, and proposed a toast, "*Bus Stops Here!*"

"*Bus Stops Here!*" echoed his new executive assistant.

"To the bus, and all who sail in her!" exclaimed Penny jovially. They drank, smiled, and looked at Nik. He looked back at them and wondered whether they would get through the show without falling out.

He had been happy to accept Chris' suggestion of Penny to produce the show. She was an old-school BBC type, full of cheery common sense and completely reliable. She was a safe pair of hands where the budget was concerned, knew everyone in the BBC and all its arcane systems, and would be invaluable as a go-between, a champion, and a general workhorse. He only worried that she might imprint her personality on the show, and give it a Blue Peter flavour. To counterbalance this he had found an energetic assistant with contemporary taste: Jack Smith. He was very young but had a degree in Media Studies, and had also won a competition with a ten-minute screenplay, although it hadn't been filmed. Nik thought he saw something of himself in Jack, and was quietly flattered when he began spelling his name Jak.

That morning the threesome had wrestled over the still-to-be-named drama series. It hadn't been easy. Penny had been quite clear about the low budget and what they could realistically expect to achieve on it. She had identified major loopholes in the dramatic logic of the series concept, and asked questions they couldn't answer. Jak had tried to dismiss her objections as fussiness, which had riled Penny to the verge of walking away from the show altogether. Nik had understood the wisdom of her points, however, and had backed her. He realised that she knew what she was talking about, and Jak didn't, so he said as much. He laid down the law: what Penny said, went. If she said it wouldn't work, it wouldn't work. Jak's function was to connect with the kids, and make sure the series was *cool*. Penny was to accommodate as much of his input as she could, but she was in charge.

This resolution satisfied Penny enough to commit to the series despite her reservations. She knew there would be a terrific scramble for work within the Drama Department from now on, so this was probably a good opportunity. She reluctantly agreed to resign from the BBC in favour of this one-year contract with Magenta. The budget was ridiculous, but given her extensive contacts and the favours she could pull in, she felt sure she could give this series the best production values without overspending. She was an old pro, and she would dedicate herself to making it work. The scheduled slot was early evening, Saturday; this kind of family viewing was her speciality.

They had agreed to develop a 26-part episode breakdown, with Penny checking costs and practicalities, and Jak checking its street cred. Nik had decided that there was no reason why these two angles should be mutually exclusive, although Penny had her doubts. Jak was keen to assemble a wish list of guest stars. How they would appear for one episode only was a problem the storyliner would have to solve, somehow. Penny had failed to persuade them that the sci-fi genre was not a carte-blanche excuse for illogical plotting. She also insisted on a story arc which would lead to an ultimate resolution, although Nik wanted to keep the show open-ended so that it could grow with each new series and potentially run for decades. Penny's views on narrative integrity were dismissed by Jak as utterly irrelevant in the post-modern, de-constructionist, *fin-de-siecle* world. Penny had no answer to this except flat denial, but Nik had managed to pull them together with the inspired reminder that since he needed both ends of the audience to enjoy the show, they must find a way to be all-inclusive, and 'Give 'em all what they want.' In this way a truce was reached, and he had brought them out to seal it over a good lunch.

"Tell me about yourself, Dik – I mean Jak," said Penny, while

Nik went to the gents. "Which university were you at?"

"Sussex," replied Jak. "It was crap."

"Oh! I thought it had a good reputation. My niece – "

"Depends what you do there."

"A pretty cool place to spend three years, I should think?"

"Boring, really. Brighton's all hippies, gays and nutters."

Penny wished Jak would at least make the effort to meet her halfway – her son's sixth-form friends had much better social skills – but perhaps he lacked confidence, and felt overwhelmed in this media restaurant. She tried again. "Nik tells me you won a writing competition?"

"Yeah."

"Are you still writing?"

"Well I'm doing this now."

She was glad when Nik returned and the oysters arrived. Working with Jak was going to be a hard slog, that much was clear. She'd thought the BBC had already presented her with every challenge under the sun, but this was a new one, she observed ruefully. At the moment it was impossible to see what contribution Jak would make to the show; he seemed nothing but trouble, but she foresaw that if she were to lose Nik's backing she'd be off the show faster than Linford Christie.

When Jon and I got back to Centre House the weekend was approaching, and the building was quiet. There was a comfortable feeling between us which I hadn't expected and I could tell he was aware of it too. We returned to our respective offices, and ten minutes later Jonathan appeared at my door with a letter in his hand.

"Have you got a moment?"

"Of course," I said. He came in and sat on my historic sofa.

"Peter's left me this note, he's gone away for the weekend. It's a bit unusual. It's very confidential."

"You don't have to tell me – "

"I think I do." He held it out to me, so I took it. It was handwritten, but crystal clear:

'Jonathan, destroy this message when you've read it. You must revise all official docs and remove any references to cannabis in The M M. Finish scripts ASAP. Peter.'

"How weird," I said. "Was it on your desk?"

"Vera brought it to me just now. It's all a bit cloak-and-dagger, isn't it?"

"Bloody hell. Perhaps he was pissed when he wrote it?" Everyone had noticed Peter's alcohol intake was rising. "What are you going to do?"

"What he says, I suppose. Vera seemed to think it was important."

"Vera always knows."

"I hope it doesn't backfire on me, what if he's forgotten all about it when he gets back?"

"I'll stick up for you."

"Thanks. Intriguing, isn't it?"

"Not half. I suppose we better get cracking, then."

"Would you mind?"

"Not at all." I really didn't. "I can work late tonight, if you like."

"Let's do that, then. We might regret it if we don't."

Chapter Eighteen

Selina was looking forward to her engagement party, naturally, and then to setting the date for the wedding, and deciding where she and Jonathan would live. They'd barely discussed it so far. They hadn't moved in together, since Daddy wanted to preserve the illusion of giving his little girl away at the altar. Humouring Daddy would certainly be to their advantage financially, so why rock the boat? Jonathan was very easy going, he was a sweetheart. He understood her parents in a way that many young men had failed to, and was content to go along with what they and Selina wanted. He seemed to know innately that opposing them would lead to far more trouble than it was worth. They'd fallen for each other soon after meeting, and since then everything had dropped into place very easily. There was a gentle, unhurried routine to their relationship that Selina found very reassuring. They always spent Saturday night together, and sometimes Friday too, and occasionally Wednesday. They remained in their own flats the rest of the week, it worked better that way. Selina hated being in the wrong place without all her cosmetics and wardrobe, and having time to herself meant she was always at her best for Jon or for work. She was glad that they weren't the kind of couple who are all over each other and can't bear to be apart. Their love was respectful and well-mannered, just like her parents'. They were perfectly suited.

Jonathan's family weren't quite so straightforward, but they were manageable. Selina had charmed his father, the retired history professor, without any difficulty although conversation had a tendency to stall unless she got him onto his favourite topic of the Plantagenets. She'd become quite knowledgeable herself as a result. Jon's mother was perfectly nice, a well-educated housewife who played the organ in their local church. She wasn't easy to get close to, but perhaps that wasn't necessary. The only member of the family she had misgivings about was Roger, Jon's younger brother.

Roger's father always referred to him with a laugh as the black sheep of the family. His mother would wince, but she never objected. Jonathan would look askance, but since family arguments were strictly taboo their father said whatever he liked. Roger was the rebellious child. He had followed his (let's face it) perfect elder brother through life being told he wasn't as good, clever, handsome, tall, or hard-working. It's unsurprising that he chose to create an identity for himself that his parents didn't care for: spontaneous, creative, sociable – qualities which translated to unreliable, unfocussed and noisy, as far as his father was concerned. His mother was more tolerant of his personality traits but also more upset by his sexuality, since she was an old-fashioned Christian and he was gay.

Jonathan and Roger were close and Selina respected that; she had nothing against Roger, in fact she quite liked him, but he made her feel uncomfortable. He seemed to go out of his way to be awkward sometimes. He was never openly rude, but he would take an alternative point of view to virtually anything his father said. Jonathan said it was a compulsion, and had something to do with being punished a lot as a small boy. Selina didn't want to know any of the details. Not at all. She found herself emulating their mother, keeping the peace and minding her own business. She didn't care for unruly behaviour either.

Selina was very pleased with her promotion at work, although she was finding it quite hard going. It was Chris who had suggested she apply to join the new Policy and Planning Department, and at first she worried that he wanted to get rid of her, but he was just thinking of her career, he said; plus he knew he could rely on her to be loyal and committed in the role. He wanted his own people in there, and who could blame him? He said she would need to be quick on her feet, responding promptly to issues as they arose. She worked directly to him for the first few months, while the new department established itself.

The whole of the BBC had been split into two sections named Broadcast and Production, which meant that the commissioners and schedulers were now completely separate from the programme makers. The latter were now at arm's length from the centre, on much the same footing as the independent production companies. Selina's role was to monitor all in-house drama production, anticipate discrepancies with policy, and head them off before they became a problem. This role had formerly been undertaken by Heads of Department, and all producers. It was still their responsibility to adhere to BBC policy, and they felt a level of suspicion concerning the real purpose of the new department.

Selina was nothing if not professional, and her conscientious nature meant she spent weeks diligently soaking up all the BBC policy documents she could lay hands on. It wasn't as much fun as being Chris' PA, although she was pleased to take on more responsibility. Much of her work would entail conferring with the Legal Department to ensure all drama programmes were safe in terms of the law. It was a huge undertaking. At least she could trust Jon not to drop any clangers where policy was concerned. For now she was concentrating on the producers who were likely to be controversial, such as Stewart Walker, who was proving to be infuriatingly slippery. He wouldn't let her see any of the projects he was working on, he promised to send her synopses but they never arrived. She was beginning to feel she was in a game of cat and mouse, where Stewart was Jerry and she the unfortunate Tom. She wasn't even sure how many projects Stewart had.

Jon was relieved that he was at the bottom of Selina's list of drama producers and that she hadn't asked him for details of *The Medical Miracle* so far, especially since Peter Maxwell had sent him that mysterious note. He and I had diligently revised all the paperwork as requested, replacing 'cannabis' with 'herbs', and shifting the emphasis from the medical issue to the economics. I spoke to Jim on the phone, and he said he could speed up the writing if we gave him a new deadline –when it comes to a situation demanding speed, being the kind of writer who only produces at the last minute is a great advantage.

Since Jonathan was the most discreet man in the northern hemisphere it wasn't difficult for him to keep quiet about it whilst in Selina's company. She understood the significance of his first full production, but for her it was about doing the job rather than the project itself, so she wasn't curious about the content. To Selina, being a producer was the important thing, regardless of what you produced – within reason, obviously. *Brideshead* was infinitely preferable to *Crossroads*, but she didn't really see the appeal of these gritty working class dramas that Jonathan was so fond of. She was assuming that *The Medical Miracle* would be another one of them.

It took a few days before Jon and I were able to meet with Peter and find out what it was all about. He was suddenly hard to get to. Vera said there were a great many meetings he had to attend because of all the re-structuring. Finally he called us to his office late one afternoon. We arrived to find a new notice blu-tacked to his door: *SMOKING COMPULSORY*. We were amused, it was obviously Peter's response to the new edict against smoking anywhere in the BBC. He was clearly not in a compliant mood as far as the senior management were concerned.

We each accepted a glass of wine for his sake. There was something sad about Peter lately. He hadn't changed, exactly, he'd just faded a little. The pillar of the department was weakening. Maybe the load bearing down on him was increasing.

Maybe a steel girder was needed.

Jonathan asked whether he'd read our re-vamped documents, and he told us yes, and they were fine.

"You'll be wanting to know what all this is about," Peter said. "It's Policy and Planning." We'd guessed as much. "The DG is centralising everything – *everything* – and he's paranoid about giving the tabloids any opportunity to go for us. The BBC has never been so insecure, apparently, and we must be squeaky clean. I'll re-phrase that. We must *appear* squeaky-clean."

"Is it mainly about bad publicity, or the license fee?" asked Jonathan.

"Politics," replied Peter succinctly. "The government would happily privatise the BBC." We contemplated this in silence for a moment.

"Not if Labour win the election, though," I said; it was expected that the country would go to the polls soon. "The Tories are a joke now, aren't they – the Sleaze Party. Surely they won't win a fifth term."

"Well, who knows, we have to survive the current storm first," sighed Peter. "And what's happening now is that we're being pruned and modernised ready for the global marketplace. Like it or not."

"And *The Medical Miracle* is liable to scare the lawyers?" Jon asked. Peter nodded thoughtfully.

"Why?" I asked. "Am I being thick here? Whatever's wrong with it?"

Jon looked as if he thought me naïve. "The tabloids will say we're promoting a Class B drug."

"But we aren't! We're raising the debate, showing both sides."

"To the Murdoch press, showing the benefits of cannabis is the same thing as pushing it."

"We're neutral, though. What's wrong with debating the issues?"

"All the politicians are terrified of talking about drugs, any drugs," said Peter. "If a party gets tagged as pro-drugs, they've had it. It's too hot to touch."

"They all want to sweep it under the carpet, pretend it's not an issue," said Jon.

"What a dreadful way to run a country! It's not about doing what's best for the people, it's about protecting the politicians!" This came out with more indignation than I intended, so I tailed off with, "Yours faithfully, Disgusted of Builth Wells."

Peter chuckled. "Okay, what we do is carry on, moving swiftly and silently, close to the wire. If we can get the show through the net and in the can while the election's keeping the press busy, we could be looking at transmission next autumn." I stared at him. It sounded like guerrilla action. "Discretion is the better part of valour, Rhiannon," he said. "This is the only drama we have left which has even the faintest whiff of originality and controversy about it, and without that there isn't much point in drama at all. In my view." He drained his glass and banged it down on the table. "Alright, leave it with me, I'll put it to the Controller at the next opportunity. I'll let you know when we get the green light. You can start drafting a schedule and budget."

I came out of Peter's office with yet another new perspective, I realised how many levels of engagement there are in making drama. The more you know the more complicated it gets. I was reminded of Shakespeare and the Elizabethans: the plotting at court, the spies, the royal patronage of the theatres, the secret Catholic priests, the coded messages, the stabbings in Deptford. At least we didn't fear for our lives these days, we could be grateful for that. There would be no execution on Tower Hill for the Director General of the BBC, only a seat in the House of Lords.

Jonathan met Selina for lunch a couple of days later; he booked a table in 'waitress service', a mezzanine area in the main canteen which operated like a normal restaurant – except that they served canteen food. You got a small table of your own, instead of sharing a larger one with all and sundry. Jon and Selina chatted about this and that, he asked how the pursuit of Stewart was going, and she shrugged.

"I don't understand the Drama Department, Jonathan," she said. "What are you all up to?"

He was flummoxed by her directness, she had pitched him onto a high fence. He teetered. Which side did his loyalties lie? Would he share the truth with his fiancée? Who else would find out, if he did? What might the consequences be? He blinked at her for a few seconds, which made her frown. Then he laughed it off. "Stabbing each other in the back, of course! You know what a lot of prima donnas we all are."

This relaxed her. "Don't I just."

"With ever-diminishing funds it's like a fight to the death," he continued. "It's like the last days of Rome over in Centre House."

"It's inevitable, I suppose, but it's all for the best. The BBC will be much healthier afterwards."

"D'you think so?" Jon asked casually, his heart sinking.

"Absolutely. The sooner we get rid of these mavericks the better. Nothing but trouble. We should be emulating the US, look at the quality of their shows."

"Look at the quantity of their investment," cut in Jon, a bit too quickly. "I know what you mean," he apologised. "It's painful while it's happening though. We all feel insecure."

Selina smiled knowingly. "You'll be fine, Jon, trust me."

"What's that supposed to mean?"

"Nothing, nothing," she exclaimed disingenuously. "Just something I heard. Play your cards right and you could be en route for a big promotion, that's all. My lips are sealed. Now. Shall we order coffee?"

Jon experienced an alteration in his world view in that moment. He'd always been the senior partner in their relationship, and now the seesaw had plunged him to the ground.

Selina was better informed than he. It was an alarming transition and it took all his powers of dissemblance to conceal his anxiety. There was something Orwellian about her. She saw the situation in simple terms; for her there was no grey area, and no discussion. Whatever came down from top management was right, and she would put it into practice. Suddenly he saw that she viewed everything in life this way, and he felt scared for his own future. He realised he was standing on quicksand and should keep very still, in case he sank deeper into a mire he wouldn't be able to get out of. He needed to think this through. The Selina he saw across the table wasn't quite the person he'd fallen in love with.

"Actually I should be getting back, sorry," he said, checking his watch. "Sorry about that. I'll pick up the tab."

"Don't worry, I'll put it on my expenses. Go on, if you're in a hurry. See you Friday."

"Okay, thanks," said Jon, kissing her. "Sorry to rush off. I should have kept an eye on the time."

"No problem darling," she beamed. "Don't be late."

Jon was relieved to escape, and walked across Wood Lane in a cloud, annoying some drivers by stepping out onto the zebra crossing without looking properly, ignoring their horns and striding up the road to Centre House lost in thought.

Back at the table, Selina was signing the bill when another figure slipped into Jonathan's empty chair: it was Chris Briggs, recently promoted again to Managing Director.

"Hello, stranger!" he said.

"Not exactly," she pointed out. "We met yesterday."

"I miss having you in my outer office," he explained, and caught himself – did that sound like innuendo? Selina didn't pick up on it. "How's it going?"

"Oh, fine. Morale in the Drama Department seems to be very low."

Chris nodded. "Bound to happen. You can't make an omelette without breaking eggs."

"No. I wish I could help though. Jonathan's suffering, anyone can see that."

"He'll be alright, don't worry," Chris reassured her. He had come to terms with what he called his 'crush' on Selina, and now saw her as a protégée. He would see to it that she survived and prospered through whatever seismic events the BBC was to encounter, and since she was planning to marry Jonathan he intended to do right by him too, as he had told her. If the boy played his cards right he could be a useful Head of Drama at some point. Chris was working on building a team of loyal, like-minded individuals.

"I know. It's not the long term that's the problem, it's dealing with the short term."

Chris nodded, "You're spot on, Selina, as usual."

"I was reading about someone who runs workshops to help people come to terms with change. I forget his name, but it sounded rather good. Maybe we could introduce something along those lines?"

"Workshops to boost morale. Good idea. I like that." Chris remembered a module he had taken at the Harvard Business School, and made a mental note to look it up.

Jonathan was wondering what Basil would make of his dilemma as he entered Block D of Centre House, so he wandered by his new office on the ground floor. Stewart Walker was in with Basil, so he loitered outside to find out whether it was a brief chat or a long one. He caught a snatch of conversation; Stewart seemed to be annoyed about something.

"It's perfectly obvious Peter's feathering his own nest, Basil."

"If he fights everything they'll find a way to get rid of him."

"It's a matter of principle!"

"I know, I know. But we have to be pragmatic."

"We need a campaign. He's going to sell us down the river."

"He's doing his best to keep as much of the department open as he can."

"There's something else going on, Basil. Help me find out what it is."

Jonathan didn't hear Basil's reply, but the door suddenly opened and Stewart strode out, scowling. Jon waited a minute and tapped at the door.

Basil was arranging his books and files, not quite his usual friendly self. He pointed to the computer that squatted blankly on the desk, and asked Jon if he knew what was the matter with it. Jonathan had a look and found that it wasn't switched on. He showed Basil how to do it, and where to find his emails.

"Aren't they sending you on a course, Basil?"

"Yes, yes," he sighed. "They keep telling me I must do one. I keep asking for a typewriter, but they've all been thrown out. By the way, they've cancelled Tony Scott's sequel. Apparently the ratings on *Down and Up* weren't good enough. Six million is too low, it seems, given the cost."

The irony of this cancellation following immediately after the Banff prize was not lost on Jonathan, and under the circumstances he didn't like to discuss his own problems with Basil. He offered his help at any time, and went on up to his office.

He hurried past Sonia who was using the photocopier with a face like a wet weekend, and went into the little kitchen to pick up a coffee from the percolator. Sally Farquar-Binns was there washing mugs at the sink.

"Hi Sally," said Jonathan, pouring a cup of stewed black coffee. "How are you?"

She turned and smiled bravely through loose hair which fell across her face. She looked as if she had been crying.

"Oh, surviving," she said. "Actually, not surviving." She turned back to the sink.

Ever the gentleman, Jonathan gently enquired what she meant.

"I'm out at the end of the month," Sally explained, trying to sound bright but ending on a semi-strangulated sob. "Morag just told me. I suppose I knew it was coming, but I thought, you know, something would turn up... "

"I'm really sorry, Sally," said Jonathan convincingly. He put a hand on her shoulder but she withdrew from him.

"You're awfully sweet, Jon, but you'll only make me howl. I refuse to give the fat old bitch *that* satisfaction."

"Was she brutal?"

"She was like that woman screw in *Prisoner Cell Block H*," said Sally bitterly. "Do you know the one I mean?"

Jonathan thought he did, and tried hard not to smile. Surely Morag couldn't have been so melodramatically cruel, this must be Sally's disappointment talking.

"You'd think she would at least *pretend* to be sorry about it, wouldn't you?"

"Yes, you would," agreed Jonathan. "Don't worry Sally, there's life outside the BBC you know. You're sure to get another job somewhere."

"Do you think so?" Sally's distraught eyes beseeched him.

He answered with all the sincerity he could muster, "Of course."

"Thanks Jonathan. I won't forget you. Selina's a very lucky woman."

Sally kissed him on the cheek and walked out like Greta Garbo.

Jim finished his second draft in a couple of weeks. Peter still wanted Jonathan's brother Roger to direct, and he was keen to do it. Jon seemed oddly unexcited though. Something seemed to have sapped his enthusiasm. He told me he had every confidence in Roger, and that he might even be a great director in the making. He was just worried about the corporate end of things, he said. He wondered, in his down moments, whether the show would ever get made.

At the time of course I had no idea what was going on between him and Selina. Mr Discretion had never gossiped about his fiancée and he was hardly likely to start now. He seemed to enjoy my company, and would often come by my office for a chat. He said it was really helpful to talk things over with me, and that he appreciated my honest reactions. I began to enjoy chatting with him myself, having realised that my first impressions had been very shallow. He was really clever, and one of the least judgemental people I've ever met. Best of all he listened very carefully to whatever I said, and was always open to changing his mind. How many people like that do you know? And to top it all off, he was very easy on the eye. If he hadn't been spoken for I might even have wasted time wondering whether there was any chance he'd go for me, but men like him don't, on the whole. Not because they don't like short dark Welsh women – I'm quite pretty, some people think so anyway – but all men like tall slim blondes best, don't they? And women like that make a bee-line for men like Jonathan, so the rest of us never get a look-in.

A week or two after this a memo came round instructing each of us to attend a one-day workshop. It said that the management had noticed staff morale in drama was suffering, and an independent consultant had been brought in to run a series of workshops. The staff approached it with scepticism as we didn't know what to expect and there was much muttering at the strain it must be adding to the department budget. Jonathan had little enthusiasm for it but didn't want it to show. He had to go to the first one, I didn't, but Maggie came up to London for it, so I was looking forward to seeing her afterwards.

It took place in the Centre House conference room. The leader was a very friendly lecturer with several books out on the fashionable new subject of 'people management', which were displayed on a table by the door. Being asked to work here was a feather in his cap, and he was keen to rise to the considerable challenge presented by the BBC in flux, and hoped ultimately to become a famous consultant. He welcomed his new clients enthusiastically and thanked them for finding the time to come, as if he thought attendance had been voluntary.

The rest of the group was composed of Donald Mountjoy, who stayed only ten minutes before his mobile phone conveniently summoned him away to urgent business; producer Gillian Makin from Pebble Mill, a dozen editors, production executives and associates whom Jonathan barely knew, and Maggie. She had mellowed considerably, and Jon now appreciated her knack of seeing straight to the heart of the problem, even if she did still tend to stick the knife in with indelicate Yorkshire bluntness. He now recognised that actually she was just like him in her commitment to high standards and ideals, and merely expressed herself differently.

The leader introduced himself as David Stringfellow, no relation, (which no-one else found amusing) and outlined the day's work, which involved analysing their work practices, discussing what the problems were, and finding possible solutions.

They divided into groups and sat on the floor with sheets of wallpaper liner and magic markers, making flow diagrams and lists. This generated a great deal of discussion and they soon overcame their initial reluctance as they found collaboration lent power to their private feelings. Truly, there was a lot that could be improved, and they began to feel empowered to do something about it.

After a break the groups assembled to present their results. They had all come to much the same conclusions, finding bureaucratic structure and lack of money to be the basis of all the problems. David began to play devil's advocate, challenging their assumptions and encouraging group discussion. Then he asked them to get together again and redraw their work process diagrams, adding in suggestions at every stage for ways in which they could increase their own efficiency.

"For instance," he said, "one of my personal problems is time management. I'm a very conscientious worker, but I tend to get on with the first thing on my list and ignore the rest till later, with the result that by Saturday I've still got half a dozen things that need doing, and the family wants me to go shopping, watch my daughter diving, and all the rest of it: now I don't see family life as less important than work, far from it, but I *do* tend to let it go to the bottom of the list. Does that ring any bells?" he looked round smiling at the semi-circle of faces but only Gillian Makin nodded and smiled back at him. Maggie was frowning.

"If several of you would like to, we can look at ways of managing your time so that you can do *every*thing, and nothing suffers. Sound good? Maybe. Okay, we'll come back to that."He pressed on and finished up with a list of possibilities they could look at, from reorganising your desk and filing system to delegating work. Then he began prioritising them.

Maggie sat frowning thoughtfully throughout, and finally raised her hand. "I'm sorry David, but can I say something? I don't mean to be negative, I can see that what you're doing could be extremely useful to a lot of people, but I'm afraid it has very little bearing on what's going on here."

Jonathan, who had found the meeting more tedious than useful and had been drifting off into contemplation, now focussed his attention on Maggie.

"The fact is," she continued, "that people here do an amazing job in the face of extreme difficulty. Their professionalism is infinite. I think I speak for all of us – do say if I don't, everyone – in that we're *already* working as efficiently as it's possible to work. Most people don't take lunch hours, they stay late in the office, they do extra work which used to be done by other staff who've been got rid of. They juggle work and home life brilliantly. The things which hold us up are not our personal inadequacies." David immediately gestured that he had never intended to suggest such a thing. "But *management* inadequacies. They sit on decisions until the last possible minute so we don't get enough time to prepare properly, or we lose the actors and writers we most want to work with. They don't know or care what making programmes is really about. They don't see it as a *creative* process at all. There's a terrible gulf developed which never used to be there in the old days – not that I've been here all that long, but that's what I understand." Maggie looked to Gillian, who nodded in agreement. "As if programmes are something you turn out by the yard." She paused, not wishing to proceed unless she was voicing a generally-held point of view, and saw her colleagues nod unhappily.

"To be honest David you should be running workshops with *them*. Suggesting that the department's problems are due to our own inefficiency is frankly very insulting."

Jonathan added his support. "I have to agree with Maggie. Without prejudice to you, it's been useful getting together like this, but low morale can't be cured by emotional Elastoplast."

David looked deeply disappointed, although he was experienced enough to know that Maggie and Jonathan were telling the truth. In fact he had made similar observations to himself already, and had been wondering how to report back to Peter Maxwell. "I'm terribly sorry if I've given you the impression that the state of morale at the BBC is in any way your own fault, I know that's not the case. And I will happily pass your conclusions on to the management, without putting any names in. Do you think that would be a useful outcome?"

They all agreed that it would, although some were very nervous that such a move might rebound back on them. Nonetheless they spent the last hour telling David all their grievances, which he listed and promised to collate and circulate to them before reporting back to Peter and his superiors.

Jonathan and Maggie left the workshop having rather enjoyed it after all. They had got a lot off their chests in the safe environment of a closed discussion, and felt fired with something akin to the spirit of revolution.

"I don't suppose it'll make a fat lot of difference, will it?"

asked Maggie.

"I doubt it," replied Jonathan. "It's all gone too far. I'm looking forward to seeing what David comes up with all the same."

"Yeah, if I'm still here. Anthea Onojaife offered me a job as producer with her new company. It's only a series for Channel 5, but I'm going to take it."

Jonathan was surprised. "Have you had enough of *Casualty*?"

"It's been almost a year now," replied Maggie. "And I really want a change. I came up to see if there was anything else available, but Morag's warned me there isn't enough to justify renewing my contract. I'm sick of the BBC. It feels like a long slow process of selling out. So I'm speeding it up – I'm getting out while the going's good. I was never a corporate player anyway. It's just not me."

Maggie's determined expression belied the disappointment in her voice. Jonathan surmised that it had been a much more difficult decision than she was letting on.

"It's all very well having principles, but they don't pay the bills," he remarked.

"That's just it, but I figure I can probably do some good stuff. Maybe my show will be the one that puts Channel 5 on the map!"

Jonathan smiled and tried to nod convincingly. They both knew that Channel 5 was an unknown quantity, a real gamble.

"Jill Watkins is going to be the lead writer on it," continued Maggie. "So at least we'll have a good time, even if we can't change the world."

He was both pleased and disappointed for Maggie; she clearly felt she had failed to make her mark at the BBC. Jonathan had been fortunate to become established in the department just before the axe began to fall. Maggie probably wouldn't be so lucky. She was making the right choice, given the state of the industry.

"Anthea's done really well for herself, hasn't she?" mused Jonathan.

"Yep. Hats off to the secretary bird, she's making waves."

Chapter Nineteen

Catherine Briggs switched on the new fifty-inch widescreen
television, drew the curtains and plumped up the sofa cushions
as Jeremy Paxman's lugubrious face filled the flat screen and, it
seemed, most of the wall.

"... her theme is that the BBC risks remaining stuck in its
past, hobbled by the imperialist culture which originally gave
birth to it. She claims there's no true pluralism in the organisation, merely colonial compromise, and that attitudes inside the
BBC are hopelessly old-fashioned. I'm joined in the studio by
the article's author, Anthea Onojaife; Chris Briggs, Managing
Director of the BBC; and Barry Goodman, Chief Executive of
the latest terrestrial channel to be launched in the UK: Channel
5. Welcome to *Newsnight*, everyone.

"Anthea. You joined the BBC as a secretary in 1985. Twelve
years on, you're running your own independent production
company, Sisters in Synch. So... what's the problem?"

"Good evening, Jeremy. The problem, in black and white
terms, if you'll pardon the pun, is that ethnic minority citizens
are desperately under-represented at the editorial and managerial
levels of the BBC, and this is reflected in the faces we see on the
screen. In fact, if you don't mind me saying so, this interview
arrangement is absolutely typical."

An ironic smile lurked behind her interviewer's stern frown,
but he conquered it. Watching together in Crouch End, Jill and
Carmen chortled and cheered. "You tell him, Anthea. Bite

the dog!"

"Three white men and one black woman: that's 25% black, a rather better proportion than you'd find in the population as a whole, I suspect."

"I'm Jewish, as a matter of fact, so you could say we're 50% ethnic minority," offered Barry Goodman smugly.

"You could hardly assemble an all-male, all-white panel to discuss this particular issue, could you Jeremy? The entire media would come down on you faster than a ton of bricks."

Anthea won the bout with this skilful blow, and Jeremy acknowledged it gracefully for a nanosecond before moving in with a fresh question. "You didn't like working at the BBC, then. Why not?"

"I found it very hard to move up the career ladder here, so eventually I gave up and left."

"That simple?"

"Yes, actually."

"Chris Briggs. Do we block our ethnic minority staff from promotion?"

"Well Jeremy, I have to say that we value all our staff very highly indeed."

"Hmm," said Jeremy, "I've certainly noticed that there are posters all over reception saying exactly that. Which seems odd at a time when so many staff are being laid off."

Chris let this pass with a pained expression. At home, Catherine sighed and put her feet up. Come on Chris, she urged mentally. Don't be a weed. It seemed to work.

"Modernisation and progress entail difficult decisions. Very many excellent scribes were put out of work when the printing press was invented, I think you'll find!"

"Let's get back to the point. Why are all the top jobs held by middle class white men?"

"It's historical, basically. I don't like it any more than you do, or Anthea does, but it takes time for these things to change. We *have* changed our attitudes, and given time, I have every confidence – "

"How long do you *want*?"

"No-one can put a time limit on a thing like this – "

"Ten years?"

"You know I can't put a figure on it, Jeremy."

"Alright," said Jeremy, unhooking him and allowing him to flop back in his chair.

Over in Wapping, Nik Mason arrived home, bolted the entrance to his loft, hurried to the television and switched on just in time to see Barry Goodman set off at his usual eighty words per minute.

"Thank you Jeremy," he smiled. "At Channel 5 we pride ourselves on being at the cutting edge of the market. We're bang on the button with dynamic, desirable entertainment. Our staff reflect this. Watch Channel 5 and you'll see we're way ahead of the other channels in terms of representing Britain in 1997."

"Are you referring to your attractive blonde newscaster or the explicit sexual material you broadcast?" asked Jeremy peremptorily.

"Ha!" Jill and Carmen clapped. Catherine smiled. Nik sneered, and poured himself a Jack Daniels as Barry attempted to weasel his way out of that one. Jeremy's attention was already on his next question.

"What do you propose then, Anthea? How is the BBC supposed to represent everyone, equally, all the time? Aren't you asking for the impossible?"

"No-one expects an overnight transformation, but I do believe you need to speed up the rate of change." Anthea looked Chris in the eye. "The BBC's lagging behind. The unions have been making this argument for years, decades even. Equal opportunities have been standard in some fields for ages, in theatre companies, for example. Why not here? There's no excuse. The BBC's not just white and male-dominated, it's Oxbridge and home counties-dominated. Outrageously so. Look at you guys!" Jeremy and Chris were both silenced by this, which their viewers all enjoyed. Even Nik agreed with Anthea on this one. Barry nodded enthusiastically but was ignored. Anthea continued, "The BBC's like the NHS, state schools, even the Scouts – it's free, it's marvellous, it's for everyone – but it's also pompous and patronising. A bit like you, Jeremy. I'm sorry." Everybody watching held their breath at Anthea's nerve. "There's no equivalent anywhere abroad, it's really important, especially the World Service, which is being cut back as we speak." She paused, hoping Jeremy wasn't offended. She hadn't really intended to be so personal. She needn't have worried, he took it on the chin, and allowed her to carry on, "If we're not careful we'll lose everything worth watching, all the new, experimental shows, our television will be exactly the same as in the US: unwatchable rubbish, wall-to-wall mindless nonsense sponsored by corrupt Bible-bashers, with a five-minute advertising break every five minutes."

Jeremy leaned back and turned to Chris. "Is that what we're going to get?"

"Of course not," smiled Chris. "It's a wild exaggeration, and it could never happen while we have the license fee."

"Which happens to be under threat."

"The license fee's a complete anachronism!" Barry leaped in. "The future of television is more choice: many many channels, offering a wide, wide range – "

"Of crap, crap shows?" Anthea's interjection raised another laugh from her scattered audience. Barry's composure began to crack. She was working for him, wasn't she?

"People are always saying the golden age of television is over," he said crossly, "I say it's just beginning. In the twenty-first century we'll see interactive television become established. It'll be democratic in the truest sense, digital technology will mean ordinary people take ownership of the medium. It won't be the property of the elite any more. The market will itself create a level playing field, where every minority interest will find its own space, have its own cable channels. There'll be 24-hour news channels, sports channels, shopping channels – and yes, sex channels, for those who want them. Why not? It's their choice. Ordinary people will have their own shows, they'll become stars in their own right. Access for all."

"To each their fifteen minutes of fame," commented Jeremy. "Is this the death knell for the BBC?" he asked Chris.

"We're a very long way from the end of public service broadcasting. This is, purely and simply, cynical doom-mongering. I don't blame Barry for talking up his new channel of course, that's his job, but let's not forget – his viewers are very few so far, and he's obliged to use, er, *tabloid* strategies to pull them in."

"The BBC will never use the equivalent of page three girls to attract an audience?"

"The Reithian principles of education, information and entertainment are still sacrosanct, Jeremy."

"What do *you* make of Reithian principles?" Jeremy put Anthea on the spot.

She didn't pause. "I don't have a problem with them at all, it would be like criticising the ten commandments. I just think we should move with the times, acknowledge progress – but not by abandoning everything we believe in and jumping on the bandwagon with the barrow boys – sorry Barry, just a figure of speech – "

"Careful babe," muttered Carmen, "don't forget who's commissioned us." Jill murmured her agreement. Nik exclaimed irritably, but he expected little else from the woman who had successfully defended Sisters in Synch from Magenta's hostile takeover bid. Her company was poised to become a major player in the next decade. He poured another drink. Catherine leaned her head back and began to doze.

"What I really care about is creativity," said Anthea firmly. "That's what gets lost in the scramble for profits. The difficult subjects tend to get ignored, along with the interesting people. It's just as damaging as favouritism towards the Oxbridge, home counties types."

"So instead of a new David Hockney we get a man who stuffs sharks."

"Exactly, Jeremy. Not that I've anything against Damien Hirst, not at all – but we need diversity. If we don't safeguard it, it'll vanish."

"But Anthea, you're contradicting yourself," said Chris. "You say on the one hand that you had to leave the BBC to move on with your career, and on the other that the free market militates against creativity – yet that's where you found your opportunity." Barry Goodman wished he'd said that.

"I think it's very sad that I had to leave the BBC. I'd much rather have stayed. And to be fair, it's not just my colour that's the problem here. Everyone's struggling, absolutely everyone. Morale in the Drama Department's at an all-time low. No-one can get anything remotely challenging commissioned these days." She looked straight at Chris, whose eyes widened slightly. Jeremy turned to him.

"Why aren't you commissioning challenging drama?"

"Aside from the fact that I'm no longer a channel controller, the BBC very definitely does commission exciting original work, and Anthea is more than welcome to bring us her ideas," smiled Chris smoothly. Jill and Carmen grimaced at each other sceptically. Catherine was now asleep with her mouth open. Nik switched his television off and put on a CD.

Jeremy turned to Anthea and asked a question with genuine interest, "If you were Director General of the BBC, what would you do?"

She chuckled at the absurd idea. "I'd try to have a better overview. I'd try to ensure a fair spread of opinions, points of view, a range of voices. I'd try to expunge the idea that 'we know what's good for you', but I wouldn't let the likes of Rupert Murdoch have it their way – I see them as worse than the old patriarchy in many ways: far more exploitative, and in a much subtler way." Barry frowned, unsure where he fitted in this scheme. "I don't know whether I'm cut out to be Director General, even if I had a cat in hell's chance of being offered it," admitted Anthea. "But I truly want to see creativity flourish in an atmosphere of equality. I mean *real* creativity, not the advertising industry kind. We need stories that tell us more about ourselves, rather than selling us back to ourselves. As a matter of fact I think there are huge creative opportunities right now. The industry's expanding like mad, and so are viewers worldwide. In future I think we'll be getting our funding from all sorts of people: banks, businesses, maybe even private individuals. I think there's going to be a big resurgence of street theatre and guerrilla art – it's beginning already; street music and fashions have always led the rest. Maybe Barry's right, and cable channels for ordinary people will be the norm in the next century. Maybe they'll start broadcasting their own shows, and amongst them will be the next Spike Lee, or Shakespeare! It's all good, in the end it doesn't matter where the new work comes from, as long as creative people can get access to an audience. I think that's an opportunity the BBC should provide. It's terribly sad that they've stopped caring about it."

"And on that note, I'm afraid we'll have to end… "

"Wow," said Jill. "Impressive. What are you doing?" Carmen's eyes were closed and her lips were twitching.

"I'm praying that Anthea will be Director General of the BBC one day."

I watched it on my own at home, almost moved to tears. Anthea was articulating what half the Drama Department thought but would scarcely admit to each other, never mind to some of the most powerful men in broadcasting and the world at large. Perhaps she'd reached the point where she no longer cared how her opinions were received. Maybe she felt she'd always been there, so it didn't matter. Part of me longed to join her, but I'd been accepted by them – the Welsh had been considered okay for a century or two so I didn't feel I had the right to complain, really. I was totally in awe of her.

Sitting soaking in the bath the next morning I wondered what was coming. 1997 felt like a significant year. The election was likely to bring us a new government, which would be a tremendous relief, but uncertain changes lay ahead. I could barely remember when Labour had last been in power. It was tempting to imagine that all our problems would be solved, but I wasn't *that* naïve, and many people were suspicious of what 'New Labour' really meant. There was no guarantee that they would bring in socialist policies. The Tories had insisted for years that the BBC was a hotbed of radicalism, full of subversives who would like to bring down the government; it was nonsense of course. There were certainly left-wing opinions broadcast, but they were more than balanced by the right.

What would a Labour government's attitude be towards the BBC? Would it change things within the organisation? I really couldn't tell. I had a feeling that we were coming to the end of something, but I also knew that *I'd* changed recently. At the ripe old age of 32 my outlook was no longer just about following my nose through life; I wasn't a bright young person any more, wide-eyed and willing. That's to say – I was, I hope so anyway, but I knew it was time to think more carefully about my future. I'd been avoiding that for a long time already.

I inhaled the lavender bath oil I'd put in, and ran a little more hot water to revive the scent. What did I want the next ten years to bring? Did I still want to stay in London, carry on at the BBC, and devote my life to making drama? Yes, I thought so. But I wasn't as sure as I used to be. I wanted to make quality drama, and I also wanted to have a family eventually. Quite how that could be achieved when my working hours were so long and variable, I didn't know. Most women I knew of at the BBC were supported by nannies, au pairs and what have you – I couldn't see myself employing people to raise my children, it would be too great a leap from my own upbringing. And of course I was still single.

I wondered whether Jonathan and Selina would be starting a

family soon. No doubt their domestic arrangements would be very comfortable. Jon was such a nice person, I sometimes wished he would crack a little, let go. I thought he deserved better than Selina. I found her a cold fish. It was hard to tell her real personality under the façade, which Jim said was grander than Selfridge's; she just seemed boringly bland to me. Jon was wasted on her. He had so much more to offer. And he was so handsome... if he was single, would he be interested in me? Best not to think about that. He liked me though, I was fairly sure. And we got along very well. Anyway, he was taken. Forget it, I told myself.

Maybe I would start looking elsewhere for work. If *The Medical Miracle* didn't get green-lit soon I might have to, as my contract would be up for renewal in a few weeks. Morag was letting people go every month. The atmosphere in the department was increasingly dire, and it was bringing everyone down. In some ways it would be a relief to leave. I wondered what Jon would do if we lost the show. Would he try to take it to another broadcaster? Might he ask me to join him? Maybe he might start up a new independent production company, and ask me to be head of development? Now that would be really nice. That could really mean the best of both worlds. Maybe we'd have an office in the West End, instead of Shepherd's Bush – in Covent Garden or Soho. That would be perfect.

My vision had crystallised into a very appealing future when I realised the bathwater was going cold. Newly oriented, I heaved myself out of the bath and threw a big towel around my shoulders as the water swirled down the plughole, sucking my old skin down with it.

Anthea received a rapturous welcome when she arrived at Sisters in Synch the morning after her *Newsnight* appearance. They had a development meeting scheduled; the writers and Maggie were already there, and they applauded her entrance, so she took an embarrassed bow. Maggie, who had gone to the

Newsnight studio with her to give moral support, had been so impressed that she feared she might be developing a crush on this Amazon. The writing team were inspired. They'd liked her before, but now they would do anything she asked. It felt wonderful.

The day sped by. Ideas were born, combined, they grew, they flew, they were captured and harnessed, they bore offspring. They were corralled into a drama series which would be challenging, surprising, funny, but above all truthful in what it said about contemporary urban life. The characters reflected the capital's racial mix, the attitudes of the young generation, the pressures of the modern workplace; they were nearly all intelligent and they were predominantly female, even though it was essentially an office-based series. At the end of the day they agreed on a title: *Sisters and Brothers*.

Jill and Maggie walked to the tube station together afterwards. Jill was anxious about whether Channel 5's Barry Goodman would take offence at the way Anthea had made him look stupid on television, and make trouble for the show. Maggie was unconcerned.

"It'll be fine. She apologised profusely to him after the broadcast, she said she'd got carried away with her anger at the BBC, and how true it was that Channel 5 had given her such a good break, and generally crawled up his bum. He was okay with it – if we give him a ratings success, he'll forget all about it. If we don't, he'll probably remember, but he stands to get all the credit if the show does what we hope it will."

"Men are weird, aren't they?" said Jill. "You can never really tell how they'll react."

"And they think *we're* the unpredictable ones."

"Maybe there's a story I can use in that."

"You're busting with ideas, aren't you?"

Jill sighed happily. "It's the best feeling in the world. A couple of weeks ago I was in development hell, I was almost ready to call it a day and get a job at Tesco. Writing was torture.

Suddenly it's like I've walked through some portal into a parallel universe. Development heaven, that's where I am now!"

Penny chose not to mention the *Newsnight* debate when she arrived at Magenta the following day; she had no doubt where Nik's sympathies lay.

Jak, however, lost no time in raising the subject the minute he entered their large open plan office. "The BBC's like a beached whale, ain't it? Too big and blubbery to turn round and get back in the sea. It's just lying there, puffing out its last gasps."

Penny observed him over her half-moon reading glasses, calculating that he'd been working on that metaphor since he woke up.

The effort was repaid: Nik was impressed. "Too right, man," he said. "Its days are numbered. The twenty-first century's going to be completely different, and I, for one, can't wait. D'you see *Newsnight*, Penny?"

"Unfortunately not. Was it good?" she enquired disingenuously.

"You missed a cracker," smirked Jak.

"The beauty of it all is… " Nik paused for their full attention, "We don't have to do a bloody thing. We needn't lift a finger. All we do is sit here, turning out hit shows by the dozen, whilst the BBC turns in on itself, chews its own legs off and eats its own insides. There's no need for us to fight them. We just wait till they're staggering around blindly looking for a bandage, and we stroll in with our fabulous series. They'll fall at our feet."

Penny regarded him with amusement, the cheek of the man! His arrogance was astounding. She returned to her computer screen, and the endless search for budget economies.

Later the three met to look at the *Bus Stops Here* episode breakdown which Jak and his team of novice writers had produced. Penny's heart had sunk on reading it, the writers' skills were disturbingly weak. Chosen for their youth, malleability, cheapness and lack of union membership, it seemed to Penny that they hadn't even mastered a basic grasp of grammar. She wished she could remove the lot in one sweep of her arm, and replace them with a couple of the experienced professionals she was used to, but she realised that criticising Nik and Jak's decisions would lead only to her own swift defenestration. So she kept her own counsel, and hoped that the boys (she allowed herself to think of them in those terms) would eventually realise for themselves that this shower couldn't write a hit series in a hundred years, never mind six weeks. She would stick to her brief, and comment only when the budget was affected.

"Nice work, Jak," began Nik. "It's looking good. I like your guest star list: Billy Crystal, Pamela Anderson, The Spice Girls... "

Penny sighed, and Nik invited her to state the obvious, "A-list celebrities charge A-list fees, that's the trouble Jak. Not a lot I can do about that."

Nik nodded, and gave Jak a sympathetic look. "Sorry mate, but we'll have to start with the lower ranks. Think of some more – the ones who've dropped off the radar and need a bit of exposure. Old pop stars, maybe. Dolly Parton. Gary Glitter. I'll leave it with you. Okay, location and set. That's a biggie. Tell us the bad news, Pen."

"Well you're right, it's pretty crucial that we find somewhere incredibly cheap, and very easy to reach, we can't pay much in travel and subsistence. I reckon we can get by with six weeks on location and another six in the studio, but there's no leeway at all, no contingency. Supposing we find the ideal location, we're going to need an experienced crew, Nik, otherwise we could end up with the most appalling shambles."

Nik had been long enough in the business to see the wisdom of this. You could scrimp and save in development and pre-production, but once the cameras were rolling money flew through your fingers, and mistakes at that point could mean binning the lot and having to start again. That was a risk too far. "We need a good crew, you're spot on there, Pen. It's a priority.

Get us the best people you know."

"The best people don't work for this kind of money, I'm afraid."

Nik simply looked at her, his eyebrows raised, "Just get 'em."

Penny frowned and sighed. "I really can't squeeze any more out of other areas of the budget. It's all skin and bone."

Nik smiled encouragingly. "You'll find a way round it. I've got every confidence in you Pen." He clapped her on the shoulder and her glasses fell onto the desk. "Sorry, darling."

Penny pursed her lips. "I might be able to call in a couple of favours, I suppose… " Nik winked, and clicked his tongue twice. Penny tried to pretend he hadn't, and fiddled with her specs.

"Title," announced Nik. "*Bus Stops Here* is killing me, it's so dull. No Yank-appeal."

"Sorry?" Penny was confused.

"Yank-appeal. Will the Yanks lap it up?"

"Oh, overseas sales."

"You've got it." Nik cleared his throat; trust Penny to be slow with the current terms. "It's essential, a snappy title. Luckily I had a bit of a breakthrough this morning. I woke up with this one, short word in my head." He paused again for effect. "BUS. With an exclamation mark."

Penny and Jak stared, nodding slowly. Penny hated it, but let nothing show.

"BUS!" murmured Jak. "Buss! What about two s'?" Nik grimaced. "You're right, keep it simple. Bus! I like it, Nik. It's short and sweet."

"Very memorable," added Penny.

"Dynamic. Simple," agreed Jak.

"And the beauty of it is the image," explained Nik. "The good old Routemaster, pillar-box red – instant recognition all over the planet. You couldn't ask for a better selling point."

"Well there you go, then," said Penny rashly. "End of discussion." Nik glanced sideways at her, noting her momentary loyalty lapse. Sarcastic old cow, he thought. You'll see. Aloud, he said, "Okay. That's all for now, let's get cracking."

Chapter Twenty

A few weeks after Peter told Jonathan and me to prepare *The Medical Miracle* as fast as possible, it was done. I had the shooting scripts ready for printing in the new paper-saving A5 format, Roger had picked his locations, and the cast and crew were chosen and waiting to sign their contracts. All we needed was the controller's green light, which would release the funds. It had been an exciting time. Jonathan, Roger and myself had spent most of it together, trying to be as discreet as we could; Peter wanted the fewest possible number of people to know about it, so we didn't talk about it with colleagues. It was even removed from the Drama Brochure, which was still under constant revision. Jon and Roger deliberately chose actors who weren't well-known faces, but whose acting skills were superb. The design was to be very naturalistic and emphasise the beauty of the landscape and there would be a score of Welsh music. It would be shot on film, rather than videotape, so that the visual quality was top notch. It promised to be a very fine production. We were twiddling our thumbs now, trying to look busy and quell our anxiety.

One morning I was sorting through my post, and found a document from David Stringfellow which summarised his conclusions following the series of workshops he had run. It seemed a long time ago already. I skim-read it; he'd put a lot of work into presenting a fair argument in favour of the proposals we had all made to improve the management of the department.

I thought it hadn't a hope in hell of being carried out and agreed with arch-cynic Stewart on this one. The whole enterprise was nothing but a sop to make us *think* we would be listened to, and keep us quiet for a few months. I opened another large envelope and found a cheaply photocopied booklet entitled *BBC Drama Brochure 1997-8*. I was puzzled. Was it Sonia's way of circulating a draft for all the producers to check? I propped my feet up on the desk and read it.

INTRODUCTION
Welcome to this year's drama brochure. If it looks flimsy, blame budget re-allocation. The launch has been delayed for the fifth time, and might happen in a couple of years in 'Stroller's Deli'. As you can see, we have a splendid array of dramatic produce on offer, I'm sure you'll find something tasty to tempt you. Enjoy!

DRAMA GROUP STAFF
At the time of going to press there were unfortunately no departmental heads expected to remain in place for more than a couple of weeks. The executive producers were in a meeting. The producers were down the job centre.

I was intrigued. It was a pretty accurate take-off of the style of the brochure. Was this Sonia's idea of a joke? If so, it was very out of character. I read on. The next season's output wasn't presented in the usual divisions of series, serials, singles and shorts, but as: *COPS AND CRIME SHOWS! DOCS AND SCIENCE SHOWS! FEELGOOD SHOWS! FEELBAD SHOWS! NICE COZZIES! VEHICLES FOR AGEING STARS!* I had to smile. As a summary of our programmes it wasn't entirely inaccurate:

COPS AND CRIME SHOWS:
THE BROKER'S MAN – Sour but sexy detective quits Fraud

Squad to investigate insurance.
DANGERFIELD – Sour but sexy police doctor with many problems acquires more.
THE CRIME TRAVELLER – Sour but sexy detective time travels to solve crimes before they happen.
DALZIEL AND PASCOE – Sour cop teams up with sexy cop.
HARPUR AND ILES – Straight cop teams up with bent cop.
SILENT WITNESS – Tough but caring woman pathologist gets offally involved with victims.
BECK – Tough but caring woman journalist turns private dick.
HETTY WAINTHROPP INVESTIGATES -Mrs Bucket turns private dick.
PIE IN THE SKY – Fat foodie as unlikely cop.
HAMISH MACBETH – Offbeat PC off beaten track.
OUT OF THE BLUE – Troubled team tecs tackle tricky tasks.
BACKUP – Top cops back up bottom cops.

I had to pause for breath. I knew we made an awful lot of police drama, but a list like this really brought it home. I read on:

FEELGOOD SHOWS!
THE HELLO GIRLS – Fifties phones, fashion, fun and frolics.
BALLYKISSANGEL – Endearing Irish endure mass celebrated by celibate Brit.
PRESTON FRONT – Trials and tribulations on the TA trail.
COMMON AS MUCK – Bin-end bin men been round again.
HAVE YOUR CAKE – Sex in the suburbs.

FEELBAD SHOWS!
EASTENDERS – Cockney crones and crooks carry on croaking.
HOLDING ON – Murder on the underground express.
THE LAKES – Lovable Liverpudlian lynched by Lakelanders
THIS LIFE – Lifts lid on lissom lawyers' wobbly world.

And last but not least… SINGLE DRAMA

Due to lack of interest/ratings/space/funds we have decided this year to present one amalgamated film:
EFFING BASTARDS – Set on an inner-city council estate riddled with gang warfare and crime, two young people who initially distrust each other fall in love as a result of being drawn together in a terrifying spiral of deceit leading to an act which is to change their lives forever. Can they escape crack addiction? Will Angel be forced into prostitution and die of AIDS? Can love survive in the futile world that is post-Thatcherite Britain? A passionate, disturbing and sometimes hilarious film from Stewart Wanker and the multi-award-winning team who made 'The Truth', the searing indictment of Thatcher's Britain which swept the board at the Grimsby Film and TV Awards in 1981.

I was really giggling now. Thank God our show was ex-directory. I turned the page and found a letter:

Dear drama colleagues,
I guess this is goodbye. It's been nice knowing you all, I just wanted to say farewell before I canter off into the sunset. I'm making my escape before I end up in a van with the men in white coats.
Love,
Sonia

My jaw dropped. Sonia was resigning in the middle of the job. She'd had enough and had decided to go out with a splash. Presumably she wasn't planning to stay in the business. I picked up the phone and dialled her office number, but the voicemail informed me that she had resigned her post and gone. It was rather upsetting, and strangely moving. I wasn't close to Sonia but I respected her, and to be honest I was rather impressed with her parody. What a waste, I thought, yet another good producer bites the dust. I wandered over to Jonathan's office to find out whether he'd received a copy.

I could see through the glass in the door that Jon was on the phone, looking tense, so I loitered in the corridor until he put it down, and then tapped on the door. He looked up and beckoned me in.

"Everything okay?" I asked. He wrinkled his nose.

"Have a seat. What's that?"

"I think it's Sonia's parting shot. Have you seen it?"

"Not yet." Clearly, he had more important news. He frowned. "I'm in a tricky situation. D'you mind if I tell you about it?"

"Of course not, is there anything I can do?"

"Maybe. I'm not sure."

I was all ears. I sat in one of his little armchairs, and he swivelled his big desk chair to face me.

"I've just had Selina on the phone. Asking me all about *Medical Miracle*. In some detail." I nodded. "She feels she's been kept in the dark. Which she has. I feel terrible about it."

"She's annoyed, is she?" I asked sympathetically, assuming this was a relationship issue. "Don't worry, I'm sure she'll understand when she knows what Peter told us... once we get the green light we can stop being so secretive, can't we?"

"Hmm." Jon combed his hands through his hair. "That's just it. Selina's the one with the switch now."

"What d'you mean?"

"No green lights without her approval."

I was gobsmacked. "*Selina* gives the green light? How on earth – "

"Not exactly. The controller doesn't say yes unless he has a stamp of approval from Policy and Planning."

"My God. Can't these people take *any* decisions for themselves?"

"Apparently not. Why make a decision on your own if you can employ ten people to take the blame if it all goes tits up?"

"Okay." I tried to absorb it. "So – what's not to like about *Medical Miracle* – what's she saying?"

"She wants to test it with a focus group."

"A what?"

"A focus group. Like they do in advertising. Get a few punters in to respond to the idea, see whether they're likely to watch it."

"Right. Don't they do that in Hollywood, to test the endings of movies?"

"Yes. But she's going to do it on the cheap, with ten people, before it goes into production."

We gazed at each other, horrified.

"How? Will she show them a synopsis or something?"

"Yes, unless we go and pitch it to them."

I groaned. "That really takes the biscuit for the stupidest idea I've ever heard in my life! Why would the opinions of ten people off the street be worth hearing?"

"It's called market research."

"I always thought these decisions were made by well-informed, experienced executive programme makers, drawing on their own considered judgement. Not a handful of people who probably only watch football and will be so excited by being asked for their opinion that they'll just rabbit all their prejudices."

"That's how it used to be," said Jon. "Welcome to the modern world of free market economics."

"They'll hate the idea, they'll say it's depressing and they're not interested in Welsh farmers, especially if we don't tell them the herb is cannabis. And we can't do that."

"I think we're stuffed."

"We've got to find a way round it, Jonathan."

He sighed heavily and nodded. "We'd better tell Peter."

We both walked along to Peter's office and asked Vera if there was a chance of ten minutes with him. She said she'd slip us in before his next appointment if we waited, so we sat down and leafed through the broadcast magazines despondently, listening to Vera on the phone to the stationery administrator. One of the new improved systems was getting rid of the stationery cupboard. Until now, if you needed a pad or a pen you could just go and get one. She needed a pencil sharpener, it seemed, and was having some difficulty.

"I only want *one* though," she said into the phone. There was a pause. "But why? What am I supposed to do with two dozen?" Another pause. "Yes I understand that we have to order in bulk, but if... well why don't *you* order two dozen and we can come to you if we need one?" She held the phone away from her ear and looked at me, shaking her head. "Okay, okay, I give in," she said finally. "I'll order two dozen. Who cares?" She hung up. "Either of you need a pencil sharpener?"

"No thanks Vera," I said. "Too risky, I might hurt myself with it. Then I'd be in trouble with Health and Safety."

Peter's door opened, and Donald Mountjoy came out. Vera looked in and asked whether we could see him, then told us we could, so in we went. Peter looked harassed, as he usually did these days.

"Bloody Policy and Planning. I'm sorry Jonathan, I know you and Selina... "

"Please don't apologise Peter. I feel just the same."

"Now I've got Donald up in arms because she wants to see all the rushes. What the hell's it got to do with her, for God's sake? She doesn't know a film from a hole in the ground. Sorry."

"No, it's true, she doesn't," said Jonathan, to my astonishment. "She likes *When Harry Met Sally* and *The English Patient*, that's about it."

Even Peter noticed that this was an unusual comment for Mr Super-Nice to make, so he invited us to sit down.

"Actually we need to talk to you about something similar," I said.

"She wants to run a focus group on *Medical Miracle*," said Jon. "To find out whether it's going to appeal to a big audience before we start production."

"That's a bit odd. I haven't heard of using them like that before," said Peter. "I smell a rat. How much does she know about it?"

"No more than the official synopsis," said Jon. "She never asked, luckily. But now she says she needs detail before she can give her approval."

"Oh dear. I hoped that wouldn't be necessary, under the circumstances." Peter was alluding to the engagement.

"Yes. She's been on the phone this morning, wanting to know about the herbs, whether there's really a herb that can treat MS. She reckons that if there is, people are going to want it, but if there isn't, they'll be angry and think it's a silly story. Either way, she says, the BBC's liable to come in for criticism."

Peter rested his elbows on his desk top and his chin on his hands. Then he got up and walked round the office. He stopped at the window and looked out. A couple of minutes went by; Jon and I looked at each other, wondering whether to say anything, and decided to wait.

Finally Peter turned and shook his head. "I'm a bit stumped, I'm afraid. Leave it with me for the moment, would you? Stall her for the time being."

"Yes, of course," replied Jonathan, and we left him in peace.

We then went across to Television Centre for lunch so that we wouldn't have to talk to anyone else.

It seemed as though we'd run into a brick wall. I felt very sorry for Jon, he was in an awful position. Peter had more or less asked him to lie to his fiancée for the sake of his project. It was a risky strategy, possibly alcohol-influenced, and it could well mean the end of the road for *The Medical Miracle*, not to mention an unpleasant row with Selina. I told Jon I thought Peter was to blame for the mess, even though it was all done with the best intentions.

"Too much intrigue," I said. "It's all very well conniving and politicking, but in the end we haven't got the power, have we? They have." He agreed miserably. "Is there any chance Selina would see it our way, and back the show?"

He shook his head. "It's too much of a hot potato, politically. She's not really interested in drama as art, you know. I hadn't quite realised that before now. She always seemed really into it."

"That's 'cause she was after you," I commented with conviction. "Now she's got you she doesn't need to pretend anymore."

"You know what, Rhiannon?" He looked at me with an expression that nearly broke my heart. His clear blue eyes were wet, and his voice trembled. He swallowed. The noisy canteen vanished from my peripheral view, as I waited for him to speak. "I can't marry Selina. It's all been a huge mistake. It's obvious now." He bit his lower lip, and looked down. I wanted to give the poor boy a hug, but it was a bit awkward with a table between us, so I gripped his forearm in a supportive sort of way, and patted it. What do you say in answer to something like that?

"You poor thing." It didn't sound great, but it was all I could think of.

"I'm going to have to break it off. I love her, but... it'll never work." He took a huge deep breath, and blew out his cheeks. "You've no idea how much better I feel now!"

"Better out than in," I remarked stupidly, as if he'd burped. "You must have needed to get it off your chest."

"Yeah." He nodded. "You're so easy to talk to, Rhiannon. Thanks, you're a good friend."

"I hope so," I said, smiling and patting him again.

"I wish Selina was more like you."

"Stop!" I said, "Don't bring me into it."

"I don't understand how you're still single."

"Oh, I'm too perfect," I said. "I frighten all the boys away!" He was looking at me with this soft expression that made my hands sweat; my heart started thumping. Oh God I thought, now I'm in the shit. I mustn't let him know what I think about him. Fuck. Now what?

"We better be getting back" I said, knowing perfectly well that there was nothing to do. Jon didn't move.

"I don't know how to handle this," he said. "I can't for the life of me think of a way to save either the show or the relationship."

"Maybe we should ring Jim and ask him to write a solution?"

Jon managed a laugh. "Wouldn't it be great if you could do that – every time you hit a problem in life, you ring up your writer and get him to rewrite it for you!"

I agreed. "Don't do anything rash. Give it another day or two."

"I'm not sure it's fair to spin it out, now I've made up my mind."

"Hello Jonathan," said a silky voice. "And Rhiannon, isn't it?" We both jumped, shocked. "Sorry, did I startle you?" said Selina, who was standing by our table, carrying a tray with used crockery on it, evidently on her way out. "You were so wrapped up in your conversation that you didn't see me wave. I was sitting over there." She indicated the other side of the room. She was very calm, but I wasn't deceived: she thought there was something going on between us. Our reactions would have confirmed her suspicion. I gawped at her, blushing, and wished desperately that my cheeks wouldn't give me away. How could I tell her she'd got it all wrong, when I knew her fiancé was going to dump her?

"See you later," she said, walking elegantly to the tray rack, even managing to look stylish as she plonked her tray on a shelf and left the canteen.

"Oh dear," I said. "I'm sorry I touched your arm, she'll have thought – "

"Don't worry. It's okay." Jon looked very pale. "Well, that clarifies one issue, at any rate. I'll have to talk to her this evening, and break off our engagement."

I tried to smile encouragingly, and started piling up the plates. What a day this was turning out to be.

The afternoon passed without further incident until five o'clock when there was an emergency producers' meeting called by

Stewart Walker. Not being one of the anointed, I went home. Jonathan attended in the Centre House conference room along with the rest; their numbers being depleted to twenty or so, there was now room for everyone to sit down. He took a place between Basil and Donald. Peter was sitting at the back of the room with a quarter bottle of whisky.

Stewart was in the chair and thanked them for coming. "I couldn't sit by any longer. Watching this department disintegrate, while we all look the other way. It's time we took some action. We should publicise what's going on, rally public opinion behind the department. Tell the viewers what they won't be getting anymore of, if we all go. I'm proposing a one-day strike to start with."

There was a pause.

"Do you really think the public would listen?" asked Gillian Makin. "As far as they're concerned, there's plenty of good drama on the box. They won't notice any difference for at least five years, so the issue's meaningless as far as they're concerned, surely? It would just sound like a load of sour grapes from a bunch of old has-beens."

Fenella also looked pained. "Stewart's right, of course. But then it's easy for *him* to make radical speeches, he's already built himself a safe little bolt-hole." She looked acidly at him. "We don't all have independent production companies to go to."

Stewart scowled back. "That's got nothing to do with it. I'll still be trying to place projects with the BBC, they'll still black-ball me if they choose to. I'm not suggesting *any*one takes risks they don't want to take."

"Well *I* don't want to, I'm afraid," said Gillian. "I'm not very confident about getting work as it is. I'll probably have to accept a pay cut, whatever I do. I can't afford to lessen my chances. If that's all you've called this meeting for, I've got more important things to do, I'm sorry." She got up to leave.

Stewart's lip curled as he replied, "That's your decision, Gillian, and I'm sure we all respect it." He looked round the room, challenging each producer. Most lowered their gaze to the table. Behind Jonathan, Peter's bottle clinked against his glass. Stewart ignored him, pointedly. Jonathan felt very nervous. He wasn't really the striking type, despite his idealism. The state of the department cut him to the quick, but he still clung to the sapling of his own promising career in the face of the hurricane.

"I agree with you Stewart," said Basil. "We should have done this a year ago, at least. We've left it too late. The die is cast, the damage is done: we've all been on the parapet fiddling as Rome burned. I don't see how we can possibly reverse it all now."

Stewart listened, and assessed the mood of the room. "Donald?"

"Basil's right old boy. As usual."

"Peter? Won't you join me for Custer's Last Stand?"

"Sorry, Stewart. I'm inclined to cling to the wreckage, myself. All may not be lost, maybe the election will be called soon. That could change everything."

Stewart snorted. "If it does I'll dance naked on the *Nine O'Clock News*."

Jonathan's view was not sought, which made him feel as if it wasn't worth hearing. He felt ashamed, and out of his depth. Where Basil's calm and cheerful presence had always given him a sense of security, his current pessimism was disturbing. The meeting drifted to a close, and Stewart apologised irritably for wasting their time. The producers left the room separately and hurried back to their offices or into their cars, keen to forget the meeting and engage their minds elsewhere. Jonathan said a casual goodbye to Basil on the stairs; it was the last time he would see him.

Suddenly, Jonathan couldn't wait to leave. The broadcasting colossus, source of his inspiration and focus of his aspiration, seemed now to be rotting and crumbling. He felt an urge to run away before it crashed around his ears and buried him in its rubble. He went home, and rang Selina: he needed to talk, he said, could he come over? She told him it wasn't convenient.

*

At work the next morning I was dying to know where things stood but I didn't want to jump in with both feet, so I found myself wandering up the corridor and into the little kitchen. I washed up a few dirty mugs and the coffee percolator jug, and then strolled up to Vera's area to read the magazines. One of the younger script editors was in Morag's office and I could hear their conversation since the door was wide open. She was asking for an extension to her contract, maybe she could even finish editing the drama brochure? Morag said that was already being taken care of. There were no other vacancies at the moment. She could always ring in later on, and ask.

"Actually," said the girl. "I'm having a baby. I was really hoping I might be able to stay until it arrives."

"No way, dear. I'm sorry. It's out of the question. We're not the Department of Health and Social Security, you know."

I was shocked by this unsympathetic response, and looked at Vera to see whether she was listening. Her eyebrows were raised but she didn't look at me. The girl in Morag's office evidently had powerful hormones pumping round her bloodstream, and she released her fury with rising volume, "No. You're the Department of *Stealth* and Social *Misery*. I've slaved here for seven years without any perks at all, and you're kicking me out four months before I give birth so you won't have to pay me any benefits. You haven't even got the grace to say Congratulations! You're an old *cow* Morag. I hope they get rid of *you* too, in the nastiest way they know."

Morag gathered herself and shrilly barked, "I'll give you the benefit of the doubt and put this down to your state of mind, but only this once!"

"You do realise I could take you to an industrial tribunal for this!"

The girl stomped out of Morag's office and slammed the door behind her. I offered her a sympathetic look, but she was too angry and steamed off down the corridor, receiving a smattering of applause from two young temps who lived in fear of Morag. Vera and I shared a shiver, and I beat a retreat to my office.

Jonathan, I discovered later, had spent the night at Roger's following an evening of brotherly bonding over a couple of bottles of claret. Roger wasn't sorry to hear that Selina would not become his sister-in-law after all; he assured Jon that it was all for the best. He also had some other ideas about the future of *The Medical Miracle*. Jon woke late with a terrible hangover, as he wasn't used to drinking heavily, and I didn't see him till much later.

I waited in my office, hoping Jon would call. When the phone did finally ring I jumped and picked it up immediately. "Hiya!" I said.

"Good morning, am I speaking to Rhiannon Jones?" Shit a brick, it was Selina.

"That's right, can I help you?"

"Policy and Planning here. Selina. We met yesterday." She was an ice queen. I felt sweat breaking out of every pore.

"Yes?" I responded cautiously.

"Just a quick question about your drama serial, Rhiannon. It's cannabis, isn't it?"

Her accusation struck like a stiletto in the neck. I froze, and hesitated. Had she worked it out? Had Jon confessed? Why was she asking *me*? Should I admit it, or lie? Was I being set up? The seconds ticked by as my brain hurtled through the options.

"Hello? Are you still there?" she sounded a bit annoyed now, and I thought there was a hint of triumphalism in her tone.

"Um, yes. I was just thinking about it. I think… well, it *could* be I suppose, the idea is that we don't actually specify a particular herb… "

"I've been doing some research. Apparently some people do use cannabis to treat the symptoms of MS."

"Oh! Do they really?" I didn't imagine for a moment that I

was convincing her, but some people always assume that they're cleverer than others.

Selina didn't seem to have a high opinion of me. "For goodness' sake, it's obvious that your writer is trying to pull the wool over your eyes. Are all Welsh people as naïve as you?"

Now, that's not a good way to talk to a Welsh woman, especially if you're a stuck-up pompous twit of a plummy public schoolgirl. I gritted my teeth, took a deep breath and put on my extra-polite voice, "Do you think so? Maybe I should have a word with him."

"Maybe you should."

"Is there anything else I can help you with?" I tried not to sound like Ruth Madoc in *Hi di Hi*, but failed miserably.

"No thank you. You've told me all I need to know."

She hung up. Oh God, I thought, what now? Have I let the cat out of the bag? I didn't actually admit anything. Might we still get away with it?

I paced my room. Maybe I should go and see Peter. But I needed to catch up with Jon first, otherwise I might screw things up even more. The phone rang again, and I grabbed it. "Hello?"

"One more thing Rhiannon." Oh God. "Is Jonathan with you?"

"No!" At least I could answer that honestly. She didn't sound convinced though.

"When he arrives, tell him to come up and see me, would you?"

"I'm not his PA. I don't know his whereabouts today."

"Tell him it's urgent."

She hung up again. I thought – you're not as cool as you make out, are you? Even down the phone, I could tell she was dying to slap my face. Just you try it, I thought – I'll have you for assault. I've done nothing wrong, nothing at all. I made devil horns with my fingers and waved them in the direction of Television Centre, whispering, 'Die, die, stupid cow!' just to let off steam. Then I remembered the glass in my door.

Jonathan was in the shower at Roger's bachelor flat in Hoxton, trying to drag his body and brain into gear while Roger made coffee and toast. He shaved with his brother's razor and borrowed some of his underwear (not entirely to his taste) then he found a tolerable shirt in the wardrobe, and sat down for breakfast.

"Alright?" asked Roger.

"I'll live. Thanks, you're a pal."

"You're welcome. You going to see her today?"

"I think I owe it to her not to string her along." Roger nodded, stirring sugar into his coffee. "And then I'll see Peter, and ask him to release the option so we can take the project elsewhere."

"Great. It'll make a fabulous film. It'll work a lot better. And instead of winning a BAFTA, we'll win an Oscar!"

"Yeah, well... there's a small matter of raising the finance first. How many years is that going to take?"

"Details, details. I might be able to rustle up a contact or two in Hollywood."

"Shut up."

"No, really. I'll talk to my agent. You and me bruv, we'll take 'em by storm. That's my boy!" He squeezed Jon's cheek, as a smile began to break out. "It's all for the best in the long run. I can feel it in my water."

Jon arrived at Television Centre looking more or less his normal self, and went straight up to Selina's seventh floor office. After consideration he'd decided against bringing flowers. He wasn't sure that was appropriate when you were about to break off an engagement.

He was surprised to find that she was expecting him: her assistant asked him to wait a moment, and then sent him through. Selina sat behind her large desk, with her hair up and wearing what he thought of as her Tory suit, making notes on a document. She didn't smile, so he tempered his own, and was obliged to stand around until she looked up. So she wasn't going to make it easy for him – not that he would have expected her to. He ran through the speech he'd prepared in his mind: 'I'm so sorry, but I've realised it just isn't going to make either of us happy... best to call a halt now before we go any further... and please don't imagine that Rhiannon has anything to do with it because nothing could be further from... "

"Okay Jonathan. Here's the situation." She startled him. "It turns out your 'medical miracle' is nothing more than a street drug. Whether you realised it or not, I don't care, frankly."

"Oh." He nodded in a manner he hoped looked wise. "You can't approve the show, then, obviously."

"No, I can't."

"That's okay. I understand. You have to do your job. It's a blow, I can't deny it, but there may be other possibilities; Roger suggested we turn it into a film – that's to say, he always thought it would work better as a single drama than as a serial."

"Yes I can imagine this project's right up Roger's street." Jon heard a hint of scorn in Selina's voice which he found rather repulsive, under the circumstances. "I'm afraid this does you no credit, Jonathan. Losing your only project for such an ignominious reason leaves you without a leg to stand on for the moment, doesn't it? And your career looked so promising. I can't see your path to Head of Drama now." Jon didn't know what to say, so he shrugged vaguely, which annoyed her. "What's that supposed to mean?"

"It means... I dunno." It means I'm trying to avoid rowing with you, he thought. Particularly in your office, with people in earshot.

"Look Jonathan, I've made a decision. The engagement's off. It's pretty clear that your interest lies elsewhere – don't try to deny it, I'm not stupid. I know how you drama types carry on. Spare me the excuses and the denials. I think the best thing is a clean break. I've brought in your toothbrush and the things you left at my flat. You can bring mine in tomorrow." She stared frostily at him, but her lip trembled. He realised that she was determined not to break down in front of him. Okay, good, it was over! He didn't have to say anything more. Really? Was that it?

"Don't stand there like a stunned rabbit, just – just leave me alone!" Her voice finally cracked, and Jon shuffled out, apologising. "Take this, will you!" He went back for the carrier bag of belongings and left, feeling ridiculous.

He stumbled round the corridor to the lift shaking his head and trying to work out what had just happened. Was that a victory or a defeat? Someone came out of an office and passed him, and he realised too late that he'd failed to respond to a pleasant greeting. He looked round and saw it was Chris Briggs. Oh well. He decided to take the stairs, in case he was called upon to converse in the lift.

Chris went directly to Selina's office. "How was it? Are you alright?"

Selina blew her nose on a tissue and smiled bravely. "Yes. I just told him straight. It's all off. He took it pretty well, considering."

"Huh," said Chris, putting his arm round her and squeezing her shoulder protectively. "He didn't react like a man who's lost everything, then?"

"No, he didn't. So that means he's keeping his cards up his sleeve, I suppose."

"He's already got someone else lined up, that's clear. Oh, sorry – "

Selina's face had creased up in pain, and she drew a deep breath with a huge effort. "Sorry Chris, no it's okay, it's just hard, you know... he's even got a plan B for the show! Turn it into a film... "

"No! The perfidious little toe-rag!" Chris longed to hug Selina and kiss away her tears, but he restrained himself and patted her shoulder instead. "I'd like to knock his block off, I really would."

"I don't like violence."

"Actually…" A thought occurred to Chris which caused him to smile. "There's one thing we could do to scupper his scheme."

Selina looked up at him. He winked at her. "Leave it with me." He rubbed her back, and suggested she take the day off, as compassionate leave.

I was trying to make sense of an invoice I'd been sent from the BBC library, which stated that the new charge for borrowing a book was now £25 per item, and consequently I owed them £50 for two volumes I'd been using to double-check my own Welsh knowledge. How could that possibly be right? There was a covering letter that said the new charges had been in force for two months. Somehow I'd missed this new policy. That's no way to keep a library in business, I thought. What's going on? Are they trying to close it, or what? Then Jonathan knocked once and charged into my office.

"There you are!" I said. "Guess who wants to see you? The ice maiden calleth. Oh, sorry, not my business."

"Don't bother, I've just seen her. I've been royally dumped."

"Oh, I'm so sorry, Jonathan."

"It's okay. I deserve it. It's better this way."

"That's very generous of you."

"Not really."

"She rang and asked me about the cannabis. I didn't say yes or no, but I think she's onto it."

"She is. And the show's been dumped too."

"No! Oh no. Oh that's terrible."

"No, it's not, it's okay." He smiled, and threw himself down on my sofa, putting his feet up on the coffee table and folding his arms behind his head.

I was bewildered. "Are you alright, Jonathan? You've had a big shock."

He laughed. "It's okay, I'm not having a nervous breakdown. I stayed with Roger last night, and he's got a great idea. If we pick up the option we can go independent and make it as a film, it could work even better that way, and we can try and get a distribution deal. He's talking Hollywood, but I can't see it selling over there myself. I don't see why we shouldn't make it here though, and quite soon: we just walk quietly away from the BBC and start our film careers with this project. Imagine the freedom, Rhiannon! It'll be great. You will join us, won't you? We'll set up an independent production company with Roger… "

"Hang on a minute." He was getting carried away, big time. "One thing at a time."

"Sorry, sorry. I've been thinking about it all non-stop since yesterday. It makes sense. You'll see it too. It's all going to work out for the best." He beamed at me, and I just gawped at him while I tried to get my head round it.

"Well, I suppose… as long as you're happy."

He sat up, and leaned forward. "There's one more thing."

"What's that?"

"Selina's made up her mind that we're an item."

"Oh well. It's all in her head, isn't it? Doesn't really matter."

"It's made me realise something though."

"Yeah?"

"I wish we were."

The moment crystallised as I replayed the conversation in my head, staring stupidly at him. I suppose that's what they mean when they say the world stops turning. It was all too much, I couldn't take it in.

"I'm sorry, I shouldn't have said that. I had no right. Why should you feel the same way?" He got up and made for the door. "I'm so sorry, Rhiannon. I – I'll see you later."

The door closed behind him, and I was still staring openmouthed.

*

That afternoon there was an even bigger shock in store. The

news came though on the Telfax system which played constantly on the monitors positioned by the lifts on every floor, and it raced through Centre House like a rip tide. The first I heard was a shriek of horror from down the corridor, so I ran out and joined the growing bunch of people gazing at the news that Basil Richardson was dead. He'd crashed his car into a wall.

Basil was one of the most popular producers in the department. He had been a treasure, a tower of strength over the years. It was like hearing that one of the royal family had died. Everyone stopped work, and stood about in the corridors wiping their eyes. Peter drank openly, and Vera was crying as she tried to persuade him to go home in case he made a fool of himself.

I went to Jonathan's office to break the news: it was so dreadful, it wiped out everything else. We hugged, which was weird, after everything that had happened. The pair of us sobbed and wept; we looked at each other and then hugged and sobbed and wept some more. It felt comforting and ludicrous and desperately sad.

"So was it an accident or not?" Jon asked eventually.

"Nobody knows. He drove his car off the road at sixty miles an hour. Doesn't sound like Basil, does it?"

"He could have fallen asleep at the wheel."

I nodded. "I suppose we'll never know."

People remained in the corridors talking about it, needing the reassurance of others, lacking the heart to get on with their work. Lots of them thought it was suicide. Basil had obviously been very depressed, had virtually lost his job, lived alone, probably felt he was on the scrapheap. Others couldn't believe he would do it. He had had such a distinguished career he should have been looking forward to a happy retirement.

As the afternoon wore on we reluctantly came to believe that it had indeed been deliberate on Basil's part. His comments at the recent producers' meeting suggested, in retrospect, a mood of despair and self-disgust at what had happened at the BBC. He probably felt a measure of responsibility, however misplaced that might seem to us. He must have felt that there was little to look forward to except an unsought-for early retirement and years of self-reproach. He wouldn't even be able to switch the telly on without being reminded of what had been lost. Basil's work was his life, and the manner of his death was, in a way, typical of him. He went without making an obvious statement, without melodrama, with an ambiguously tragic ending.

Jon and I parted with a kiss when we left work, but it was a friendship kiss on both cheeks. It didn't need saying that the time and place was not now, not here.

*

For the next couple of weeks things were very quiet at work. We had a meeting with Peter to talk over the *Medical Miracle* debacle, and he said it had been worth a try – some you win, some you lose. He would be happy to put the show in turn-around and release the option so we could pick it up ourselves. He wished us well.

We kept everything low key, especially our relationship. How could we jump into bed at a time like this, amidst all the wreckage? We spent time together but it was like mourning. It was the strangest start to a romance I've ever heard of. We tried to avoid Selina of course, which wasn't difficult as long as we didn't go in Television Centre. We each met with Morag and accepted that our contracts would run out in the next couple of months. We met with Roger, which was a lot more cheerful, and talked through setting up our company; that felt great, although I had major reservations about going into business with a new boyfriend. On the other hand, my intuition said it was the right thing to do.

Unfortunately we hit a snag when we tried to buy the option on *Medical Miracle*. Even though Jim was fully on board, we were unable to buy it. It turned out that the BBC had a ten-year option which they were unwilling to sell. This made no sense at all. If they didn't want to make it, what was the point of hanging onto it? We were all at Roger's flat, ready to negotiate the fee, when this bag of manure burst open. I was on the phone to the man in the rights office, who said he was sorry, there was nothing he could do as the project had been specifically frozen by Chris Briggs. He didn't know why.

"I know why," said Jonathan dully, head in hands.

"Let's go and see him," said Roger. "We can talk him round."

"Forget it," said Jon. "God, I'm so sorry everyone. This is Selina's work. She's done it to spite me."

"Hell hath no fury like a woman scorned," I murmured, realising the truth of the quotation for the first time.

"It's my fault," said Jon. "I should have kept my fucking trap shut. I told her you wanted to do it as a film."

Roger was incredulous. "Why? Why would you do that? What's it to her anyway?"

"I wasn't thinking straight, I had a hangover, it was all a complete nightmare. I had no idea I was telling her something important! Jesus… "

I went and hugged him. "Never mind," I said. "You weren't to know. It's not your fault."

"That's the end of it, then. No film. No work. I'm really, really sorry, both of you."

Roger threw his cigarettes at the wall. Then he clapped Jon on the shoulder and squeezed it. "I'm going out for a few hours, the flat's all yours. Stay here if you want. If I were you I'd fuck each other's brains out."

I stared catatonically into space as he collected a few things and left, contemplating an abyss of unemployment. As the front door closed behind him, Jon lifted his head. "What did he say?"

*

There was a memorial service two months later in the BBC church in Langham Place. It was attended by hundreds of people; staff, ex-staff, actors, directors, many famous faces.

Press photographers waited outside. Officially, his death had been accidental, just another tragic road death statistic. Those who thought otherwise held their peace, there was little point in pursuing it, and it seemed disrespectful to Basil to gossip about him after his death.

Jonathan and I sat with Maggie a few rows behind Vera and the drama producers. We watched Peter Maxwell nervously as he stumbled on his way up to the front where he was to address the congregation.

"Welcome, friends," began Peter, loud and clear. "Thank you all for coming to celebrate the life of our dear friend and colleague, Basil Richardson." To our relief he didn't sound too pissed. "Basil worked in BBC Drama for thirty eight years. Even longer than I have. Even longer than my esteemed PA, Vera Ainsley." He smiled in tribute to Vera, who was flattered.

"In those early years, which commentators like to call the golden years of television drama, an extraordinary revolution took place in the culture of our country. Basil's contribution was to make wonderful programmes, broadcast *live* remember, to staggeringly large audiences – there were of course only two channels to choose between in those days. In the years that followed Basil carried on making drama that showed what was really going on in ordinary people's lives, work that mattered, work that made you want to change the world and throw out all its injustices.

"I've made a list of some of the shows I consider to have been the best during his time. Basil didn't work on all of them by any means, but he was part of the department which made them, and as we all know, making top class drama isn't like buying a potted plant off a shelf; you need a well-run nursery, you have to sow many, many seeds, prick out the strongest seedlings, and nurture them in fine, cultivated soil. Here they are, then. This roll call is a tribute not just to Basil, but to all those of his ilk: *Cathy Come Home. Z Cars. The Price of Coal. Dr Who. The Forsyte Saga. I, Claudius. The History Man. Threads. The Singing Detective. Auf*

Wiedersehen Pet. Edge of Darkness. Boys From the Black Stuff. The Monocled Mutineer. A Very British Coup. A Very Peculiar Practice. The Firm. Our Friends in the North. In my humble opinion, these programmes are peerless. They were all groundbreaking in their time. They and many more have inspired countless writers and producers, and enriched the lives of millions of viewers. Forgive me for leaving other worthy programmes out."

The congregation, expecting a standard eulogy, found itself fully engaged by Peter's sentiments as he unconsciously patted his bald patch and stared at the arched ceiling.

"My only regret is that, today, I see precious few shows on our books to match them." He paused and cast his gaze around the church. His expression was solemn. "No disrespect to all of you still working in the department, but we all know why, and should perhaps have said so before: the conditions no longer exist at the BBC for truly groundbreaking drama to be developed, produced, or broadcast. Our highly-decorated Director General has given us a new culture of competition. We must be correctly positioned in the new electronic marketplace, apparently, or we'll lose our audience. He seems to forget that it was the BBC's reputation for making the *best programmes* which made it the brand leader around the world. Instead of concentrating the corporation's efforts on making sure the best programmes *continue* to come from the BBC, and making commercial companies compete with *us*, he has sold our inheritance and instead competes with them on *their* terms. He talks of giving viewers more choice, but *his* idea of choice turns out to be more opportunities to watch the same repeats, and the same kind of derivative, generic drama we see on other channels. Perhaps the time has come for Channel Four to take the baton? I don't know. All I know is that I can't carry it any longer. Ladies and gentlemen, I hereby tender my resignation. I think Basil would have approved."

Many of us gasped at Peter's announcement; a handful of

journalists were already scribbling furiously. Jonathan and I gripped hands as tears rolled down my face. Maggie was sniffing. My heart pounded; we felt absurdly proud of our old boss as he left the dais and walked down the aisle, looking shell-shocked. A light patter of inhibited but heartfelt applause spread across the church, gathering intensity as he left. The organ began the introduction to *To Be A Pilgrim*, and choir began to sing. By the end, the whole congregation was belting it out with gusto.

There's definitely an important catharsis about a church service, regardless of your religious beliefs. I wouldn't have missed it for the world.

"What do you think of the name Basil?" Jon muttered in my ear as we left.

"For a baby, you mean?"

"Yes."

"Well. Perhaps it'll grow on me."

We dived into the nearest pub, and not surprisingly, we found Peter at the bar. He noticed that we were holding hands.

"At last," he said. "I always thought you'd make the ideal couple. You fit together like two pieces of a jigsaw." His judgement was spot on, as ever.

Chapter Twenty-one

By the time *Bus!* was in the can Penny had lost over two stone. Normally she would have been thrilled by this, but since she'd also developed high blood pressure it didn't seem so great. In fact she was already nostalgic for the days when she'd been cheerful and relaxed enough to sit back and put away a decent bottle of wine and a plate of French cheeses. She had also developed the kind of smoking habit which is harder on the bank balance than the lungs, getting through two packs of lowest-tar cigarettes a day, but only smoking half before stubbing them out, and hardly inhaling at all – hoping that this would mitigate against their harmful influence. It was a nervous habit, she acknowledged that, and planned to stop when the show was finished.

Although accustomed to long hours at the BBC, she'd found Nik's expectations almost impossible to meet: sixteen hour days, seven days a week. He'd pointed out that she could rest as much as she liked at the end of her contract. Even her journey to work seemed a self-indulgent luxury. In fact as time went on, she looked forward to it as a brief period twice a day which was hers alone; being uncontactable for an hour became a joy to cherish. It was all down to reducing costs, of course; her professional standards wouldn't allow her to cut the cloth according to the budget. She was producing a high quality show through sheer willpower. Her reputation was such that expert production staff agreed to work on the show for half their normal rate just because they liked and respected her – and their jobs at the BBC had vanished. They loved their work enough to sacrifice themselves. Penny being Penny, she felt guilty and responsible with every reduction of their working conditions, which worsened as the schedule rolled on. They knew it was out of her control and appreciated her care, but the strain took its toll on her nonetheless.

Nik's earnings were far beyond anyone else's on the team. He piled on the pressure, but Penny didn't complain. She didn't pass it on down the line either, seeing herself as a buffer protecting the creative team as much as she could. She suffered enormous guilt for exploiting her old colleagues, even though they knew exactly what they had signed up for. Somehow the struggle for good working conditions didn't apply at Magenta, it wasn't relevant. It was difficult to say how this had happened, given that a Labour government was finally in power again. There were no unions, no proper rights for employees; there was health and safety, and insurance, but everyone was on a short-term freelance contract which they either signed or turned down. Very few in the industry could afford to say no. It felt like a new world, a new way of life, to the old guard. The comforts of life were over and gone, even the glorious camaraderie continued to exist only as personal relationships between those who had worked together for many years. There was no longer a sense of playing your part in something so big and strong that it was greater than the sum of its constituents, and which would repay your loyalty. Now it was everyone for themselves, the life of the freelance, which was not a million miles away from the old world of the day-labourer who turned up at the dock gates at dawn each day, hoping for a few hours' work.

Penny's consolation was a great satisfaction derived from the show itself, since she knew perfectly well that the sow's ear Nik had given her had been transformed into a beautiful silk purse by her skilful needlework. She had quietly brought in a hugely experienced series writer to knock the scripts into shape, without embarrassing Jak and his team. The lighting cameraman had dozens of films to his credit, and was able to achieve magnificent visual quality with cheap video technology. The director had forty years' experience. An ideal location was obtained for peanuts through another old contact; the list went on.

Penny was truly proud of the show. Its rather silly premise was handled in such a way that it felt perfectly normal. The old adage concerning the audience's 'willing suspension of disbelief' applied. It was fun, a family show, not very demanding, heartwarming without sentimentality – the key was that it didn't take itself too seriously. Even the guest stars were slotted into the storylines without too much contrivance.

Nik recognised the show's quality, but he had no concept of how exceptional the achievement was. He assumed it was all normal, that any producer could do the same, that the crew were standard and their experience average. He treated them all the same as any other Magenta employee and saw no reason to bestow praise on someone simply for doing their job. He expected everyone to work willingly and cheerfully. He interpreted tiredness as weakness, and irritability as resistance. Consequently, as Penny's tolerance and generosity wore thin under the pressure of constant effort and exhaustion, she began to wear a strained expression and a fixed smile which Nik found intensely aggravating. He decided she had an 'attitude problem' and imagined she thought herself superior, too good for Magenta and for him. Naturally, he never mentioned it to her. Just to everyone else.

Ever the professional, Penny put all she had into the show, but as the scheduled days were ticked off she felt something draining out of her, as if a plug had been pulled on her reservoir of enthusiasm. By the time the end of the project was in sight she was longing to escape, and was quietly planning a new life in Cornwall: semi-retirement, or 'downshifting' as it was known in the Sunday papers she had no time to read. There was a lot of regret, but having tasted the new world of broadcasting she knew she had no appetite for it. Best to go before her heart packed up altogether.

With the series safely signed off, Nik found his welcome at the BBC a good deal warmer. In fact he began to believe he was now accepted. Then a head-hunting firm called, and met with him to discuss a possible post at the BBC. They told him that there was a vacancy for Head of Drama, and that the management were very impressed with his work at Magenta, in particular *Bus!* They thought it had the same high production values of an in-house show, but somehow Nik had achieved it for half the price. This was precisely the skill they needed in the Drama Department. Could he do the same from inside the corporation? Of course he could. Could he halt the decline of the department? Of course he could. Would he leave Magenta and pass up his share options? Of course he wouldn't. Did they think he was mad? After a few weeks of secret meetings and interviews, Nik accepted the job on condition that his position at Magenta was suspended only for the duration of his tenure at the BBC, and that his income as a director of the company would be uninterrupted.

Nik was enormously flattered, although he understood that his role was to be the hatchet-man. They needed him to sweep out the old crap that remained, and re-establish the corporation in the modern marketplace. The old values were dead or dying. Time for a new approach, ready for the new millennium, which was almost upon them.

Magenta was in any case undergoing a major shake-up. Rex, who had been sent on a year-long sabbatical by the chairman of the board, had cleaned up his act, cut down his boozing and gambling, and had spent a month in a California clinic having his body re-moulded. He returned with toned muscles, tanned skin, white teeth, and a flat stomach which he was quick to admit he owed to liposuction. In fact he proudly lifted up his shirt for anyone brave enough to take a closer look. He was in good enough shape to take over his old post at the head of the company, and had made several valuable new contacts in LA. He was setting up a Magenta office over there so that he could expand into the American market, and had already sold two quiz show formats to US networks.

Haris' enthusiasm for taking over smaller production companies had stalled at the first bend, since Anthea Onojaife at Sisters in Synch had resisted Magenta's hostile takeover bid much more strongly than he had anticipated. One or two little production companies had subsequently been absorbed but the strategy was suddenly overshadowed by a bid for Magenta itself, made by a vast entertainment conglomerate; they were bought out for a sum so massive that they couldn't believe their luck. Rex and Haris retained their posts and were perfectly content to accept the guidance of their new mothership from now on. They and Nik became millionaires.

*

Vera wasn't sure about her new boss. He seemed very young. He was dressed in a beautifully cut slate grey suit and a yellow silk shirt, he wore his dark hair razored and heavily gelled, and he was very attractive judging by the body language of the young office secretaries. She greeted him politely, hoped he would enjoy working there, and sent one of the girls out to get the Perrier water he wanted instead of coffee.

He entered Peter's old office critically: it hadn't been used by the Acting Head of Drama who had filled in over the fifteen months since Peter's resignation, during which the top brass had struggled to find a senior figure willing to take on the post.

"Hmm. That corduroy sofa has to go, what an eyesore! I suppose if we get some decent furniture, get rid of all the books – we'll keep the certificates – some nice lights and a couple of big plants, maybe a little water feature, what do you think?"

Vera was lost for words.

Nik suddenly laughed. "Joke!"

"Oh!" she felt silly.

"Water features are a pain in the arse. Just ask someone to remove the old stuff and get me a Heal's catalogue, would you? I'll camp out for the time being."

He gave her a reassuring smile and put his laptop down on the desk. He looked for the nearest socket and found it was too far away.

"Peter didn't have one of these, then," he observed, and Vera looked round until she found a cable extension.

"Doesn't matter," said Nik. "I'll have the desk moved anyway. I'm meeting the gang at eleven o'clock, right?"

"Yes, everyone knows about it."

"Good. We'll have real coffee, Perrier, and some nice cakes from Maison Blanc. Get a couple of dozen."

"Er, actually I've ordered the usual from catering… "

"Cancel it. Or give it to the homeless, I don't care." He switched on his laptop, which made a series of dramatic whoops, spread his hands on the desk and looked directly at Vera for the first time. "First impressions, Vera. Very important."

"Whatever you say, Nik!"

"Sweet," he smiled. "I'm sure we're going to make a great team. When's your birthday?"

"Oh! um… April 30th."

He stood up and typed into his laptop, then winked at her. "I won't ask how many – ladies' privilege. Right. I'll call if I need you."

"Fine."

Vera turned and left the room, thinking Nik was nothing if not dynamic, and his energetic approach would be a breath of fresh air. She might even learn to like him, once she got used to him. She would try, at any rate.

The remaining editorial staff were few enough in number to fit into Nik's office for his introductory address. The two producers, Fenella Proctor-Ball and Donald Mountjoy, sat on the familiar, comfortable corduroy sofa. Morag claimed one of the armchairs, the three script editors and readers sat on desk chairs, and a newcomer occupied the other sagging armchair. Nik introduced him as his development executive Jak Smith, whom he had brought from Magenta. He looked like an even younger version of Nik, and Fenella exchanged a surreptitious raised eyebrow with Donald. They all cooed at the patisseries and helped themselves at Nik's invitation.

"It's a special day," he said. "I've just hit the big three – O!"

The younger women murmured "Happy birthday," but Morag, Fenella and Donald remained stony-faced. Nik made a brief phone call at his desk before joining them with his high-backed chair, removing his jacket and hanging it carefully behind him.

"Hello everybody, nice to meet you, I'll get to know you individually very soon. Today I just want to introduce myself and outline the plans I have. We're a small, tight team here and I want us to work very closely together."

They all gazed at him blankly. He rubbed his palm around the back of his neck, stroking his stubble.

"I'm very pleased – and honoured," he added for Donald's benefit, "to have been asked to come to the BBC. I'm going to sort out some of the problems we've got here, but I need all of your support."

They all nodded supportively.

"Okay. Well, I'll just outline my chief aims and objectives for the first few months, and Jak will prepare some more detailed papers for you all soon.

"Obviously we have our soaps, which are chugging away in the suburbs; I shall be visiting them as soon as I can. And our returning series, which are all in hand.

"One of the most vital items in my strategy is to maximise our exploitation of these assets. In other words, I want spin-offs."

Jak smiled at his boss and looked round to make sure the subtle dig was appreciated. It was obvious to any moron that the BBC had been painfully negligent in creating new hit series for its soap stars.

"The reason you haven't managed it before," Nik explained. "Is that you always devise an entirely new show. The character changes, the actor's seen in a different light, audiences aren't convinced. They want to see the familiar character, their old mate. So we'll look at ways of starting a new soap with characters from old soaps. Anyone seen *Frasier*?"

Everyone except the producers had. They all nodded anyway.

"A superb sitcom created from another superb sitcom." He drily explained, *"Cheers"*, suspecting they might not know this basic fact. "Jak will be running that project. You'll be hearing from him. Next, novel adaptations. Obviously I bow to your greater experience," he deferred to Donald. "And I understand there are a few more classics in the works. Fabulous. I want us to look in a different, contemporary area as well. We want some real blockbusters, thrillers, sex-and-shopping – why not? Bank Holiday entertainment. Nothing too expensive, of course, we can't afford to make James Bond, just some really cracking airport novels." He made eye contact with each script editor and reader. "That's your job. That about covers it for now. Any questions?"

No-one wanted to ask any questions.

"Okay, thanks for your time, I'll get Vera to give you each an appointment with me later in the week."

They all filed out except Jak, who remained in his seat.

Morag returned.

"I just wanted to mention," she said apologetically. "That we urgently need a new producer on the mortuary series. Obviously, you're not really prepared yet – I was going to suggest Penny Cruickshank might be available. She knows the show, and – "

"Jesus, not that toffee-nosed cow again," snorted Nik. "No. I don't want her here, she's useless." Jak looked askance to show agreement. Morag blinked through her heavy spectacles, her mouth open.

"Oh, sorry." She recollected herself. "I thought as you'd just been working together you'd – "

Nik stopped her with a look. "Morag. Just between you and me, the woman's a total waste of space. I *carried* her on that show. Never again."

Morag nodded. "Of course, sorry Nik. I was just trying to help."

"I'll get on the phone later and see who's free. I'll get back to you."

"Great, thanks," replied Morag, and withdrew to puzzle over Nik's views on Penny, which were in conflict with everything she knew or had ever heard about her. Evidently they had not got on at all.

Nik threw himself on the sofa. "Phew!"

Jak grinned. "I think they got the picture."

Nik took a bite of a chocolate eclair. He looked at it appraisingly. "It's nice," he said. "But not as nice as a line." He looked slyly at Jak. "It's not done here. Or is it?"

"I wouldn't be surprised," answered Jak, looking hopeful.

"Not on my first day. Not before lunch, anyway."

Jak chuckled. "You'll have to get a glass coffee table."

Nik finished his eclair, drank a glass of Perrier straight down, belched in a restrained manner, and addressed his development executive.

"Let's make a list. Of all the women who are young and hot."

"A pleasure." Jak shook his head in admiration of his boss' cool, and got a pad and pen out of his briefcase.

"We'll take them to Groucho's, and then we'll make them stars," said Nik dreamily.

"And then what?" sniggered Jak.

"Behave. Right. Who's the hottest babe you can think of?"

"Cameron Diaz."

"Get real. We're talking television."

"Daniela Nardini?"

"Leave it out, she's disgusting."

"Martine McCutcheon."

"That's more like it, we can get her no trouble. Who else?"

*

Nik had a lunch appointment with the Deputy Director General, Chris Briggs. They went in Chris' chauffeur-driven Mercedes to a discreetly café-styled expensive restaurant in Notting Hill, and relaxed at a screened table.

Chris was still slightly uneasy in the company of this confident, fashionable young man of the world. Nik was quite friendly, but Chris had failed to find any common interests which would enable them to get to know each other, so he was obliged to fall back on a more formal preface of small talk. When the starters had been cleared away, he got down to business.

"We need to discuss the Drama Department's future," he began. "In terms of the over-arching plans the DG has set in motion for the twenty-first century."

Nik was all attention as he leaned back in his rattan chair, sipping a glass of Chablis.

"That's not the same as your personal future, of course. It goes without saying that, if you succeed in resolving the situation in line with the DG's aims, he'll ask you to rise to a new challenge, perhaps in a different role."

Nik inclined his head in acknowledgement.

"I believe part of your work at Magenta included taking over production companies and turning them around."

"That's right. I appraised their current business and their potential, and acted accordingly. Some just couldn't be made financially viable." Nik had mastered the knack of implying he'd done far more than he really had.

Chris smiled and nodded. He sipped his wine, put it down carefully and lowered his voice further. "We've known for a long time, a *long* time, that the Drama Department has major problems."

Nik responded with a shrewd gaze. "I realise that."

"The point about the BBC is that it occupies a unique position," continued Chris. "No change can ever be made suddenly without frightening the horses, as it were. The press are on your back before you know it, there are letter campaigns from retired colonels, even questions in Parliament. It's very, very sensitive. I want to be absolutely sure that you appreciate this. We're not in Wardour Street here."

"Believe me Chris, I *do* understand. I wouldn't dream of taking any action which would create opposition."

"The new government has pretty much left us alone, so far. It may be that they have more urgent business to attend to and that, sooner or later, they'll give us more attention than we really want. We mustn't precipitate a reaction."

"I understand."

"The licence fee is always under threat."

Nik smiled confidently, one eyebrow raised. "Personally, Chris, I wouldn't worry about it. Subscription would be a much better system in many ways."

Chris frowned.

"Of course," continued Nik. "We want to keep the licence fee for the foreseeable future, I agree completely." He nodded very seriously.

Chris spoke quietly with determination. "I'd like you to discuss your strategy with me, when you've had time to think it through. As a safeguard. To make sure you don't inadvertently contradict our underlying policies."

"Certainly. No problem, Chris."

"Would you like to share your first impressions with me?"

Nik smiled. "Sure. My *first* impression, which I have yet to confirm, of course, is that the tired little outfit in Centre House should be put in a boat and shoved off down the river." He laughed. Chris watched him intently. "Current shows I have no problem with. There's really no need for them to be managed from the centre, they can be privatised and run themselves. New shows, that's the crux of it all. I shall have to see what I can do to kick-start development. I wonder though, in the long term, does the BBC really *need* to develop new shows? The country's full of independent producers furiously working away at new ideas and queuing up outside the door to show them to us. All we have to do is pick and choose. Why should we have rooms full of people doing the same thing, *on salary*?" Chris nodded slowly. "And home-grown shows tend to carry other baggage with them. Such as copyright problems with writers and producers. At Magenta we held all the rights in every script we commissioned."

"Didn't you have trouble with the Writers' Guild?"

"We would have, so we didn't go near them. It meant we had to use less experienced writers most of the time, that's all. It doesn't take long before they *are* experienced. We had to get rid of a few along the way, but it was all worth it. We're – I mean, Magenta's on a nice little earner now, thanks to me."

Chris seemed impressed. "Jolly good, I think we'll get along pretty well, Nik. Tell me, have you ever visited the Harvard Business School?"

Chapter Twenty-two

Jonathan and I became an item very quickly. I suppose we already knew each other pretty well, and were grown-up enough to deal with it maturely. By the time our BBC contracts had run out we were a secure couple, not living together yet but virtually. Jon said one of the things he loved most about our relationship was the complete absence of ceremony. I shuddered to imagine what going out with Selina had entailed. We'd circumspectly enquired about each other's hopes for the future, and had established that we both wanted to marry and have children. We both felt satisfied with that and didn't jump the gun. There was an unspoken understanding between us that, all being well – and we had no illusions about the possibility of circumstances intervening – that's what lay ahead for us. We were very happy. Which was lucky really, since we were soon to be unemployed.

We did the usual rounds looking for new contracts, but it was very hard as so many people were on the same circuit. We tried a couple more times to buy the rights to *The Medical Miracle*, but it was impossible. I had a nasty feeling that they might be for sale to others, but we had to give up on it.

Finally, BBC Wales advertised for a drama development team. I wasn't sure I wanted to apply. It was too much like going home to our street, and I thought it would be far too boring for Jon. Once again he surprised me, he was perfectly happy to give it a go, so we both applied, and were both accepted. This time I was senior to him; my Welshness put me in the lead as Head of Development, with Jon as Senior Script Editor. How's that for a result?! Laugh? I nearly wet myself. I tell you, there aren't many blokes who could cope with that kind of reversal and keep the relationship intact.

We moved to Cardiff in early '98, and rented a flat to start with. My family took a while to get used to my posh Englishman: posh Englishmen haven't been that popular in Wales, down the centuries. What tipped the balance with my dad was when we were all in his favourite pub one winter evening, with a roaring fire and rain dashing against the windows, all very Dylan Thomas, and some of the fellers started a sing-song. Nothing formal; they just felt in the mood. Being Welsh they knew all the traditional songs, and so did the rest of the pub. It was one of those spine-tingling evenings that happen – well they happen every week in Welsh pubs, but Jonathan didn't know that. As the gorgeous harmonies swelled and filled the room, tears rolled down Jon's face, he was incapable of holding them back. He felt a complete idiot, but my dad and I loved him for it. After that he was one of the family.

Our lives at work were very enjoyable. There was less pressure and tension, and a lot more real drama development. We benefitted from our status as a regional centre in that the public service element meant we were securely funded, so we could settle into developing Welsh writers and solid, family-oriented drama. We gradually stopped caring what was going on in Shepherd's Bush. The longer we lived in South Wales the more absurd London seemed; the long hours, the politics, the back-stabbing. Not that Wales was entirely free of that kind of thing. It was rife in some areas, to be honest. But it didn't get in our way. Or perhaps we were more adept at dealing with it.

It was always fun to hear the news from London, and Maggie was a great source of gossip. She continued to be very happy at Sisters in Synch with Anthea. They weren't making a lot of money but the company was establishing itself. Jill and Carmen both wrote for them regularly. Jill's ex-husband had been elected as a New Labour MP, we looked out for his name, but he didn't seem to be one of the Blair Babes. Right time, wrong sex, I suppose. Isn't it a shame when men are sidelined just because of their gender?

Stewart Wanker (as we'd referred to him since Sonia's brochure) had set up an independent production company which was busy making controversial films designed to make waves in Cannes. Penny Cruickshank had retired and gone to breed spaniels in Cornwall. I liked to imagine her striding the cliff-tops with a dozen golden cocker spaniels bouncing around her, their ears flapping in the wind. Peter Maxwell was now on the boards of several august film and television institutions. Chris Briggs was Deputy Director General, and it seemed inevitable that his career trajectory would continue to carry him upwards. Selina was in charge of Policy and Planning. Whether she was also sent to the Harvard Business School we never found out. Nik Mason settled into his post running the Drama Department and made a surprisingly effective job of it. Everyone hated working for him, but no-one could deny that he brought a number of successful shows to the screen, and re-established BBC1's core position. If the hit shows were derivative and obvious, so what? It was a cut-throat industry now.

As the millennium approached the country became fascinated by the prospect of a new century, as if no-one could have predicted its arrival. It was rather like when we hit 1984, a year that had been imprinted on us all as a symbol of everything terri-fying and futuristic. You'd think we'd have learned from that, but no. It was much more fun to picture the world falling apart because of the millennium bug, or even better, the End of the World. Plenty of cults believed they'd be off in a cable car to heaven as soon as the Big Ben bongs died away.

Jon and I were chuffed to be invited back for a special televi-sion awards ceremony in December 1999. The powers that be had decided that everyone who was anyone in television should all get together and see the century out with a spectacular bunfight; there was money to burn in those days. The government was burning as much as possible at the Millenium Dome. The Mayor of London intended to burn it all the way down the Thames in a River of Fire, but it didn't work. Maybe the blue touch paper got damp.

We'd recently got married, and I was pregnant with our first child. I was still Head of Development in Cardiff, but Jon was now a producer on our newest series which promised to be very exciting, a show that combined Welsh wizardry with contemporary science fiction, and was witty and fun too. We were quietly confident that it would be a big success, and would burst out of the quiet provinces to take the country by storm. It's surprising how little time it takes for your allegiances to root themselves in the country where you're given a warm welcome.

The awards event took place at the Café Royal in Regent Street, a huge hall with a long history. (Don't go looking for it – it's gone now.) Sixty tables were packed with nominees and guests, all knocking back the wine too fast, wanting a fag, and resolving to have their formal outfits let out by a couple of inches. I was wishing I'd splashed out on a maternity frock, but I'd thought I could just about get away with wearing my little black number and save the money. We were sitting at the Regional table, which was, inevitably, situated at the edge of the room.

Hundreds of flushed faces bearing new haircuts and sparkling jewellery chatted nervously. The clatter of cutlery and china rose in a cacophony to the top table where Nik was seated alongside Chris Briggs and his wife Catherine. There was no-one he was interested in talking to on his own table apart from the delectable Head of Policy and Planning, Selina, but she was too far away for comfortable conversation. Already bored, Nik cast his gaze around the room frequently and swiftly, since he was keen to avoid catching the eye of many people present. The Magenta table was near the front – Rex was schmoozing happily, and

Haris had for once decided to taste the high life, and had even brought his wife along. Nik had never met her. She looked much more intelligent than he had imagined a stay-at-home wife would be, and she clearly had plenty to say to Penny Cruickshank, who was deep in conversation with her over some photos of what looked to be dogs.

Geordie Boy was sitting at a table full of comedians, dressed to kill and having a whale of a time. To Nik's chagrin, Geordie had taken the idea he'd rejected as too camp for Magenta to a well-known gay theatrical entrepreneur who had set up a new production company entirely for the benefit of his friends, as far as Nik could see. He didn't expect it to remain commercially viable. However, Geordie's new show had wowed them at Channel Four and it now had a cult following; it was nominated for Best Comedy Series. It was many months since they had spoken to each other.

After the first course Geordie passed close by Nik's table and paused to say hello. He was polite and restrained, congratulating Nik on his job at the BBC and wishing him well. Nik responded minimally, seized with tension; he was anxious to avoid being seen by the BBC bigwigs with the debris of past relationships dangling from his nose. After Geordie had gone, Nik realised that the correct thing to do would have been to congratulate him on his nomination and wish him luck. Too late now. He turned his attention to his companions.

Over at the side of the hall the atmosphere was more relaxed. There were cheerful reunions between us and the adjacent Sisters in Synch table; they were nominated in the Best Film category. Jonathan made a point of shaking Anthea's hand and wishing her luck. He'd been massively impressed by *The Prosecution of Justice*, and hoped her achievement would be recognised. He was embarrassed, as he'd never spoken to her when she worked at the BBC. She gallantly ignored this, quietly enjoying the fact that her status was now higher than his; to her, Jonathan was no better and no worse than anyone else, and she no longer cared what the BBC got up to.

Jill Watkins was there, looking exactly the same as ever. Some people don't age, do they? She'd barely altered at all. I noticed her tense up when Tony Scott came over to the table to chat. He sat next to her and she started fanning herself with a napkin. Poor thing, I thought, hot flushes. If Tony noticed, he didn't show it. He'd heard that her ex-husband had been elected as a New Labour MP, and asked where he stood politically.

"Wherever there's a spotlight," was her answer.

"Follows the trend?"

"'Fraid so. He's an economist."

"Ah! The world seems to be run by lawyers and economists these days."

"What about the workers?"

"Exactly! And the writers!"

Carmen leaned across to join in, "You two make a lovely couple."

"What?! Mind your manners, Phillips!" Jill was mortified, blushing furiously. Carmen chortled wickedly. Tony leaned back and sipped his wine, head tilted to one side. He thought Jill was rather lovely, in her way. If he weren't married he would ask her out, he didn't mind telling her.

Maggie stepped in to cover Jill's embarrassment, "Doesn't everyone look fabulous tonight! *Sooo* handsome in your DJs, boys! And so glamorous in your frocks! I couldn't bring myself to wear one. D'you like my outfit?" She displayed her white men's dinner jacket and over-large trousers held up with a wide belt. "I call it my James Bond look."

"Very nice, Maggie," said Jill. "Moss Bros?"

"No, Oxfam. Well, isn't it good to know that there's life beyond the BBC? You all look a sight better than you ever did in Shepherd's Bush."

"Even me?" I asked, listening in.

"Even you. I say," Maggie said impulsively, leaning over the table. "D'you want a tasty bit of gossip?"

"Yes, go on," we chorused.

"You see that Chris Briggs?" she indicated him at the top table. "I've had him, I have!"

The effect was rewarding, as every jaw fell table-wards.

"Come off it," said Carmen. "I can't see you two together in a million years."

"You'd never fancy a bloke like him, Maggie," I said.

"Not even Roger would fancy him," added Jonathan.

"I don't know," mused Maggie. "He used to have a certain *je ne sais quoi*. He carries his authority well, don't you think?"

"Anyway – where and how, Maggie?" demanded Jill.

"In Edinburgh. August 1985 I think. Chris was with us that day when we got arrested for disturbing the peace. He's the one who got us out of the police station. I went back to his hotel room afterwards."

There was a short pause and then a howl of glee, which caused half the room to turn and look.

"You sly dog!"

"She's got no shame."

"Didn't get you anywhere, did it!"

"What was he like?" Jill leaned over, conspiratorially.

"Jill!" I remonstrated. "Spare us the details, Maggie."

"No, tell us everything!" yelled the others. Maggie beckoned us in, and spoke in a stage whisper.

"He was okay. Nothing spectacular. A bit clinical. Very well-mannered, though. Asked me if I'd had a satisfactory orgasm!"

We all howled with laughter and couldn't resist looking round at Chris, chatting urbanely with his colleagues. Only Nik noticed us and wondered what it was all about.

Jonathan coughed. "Actually," he said. "I was there too."

"You what?" We stared at him.

"It was in Princes St Gardens, right? Someone was making a speech, and there was a bit of a fight. We all got arrested. I was still at Cambridge, I had a costume and make up on, I'd directed *Henry V*."

Jill and Maggie gawped at Jonathan, stunned.

"Unbelieveable."

"I'd never have recognised you two," said Jonathan.

"Same here. Small world, eh? "

"You can say that again."

"D'you remember the other one? A kid from a youth theatre or something."

"Yeah," said Maggie. "Very young. Bit of a squit, wasn't he?"

"He certainly was," confirmed Jonathan. "Looking for a fight."

"Very touchy, as I recall," mused Jill. What was his name?" No-one could remember. "I wonder what happened to him?"

"Probably behind bars, if he carried on like that," said Jonathan. "Wasn't it all his fault?"

"You know who looks like him?" pondered Maggie. "Nik Mason." The others grinned, she did have a point.

"Nice try," said Jill. "But you're pushing it too far now."

Just as I was going to add my own contribution a handbell was rung on the platform, and the MC called silence for the host. The assembly returned to their seats and faced the front, affecting nonchalant attention as he formally opened the proceedings.

It was an hour before the Best Drama Series category was reached, for which *Bus!* was nominated. Penny was certain they wouldn't win. The show was popular, and a third series had already been commissioned, but in her opinion it was too light-weight for an award. Rex was more hopeful and Haris forebore to offer an opinion. Nik's face was immobile but his hands sweated as the four short-listed clips were played for the audience to admire. The senior colleagues and governors at his table smiled encouragingly, which wound him up; he fought against his resentment of their patronising attitudes. Familiarity had led him to realise that their intentions were generally much more genuine than he had previously believed, but the old reactive instinct still lurked deep inside him, and he had to suppress it on a daily basis. It was tiring but necessary, as his ambitions now extended to the very top. He wanted to be Director General one day. Perhaps Chris would get there first, he was willing to concede that, and was beginning to grasp the virtue of patience. 'Rome wasn't built in a day' was the first unspoken rule of BBC management. However, he had a long road to travel first. He hadn't won any awards yet, and he wanted one desperately. He was fiercely jealous of every joyful recipient who mounted the platform.

He was disappointed again, especially since his rivals at ITV beat him to it. Then he discovered that the top table was the worst place a loser could sit. Being in view, he was obliged to force a smile to his lips and clap the bastards, and then to shrug with cheerful resignation across at Rex, Haris, Penny and the rest, as if they had merely lost a charity raffle for a basket of fruit.

Next came the award for Best Writer. Carmen Phillips was nominated for her screenplay, *The Prosecution of Justice*. Carmen had no truck with affecting not to care, and crossed all her fingers: this award could change her life. When her name was called she had to be helped to her feet. Jill hugged her and pointed her towards the stage, and she stumbled to it in a daze, overwhelmed by the cascade of applause. Her speech was unprepared but simple and heartfelt, her thanks to Anthea generous.

The Best Film award was hotly contested as all four were very strong. Anthea feigned calmness, only her eyes blinked nervously, gazing into the middle distance. Carmen bit her nails, willing their film to win, but it didn't. Donald Mountjoy won for a particularly fine version of *Northanger Abbey* made not at the BBC, but at Granada for ITV.

Nik applauded dutifully, wishing the stunning black woman had won. He had no favourites amongst the films, but Mountjoy had always got on his nerves and he'd been relieved to see the back of him. He typified the Oxbridge tossers who swanned effortlessly into the BBC and up its ranks. They had the contacts, knew the ropes, and won everything. He sighed, there was more to it than that, he was willing to acknowledge it now. Plenty of others with an equally privileged background failed to make it, there was only room for a handful of people at the top of any career ladder. Carrying a chip on your shoulder only weighed you down, he realised, 'Dump it!' he told himself. 'Get over yourself. Recognise talent when you see it.' He watched Donald receiving his due reward of hugs and handshakes, and tried to like him. He failed.

Stewart Walker stepped up on the platform, looking louchely handsome in an immaculate tuxedo, holding one of the little bronze models and crooning into the microphone. "It gives me immense pleasure to present the Basil Richardson Memorial Prize for Most Promising Producer to... Anthea Onojaife for her extraordinary, challenging Channel Four film inspired by the Stephen Lawrence murder investigation, *The Prosecution of Justice*."

A cheer went up from Anthea's table, and Nik saw her jump up from her chair. She hurried to the microphone, excitedly tripping on the step in her high heels and tight skirt, and beamed a gleaming smile that few of the people who remembered her as a BBC secretary had ever seen. Nik didn't pay much attention to her speech, but he wished he could get her back into his department. He made a mental note to lunch her.

Nik grew increasingly bored. These BBC people were so dull. His former lifestyle had been far more glamorous. These nobs were stuffy and uninspiring. He felt as if he were trapped inside Radio 4. Would it always be like this? Maybe he could change the place around him as he rose through the ranks? Bring in more people like himself, widen the workforce to include more real people, as he saw it. He was greatly impressed by Channel Four's new reality game show, *Big Brother*, and felt certain this innovative format would have a tremendous impact on all broadcasters. It was a new genre on its own, and the possibilities were endless. Channel Four was doing too well lately. He needed to re-position BBC Drama again.

His reverie was interrupted by Geordie's arrival on the podium to collect the Best Comedy Series Award. Nik could see him hyperventilating in his astonished joy. He waved his arms about and kept saying, "Howay! I canna believe it!" playing to the gallery as usual. Nik found it in himself to be pleased for his former friend, as Geordie embarked on a lengthy list of thank-yous during which he calmed down.

"Finally I'd like to dedicate this award to a very special person. He's here tonight." To Nik's alarm he realised Geordie's eyes were seeking him out, and he reddened, afraid of what was coming next. "Nik Mason, ladies and gentlemen, gave me wonderful support in my first years in television. Wonderful in every position. I mean way." Geordie sighed theatrically and fanned himself, raising a laugh. "And then, when I was poised to launch the new me, the *real* me, he helped me again. He said, 'No Geordie, you can't camp around in *my* company. Piss off and do it somewhere else!' So I did, and it's the best move I ever made. Thank you Nik darling, and I hope that closet isn't making you feel too claustrophobic." Geordie left the stage to cheers, whoops, and a buzz of intrigue.

Jill and Maggie exchanged astonished looks.

"The personal is political, eh boys!" Maggie observed.

Nik sweated in his seat. He had been outed – he couldn't believe it. It had never crossed his mind that such a thing would ever happen so publicly, and he had no idea how to handle it. There had been just enough malice in Geordie's tone to make his message crystal clear, so he couldn't brush it off with any conviction. He hadn't even brought a woman along with him tonight, as he often did. He sat rooted to his chair, crimson-faced, staring into his glass to avoid everyone's eyes.

His fellow diners were equally embarrassed, so they

pretended to chat together as if they hadn't noticed. The Chair of Governors, Philip Townsend, gripped his arm and said quietly, "Disgraceful! It's men like him who give gays a bad name. Don't alarm yourself Nik. Rise above it. That's what I do." Nik forced himself to smile back at Philip, who was a lean, bespectacled sixty-five year-old, fighting the urge to tell him to fuck off.

Catherine Briggs felt sorry for him. "What a mean-spirited thing to do! Don't worry, he's obviously had too much to drink. No-one will take any notice."

Chris coughed. "Personally," he said, "I detest discrimination in any shape or form. So does the BBC. In fact our policy is to try to represent all minority groups at every level of the organisation, even senior management. So if that old queen thinks he can turn us against you, he's missed by a mile." He looked at Nik encouragingly. "These days it often seems to me that it's a positive advantage not to be a white, middle-class Oxbridge-educated heterosexual male!"

The little group chuckled appreciatively, Selina among them: she made a point of sending him a sympathetic smile of support across the table, which Nik returned with what he hoped was a charming shrug. He took a deep breath and swiftly scanned their faces as he gulped a mouthful of wine. They were well-disposed towards him. How extraordinary. Maybe he could ride this storm out? He smiled tightly and shrugged as he put his glass down, feeling he should say something but unable to find any words.

Chris sought to help him out. "I'm reminded," he said anecdotally. "Of something that happened to me once in the eighties. I was in Edinburgh for the television festival, and I went for a walk in Princes St Gardens. There were lots of street entertainers and so on, and it was very busy, and hot, as I recall. Anyhow, there was a young boy there in some sort of dispute with a skinhead who was trying to make out this kid was gay. And do you know what this kid did?"

The others shook their heads. Nik's heart missed a beat as he recognised Chris. His jaw began to tremble and his eyes fixed on Chris' mouth, terrified what would come out of it next.

"He went straight up to the skinhead and head-butted him, just like that, really hard – knocked him flat on his back!" Everyone laughed.

"Go on Nik, why don't you try it on Geordie?" suggested Catherine playfully.

Nik forced his lips to move, "I don't think so, that's not really my style."

They all murmured supportively. He hoped desperately that Chris would not suddenly recognise him. If so, he would run for the exit – sweat was already trickling all over his body.

"What happened then, Chris?" asked Catherine, to keep the conversation flowing.

"Well, a fight broke out actually, and then the police rolled up. Several people were arrested, including me, would you believe!" he hooted with laughter at the idea.

"No, really?"

"Yes! We weren't charged, though. We had to sit in a cell for a few hours, that's all. I managed to explain things satisfactorily to the sergeant" he said modestly. Nik was all ears. "I told them the kid was my brother and he was a bit brain damaged. I'd only left him alone for five minutes and he'd got into a fight. I promised not to let him out of my sight again."

"Ah," said Catherine. "That was nice of you, getting him out of trouble. He must have been very grateful."

"As a matter of fact, he was extremely rude!"

They all tutted, whilst Nik felt a powerful sensation of floating above the table. What planet was this geezer from? *Brain damaged*? He felt utterly patronised. Twice over. This twat thinks he's Jesus bloody Christ, he thought. And now I'm his little project. Maybe I overdid the chirpy cockney bit. Well, I'm sick of being a protégé, I've arrived now, and I'm going all the way. He'd better watch his back.

He rallied his strength and excused himself, to avoid blurting out something regrettable. In the gents he took a line of coke and several deep breaths. He needed to stay well in with Chris and the other stuffed shirts if he was going to make it to the top. He had to accept their ways for a while. He was up to it. It was worth it. Hang on in there, there's nothing to lose, he told himself. He remembered his father and reminded himself that patience was essential. Some things had to be waited out. He'd managed not to lose it back there at the table. Maybe no-one would ever connect him with the NYT With No Future. He ground his teeth at the memory of it.

When he left the gents people were beginning to go home, so he took his chance to end the awful evening. He shook hands with Chris, who said, "You know, Nik, you can have a terrific influence at the BBC, and I mean to do all in my power to help you." He squeezed Nik's shoulder in a brotherly manner, as Catherine warmly invited him to dinner soon.

"That would be very nice, thank you," he said politely. "Cheers Chris, I… "

"See you Monday, Nik. Take care."

Nik walked up Regent Street aimlessly as others left in groups, en route to clubs and parties. A black cab went past with Magenta people in it, and he waved carelessly to them. A minute later another cab pulled up next to him, and Geordie leaned out.

"Howay bonny lad," he said. "Wanna be pals?" He smiled sadly. He meant it. Was Nik man enough to conquer his insecurities? "Come on. We're going to a party. Lots of celebs'll be there."

He thought about it, which way should he jump? He stared, bit his lip, couldn't decide. Getting in with Geordie meant coming clean, admitting to their relationship, and looking a complete fool. Part of him wanted to unload the burden and forget his ambitions, but they were still as strong as ever. In any case, he wasn't a hundred per cent homosexual. He had ideas of marriage and even kids, in his softer moments. All these thoughts raced around his mind as Geordie watched him stand spellbound on the lamplit pavement.

Eventually Geordie decided for him, "Fine. If that's the way you want it, that's okay. Happy New Year." His tone was pleasant, calm and a little sad, but for Nik, not for himself. He pushed the window up and sat back as the taxi drove off.

Nik sighed and, too late, raised his hand to wave at the departing cab. Then he carried on up Regent Street, trying to be glad that he wasn't in that cab on his way to a party. A few minutes later another car pulled over, this time it was a silver Rover, and Chris Briggs leaned out.

"Can we offer you a lift? We're taking Selina home, we could drop you off near your place." Selina sat on the roomy back seat, smiling pleasantly. The streetlamps lent a dramatic chiaroscuro to her perfect bone structure, and her luscious cream evening gown draped her like a Madonna.

It flashed into Nik's mind that there were many ways to get on in life, and very few fixed rules. In fact, you could make the rules up as you went along. Nothing was forever. People changed. *He'd* changed. He'd grown up, moved on. He was still changing, still moving, still succeeding. There was still a long way to go, so much more to see and experience. He smiled, "Thanks very much, that's extremely civil!" Then he opened the back door and climbed in next to Selina, who looked as perfect as she had at the start of the evening.

The car accelerated imperceptibly and they moved smoothly out into the early morning traffic of the twenty-first century. The world was full of opportunity, and it was all to play for.

A Last Word

May 2011, Penarth, Wales.

There's a saying, I think it's ancient Buddhist wisdom, about spending a lifetime travelling the world in search of something, only to return home and find it in your own backyard. It's true: I've proved it. Here I sit, looking out over Cardiff Bay, as happy as I could ever have hoped to be. I have a nice old desk in the attic of our big family house where I can escape to write while the kids are at school. Jon is Head of Drama at BBC Wales. I gave up on my career when our first child turned three. I realised I wanted to be at home for them, and you can't do everything – don't listen to the women who say you can have it all; it's rubbish. Well you might get it all but you'll be letting some people down, starting with your kids. Turning forty also brought me to the mental place where the idea of writing a novel became a pressing need. It's a lovely thing, if you haven't tried it you should. It's a great freedom to be able to enter and discover a world that's entirely yours and under your control.

You're probably wondering what happened to everyone since the dawn of 2000. Maggie went to Sydney, and is now a big shot in Australian television. Poor old Jill still lives alone in her Crouch End flat. Her son followed his dad into politics but joined the Tories, which hasn't done anything for Jill's nerves. Penny's spaniels are very highly regarded, in fact we bought one ourselves; Basil is adored by all of us. Anthea's a leading film producer now, and Carmen won an Oscar a couple of years ago and moved into the Hollywood stratosphere.

So who became Director General? Chris Briggs, of course. The managers' manager secured the flag whilst the arty lot and the money-men were preoccupied with screaming at each other. It's the triumph of the uncreative. A management style that engulfs the firm like a suffocating fog, and – most astonishingly – enriches itself beyond anyone's wildest dreams. He doubled his own pay in just a few years. How did he get away with it? Because, it turns out, everyone was doing it, from the peers of the realm to every banker in the city. To give him his due, he did manage to steer the BBC through an endless storm of disasters without allowing it to sink, although an awful lot was thrown overboard to keep it afloat. He's Lord Briggs of Banbury now, of course.

Through the twentieth century the old BBC played a vital role in the country, binding us together in a common culture. However maddening it was for many of us, it was essentially benevolent. What holds us together now? Do we have shared values anymore? We seem to be having an identity crisis. It came as a bit of a shock when I realised that all three main party leaders are now younger than me – we're not ready to hand over yet, everything's still in such a mess!

Nik Mason is still rising upwards through the BBC. He turned the Drama Department into a slick commercial operation, churning out sharp, efficient drama series by the mile. They sell all over the world and bring in a vital source of revenue that helps keep the Beeb afloat; the license fee is eternally insecure. He moved across to senior management after a few years, and married Selina. She worked wonders on his social skills. They're civil to me and Jonathan if we meet at the occasional function, but we don't stay in touch. It'll be interesting to see whether he makes it to DG, and if he does, what will become of the BBC. Will it retain any of its character, or will it turn into an American-style media Godzilla?

Nowadays precious few of the top brass have even made a programme. They give BAFTA fellowships to drama heads who've never produced anything at all. The commissioners' artistic judgement isn't a patch on the old school drama folk; they fill the schedules with similar generic programmes as if they were stacking produce on supermarket shelves. They don't even try to present a balanced evening's entertainment for a loyal and discriminating audience. They only care about flogging more items to more faceless trolley-pushers than the other channels – you must have noticed this yourself as a viewer.

One of my personal bugbears is the loss of narrative integrity. It started with *Twin Peaks* and got much worse by the time we got *Lost* (pun intended). Instead of telling us a proper story, by which I mean that the plot unfolds towards an inevitable but surprising conclusion, they just make up something sensational for every episode, and if it doesn't connect at all with what happened at the beginning, who cares? As long as you've hooked a rope through the ring at the end of the audience's nose, you can lead them anywhere. Well sooner or later audiences will get wise to it. When they realise there's going to be no satisfaction at the end of the story, they'll stop watching. Simple as.

Then, perhaps, creativity will come back into fashion: originality, ideas, content that leaves you with something to think about. Creativity needs careful nurturing – I think I've mentioned this already, sorry if I'm labouring the point. Over in London they've stopped bothering, it seems to me. The good old Drama Script Unit closed years ago, the slush pile isn't taken remotely seriously now (despite what they tell you) and to be fair, the number of prospective writers these days is absolutely staggering. So where does the original work come from? It's true, fantastic new programmes do get made. Not everyone decamped into the film industry. It's often the independents that bring in the best original work, they get less top-down interference. There are still vibrant pockets of production here and there, I'm proud to say we're part of one here in Cardiff, one of the finest. Most of the really good work has a lot of humour in it – which is ironic, given that drama has traditionally looked down on comedy. I've never understood why that is. I reckon it's dead easy to make an audience cry, but making them laugh takes a dash of genius.

In our out-of-the-way Welsh corner we've had it good, these last ten years. We've been able to run things the way they should be run, and we've proved it works. Our shows are some of the BBC's best and most popular new drama series. It's funny how the best opportunities turned out to be in my own boring old home town. Don't tell anyone, will you? Now that the BBC management are de-centralising and moving whole departments out to the regions, we're a bit worried that they're all going to turn up here. We're keeping very quiet. The last thing we want is an official management-sponsored 'creativity partnership initiative' round here.